WITCHLING

MEET THREE
SEMI-SUPERNATURAL
SISTERS OUT TO SAVE
OTHERWORLD...

YASMINE GALENORN

BERKLEY

ISBN 0-425-21254-6

9 780425 212547

5 0 6 9 9 >

EAN

ALL BUSINESS

"You aren't going to believe what happened. Jocko's been murdered." Chase glanced around the store. "Are we alone? I don't want any of this getting around." Normally, when Chase wanted to discuss something with me privately, he was trying to get into my pants. A letch, he'd been after me since the first day we met. I, on the other hand, had found it easy to resist his charms. Chase wasn't my type. For one thing, he was an FBH—a full-blooded human.

When the Otherworld Intelligence Agency had assigned Delilah, Menolly, and me to live Earthside, we figured we were one step away from being fired. As the months wore on with no real word from them, we began to relax and think that we'd just been placed on an involuntary sabbatical. But now, with our fellow operative dead, we'd be responsible for stepping in and cleaning up the mess. And if he had been murdered, the OIA would want answers . . .

Witchling

YASMINE GALENORN

BERKLEY BOOKS, NEW YORK

THE BERKLEY PUBLISHING GROUP
Published by the Penguin Group
Penguin Group (USA) Inc.
375 Hudson Street, New York, New York 10014, USA
Penguin Group (Canada), 90 Eglinton Avenue East, Suite 700, Toronto, Ontario M4P 2Y3, Canada
(a division of Pearson Penguin Canada Inc.)
Penguin Books Ltd., 80 Strand, London WC2R 0RL, England
Penguin Group Ireland, 25 St. Stephen's Green, Dublin 2, Ireland (a division of Penguin Books Ltd.)
Penguin Group (Australia), 250 Camberwell Road, Camberwell, Victoria 3124, Australia
(a division of Pearson Australia Group Pty. Ltd.)
Penguin Books India Pvt. Ltd., 11 Community Centre, Panchsheel Park, New Delhi—110 017, India
Penguin Group (NZ), Cnr. Airborne and Rosedale Roads, Albany, Auckland 1310, New Zealand
(a division of Pearson New Zealand Ltd.)
Penguin Books (South Africa) (Pty.) Ltd., 24 Sturdee Avenue, Rosebank, Johannesburg 2196,
South Africa

Penguin Books Ltd., Registered Offices: 80 Strand, London WC2R 0RL, England

This is a work of fiction. Names, characters, places, and incidents either are the product of the author's imagination or are used fictitiously, and any resemblance to actual persons, living or dead, business establishments, events, or locales is entirely coincidental.

WITCHLING

A Berkley Book / published by arrangement with the author

PRINTING HISTORY
Berkley edition / October 2006

Copyright © 2006 by Yasmine Galenorn.
Excerpt from *Changeling* by Yasmine Galenorn copyright © 2007 by Yasmine Galenorn.
Cover illustration by Tony Mauro.
Cover design by Rita Frangie.
Interior text design by Stacy Irwin.

ISBN: 0-425-21254-8

BERKLEY®
Berkley Books are published by The Berkley Publishing Group,
a division of Penguin Group (USA) Inc.,
375 Hudson Street, New York, New York 10014.
BERKLEY is a registered trademark of Penguin Group (USA) Inc.
The "B" design is a trademark belonging to Penguin Group (USA) Inc.

PRINTED IN THE UNITED STATES OF AMERICA

10 9 8 7 6 5 4 3

Dedicated to:
Samwise. For love. For life.
I promised you a touch of my magic as
part of my wedding vows.
I think we've managed that.

ACKNOWLEDGMENTS

Thank you to: Meredith Bernstein, my agent. You truly believe in me. Thank you for that, more than I can ever express. To Christine Zika, my editor, who saw the potential in this series. Thank you to my husband, Samwise: Honey, it's just getting better with every year.

Thank you to Glen Hill for helping me with the Japanese translations and information I needed. To Lisa Croll Di Dio, Brad Rinke, and Tiffany Merkel, each of whom listened to a little of this crazy world I've managed to create here and convinced me that my trip into la-la land was worth the journey.

Thanks for the support from my Witchy Chicks Blogging Group. To Mark W. and his furble Maggie, the feline inspiration for Maggie the gargoyle. To my own cats, my little Galenorn Gurlz. To Ukko, Rauni, Mielikki, and Tapio, my spiritual guardians.

Thank you to my readers, both old and new, for spreading the word about my books, for continuing to follow me on this trail of words I leave, for reading in a world filled with other entertainment options.

You can find me on the net at Galenorn En/Visions: *www.galenorn.com* or you can write to me snail mail (see website or via publisher). Please enclose a stamped, self-addressed envelope with your letter if you would like a reply.

In all chaos there is a cosmos, in all disorder a secret order.

—CARL G. JUNG

How do you commence to start to begin an almost new kind of writing, to terrify and scare?
You stumble into it, mostly. You don't know what you're doing, and suddenly, it's done.

—RAY BRADBURY

CHAPTER 1

Seattle is gloomy most any day of the year, but October can be especially rough in the bad weather department. The rain pounded down from silver skies, slashing sideways against the windows to form rivulets that trickled down the glass. The water pooled at the bottom in puddles, collecting in the depressions where the weeds had thrust through the cracked pavement. Luckily, the door to the Indigo Crescent was elevated by a slight ramp, just enough to keep customers dry as they entered the shop. That is, if they didn't manage to slip off the edge and land their besandaled foot in the puddle like I had.

I shook off the rain as I entered my shop and punched in the security code. Thanks to my sister Delilah, the alarm not only kept an eye out for thieves, it picked up on spies too. And we needed that peace of mind, considering just who we were and where we were from.

My foot made a squishing sound as I limped over to my favorite chair and slid off my four-inch heels, picking up one of the strappy sandals. As I wiped off the designer shoe, it crossed my mind that being half-Faerie had its perks.

I hadn't spent a fortune on the shoes. In fact, they'd been a gift from the local Faerie Watchers Club members who liked to frequent my shop.

When they saw me coveting the shoes in a catalog, they'd shown up a couple days later with a bag from Nordstrom. I'd debated accepting the gift about thirty seconds; then desire won out, and I graciously thanked the club for their gesture while sliding into the shoes, which were a perfect fit, I might add.

I examined the sandal, deciding that it had suffered no permanent damage. After drying my feet and reuniting them with their favorite heels, I took out my notebook and looked over my to-do list. I had books to shelve and orders to fill, and I'd agreed to play hostess to the Faerie Watchers' monthly book club meeting. They'd be here at noon. Delilah would be out on a case the greater part of the day, and of course my other sister, Menolly, was asleep.

Might as well get to work. I switched on the stereo and "Man in the Box" by Alice in Chains echoed through the store. Later, I'd switch to classical, but for early morning when the store was empty and I was alone, it was all about me. Longing for something interesting to happen, I grabbed a box of new paperbacks and had begun to shelve them when the bell over the door jingled, and Chase Johnson dashed in. *Not* the kind of interesting I was hoping for.

He folded his umbrella, then dropped it into the elephant-shaped stand by the door. As he slid out of his long trench and hung it on the coat rack, I studiously kept my eyes on the book I was sliding onto the shelf. Great, just what I needed to make the day brighter. The letch of the year dogging my tail again. Appreciation was nice. Glomming, not so much. Chase was far from being my favorite human; he didn't even make the top-ten list, and I did my best to frustrate him whenever possible. Nice? Maybe not. But fun? Definitely.

"We need to talk. Now, Camille." Chase snapped his fingers and pointed at the counter.

I fluttered my eyelashes at him. "What? You aren't going

to try to sweet-talk me first? I'm hurt. You could at least say please."

"Your attitude's showing again." Chase rolled his eyes. "And can you turn down that racket?" Shaking his head, he snorted. "You come all the way from Otherworld, and what do you listen to? Heavy metal crap."

"Eh, shut up," I said. "I like it. Has more life than a lot of the music I grew up on." At least he hadn't tried to grope me, although the lack thereof should have been my first clue that something was wrong. If I'd paid more attention to my intuition rather than my irritation, I'd have packed up my gear, turned in my resignation, and headed home to Otherworld that very afternoon.

I reluctantly set Grisham down on the table next to Crichton so they could have a nice little chat and slipped behind the counter, turning the stereo down but not off. The Indigo Crescent was my bookstore as far as anybody on the outside was concerned, but in reality, it was a front for the OIA—the Otherworld Intelligence Agency—and I was one of their Earthside operatives. Lackey, if I wanted to be honest.

I glanced around. Still early. No customers. *Lucky me.* We had leeway to talk in private.

"All right, what's going on?" I sniffed, aware of a pungent odor that was emanating from Chase. At first I thought he must have just come from the gym. I'd smelled a lot of things off of him in the past: lust, testosterone, sweat from his workouts, his ever-present addiction to spicy beef tacos. "Good gods, Chase, don't you ever take a shower?"

He blinked. "Twice a day. Smell something you like?"

I raised one eyebrow. "Not so much," I said, trying to pinpoint what the smell was. And then I realized that the odor coming off of him was fear. This was not a good sign. I'd never smelled this much worry off of him before. Whatever he had to tell me couldn't be good.

"I've got some bad news, Camille." He cut to the quick. "Jocko's dead."

"You have to be kidding. Jocko can't be dead." Jocko was a giant and an OIA agent, albeit just a tad vertically challenged. He barely cleared seven three, but there was nothing wrong with his biceps. "Jocko's strong as an ox. What happened? A bus hit him?"

"Actually, he's been murdered." Chase looked dead serious.

My stomach lurched. "Well, hell. What happened? Some jealous guy find out Jocko was fooling around with his wife and shoot him?" It had to be. No normal human could take down a giant without a big-assed gun, not even one Jocko's size.

Chase shook his head. "You aren't going to believe this, Camille." He glanced around the store. "Are we alone? I don't want any of this getting out until we know exactly what we're dealing with."

Usually when Chase wanted to discuss something in private, he was trying to get under my skirts, but I found it easy to resist his charms. Chase wasn't my type. For one thing, he was obnoxious as hell. For another, he was an FBH—a full-blooded human. I'd never slept with an FBH and had no incentive to start doing so.

Dressed to the hilt in black Armani, Chase stood six one, with wavy brown hair and a smooth Roman nose. He was handsome in that casual way that suave men have, and when my sisters and I first met him, we thought he might have a little Faerie blood running in his veins. A thorough background check had quashed that idea. He was human to the core. Good detective. Just lousy with women, including his mother, who was constantly calling him on his cell phone, asking him when he was going to be a good son and pay her a visit.

"Where's Delilah?" His eyes flashed.

I grinned. I knew just what he thought of my sisters, although Delilah startled rather than frightened him. Menolly just creeped the poor guy out, and she usually did it on purpose.

"She's out on a case. Why do you want to know? Worried she's going to jump out and say *boo*?" Delilah didn't mean to alarm people, but she walked so softly she could sneak up on a blind man and he wouldn't hear.

He rolled his eyes. "I really need to discuss this with all three of you."

"Yeah, okay, that makes sense." I relented and flashed him a smile. "You know we'll have to wait until after dusk. Menolly can't come out to play until then. So have you contacted the OIA about Jocko yet?"

Not that I expected much in the way of a response from them. When headquarters had assigned Delilah, Menolly, and me to live Earthside, we figured that we were one step away from being fired. While we were hard workers, our track record left a lot to be desired. One thing was for sure: none of us would ever make employee of the month. But, as the months wore on with no real word or major assignment from them, we'd begun to relax and decided that involuntary relocation wasn't altogether bad. At least we were having fun getting used to Earthside customs.

Now, however, with Jocko dead, we'd be responsible for cleaning up the mess. And if he'd been murdered, the OIA would want answers. Answers that we weren't likely to find, considering our lack of results in the past.

"Headquarters is blowing me off," Chase said slowly. His lip twisted into a frown. "I contacted HQ this morning, and all they said was to turn the case over to you. I'm supposed to help out in whatever way you need."

"That's it?" I blinked. "No guidelines? No lengthy bureaucratic regulations that we have to observe in our investigation?"

He shrugged. "Apparently, they don't consider Jocko's death a priority. In fact, the person I talked to was so abrupt that I almost thought I'd said something wrong."

While it wouldn't be the first time Chase put his foot in his mouth, HQ's reaction was strange enough to make me take notice.

I glanced at the empty aisles. Still no customers, but in a little while the place would be jumping when the Faerie

Watchers book mavens arrived. Entertaining a pack of gawking, camera-happy fans wasn't on my top-ten list of favorite activities, but hey, it paid the bills and helped Otherworld-Earthside relations at the same time. And the women were nice, if a little giddy.

"Come on, let's talk. The FWC contingent won't arrive until noon, so I've got some time to kill."

"The Faerie Watchers Club?" It was Chase's turn to grin. "Oh come now. Don't tell me you finally gave in to them? Don't you just love being a celebrity?"

I snorted. "Oh sure, I *love* belonging to the Anna Nicole Smith set. All Earthside Faerie live in tabloid land, you know." In fact, yellow journalism had gotten a huge boost when we showed up, our presence infusing new blood into the *Enquirer*, the *Star*, and numerous other tabloids. "Hey, it could be worse. I could have the Guardian Watchdogs breathing down my neck."

"Heaven help us from that," Chase said under his breath.

A vigilante watchdog group, the Guardian Watchdogs considered anybody who wasn't an FBH to be an "alien." They called themselves the "earth-born" and lumped everyone from Otherworld together as a threat to society, a threat to their children, and a threat to morality in general. Wouldn't they be surprised to find out who was lurking in the shadows long before we'd ever opened up the portals on our side? Earth had its own tidy measure of vampires and Faeries, along with a few other creatures that didn't show up in the storybooks.

The Watchdogs took it upon themselves to keep track of any incidents involving the Sidhe and their kin and then exploited them for their own ends. They were a whole lot scarier than the Faerie Watchers Club, who just popped a dozen flashbulbs in our face every time we turned around and asked for an endless string of autographs.

"Say, you don't think they could have had something to do with Jocko's death, do you? The Guardian Watchdogs, that is?" I asked as I led Chase to a folding table that sat beside a shelf filled with obscure foreign novels. Pushing away the remains of my morning egg-sausage muffin and venti mocha, both of which I'd become thoroughly addicted to, I motioned for him to sit down.

"I don't think so," Chase said. "They're pretty much all talk and no action, other than their never-ending protests and picket signs."

I settled into my chair and propped my feet on the table, crossing them at the ankles while I made sure my skirt was covering everything Chase might want to see. "Do you have *any* idea who killed Jocko? And how did he die?"

"New shoes?" Chase asked, raising an eyebrow.

"Yeah," I said, not about to tell him where they'd come from. "So do you? About Jocko?"

Chase let out a long sigh. "No. And he was garroted."

Garroted? My feet hit the floor as I straightened my shoulders. That didn't track right.

"You're sure you told headquarters how he died? And they blew you off?"

"That's what I said." He leaned back and slid his hands in his pockets. "But I've got a weird feeling about this. I don't think we're dealing with humans, and there's nothing that I can tell you that would explain why. Just a hunch."

"If he was garroted, you're probably right. Sometimes the dregs from Otherworld slip through the portals. And not all of my kin in OW play by human rules." I frowned. "Maybe somebody has a grudge against giants, or got drunk on a bad batch of goblin wine? Or maybe somebody was just in a bad mood and decided to pound on the bartender? Could be this is just a case of some OW thug taking out his frustrations while he's Earthside."

"Could be," Chase said, slowly nodding. "But I don't think so."

I squinted, staring at the table. Chase was right. I knew I was howling at the wrong moon. "Okay, let's look at this logically. Nobody Earthside has the strength to garrote Jocko. At least no one who's human. Did you find *any* sign that one of the Sidhe might have had a hand in this?"

"Not that I noticed. Of course, I might not know what to look for. I did, however, find the cord used to strangle him. Here." Chase tossed a braided leather thong on the table. It was spattered with blood. "There's a feeling I get when I touch this . . . I thought you might be able to ferret something out."

It occurred to me that Chase had a touch of second sight. Picking up the braid, I closed my eyes. The faint scent of sulfur hit my nose as a dark miasma slowly began seeping out of the woven strands, oozing over my fingers like burnt oil. I jerked away, dropping the rope back on the table as I drew a sharp breath.

"Bad news. Big bad news."

"What? What is it?"

I swallowed a lump that had suddenly risen in my throat. "Demonkin. That rope has demonic energy infused into the fiber of every strand."

Chase leaned forward. "Are you sure, Camille?"

I folded my arms and leaned back. "Positive. There's no feeling in the world that even comes close to demon energy. And this rope reeks of it." Which clinched matters. We weren't facing some disgruntled Faerie or dwarf, or any of the other numerous inhabitants of Otherworld who could easily be captured and deported.

Chase stumbled over the same thought. "I thought demons were banned from Otherworld."

"They are, for the most part. Oh, we have some gremlins, imps, a bunch of lesser vampires and the like, but nothing on the order of what it would take to produce this strong of an aura." I stared at the murder weapon. "I hate to even give voice to the thought, but there's a chance that a demon has made its way up from the Subterranean Realms and slipped through a portal."

"That's not supposed to happen." Chase sounded so plaintive I almost felt sorry for him.

"You're right, it's not." When we'd accepted our post, the OIA had guaranteed that demons from the Sub Realms couldn't get through. All the reports said that throughout the hundreds of years they'd been watching the portals, not a single demon or ghoul from down under had made it topside. But then again, the OIA promises a lot of things they never follow through on. Humans have *nothing* on the Sidhe when it comes to bureaucracy.

He tried again, skirting to find another angle. "You're positive your inner . . . magic . . . ticker just isn't off?"

"*Inner magic ticker?* Oh please, you can do better than that. Chase, you asked me, and I told you. This rope belongs to one of the Demonkin. You can believe me or not as you choose."

"Okay, okay," Chase said with a grimace. "I just don't like the sound of that. What should I do about the OIA? Tell them about the rope and what you sense off of it?"

"Yeah, give it a try." I snorted. "See if that kick-starts their butts. I advise contacting them again as soon as possible."

The Wizards Guild, the IT workers of Otherworld, had set up a communications network for OIA's Earthside contingent. Trouble was, when headquarters didn't want to take a call, they just ignored the message. Of course, when *they* needed to contact *us*, we'd be in deep shit if we didn't answer.

Chase glanced around. "Are you sure it's safe to talk here? I can just imagine what would happen if the papers got hold of the news that a demon's running around. It's dicey enough with you Faerie folk and the like."

I didn't bother to remind him that I was half-human and had as much right to be on Earth as I did to be in Otherworld. "You're like a fussy old mother hen, Chase. Chill. I just warded the store against snooping yesterday. We should be safe enough."

"Uh-huh, sure you did. You positive you didn't turn the place into a bullhorn by mistake?" He laughed so loud it turned into a snort.

"Excuse me?" I leaned across the table and flicked his nose. "It was bad enough back home, but now I should put up with this crap from an *FBH*? I don't think so! I happen to be magically challenged. You have a problem with that?"

"*Magically challenged*, so that's how you're describing it now? Hey, far be it from me to give you grief, but I'm not the one who ended up nekkid for the whole world to see," he said, grinning as his gaze ran up and down my body.

"Get your mind off my naked body, Johnson. While you're at it, let's see you try your hand at a little magic," I said curtly. "Care to show me what you've got, Superman?"

That shut him up. One thing I'd discovered since we arrived in Belles-Faire, a seedy suburb city of Seattle, was that Chase craved power. He couldn't wield magic himself, so he did the next best thing when he found out about the OIA. He went to work for them. Sometimes I thought he actually enjoyed it when my spells backfired.

He held up his hands to ward me off. "Sorry! I didn't mean to strike a sore spot. Truce?"

I let out a long sigh. Tactless or not, he had a point. And with the pall on that rope, we had bigger fish to worry about than my ego.

"Yeah, yeah. Truce. As to my warding, don't have a hissy fit. To back up my magic, Delilah installed an electronic surveillance system. She has a knack for your technology, and she rewired it to pick up on any bugs or other listening devices that may have been planted around here."

I didn't tell him that she'd also blown a fuse and sparked herself a good one. The resulting flash of electricity threw her across the room. But Delilah was no quitter. Eventually she'd figured it out and got it working.

"Good girl. I knew you wouldn't let us down."

"Girl?" I gave him a long look. "Chase, I'm old enough to be your mother."

He blinked. "I tend to forget that. You don't look it."

"I'd better not look it," I said, raising an eyebrow. I was damned proud of my looks and took pains to accentuate the positive. One perk about living Earthside: the makeup was fantastic. For one thing, it didn't stain like cosmetics made from herbs and berries. Back in Otherworld, I'd spent longer than I'd ever planned to looking like a Pict when

I tried out some face paint made out of woad. Never again. When I returned home, I'd be carting a butt load of M•A•C cosmetics with me, especially tubes of Verushka lipstick and tubs of Soft Brown eye shadow. I nurtured my little vanities.

Chase coughed, and I saw the glimmer of a smile behind his eyes. "All right," he said. "Here's how it went down. This morning I took a call from one of the homeless guys who live in the alley around back of the Wayfarer. He found Jocko's body. The dude's been one of my informants in the past and was scrounging for a few bucks. So I got there first, which was a good thing, considering Jocko wasn't looking all too pretty. Of course, I immediately activated the FH-CSI."

I stifled a smile. The Faerie-Human Crime Scene Investigations team was Chase's brainchild and was a mix of human and Otherworld agents, specially trained to deal with the problem of crimes against OW citizens. Chase had initiative and foresight, I had to give him that. It was unfortunate that he had to answer to Devins, a real prick who was a few offices higher up than Chase, but usually he was able to keep his boss out of the loop.

"We're using an OIA medical examiner, and all the info has been sealed."

I slumped. Suddenly it all seemed too real. The thought of Jocko meeting his end in a back alley made me cringe. He may not have been the brightest bulb in the socket, but he made up for it in congeniality, and I'd genuinely liked the gentle giant.

"Jocko was one of the most even-tempered giants I've ever met. That's why he got the job, you know. He could interact with others without pounding them into the ground when he got irritable. He was a good-hearted man who did his best. I'll miss him."

"He wasn't a man," Chase said, wrinkling his nose. "He was a giant. And he was crude, loutish, and made fun of my suits."

"As you said, he was a *giant*. Giants are like that, only most are much worse. What do you expect?"

Chase gave me an exasperated look. "I have no idea. I don't know any other giants. I never met a vampire or a lycanthrope either, until I met your sisters, so give me a break if I don't react with much enthusiasm. Giants and bloodsuckers and werewolves—"

"Were*cat*. Lycanthrope means were*wolf*. It's not synonymous with Were. Delilah would scratch your eyes out if she heard you lumping her with the Canids."

"Right, werecat. What was I thinking? Sorry," he said, his voice anything but. "Section five of the handbook. *Not all Weres are the same*."

"Damned straight they aren't, and don't you forget it. Some of them would slit your throat for even suggesting it." I was giving him a hard time, but better that than let Chase learn the hard way. The point of a sword or fang was a whole lot sharper than my tongue.

"Whatever. What I'm trying to say is that all of you were simply tales of myth and legend until a few years ago, when you crawled out of the woodwork. Even you—you're a witch. And half-Faerie at that. I'm still wrapping my mind around all this."

"Point taken," I said, grinning. "I guess we do come as quite a shock, especially when you've been taught your whole life that we don't exist. Okay, back to business. Tell me more about Jocko's death."

"Well, other than the fact that the killer had to be at least as big and as strong as he was, there's not much to tell. Nothing in the bar to give us any idea what happened. Nothing in the portal log to indicate that somebody new came through last night. Basically, it boils down to the fact that the Wayfarer is out one bartender, and HQ wants you to take care of it."

The Wayfarer Bar & Grill, like the Indigo Crescent, was OIA run and operated, and part of a worldwide network of safe houses and portals. The bar was also a hub for FBHs who wanted to meet the Fae. And there were plenty of admirers who lined up for a chance to see, or talk to, or screw us. The crowds were thick and the partying hard.

My sister Menolly worked night shift at the bar. She listened for gossip and rumors that might be important among the travelers who came through from Otherworld. Having her there was a good way to spot potential trouble, since the grapevine always ran faster than official channels. It was also one of the few night jobs she could find, and she was strong enough to stand in for the bouncer if need be.

Chase pulled out a pack of cigarettes but stuffed them back in his pocket when I shook my head. Cigarette smoke raised havoc with my lungs and was even worse for Delilah. Menolly didn't care anymore. She was dead. Well, undead. The only things she could smell were blood, fear, and pheromones.

I glanced at the clock. "I can't wake Menolly until dark. Delilah's out on a case and won't be back until late afternoon. Why don't you meet me here at six, and we'll go back to the house? That way you'll have had a chance to contact HQ again. And by then the sun will be set."

"Can't you wake Menolly up now since it's overcast?" Chase said.

"Chase, get a grip. Vampires and daylight just do not mix. Besides, it's rough on her to be locked in the house all day. Better for her to sleep as much as she can; it keeps her from getting claustrophobia. Menolly hasn't been a vampire very long, not by our standards. She's still learning to adjust, and we're making it as easy as we can on her. I'm doing my best to help her, but it's rough going at times. In fact, I'm working on a surprise that she'll probably hate me for, but it will be good for her."

"I see your point," Chase said, musing. "All right, I'll try to raise HQ again and tell them what you said about the rope. But if I were Menolly, I'd call in sick tonight. If there *is* a demon behind this, he might be after OIA agents. And if he had inside help, then he might know that Menolly is an operative."

An inside job? That thought hadn't crossed my mind. "Great, that's all I need to think about," I said, grinning. "Okay, see you tonight."

Chase headed for the door. As I watched him leave, a shadow seemed to pass through the shop, and I reached out to touch it, but it shuddered and dissipated into the gloomy day. Jocko's murder had set in motion dangerous events to come. I could feel it on the wind, though any clear picture eluded my sight. I went back to my work, trying to muster up a smile for the Faerie Watchers who would be here in full force in less than an hour.

CHAPTER 2

After I finished shelving the box of books, I grabbed the phone and punched in Delilah's cell number. I wasn't sure what case she was working on, but no matter. Jocko's death was more important. That rope smelled like demon, and I knew my nose wasn't playing tricks on me. But it left me wondering: Just what sort of creature had managed to sneak through? And why was it here?

Delilah picked up on the second ring. I told her what had happened.

"Get your butt back here by six. And whatever you do, don't go near the Wayfarer until we know what we're dealing with."

"Poor Jocko, he was a sweetheart," she said. "Do you think he was killed because he was an OIA agent?"

"I hope not," I said. "But on the off chance, we're keeping Menolly home tonight. As good of a guy as Jocko was, he was also dumb as a fence post, and he might have let it slip that both of them are from the agency. Make no mistake about it, there's trouble on the way. And we're standing right in its path."

"You thinking the Subterranean Realms?" Her voice begged me to say no. Delilah was an optimist, always wanting things to turn out with a happy ending. How she managed to stay in the OIA and retain her naivety, I had no idea, but somehow she always pulled through with a smile.

I squinted, mulling over the growing sense of dread in my chest. My powers came from the wind and the stars and the moon and, while I couldn't always foresee the future, I could sense when great beings awoke. And if a secret was whispered to the wind during the night of the full moon, I might be able to catch it if I listened hard enough.

"I don't know for certain, but something's stirring."

Delilah squeaked. "I have to go! I'm on a photo assignment, and my target just came out of the school."

I groaned. "You're taking pictures of a child? What have you gotten yourself involved with now?"

"No, goose. I'm photographing a teacher. Her husband thinks she's messing around on the side and wants me to follow her. She's supposed to be in a meeting during lunchtime, but she's headed to her car right now. I'll see you tonight!" With a happy laugh, she hung up.

So, who am I? Well, my name is Camille D'Artigo, and I'm a witch. I'm half-Faerie, and half-human. I suppose a little background is in order. The oldest of three, I was born in Otherworld. Of course, we have our own name for our land, but it's just easier to call it OW while we're Earthside. Most people on Earth thought "Faerie Land" was a myth until we snuck up behind them and yelled "Boo!" And when we came out of the broom closet, we came all the way.

A hop, skip, and dimension away, OW is populated by the Sidhe, along with a variety of dwarves, elves, Faeries, unicorns, Weres, lesser vampires, dryads, nymphs and satyrs, gargoyles, dragons, imps, and other marvelous beasties so strange most humans have never heard of them. Growing up in OW was like living in a storybook, though sometimes our world seems founded on Grimm's nightmares rather than Mother Goose's rhymes. But we love it, monsters and all.

Until the past few years, we seldom crossed through the portals in any great number. So anybody who happened to meet one of us Earthside either kept their mouth shut, or ended up being labeled nutty as a fruitcake. Or worse. Now, of course, we're tourist attractions. People come to my shop to gawk and take pictures. It's good for business. Most everybody buys at least one book to take home with them, so I give them a cheesecake pose and wink at the camera.

Once in a while a rare soul takes it into his head to go trophy hunting because he's decided we're the spawn of Satan, but luckily for us, that doesn't happen very often. No, for the most part, our kith and kin are sought after as party guests, bedmates, and status enhancers. The attention can get a little wiggy, but in the name of Earthside-Otherworld relations, it's all good.

Together with my sisters Menolly and Delilah, I grew up in the outer courts of the Queen's palace. Our mother, Maria, was mortal, and it's her last name we bear here on Earth: D'Artigo. Our father is of Sidhe blood.

I say she was mortal, but it would be more accurate to say she was human, because most of the inhabitants in OW are mortal. Long-lived, yes, but mortal and all too capable of dying. The only true immortals are the Elementals, who have as little to do with flesh-and-blood beings as possible. Oh—and we can't forget the gods. But the gods aren't talking much as of late, and they tend to stay in their own little worlds.

I hear rumors that Demeter's wandering the Earth again. Sometimes she gets a little foggy and forgets that Persephone is a grown woman and quite happy as Queen of the Underworld. During her forgetful periods, she'll go looking for her lost child until her brother Zeus finds her and gently guides her back to Olympus. However, the majority

of gods turned their backs on humans when humans turned
their backs on them. The lack of worship bruised a few
egos.

Anyway, our mother was from Seattle. An orphan, in her
third year of college she moved to Spain to work on her art
degree and track down what remaining family she might be
able to find. World War II erupted, and she dropped out of
school to work in a factory until the day she met my father
on the outskirts of Madrid, where he'd recently been posted
to an assignment.

It was love at first sight, and he broke down and told her
the truth. Mother packed a bag and returned to Otherworld
with him, where they married under the disapproving eyes
of the Queen. In the years following, the three of us were
born. When Mother was in her fifties, she was thrown from
a horse on a hunting trip and died, and Father took over
raising us.

Growing up as a half-human in Otherworld was rough.
For one thing, we were teased incessantly because we were
half-human. But bigotry was the least of our problems. It
didn't take our parents long to discover that the gifts we inherited from Father's line had gone drastically awry because of our mother's human blood.

As I said, I'm a witch, but my spells and charms have a
nasty tendency to backfire. Sometimes they're spot-on, but
other times . . . not so much. Like last month when I tried
to turn invisible to avoid being seen by an annoying customer. Things went haywire, and I ended up nekkid. Not
just naked, but leave-nothing-to-the-imagination nekkid.

To make matters worse, for the first few hours *I* could
still see my clothes. Just nobody else could. My 38 DD
boobs gave the world a real show, along with my hourglass
figure, long raven hair (it's blue black on *all* areas of my
body, as everybody now knows), and JLO-esque butt. My
regular customers were more than happy to line up and
chat with me until I figured out what had happened. The
spell lasted for a week, during which time I had to leave

Iris, my assistant—a Finnish house sprite—in charge. The winks and nudges still haven't worn off, but I'm a good sport about it.

Delilah and Menolly have their own problems. Although our handicaps keep us from being ideal agents, we try. So we were sent Earthside where the higher-ups figured we'd keep out of trouble. Boy, were they wrong.

The local branch of the Faerie Watchers Club was due any minute. I gave the store a once-over, but it was as tidy as it was going to get. Iris had done a wonderful job on the dusting and cleaning, and I made a note to treat her to an afternoon shopping at the fabric store. House sprites had come a long way in the past hundred years, including a clause in their contracts that they would now accept money for their services, but Iris still loved a good length of silk.

As the doors swung open precisely at noon and the Faerie Watchers filed in, I grabbed a quick look in the mirror to make sure my lipstick wasn't smeared and lowered my glamour, allowing the shifting silver flecks to peek through the violet of my eyes. With a smile, I went to welcome my visitors.

Erin Mathews, the president of the local order, sidled over to me. As humans went, she was a good sort, and I enjoyed her company. She ran a lingerie store a few blocks from the Indigo Crescent, and we'd met when I went shopping for bustiers. After that, we occasionally got together for coffee and to chitchat. I thought her friends were a little balmy, but when I thought about it, most of my friends back home had issues, so who was I to judge? Baggage was baggage, no matter which side of the portal you lived on.

"Camille, we were wondering if you'd do us the honor of joining us for a group picture?" She flashed me a hopeful smile that said she knew how many requests of this nature I received.

"Of course. You don't even need to ask," I said, suddenly humble in the face of their enthusiasm. Humans were more generous with friendship than my father's people.

They lined up in three rows, splitting on either side so I could stand in the center, and Iris took the picture before popping back on her stepstool that allowed her to see over the counter. A junior member of the OIA, Iris was technically a Talon-haltija. She guarded the store at night, worked the counter when I needed her, and tidied up. Short and squat, she had a fresh, appealing face and a personality to match. She was also a real draw with our customers, enchanting them with her cups of tea and freshly baked stollen that always graced the store.

The group of fifteen women—and one man—gathered around me. Erin took a deep breath and then held up the book—a copy of Katharine Briggs's book, *An Encyclopedia of Fairies.*

"So tell us," she said, "What's true and what isn't?"

With a silent groan, I took the book. This was the part I hated: being the teacher who had to explain just where the line fell between legend and fact.

By the time Delilah returned, the club had vacated the premises and the only customer left in the shop was Henry Jeffries, one of my regulars. Delilah gave us both a quick wave and jogged up the stairs to the seedy little rooms she used for an office. The OIA owned the entire building, and they'd given Delilah the upstairs suite in which to set up her PI business.

The offer might sound generous, but the rooms were dark and grimy, and it was implied that she was expected to keep the rat population down as part of the deal. She complied but stopped short at eating them. Every day or so she'd open one of the windows in her office that overlooked the Dumpster in the alley and toss out a dead rat or two. As she put it, "Who knows where those things have been? Eat a city rat? You've got to be kidding!"

"Your sister sure looks different than you," Henry said as he wrote out his check. He was a sweetheart, reminding me of one of my uncles, except Henry couldn't talk to trees, and he was younger than I was, even though he looked a good deal older. He also treated us with a courtly respect that I found sorely lacking Earthside.

I finished bagging his books—Henry was an avid SF and fantasy reader and zoomed through at least a half dozen a week—and handed him the sack. "I resemble our father. She takes after our mother, who was human."

True, although far more than in just appearance. Delilah, the golden child, would always be closer to human than I. She had a soft heart and believed in the innate goodness of people. I worried about her sometimes. As for our sister Menolly, nobody knew where to trace her looks back to. The red hair was a recessive trait in both of our parents' lineages, but we hadn't ever figured out just which side held sway. The fact that she'd been turned into a vampire just complicated matters.

I escorted Henry out, flipped the sign from Open to Closed, and leaned against the doorframe. The rain was letting up, although the last of the drizzle still spattered against the pavement. I ducked out from under the awning and caught a drop on my tongue, then grimaced at the acidic taste. Otherworld's rain ran pristine and mineral thick, like glacier water. Yet another thing I missed from home.

Sighing, I closed the door and returned to the counter. Almost dark. Night, with its cloud cover, came early in the Pacific Northwest—one of the advantages to living in the area. By the time we reached the house, it would be safe to wake Menolly.

As I tallied up the receipts, Delilah scampered down the stairs. "Chase here yet?" she asked, hopping up to perch on the counter while I tucked away the receipts and locked the cash register. She wrapped her arms around her knees and cocked her head to the side, watching me. I could swear her ears twitched.

I glanced at the door. "No, but you can bet he's on his

way. Chase is never late unless an emergency crops up. So, how was your stakeout? Catch her in the act?"

Delilah grinned. "Nope. Turns out the woman has been spending her lunch hour volunteering at the Wilson Street Orphanage. I did a little prying and found out that she wants children, but her husband is sterile. I think she's looking to adopt but doesn't want to spring it on him yet."

"What did you tell him?"

"That she wasn't cheating. That her meeting was off campus. To quit worrying and appreciate his wife more." She snickered. "He didn't like that very much. I think he was hoping for an affair so he'd score one up on her. You know, sometimes I don't understand the culture. If she loves *him*, why should he be insecure if she mates with someone else?"

I laughed. "I don't think we'll ever figure everything out. Not entirely. I have no idea how our mother managed to fit into this world. Of course, she was one hundred percent human, when it came down to questions of fidelity," I said, thinking about the sharp-edged tongue that she'd unleashed on Father every now and again. "You know very well that she would have raised a riot if Father slept with another woman."

"That wouldn't have happened. Father never even looked at another female. I can't remember a single time, not in all the years we were growing up, that he commented on another woman's looks." Delilah sniffed. "I wish he was here. I'd feel safer with him around."

I grinned. "You're a trained OIA agent and yet you want your daddy here to protect you?" She blushed, but I waved away her embarrassment. "To tell the truth, I wish he was here too."

Delilah's eyes twinkled. "I miss Mama. I wish she hadn't died so soon. I wouldn't mind knowing more about our human side, and she could have taught us so much more than she did."

"That she could have." I gently pushed Delilah's bangs

out of her eyes. "Maybe while we're here, we can find out more about her family—our family."

All my instincts warned me that would be a mistake, but right now Delilah needed reassurance. Of the three of us, she missed our mother most. I was the oldest; I'd taken over when Mother died. Menolly was born independent. But Delilah . . . Delilah had clung to Mother's skirts for a long time before cautiously making her way into the world.

She wrinkled her nose. "I think humans must have bravery in their blood, don't you? After all, Mother followed Father home to a world she'd never known existed until he told her about it. That took courage."

"Don't forget how she managed to make herself welcome in OW, not an easy task for a full-blood human." In fact, it was damned amazing. Very few FBHs had ever made an impact on the Court. I shrugged into my coat. Like most of my clothes, I preferred the dramatic and had found a gorgeous vintage black opera coat in a consignment shop on Pike Street. It had been a steal at thirty dollars. "You're a romantic, Delilah. You always have been. All fluff and kittens and hearts."

"Hey! I can be a real tiger when I want to." She handed me my handbag, a beaded affair that matched the opera coat, and sniffed. "I just prefer to sheath my claws unless necessary."

I laughed. "Oh sweetie, don't fret. You're just as brave as our mother was. We all are. We left our home for a new world, just like she did. And our work is helping OW in the process."

"We're explorers," she said with a grin, which showed off the tips of her fangs. Unlike vampires' fangs, Delilah's weren't retractable. She received a lot of attention from men who liked dangerous women.

"Adventurers!" I countered, returning her smile.

"Lackeys in a two-bit government agency that thinks we're deadwood!" She thrust her arms in the air in a victory salute.

I sobered. "Too close to the truth for comfort. The OIA's as slow as a lumbering sloth, and one of these days, that will be its downfall. While we're on the subject, don't forget to add that we're crazy out of our minds for accepting this post." A movement outside the window caught my attention. "Here comes Chase. He looks worried."

The buzzer sounded as Chase hurried in. "Sorry I'm late," he said, his voice brusque and not inviting conversation. "I contacted HQ again, but save your questions till we're all together and in a secure place."

"Ready to go?"

He nodded. Delilah swung off the counter and slipped on her bomber jacket. At a hair over six feet and wearing tight jeans and stiletto boots, she was a sight to behold—both impressive and intimidating. After arming the security system, we headed for our respective cars.

The house in which we lived was a huge old Victorian, three stories high not counting the basement. Menolly slept there, hiding from the sun. I lived on the second story, and Delilah took the third. We shared the main floor, eating our meals together. Well, Delilah and I ate. Menolly just kept us company.

Set toward the back on five acres of land and next to a strip of woodland that led down to a large pond, the place hadn't come cheap. Lucky for us, Father had stockpiled a good sum of dollars from his time Earthside, keeping it in a secret account started years ago in a bank that had managed to keep itself afloat during the intervening decades. He gave it to us when we were assigned to this post, and over the years, interest had accrued. Along with the accounts Mother had left, we had enough to buy the house, furnish it, and keep ourselves going in a simple but comfortable fashion.

By tradition, we'd been given our mother's last name, even though she was human, and years ago, when we were born, Mother had insisted on getting Social Security cards for us. Father had brought her back Earthside to fill out the documents, and so when we'd arrived for our new posts, we'd been able to set up bank accounts and—after a lot of nail biting and practice—get our driver's licenses.

Thanks to our parents' foresight, we'd dodged one of the worst fates an Earthside OIA agent could be subjected to: living in one of the OIA's convenience suites. Read: slang for a cheap room in one of the roach-infested hotels owned and operated by agency flunkies.

Only OIA members were allowed to live there; a subtle way of keeping humans out of the loop, but not so subtle in reminding agents that they were a long ways from home and that the OIA owned their butts. Of course some operatives—giants like Jocko, and some of the goblins—were overjoyed with the conditions. They were used to living in hovels or caves that would make a skunk turn up its nose, but to the Sidhe, the grunge was positively appalling.

The drive into Seattle was the one drawback to living in Belles-Faire. It took half an hour to commute into the city in the morning, and another thirty minutes at night, if traffic was light. We were also five miles away from the nearest portal, which was hidden out in the woods, protected by one of the Hags of Fate. So slipping back to OW wasn't our first option should trouble arise. Otherwise, we had privacy, comfort, and a place where I could grow the herbs I needed for my spells.

Delilah kept down the mouse population, although she always complained they gave her indigestion. Another perk that came with living on the edge of a grimy suburb was that it made it easier for Menolly to hunt undetected. She did her best to confine herself to the dregs—thieves and the like—but I suspected that Chase would be pretty pissed if he really knew how she got her meals. We'd told him that she hunted stray animals. Which to us was close to the truth, considering the scum she went after.

I headed toward the porch as Delilah jumped out of her truck. Chase was close behind. I turned around and called back to her, "Why don't you get Chase a drink while I wake up Menolly?"

Chase looked like he wanted to protest, but then he shrugged and followed Delilah into the living room.

I slipped through the secret passage in the kitchen when I was sure he couldn't see me. We'd hidden the entrance to the basement for Menolly's safety—there wasn't much she could do in her sleep to protect herself. My skin prickled as I quietly tiptoed down the stairs. Sneaking into a vampire's lair was never a delight, even when the vamp in question was my own sister.

At least Menolly stayed away from stereotypes. The walls of the basement were painted a muted ivory, and she'd chosen a sage green toile for her bed linens and chair seats. She'd gotten the idea from an old episode of *Trading Spaces*, and by the results, it made me think she should go into interior design. But then, Menolly had an artistic bent. Unlike a number of vamps, she eschewed the tacky and kept herself meticulously clean, both in body and clothing.

She slept in a real bed, not a coffin, and we'd fashioned a blood room, accessible through a ventilation shaft, where she could hose herself off after feeding so she wouldn't track stains into the house. I appreciated her neatness, since most of the housework fell on my shoulders. Delilah always managed to conveniently stress out when it came time for chores, and Menolly did what she could at night, but even she had her limits for dusting and vacuuming. I kept asking the OIA to assign us a housekeeper. Probably a pipe dream, but I could fantasize, couldn't I?

As I approached the bed, I gauged my distance. Long scars forever embedded in my arm were a good reminder of the power a waking vamp could wield. After the first time, I stayed out of reach. Of course Menolly felt horrible about it, and I wasn't one to hold a grudge. But I wasn't stupid either, and now I stood well away from the bed whenever it was time to wake her up.

"Menolly? Menolly?"

The waxen expression on her face stirred. Lovely and

delicate, there wasn't a wrinkle in sight, and there never would be. She was far too pale, of course, but there was nothing we could do about it. We'd tried a bronzer for her skin, but it just turned her a bad shade of orange to match her hair—clouds of burnished strands caught up in dozens of beaded braids. Bo Derek of the vampire set. We watched a lot of old movies to catch up on pop culture.

"Huh?" She shot straight up in bed, blinking, and I jumped. Once bitten, twice shy. Her eyes shifted to red, then back to frost blue when she saw me standing there.

"Camille? Is it time to get up already?" She squinted at the clock. "Barely six thirty? Has the sun gone down?"

"Just now. You're safe. Something important happened, or I would have let you sleep longer. Chase is upstairs. HQ has assigned us a case."

She stretched and slipped out from under the covers. Where I was curvy and buxom, she was willow-thin and petite, the top of her head barely coming up to my nose. Delilah had us both beat, topping out at an inch over six feet, a good six inches taller than me, and athletic to boot. The girl would put Sarah Conner to shame. I just hoped that Jocko's death didn't foretell a meeting with our very own Terminator.

Menolly slipped into her jeans and a hunter green turtleneck. No shifting the jeans to fit her butt, no adjusting her boobs in her bra. In fact, she didn't have to wear a bra. No, she was like a beautiful porcelain mannequin, who would never fade, never gain weight, never have to face the world of underwire.

"What happened?" she asked, shaking her braids into submission. The beads clicked, and she grinned at the noise. She had confided in me that it made her feel alive again. Vamps moved in silence, and it drove her nuts.

I sat cross-legged on the bed, playing with the edge of the quilt. "Jocko's been murdered. HQ has pawned the case off on us. They say it's random, but I smell demon behind it. You're not going to the bar tonight—I called in for you this afternoon."

"Murdered? A demon killed Jocko?" Although her expression remained frozen, I heard the catch in her voice. She and Jocko had become good friends over the past few months, as good as a vampire and a giant could be. Both felt their handicaps keenly—Menolly hadn't asked to be a vampire, and Jocko had been born stunted.

I nodded. "I'm sorry." Leaning over, I wrapped my arm around her shoulder, and she stared at her hands. I could tell she was fighting off the tears—vampires' tears were red as the blood they drank, and she hated the stains that they caused.

"How? And who the hell would kill him? Jocko never hurt anybody who didn't ask for it." She let out a long sigh. "This just sucks."

I kissed her forehead. "I know it does. Somebody garroted him, a really bad scene. Chase will fill you in. He went to talk to HQ again after I smelled the scent of demon on the murder weapon. He said he managed to get a call through to them, though who knows what good it will do." I put my arm around her shoulders. "And on another subject, I have a surprise for you. I'm going to take you somewhere tonight, but I don't want you to ask why. Promise you'll go?"

"You aren't taking me to another strip bar, are you?" She glared at me. "After that last fiasco, I hope you learned that combining lots of bare skin and a hungry vamp is a recipe for disaster."

Not all of our attempts to understand Earthside culture had turned out to be good ideas. After I had managed to drag Menolly out of the bar and shake her out of her glazed state, I decided that the last thing she needed was to look at naked bodies. Which meant no Chippendale shows, strip clubs, saunas, locker rooms, or anything else of that ilk.

"Trust me, we're not going through that again. No, it's something quite different. Promise you'll go?"

She sighed as I led her toward the stairs. "Oh, all right. I promise. But it had better be as entertaining as the shows I get at work."

Chase and Delilah were waiting at the kitchen table. Chase had a bottle of beer in front of him, Delilah a glass of milk. Both looked so relieved when we appeared that I snorted. "Not much to talk about, huh?"

Delilah whistled and stared at the ceiling. Chase stared at his drink.

"Let's get this show on the road, then." I slid into my place, shivering as the warmth from the oak resonated through my body.

Chase was staring at Menolly, and for once, lechery wasn't even in the equation, a good thing for him. He was right to respect her. She could make quick work of him with a single bite.

I poured myself a glass of wine. Menolly didn't drink when we had company. Even though blood looked a lot like tomato juice and we kept some spare in the refrigerator, it could get a little awkward. And the smell had a tendency to put off people who weren't used to it.

"Okay, here's the scoop." Chase cleared his throat and pulled out a notebook. "Camille already knows some of this, but I'll start from the beginning to catch everybody up. This morning at five thirty, a wino—an informant—in the alley behind the Wayfarer stumbled over Jocko's body. He called me, and I arrived not more than ten minutes later. Jocko had been garroted. Whoever killed him had to be a strong motherfucker because Jocko's big, and it was obvious that he put up a fight. But the medical examiner agrees with me that he was probably killed inside the bar and then dumped out back. There was a trail of tipped-over chairs, and the back door was standing open."

Delilah winced. "Poor Jocko. What else did the medical examiner say?"

Chase consulted one of his notes. "Not much. They found traces of nonhuman energy signatures on him. Once Camille told me she smelled demon on the rope, I went back and asked them to check it out. Unfortunately, the OIA agent who did the autopsy doesn't recognize demon scent, and so we're waiting for a specialist to verify it."

"That somebody is big enough and strong enough to strangle a giant is a sobering thought." Menolly raised one eyebrow and nodded toward Delilah. I glanced at our blonde goddess of a sister.

The subtle signs of stress were playing out across her face. She was taking Jocko's death harder than I'd thought. Or maybe she was just tired—the full moon was coming up in a few days and she always got PMS—pre-moon-syndrome—before it hit. I tapped her on the arm.

"Drink your milk, honey. It will relax you."

She picked up her glass and lapped at it gently before taking a full sip.

Menolly propped her elbows on the table as she stared at Chase. "So, no idea of who or what killed him beyond demon scent?"

He shook his head. "No, but as I said, I got through to HQ once I talked to Camille. They're keeping close-mouthed on it, but they did ask if you'd overlooked reporting anything suspicious happening at the bar?"

Menolly sucked in a deep breath—more for show than any need of air—and pushed back her chair. "Just what are you hinting at, Johnson? That I screwed up or that I'm a traitor?"

Oops. I could see the impending signs of a blowup. The last thing we needed was a fracas between Menolly and Chase. I cleared my throat. "I don't think he was implying anything. HQ was the one who asked." I shot Chase a quick look that said, *Think first; speak later.*

He blinked, realizing how close he was to becoming dinner. "No, no! I wasn't implying anything of the sort," he said. "No offense meant."

"Then *HQ* thinks I messed up," Menolly said, her gaze still fastened on Chase's face.

Delilah picked up on the tension. "Please don't argue! I don't like it when you're mad." A stricken look crossed her face.

I pushed back my chair, but before I could reach her side, a wave rippled through the air, colors shifting and melding. The image of my sister folded in on itself, limbs shortening, body morphing. It was hideous to watch and looked incredibly painful, though Delilah denied that it hurt. A shower of golden light sparkled around her, and in her place, an orange tabby cat placidly sat, a sweet, blank look on its face.

CHAPTER 3

"Oh Great Mother, look what you two have done!" I cautiously approached Delilah and knelt down, holding out my arms. "Delilah? Kitty, kitty, kitty . . . come here."

Chase stared at the cat, transfixed. "Holy shit." He'd seen her in cat form but had never before witnessed the transformation process. "What happened? Is the moon full?"

"No, but certain stresses—especially when it comes to family altercations—also force her to shift. Sometimes, she's able to control the transformation, but not always." I pounced for the bewildered cat, but she slipped away, clawing her way up the curtains. Leaning against the fridge, I let out a long sigh. "Menolly? Some help, please."

Menolly snorted. "Good going, Johnson," she said as she approached the window. "Delilah, honey? I'm coming up. Don't be scared!" She slowly began to rise through the air as if she was standing on a pad of air. Delilah meowed but didn't try to escape as Menolly approached the top of the curtains. With a firm hand, she reached out and grasped Delilah by the pale blue collar that embodied Delilah's clothing. "Come on, you little twit," she said fondly.

Menolly held her tight until she hit the ground and then handed Delilah to me. As Delilah snuggled against my shoulder, I scratched behind her ears. "Poor baby, it's okay. It's okay," I said softly.

Chase cleared his throat, his eyes wide. "How long till she turns back to normal?"

"Once she calms down, she'll be okay," I said.

"Was she born that way?" he asked.

Menolly surprised me by fielding the question. "Delilah was born a werecat. Unlike others of her kind, she doesn't change into a big cat. Just our gorgeous little long-haired golden tabby." She laughed then, throaty and deep. With a glance at Chase, she added, "The children teased her about it when we were little, and sometimes they forced a change in order to 'play with the pretty kitty.' It got so bad our father and mother pulled her out of school."

Chase shook his head. "There's a lot I don't understand about the three of you yet."

"What exactly sets her off is hard to determine," I said. "I've seen her face down some of the nastiest criminals in OW and remain calm and in control, but let the three of us get in an argument, and she's a mass of fur and razor blades."

Delilah meowed in my ear. Loud. I turned to Chase and Menolly and, in a low voice said, "Okay, so the two of you need to tone down your spats because if you don't, I'll take matters into my own hands."

Chase rolled his eyes. "Uh-huh, you and what army? What are you going to do? Take off your clothes and dance nekkid, maybe?"

"Get your mind out of the gutter, and me with it, Johnson." I kept my voice even, but he knew I was pissed. "I may not be able to do much to Menolly, but *you* I can cast a spell on. Ever thought of what it would be like to be a toad? Or a mouse, maybe? Want to see what Delilah does to cute little mice?"

Menolly grinned, baring her fangs as Chase blanched. "She means it, Johnson. And considering the chance for backfire, I think I'd apologize."

"Why me? You're just as much to blame—"

"Oh cripes! Can't you two be in the same room together for five minutes without picking a fight?" Startled, Delilah tried to claw her way up my shoulder, resulting in a couple of deep scratches, but I stroked her neck, calming her down. "Can you quit bickering for one night? Please?" I stared pointedly at Chase.

He let out a long sigh. "Okay, I'm sorry. I'll play nice."

Menolly shook her head. "As usual, Camille, you're the voice of reason." She graciously extended a hand to Chase. "I'll pull my fangs in." She leaned toward Delilah and added, "Delilah, honey, you don't have to worry, I'm not going to have a Chase cocktail for dinner."

Chase drummed his fingers on the table. "Perhaps it's none of my business, but if Delilah was born a werecat, were you born a vampire?" he asked softly. "Nobody ever filled me in on your backgrounds, other than the fact that you're half-human and sisters. Hell, until a few years ago, I didn't even know vampires really existed. Witches or were-cats either," he added with a smile.

I glanced at Menolly. She shrugged and headed for the kitchen. "Tell him," she said on her way out.

Chase waited till she was out of the room. "Touchy subject?" he asked.

"You might say that. Nobody's born a vampire. You have to be made one, and almost anybody can be changed. Menolly was a top-notch acrobat; she could climb anything. Most of the time. Shortly after we joined the OIA, they assigned her to spy on the Elwing Blood Clan, a group of rogue vampires who refuse to play by Otherworld's rules. They were sheltering a greater vampire who was due to be deported to the Subterranean Realms. The Elwing Group has always been trouble; they give a bad name to all vampires."

Chase raised his eyebrows. "Aren't all vampires bad?"

"They have their place in the scheme of things. You'd be surprised how many were already here Earthside when we came over. But, as I said, the Elwing Blood Clan won't play by the rules. Menolly was collecting information on them when her ability to climb walls short-circuited—that half-human problem again. She slipped off the wall, and the Clan caught her. When they found out who she worked for, they didn't go easy on her."

"Bad, huh?"

"Bad doesn't even cover it. The techniques they use can shatter the psyche as well as the body. After torturing her, they turned her into a vampire."

I closed my eyes, remembering the morning she'd come stumbling home, body shattered, her soul no longer her own. She started toward me, then raced into her room and locked the door, screaming for me to get help. That was the last sound she made for weeks. It took the OIA months to restore her sanity.

"Oh Jesus, that's nasty."

"Yeah, it was. The scars they left on her body will be there forever. I'm hoping to help ease the scars in her heart."

"And OIA let her stay on?"

"It's a long story," I said, sighing. "Someday, I'll tell you the rest. Right now, I'm trying to help her adjust. To have fun even though she's . . . well . . . dead."

"Don't you mean undead?" Chase asked.

I grinned. "Definitions are a slippery slope."

After another awkward pause, Menolly returned from the kitchen. She paced the length of the dining room, her boots clipping a staccato beat against the hardwood. "Here's the deal. I know that I reported everything that seemed out of place. If there's an inside man, then he's damned good at hiding. I can smell undead like you can smell pussy—"

Chase blinked.

She snorted. "Oh, don't give me that innocent look. You've been sniffing after Camille's ass ever since we arrived. I don't really care what you're thinking, as long as you don't touch. She doesn't want you, and the sooner you accept that, the better. My point is, I can ferret out undead.

I can also pick up on some demons, though I'm on a learning curve there."

She leaned over his shoulder and tickled his neck with her hair. "I recognize the undead because I *am* one of them."

As her hand landed on his shoulder, nails digging in ever so softly, Chase paled. "Yeah, so I understand."

Menolly blew on his ear, tickling it with her tongue before flashing him a dark smile. Chase managed to look both terrified and turned on at the same time.

"Good." She sauntered back to her chair. "What I'm trying to tell you is that I'm the only member of the ooo-spooky set at the Wayfarer. There aren't any other undead there. And if the killer is a demon—whether from the Subterranean Realms or somewhere else—it has to be one of the races I haven't learned how to read. Most of those are Greater Demonkin."

Another awkward pause, and Delilah's purr stopped. She twitched her nose, her whiskers brushing my hand, and her fur started to ripple. Quickly, before we reenacted a mishap I didn't care to repeat, I plopped her on the floor next to my chair. The air shimmered and Delilah stood there, blinking.

"Sorry," she said, stretching her neck. With a quick lick of her hand, she said, "Didn't mean to do that."

"Don't apologize," I said. "Menolly knows better than to scare you."

Menolly grinned and stared at the ceiling.

I tapped my goblet with a spoon. "Attention—now that the excitement is over, can we get back to business?" I looked up to find Chase staring at Delilah, his eyes dark and unreadable. Pointing toward his notebook, I said, "What else have you got for us?"

He flipped open the binder. "There's one other thing. The person I was talking to at the OIA left his station for a moment, and somebody took his place. Guy with jet-black skin and silver hair—dangerous-looking dude. He gave me a message directed at you specifically, Camille." Chase swallowed. "He said he'd twist my balls off if you didn't get it."

The look on his face was priceless, but I couldn't even dredge up a smile. My pulse started to race, and a flurry of images flickered through my mind, dark and passionate. Shit. I knew exactly who Chase was talking about.

"Trillian is working for the OIA? That isn't possible. They wouldn't hire him." I glanced over at Menolly and Delilah, both of whom were frowning.

Chase stared at me, a scowl on his face. "You know who this guy is?" Without waiting for an answer, he continued. "He said, and I quote, 'Rumor has it something big is going down in the lower depths. There's a new ruler, and he's far more ambitious than the Beasttägger was. Don't count on help from home.' "

The skin on my arms rippled. "The last I heard, the Beasttägger was in charge. Promotions down there come at the expense of a superior's life, so the Beasttägger probably whispered hello to the point of an assassin's knife. Did Trillian say anything else?" On one hand, I prayed he'd sent me a personal note. On the other, any step closer to that dark, murky pool from which I'd barely managed to extricate myself would be asking for trouble.

Leaning back in his chair, Chase stuck his hands in his pockets. "Yeah. He said, 'Tell Camille that Shadow Wing's in charge now. And he's on the warpath.' That mean anything to you?"

Menolly sucked in a deep breath, and Delilah let out a little "Oh" of fear. I returned Chase's stare. "Shadow Wing? Are you sure?"

He nodded. "What's wrong? You look like you've seen a ghost." He grimaced. "Strike that. You're probably best friends with one."

I sank back in my chair, all thoughts of Trillian slipping to the side. Shadow Wing's name was well known throughout Otherworld. A powerful demon overlord, he'd risen through the ranks in the lower depths with a ruthlessness that defied understanding. Nothing stood in his way. He went after what he wanted, and he never failed. His name had been feared in OW for hundreds of years, though from a distance.

According to everything I'd heard about him, Shadow Wing made it abundantly clear that he thought humankind should be razed to the ground. Father had told us that the OIA had been begging the Court and Crown to pay attention to the growing unrest for years, but the Queen was too caught up in her opium dreams to care. Now, with Shadow Wing in power, both Earth and Otherworld were at risk.

"I'm thinking OIA may not want to even consider this, but do you think there's a chance that Jocko's death might have something to do with Shadow Wing?" I glanced at my sisters, wincing.

"Oh crap," Menolly slumped back in her chair. "That's the last thing I needed to think about."

Delilah blinked. "Maybe we're overreacting? Maybe it's just a random strike by some idiot demon who got himself trapped Earthside?"

I stared at her. "Did you even *hear* the message Trillian sent?"

She shrugged. "It came from Trillian. What can I say?"

I let it drop. Neither one of my sisters liked my ex, but a voice inside whispered to me that we were standing at the tip of the iceberg, staring at an enemy far greater than anything the OIA had ever faced.

After escorting a subdued Chase out the door, we sat around the table, mulling over the situation. With Shadow Wing riding at the helm of the Subterranean Realms, our job had taken a turn for the dangerous. Not to mention that I had a personal stake in the matter. Trillian was back, and he had singled me out. How had he hooked up with the OIA? They didn't accept Svartans in their service, any more than my family had accepted him.

My stomach rumbled and, hungry, I shoved back my chair, went to the refrigerator, and pulled out a loaf of whole grain bread, a packet of sliced chicken breast, sliced

Swiss cheese, and a bowl of tomatoes. Delilah perked up when I fixed a couple sandwiches and handed her one.

"So, we've got some decisions to make," I said, settling back into my chair. "I know that Jocko's murderer either was—or had close contact with—a demon. That rope is permeated with the stench."

Menolly's eyes narrowed. "The question is, does Shadow Wing have a hand in this, or is the demon a rogue? And are there any mortals involved? Humans, Sidhe, somebody discontent with the status quo?"

"Anybody new check in at the Wayfarer the past few nights, however unlikely a suspect? Maybe a shape-shifter?"

She frowned, tapping her taloned nails on the table. "A few, but they all cleared through as being from Otherworld. Of course, that doesn't mean that they're on the up and up. There are some shady characters back home."

I nodded. While the Subterranean Realms were home to the biggest, baddest beasties, OW had its share of malcontents, and not all of them fit the stereotype. "Did Jocko have any friends here?" I asked.

Menolly snorted. "He was popular with the women. He was hung like a horse and apparently FBH women loved him. I know for a fact that he spent a lot of time hanging out with one woman in particular. Her name's . . . give me a minute," she said, thinking. "Oh yes, Louise. Louise Jenkins."

"Do you know where she lives?" I asked.

"Not a clue." Menolly shook her head.

"Okay, here's the plan. Delilah, you're the detective. Find out whatever you can about this Jenkins woman. Where she lives, who she hangs out with, if she was seen with Jocko anytime in the past day or so. Anything that seems remotely important."

Delilah grinned. Sometimes I think she loved her cover job playing detective more than she loved her real job working for OIA. "Will do, Chief."

Menolly looked at me expectantly. "What should I do?"

"There are a lot of gang members and derelicts that frequent the alleys around the bar. I think you should pay them a visit later tonight and see what you can find out." I gave her a long look. She knew what I meant.

A slow smile spread across her face. "I am hungry," she said softly.

"Take only what you need to quench your thirst," I warned her. "Wipe the memory of the others. We don't want to leave a bunch of bodies around a recent murder scene, and we don't want Chase on our backs."

She nodded, laughing, and the ivory beads of her braids sounded like dancing bones. "And you? What are you going to do?"

I closed my eyes. "The only thing I can think of. I'm going to pay a visit to Grandmother Coyote."

Menolly and Delilah stared at me, openmouthed, but I stopped any protests with a raised hand. "I know, I know—the Hags of Fate are dangerous, but we have no choice. Grandmother Coyote may be able to tell us whether Jocko's death is connected with Shadow Wing."

Menolly stood. "If I'm going to hunt, I'd better get ready."

"Not so fast." I stopped her. "Wait till after midnight when there won't be so many people out and about. Besides, you made a promise, and I'm holding you to it."

She squinted, staring at me for a moment, then turned to Delilah. "Hey, Kitten, do you know where Camille's planning on taking me?"

Delilah got very busy, very fast, studying her fingernails. "I need a manicure. My nails are growing too fast again." She began to whistle.

Menolly cleared her throat. "I asked you a question."

"And I didn't answer!" Delilah said, hopping off her chair. "Don't blame me, Menolly—it's all Camille's idea!"

"Traitor!" I yelled after her, laughing as she raced up the stairs. I glanced at Menolly, who was giving me a long stare. "Get your coat and let's go."

"I don't need a coat. I don't get cold," she said dryly.

"But you can get wet, and it's pouring out right now." I slipped into my opera coat and picked up my keys. Menolly silently followed me out to the car. As I started the ignition, she popped a CD in the slot and we went sailing down the road to the wailing tunes of Godsmack.

Our destination was the basement of an old school turned community center. Goose bumps rippled along my arms as we descended the stairs, and Menolly once again hissed in my ear, "What is this? Where are you taking me?" she asked for what had to be the hundredth time since we left the house.

"Will you just shut up until we get there?" I knew she was going to be pissed. "You'll see soon enough. Please, just go along with this? For me?"

She let out a low sigh. "All right, all right. You owe me a big one."

"And I know you won't let me forget it." I flashed her a grin, and she rolled her eyes. As we came to the end of the stairs, a set of double doors faced us. On the door was a poster, and in the dim light it read V.A. Meeting, 10:00 P.M.

"This better not be what I think it is—" she started to say as I pushed open the doors. We entered the room, and with a quick look around, Menolly let out a groan. "Holy shit. Camille, what the hell were you thinking?"

"Would you quit whining and give it a chance?" I said. "Now find a place for us to sit down. And make sure we're sitting together. I don't feel safe here without you next to me."

"Serves you right," she muttered but then grabbed my arm and looked around. "There are two seats in the third row. You'd better sit next to the aisle. You're prime meat at this meeting, you know that?"

I knew she was right, but I also knew she'd never have come on her own if I'd just told her about it.

The room was about thirty by thirty feet, with four rows of chairs facing a lectern covered with a bloodred cloth.

A folding table to one side held what looked like bottles of warm blood. There was a plate of cookies and some coffee for family members. The basement had no windows, and an emergency exit offered passage to the sidewalk, probably a good idea, considering the nature of the meeting.

The other guests milled around the room. A few hovered near the ceiling, looking almost in trance. Everyone I could see was as bone-pale as Menolly. Some were dirty and matted and smelled like they could use a good bath. Others were fastidiously clean.

One woman with shocking silver hair and a figure to die for wore a black Yves St. Laurent Rive Gauche dress and Chanel ballet pumps with ribbons that wrapped up her legs. She looked stunning, even more so due to the brilliant crimson on her lips and nails that contrasted with her wan complexion. I blinked. That was Sassy Branson, the reclusive socialite mentioned in last month's *Seattle Magazine.* I read several local magazines to keep up to speed with the city and recognized her picture from an article about some big charity fund-raiser held a few months ago. So Sassy was a vampire? Who would have guessed?

A couple of the other vamps in the room were staring at me with obvious interest, their nostrils flaring, but when Menolly put her arm around me, they kept their distance. One of them, a geeky-looking man with a ponytail and a layer of thin fuzz covering his chin, was dressed in a Microsoft T-shirt and a pair of holey jeans. He slowly winked as he caught my gaze and raised his bottle as if in salute.

I swallowed and pressed closer to Menolly. "Maybe this wasn't such a good idea—"

She snorted. "You think? But now that we're here, why don't we stick around for a little while and see what's going down?" Her eyes flashed, and I had the feeling she was enjoying watching me squirm.

I cleared my throat. "Am I the only one alive here?" Somehow I'd expected more family support to show up.

"Don't let it bother you," a voice said from behind us. "Members are prohibited from drinking from the other guests while on the premises. You'll be safe enough, at least in body. We don't control the fantasies of our participants."

I whirled. The man who had spoken was of average height with bleached blond hair. He wore a tweed jacket with leather patches on the elbows, a pair of tidy jeans, and plastic-rimmed square glasses.

Before I could stop myself, I blurted out, "I didn't know vamps ever needed to wear glasses."

"Force of habit," he said. "The glass is purely for show. I can't seem to get used to going without them. I'm still a relative newborn. In fact, I'm the one who started this group." His gaze slid over Menolly, slowly drinking her in. "If you don't mind me saying so, you're stunning."

She looked startled, and I knew what was running through her head. It had been a long time since anyone but Delilah and I'd said that to her. Humans found vampires irresistible, but it was that old undead charm that did it. For a fellow vamp to comment on her beauty was quite another matter.

"Thank you," she said slowly. "I'm Menolly. This is my sister, Camille."

He nodded. "And you're both part Faerie, if I'm not missing my guess. We're about to get started, so please take your seats, ladies."

As we made our way to our chairs, Menolly was quiet. I expected her to make some catty comment regarding the seedier-looking members of the audience, but she seemed preoccupied.

The vampire we'd been speaking to took the podium and gazed out over the twenty or so members of the audience. "Welcome, children of the night and their guests, to the regular weekly meeting of Vamps Anonymous. For those who are new, let me explain why we're here."

Menolly squirmed in her seat, glancing around. Nobody else seemed out of place, so we were probably the only newbies around.

"We're a group of recently transformed vampires—along with supportive relatives—who are all facing the difficulties inherent with adjusting to a new way of life. Or death, if you prefer. I used to be a psychiatrist before one of my clients decided I'd be better off as a vampire. Now I counsel my peers. I'll begin the introductions." He held up a hand and waved. "Hi, I'm Wade, and I've been a vampire for five years."

The audience rang out in unison with a resounding, "Hi, Wade!"

Menolly blinked, and I could see her fighting back a smile. The enthusiasm in the room, which had been so lacking before the meeting started, now reverberated from the walls as each person—vampire—gave their name and the standard speech and was met in return with a hearty welcome.

When the round-robin came to Menolly, she grabbed my hand, giving me a *Please don't make me do this* look.

Wade must have noticed her reluctance because he called out, "Please, don't be nervous. I know this may feel silly at first, but it's a relief to have a place where we can discuss what it's like to be undead. These weekly meetings are open to both vamps and their living family. We also have a private vamp-only meeting every two weeks for discussions of a more personal nature."

Slowly, Menolly let go of my hand. She stood up, looking like she'd rather be anywhere but here, and in a clear voice said, "Hi. I'm Menolly. I'm half-Faerie, half-human, and I've been a vampire for twelve Earthside years."

As she sat back down, everyone shouted, "Hi, Menolly!" and that faint smile crept back across her face.

By the time the meeting was over, the vampires were doing their best to be civil to me and not stare like I was a Big Mac with fries on the side.

Menolly exchanged a few phone numbers. Sassy Branson, the socialite in the Rive Gauche dress, seemed especially attentive. She still retained enough of her humanity to be taken in by our Sidhe charm, and we found ourselves—Delilah included—invited to her annual holiday cocktail party in early December. It crossed my mind that we'd be a definite social coup for her, though she did caution us to avoid mentioning that both she and Menolly were vampires.

"My friends haven't figured it out yet, and I'd like to keep it that way," she said, a savvy look on her face. "They just thought I'd taken ill for awhile, and I play up my eccentricities to keep them guessing. It was lovely to meet you, girls. Camille, you're a good sister to bring Menolly to the meeting."

Wade also made sure to get our number, and Menolly seemed only too happy to give it to him. On the drive home, I glanced at her.

"Are you mad at me for taking you there?"

She stared out the window. "At first I was, but now . . . I suppose not." She shrugged. "You might be right. It might be good for me to know a few other vamps who don't seem hell-bent on playing the big, dark, and ugly like most of the ones back in OW. Sassy sure doesn't dress down."

And with that, I knew that I'd been forgiven.

CHAPTER 4

By the time we arrived home, it was close to eleven thirty. Delilah peeked out from the parlor. "Is it safe to come out?" she said.

Menolly grinned. "I'm not going to bite, and Camille is still in one piece, so get your ass out here, Kitten." When Delilah joined us, Menolly added, "I notice you weren't there lending me your undying support tonight."

Delilah let out a laugh that was almost a purr. "*Undying* is the operative word. I thought that I should stay home in one piece to pick up what was left of Camille when you got done with her. I'm glad that you aren't upset, though. Next time—if you go—I'll be happy to go along."

Shrugging, Menolly said, "I'm not sure if I'll go again. Maybe. We'll see. I'm going downstairs and change. It's time to go hunting." She blew us a kiss and disappeared through the secret passage that led to the basement.

I watched her go, feeling the bloodlust surround her, the hunger a palpable force that radiated like a brilliant gem from her center. It had filled the room at the meeting earlier, and it was fascinating to feel the different levels of thirst that rolled through the room. After a moment, I turned back to Delilah.

"Find anything out about the Jenkins woman yet?"

She stood and stretched, her face a mask of bliss as she rolled her neck and arched her back. "Nope. I was watching *Sex and the City*, but I'll get to work now. I can surf the net on my laptop while Tyra's on."

My sister napped off and on through the day in her office, but like any cat, she spent part of the night awake. She'd developed an addiction to late-night TV, a realm that I avoided at all costs. I loved movies and had been gorging on them since we first crossed over Earthside, but Delilah had a taste for the lurid that eluded me, an odd contrast to her noncombative nature. At least at night I was usually asleep. Delilah liked company during the wee hours, and she'd cajoled Menolly to sit through more episodes of *Jerry Springer* than I wanted to count.

"Louise shouldn't be too hard to track down. When are you leaving to visit Grandmother Coyote?" she asked, giving a little shudder. "I don't envy you, that's for sure. Those Elementals scare the hell out of me."

"You are such a wuss," I said fondly. "But I love you anyway." I stared out at the blustery night. The wind was whipping leaves off the trees. We had less than a week before the full moon. Delilah would be useless that night, Menolly would be on the prowl, and I would be at the zenith of my power and more than a little crazed. "I'd better go now. I don't think she hangs around the woods during the day—too much chance some idiot with a gun might catch her."

Delilah shuddered. "Better you than me. Be careful, Camille. People prowl these woods too, and humans can be as dangerous as Elementals. There are a lot of evil men in the world."

I gave her a long look. Since we'd arrived Earthside, Delilah's unfailing optimism had started to crack ever so slightly. "I'll be careful, I promise." I gave her a kiss on the forehead before heading toward the stairs. A veiled shriek from the wind caught my attention, and I stopped to glance out the window at the leaves that rustled and whirled to the ground.

She followed my gaze. "There's an ill wind blowing tonight."

I closed my eyes. Delilah was right. The wind was filled with graveyard dust and the footsteps of the dead walking. As I headed up to my room, I thought about the events of the evening. We might have been considered disposable before, but with Shadow Wing looming in, the OIA was going to need every hand at the ready, even if they didn't realize it yet. And we were leading the brigade.

My apartment on the third floor reflected my many moods. Four rooms and a bath, I'd turned one into a magical sanctuary, which included the only balcony in the house. With a table and chair under a rainproof awning, I could sit beneath the starlight and recharge myself.

As I slipped out of my work clothes, framed by the chill of the night, my body ached. Last time I'd had sex had been back in Otherworld. Too long for my tastes, but no one Earthside had caught my fancy. In fact, nobody had touched me since my last meeting with Trillian. And now he was inching back into my life, even if only through a lone message.

A Svartan, he was one of the dark Fae from Svartalfheim, a city in the Subterranean Realms. But Trillian had turned sides and moved to Otherworld. We met under a dark moon one night when I was feeling particularly vulnerable, and from the first touch, he'd left me spoiled for anyone else. Trillian had stolen my heart as easily as he'd claimed my body. I'd ripped myself away from him when I realized what was happening, but once you've been with a Svartan, there's no going back.

He'd pursued me for months, and I finally ended up taking some time away from work, hiding at home protected by my sisters until I felt strong enough to stand on my own. But since then every man had paled in comparison, and

I still craved the passion with which Trillian had chained me. He was a bad boy and I knew it, but I missed him.

I ran my fingers down my body, lingering over my breasts as my nipples stiffened. Catching my breath, I forced myself to drop my hand. I didn't have time to indulge my fancy. I had work to do.

I opened my closet and dug through until I found what I was looking for—an ankle-length black skirt, a long-sleeved blouse that would keep me warmer than a fur coat, and a spider-silk cape that reached my knees. All were Otherworld garments, woven to glide through the forest with ease and to keep out the cold.

Sliding into the skirt and top, I laced up a pair of leather ankle boots and stared at myself in the mirror. My face was a pale shadow against the flowing cape that would offer me easy passage through the woods, unfettered by the thick undergrowth that grew in this area. And my eyes glowed brilliant violet against the raven hair and pale skin. At times they were flecked with silver—when I had been working magic for a long time, or when I walked the paths of Otherworld.

With a sigh, I sank to the edge of the bed, homesick. Earth might have been my mother's home world, but it wasn't mine. And yet, neither was Otherworld. I knew Delilah and Menolly felt the same way. We were caught between worlds, caught between races, caught between dimensions. When we were children our playmates taunted us, calling us Windwalkers—beings who never settled in one place, who never belonged to a land or a clan.

When we'd joined the OIA, we'd hoped that it would bring us closer to our father's people. But our strangeness had only been accentuated since Menolly had been captured and transformed. And now . . . now there was no going back, even if we wanted to.

Bracing myself, I strode to the door and raced out into the night. I jumped in my Lexus—a steel-gray shadow hidden in the mist that was rising—and pulled out of the driveway, glancing up at the moon, who was peeking through a break in the clouds. We were bound, she and I, by the oaths and trials I'd taken during my initiation. I could always count on the Moon Mother to watch over me and to drive me into a frenzy when she went full and the Hunt was on the prowl.

Grandmother Coyote lived in the woods on the outskirts of Belles-Faire. She'd been drawn to this place because of the portals, and she guarded one outside of the OIA's jurisdiction. By day she was just an old woman reading fortunes in a dim little shop on the wrong side of town. By night, she came into her own, because Grandmother Coyote was one of the Hags of Fate. She neither wove nor created destiny but simply watched it unfold. Sometimes, for a price, she would look at the strands and read what was most likely to happen.

Once I reached the edge of the wood, I stepped out of the car and closed my eyes, dropping my head back to catch the wind. "Show me the way," I whispered, and the stars heard me from behind their cloud cover and answered. The sound of singing echoed from deep within the stand of cedar and fir.

I moved through the bushes like a fish through water as branches slid away from the material of my cape. Creeping around thick cedar and fir trunks, I clambered over a leaf-strewn windfall that blocked my path, taking down a spider's web strung between two trees. The arachnid landed on my hand, and I gave her a little tap and sent her on her way, watching as the striped orb weaver clambered along one of the remaining threads and began reweaving her net. Like all of my father's kin, I could see in the dark, perhaps not quite as clearly as a full-blood Sidhe, but enough to recognize colors and shapes with little difficulty.

After a few minutes, the huckleberry and bracken fern gave way, and I entered the center of a small grove, circular and mossy and open to the sky. I paused, feeling my way through the energy. Magic ran thick here—the magic of old woodlands and dark lords and deep secrets. Some

FBHs could feel it. Some of the human witches and pagans had flocked to my store, their eyes shining because what they so long believed had come true, though in ways that often shocked them.

I reached out, searching, and then I felt her. *Grandmother Coyote*. She was watching from behind one of the lone oaks that dotted the copse.

"Come out, come out, wherever you are. I have questions and concerns for you, Grandmother. You are needed," I whispered.

Within moments the undergrowth on the other side of the glade rustled, and out stepped an old woman. Clad in a long gray green robe, she moved silently across the lea to stand beside me. Her hair was hidden beneath a hood, but wisps of white fur peeked out from the edges to frame her face, which was so ridged with wrinkles it was difficult to imagine that she'd ever been young. Cracks on the road map of eternity.

She might have been born old. One of the Elemental spirits, Grandmother Coyote was bound to Earth but served all realms. She lived outside of time, immortal. Or as immortal as the planet allowed her to be. When the earth died, so too would she. No demon could kill her, no human could harm her, no one from Otherworld could charm her. Outside of reach, she was in touch with everything that wandered the planet, every event that took place on its surface.

She looked into my eyes, and I stood still, allowing her to probe my essence. Grandmother Coyote would speak or not as she willed, but my behavior would determine how much she might be willing to tell me.

"What is it you seek, daughter of Y'Elestrial, and of Earth?"

Y'Elestrial . . . my homeland in Otherworld. I knelt, genuflecting.

"Very pretty," she said, her voice a smidgeon above a cackle. "But you know as well as I do that actions can be deceiving. All the pretty manners in the world won't cover an empty soul. Stand and let me listen to your heart."

I rose from my knees and sat beside her on one of the windfalls while the clouds parted and the gibbous moon flared through the trees, its silver beams illuminating our faces.

"I'm with the OIA, and I'm looking for answers to a murder, and a recent shift in power. We need to know what's happening. Will you help me?"

Grandmother Coyote stared at me, her gaze splitting me wide as she viewed every atom within my body, every thought within my soul. I felt like I was naked, tied spread-eagle to a stone under the starry night, open for scrutiny, every flaw and strength exposed.

After a moment she motioned for me to follow her to the base of one of the nearby trees. The trunk was huge—wide enough to fit several men—and when she approached, a light shimmered as a doorway formed. She ducked her head, entering, and I followed.

Within the trunk we strode along a dirt path lit by dancing lights and shrouded on both sides by mist and shadow. Near the end, we came to a cave within which rested a small table and two chairs carved out of oak. The knots and burls blinked as I took the chair opposite her. I had the uneasy feeling I was sitting on somebody's face but pushed it aside. Now wasn't the time to question seating arrangements.

Grandmother Coyote sang a few notes, and a candle sprang to life. On the oaken table rested a crystal ball almost as big as my head. Grandmother Coyote leaned close and blew a long, slow breath on it, the mist from her lungs enveloping the orb like fog. A spark flared in the center of the crystal, radiating out. She opened a velvet pouch that hung on her belt and held it out to me.

"Let's see what the bones have to say," she said. "Choose three."

I cautiously reached within the darkened pouch, and my fingers met a smooth surface that felt like polished ivory. The bag was filled with finger bones from all different races and species. Swallowing a lump that rose in my throat,

I let my fingers close around three of them before withdrawing my hand.

"Place the first on the table."

I opened my hand, and the first bone, a long, narrow digit etched with symbols that I couldn't read, fell onto the table. Grandmother Coyote gazed at it for a moment, then looked deep into the crystal ball.

"A great shadow arises. He intends to rule all three worlds. Born from the fire, his nature is greed." She jerked her head up, and even though I knew she was immune to fear, I imagined a quaver in her voice as she said, "*A Soul Eater*. He charms the birds from the trees, the fish from the water. He unites those who will not be united into a great force, and they are sending out scouts even as we speak . . . to look for . . ." She paused, then shook her head. "I'm not sure what he's looking for yet."

Shadow Wing. She had to be talking about Shadow Wing. Soul Eaters were the biggest of the big bads. They devoured the very essence of their enemies, casting the souls into oblivion as they absorbed their opponents' power. Among the highest order of demons, Soul Eaters were rare, and they usually managed to charm their way into positions of authority. Once there, they turned tyrant, and the resulting rule was always bloody. By the time their minions realized what was going on, it was too late.

"The second bone," Grandmother Coyote said. I dropped the second bone in front of her. It was a finger from a Brownie. Shuddering, I jerked my hand back as she picked up the digit and closed her eyes.

"Long ago, the Elemental Lords were given guardianship over the spirit seal, which was broken into nine parts, fashioned into pendants. The Lords grew lazy, and the seals were lost. Eventually mortals found them and took possession. These are what the scouts seek. When they find the seals, they will take them into the depths where they will be joined back as one, and the Soul Eater will rip open the portals that separate the worlds."

Spirit seals? I must have looked confused, because she paused. "You don't know what the spirit seals are?"

I shook my head. "No, I've never heard of them."

"No accounting for the school system, either in OW or here," she said, disgruntled. "But that doesn't surprise me. Whenever mortals of any kind are involved, they forget the past and repeat mistakes." Grandmother Coyote looked as if she was debating whether to tell me more. She held up a hand. "Wait here," she said, rising to disappear into the shadows that surrounded the table.

I slowly opened my hand and stared at the remaining bone. It was the finger of a human—a woman. That much I could read off of it, but more I couldn't see. I started to stand, intending to stretch, but the chair wrapped a branch around my waist, holding me fast.

"Hey! What are you doing?" I squirmed, trying to get free, but the limb anchored me firmly in place. Apparently, I wasn't allowed to wander around. At least it wasn't trying to feel me up. I relaxed, and the branch relaxed. I tried to stand again, and once again found myself slammed back into the seat. "Okay, okay, you win," I mumbled.

Just then, Grandmother Coyote reappeared. "Getting fresh with you, is it? No worry. I just don't want strangers wandering through my labyrinth."

She flashed me a smile then, the first I'd seen from her, and I cringed. Her teeth were razor sharp, shining steel in the night. Menolly's fangs looked like baby teeth in comparison to Grandmother Coyote's metal mouth. Either she didn't notice or she chose to ignore my response, because she held out a book. "You can have this. It will teach you the history of the spirit seals, at least enough for you to understand what you're up against."

I murmured a thank-you and took the book. The cover was hand-tooled leather—dragon leather. I ran my fingers over it, feeling the low rumble that still emanated from the skin. I hadn't heard of a dragon slaying in a long time. The book must be ancient. I carefully set it aside and tossed the third bone on the table. Grandmother Coyote fingered it for a moment, then shook her head.

"Out near Great Mother Rainier, you will find one of the seals. That is, you will if you get there before the Soul Eater's scouts."

"What does the seal look like?" I asked, thinking of Mount Rainier and just how vast the national park was.

Grandmother Coyote snorted. "A talisman of energy, a swirl of souls. Look for the pendant around the neck of a man known as Tom Lane." Her eyes began to spin, and I blinked against their kaleidoscopic brilliance.

A guardian, or an unwitting accomplice to fate? "Is he human?"

"Yes and no, but that's all I'm going to tell you. And now, the bill for my services."

I winced. She had every right to demand payment. I just hoped it wouldn't be something I needed in order to live. "What do you want?"

She gave me a lazy grin. "I have yet to collect the finger bone of a demon."

Oh yeah, that sounded doable. I coughed. "I don't know any demons. And I sincerely doubt that they'd give up a finger bone for my sake."

"A free prediction, my dear. Over the coming years, you will know far more demons than you ever hope to. If you survive the coming onslaught, you'll have plenty to choose from. Bring me your favorite," she said. "And if you don't, then one of your fingers will do *just fine*."

Before I had time to sputter, I found myself standing back in the center clearing of the grove, alone. I whirled around, looking for Grandmother Coyote, but she'd disappeared, and I couldn't pick out which tree was hers.

For a moment, I wondered if I'd imagined the whole thing, but when I looked down at my feet, I saw four objects: the three bones gleaming in the moonlight and the book. I scooped them up and, feeling the need to be out of the woods as quickly as possible, ran through the trees, glancing at the moon over my shoulder. The Huntress was racing the night winds, the Hunt only a few nights away. I couldn't afford to get swept up in the primal chase with this mess looming over our heads, but when the Moon Mother called, I answered.

At my car, I took one quick look back at the forest. For a moment, a hundred red eyes peered out of the gloom, staring in my direction. Needing no further hint, I slid into the driver's seat and pulled back onto the road. As I headed for home, I wondered just where in the world I was supposed to find a demon willing to part with his index finger. Because I sure as hell wasn't ready to give up one of mine.

The night was waning by the time I slammed the front door behind me. I slipped into the living room, startling Delilah. Menolly sat by her side, apparently back from hunting. A glance at the TV made me flinch.

"*Blind Date*? Honey, you've got to develop some viewing taste. Maybe we should make you watch PBS?"

Delilah snorted as she fished another corn chip out of the bag of Fritos. "You and what army? Mr. Big Bad Demon?"

With a laugh, Menolly burped. She flipped off the TV, looking sated. Obviously, she'd fed well. Delilah beamed, waving a packet of papers.

"I found Louise Jenkins! You want to pay her a visit tomorrow?"

"Hold on a few. Let me get out of these clothes first," I said, dashing up the stairs. I changed into a long satin nightgown and slipped on a matching robe, again blessing Earthside clothing designers. Victoria's Secret was my secret playground. My thoughts flickered briefly to Trillian. He loved silk and satin.

Sighing, I brushed out my hair and slid on a pair of fuzzy slippers. By the time I returned to the living room, the knots of tension from my encounter with Grandmother Coyote were beginning to ease, but my shoulders still hurt like hell. I plopped myself down on the floor in front of Menolly.

"Neck rub?" I asked, leaning back. She wrinkled her nose and smiled. I noticed her fangs were retracted, but there was a smudge of blood on her lower lip that she'd missed. I silently handed her a tissue and tapped my chin. She wiped her mouth. "I take it you had a good night?"

"Very good," she said, rubbing the kinks out of my shoulders. Her fingers were so strong that it occurred to me she might look into becoming a masseuse. Cancel that. The image of her massaging a stranger's neck brought up other thoughts—not so good ones. I backtracked from the idea. Menolly had self-control, but even the best of us could experience a weak moment.

"I found out more than I expected to, and the world now possesses one less perv," she said. "He was about to slice up a hooker who works the back alley around Jocko's. I wiped her memory after I took care of her would-be suitor. In fact, I wiped her memory and told her to go find a good job as a waitress. When she comes to, maybe she'll get herself off the streets." Menolly had a penchant for tracking down the whack-jobs of the world. Since we'd been here, she'd saved the police a great deal of expense and trouble, even if they didn't know it.

I grasped Menolly's hand and gave it a quick kiss. "Good work," I said. "So what did you find out?"

Her eyes glistened, flaring crimson before fading back to the icy gray they'd turned when she'd died. "I talked to one of the men who sleeps in a box next to the restaurant—not Chase's informant, but a buddy who was drunk when Chase interviewed him. He told me what he forgot to tell Chase. Seems three figures came racing out of the back door in the wee hours of the morning, dragging Jocko by a rope. They left him in the alley before fleeing. My man was sleeping it off behind a pile of cardboard boxes. But it's bad. Big, bad news."

I held my breath. "As in?"

"As in a trio of demons. From the descriptions, I figured out what we're looking at. Starting with a Psycho Babbler."

"Oh great," I moaned. Psycho Babblers were reptilian, able to shift into the most gorgeous of mortals. They were similar to incubi, but they never bothered to have sex with their victims. They just charmed them into a violent and bloody death. And they were stupid. Real stupid.

"It gets even better," she said with a grim smile. "The second one's a harpy, and that's just nasty. But the third . . . we're in worse trouble than we thought." Her nostrils flared, and her fangs extended just a smidgen. Something had my sister excited. Delilah put down her book, looking grave.

My spirits sank. Grandmother Coyote said Shadow Wing had sent scouts through the portals, and it seemed she'd been telling the truth. Maybe I had more chance to find that demon finger than I thought.

"Okay, I'll bite. Who's our third man?"

"Remember when Father told us about a demon he'd fought on one of his scouting missions? The one who killed Uncle Therasin? He showed us the demon's image in the Crystal Mirror."

"Oh hell," I said, leaning back. "Bad Ass Luke."

Menolly nodded vigorously, her beads clicking loudly. "That's right. Ladies, Bad Ass Luke is in town."

As I set the book and bones on the coffee table, Menolly's eyes widened. Delilah leaned in for a look.

"Okay, let me add fuel to the fire," I said. "Grandmother Coyote told me that Shadow Wing is sending scouts through the portals—hence our lovely trio of miscreants. Trillian was right—Shadow Wing's on the move. Not only that, but I found out what kind of demon he actually is. Ladies, we now have a Soul Eater at the helm of the Subterranean Realms."

It got very quiet for a moment, then all havoc broke loose as the front door burst open. In a blur of movement, Delilah was standing, holding a gun in one hand, a long knife in the other. Menolly hissed and soared up to the ceiling, her arms spread to dive in attack. Running on instinct, I called out to the Moon Mother, and energy raced into my hands, crackling as I armed myself with the silver lightning.

"Show yourself or you're a dead man," I yelled, hoping that my shout would make up for my lack of confidence.

"Gladly." The figure stepped out from the swirl of rippling energy.

I lowered my hands. Oh hell. I did not need this—not now. Not ever. My heart started to pound, and my knees turned to rubber as Delilah lowered her weapons and Menolly sputtered something I couldn't catch.

"Please tell me I'm imagining things," I said, fighting my instinct to race over and dive into the Svartan's arms. Trillian bowed, his lips full and pouting. I wanted to bite into them right there but managed to restrain myself. "What are you doing here?" I asked. "Who told you that you were welcome in our house?"

"Your father asked me to check up on you and deliver a message for him. He's decided that you need somebody outside the agency to play delivery boy and bodyguard. There's a bad wind on the rise, my sweet, and you and your sisters are right in its path."

As he stepped fully into the light, I could see that Trillian hadn't changed since I'd last seen him. He was as gorgeous as ever. Svartans—the dark-souled cousins of the Sidhe world—were creatures of beauty. With skin the color of obsidian and hair that shone somewhere between silver and blue, they were luminous, radiating sex and power and chaos. And I knew all too well how deep this particular Svartan's beauty ran. I'd seen him naked too many times. Or too few, depending on how I looked at it. Whatever the case, from the top of his head to the tips of his toes, Trillian was a magnificent sight.

I struggled to gather my wits as I stared into my nightmare's eyes. He grinned, then leisurely reached out and wrapped his arm around my waist, pulling me tight against him. I should have fought. *Shoulda-woulda-coulda*. His other hand gripped my hair, tilting my head back as his tongue parted my lips, and I fell hopelessly in lust with him again as he pulled me in for the deepest, darkest kiss I'd had in a long, long time.

CHAPTER 5

The kiss went on and on. He ground his hips harder against mine, and I could feel an edge of desire rise that had been missing from my life for so long. Two seconds away from ripping off my nightgown, I stumbled and pushed against his chest. He loosened his grasp but didn't let go, gazing down into my face with eyes that knew me inside out.

"You shouldn't have left me," Trillian said, his voice rough.

I swallowed the lump rising in my throat. "You know I didn't have any choice. You're Svartan." And that said it all.

Trillian, however, wasn't ready to let the matter drop. "I wasn't the one who made the first move. You chose to bind yourself to me. You're mine, no matter what you think or say or do."

I bit my lip, drawing blood. He leaned down and pressed his mouth against mine, sucking gently. After another moment, he stepped back, letting me go, and I wavered. As I fought for control, Delilah grimly sheathed her knife and holstered her gun. Menolly drifted to the floor, never taking her eyes off of Trillian. Neither she nor Delilah had approved of my affair with him, but they wouldn't interfere unless I asked for help. At least not overtly.

I wiped my mouth, unable to tear my gaze away. What I'd suspected was true. Trillian still held me in thrall, a disconcerting discovery to say the least. I wasn't even sure I'd ever *liked* him, but I'd fallen hard. He was one of those dark golden boys that shimmer with the promise of heady nights and summer wine.

"Camille? Camille?" Delilah's voice brought me back to the present. "If Father asked Trillian to play messenger, then something must be drastically wrong at home."

Trillian took another step in my direction, and I stumbled back, almost tripping over the coffee table in my haste to avoid his hands. Damn it. The last thing I wanted was for him to realize he still had control over me, but I had a feeling that was one secret I wasn't going to be able to keep. He read my expression and laughed. It wasn't a pleasant sound.

"So glad to find that you haven't forgotten me," he said. "At least I'm not alone in my obsession."

I jerked my head up. "What are you talking about?"

He licked his lips, and I had to force myself to keep from flying at him again. "You're the only one who willingly walked away from me."

So that's what had him in a lather—I'd left before he'd had a chance to get bored with me. It had taken every ounce of self-discipline I had to make the break, and I wasn't sure I could do it again. When he suddenly disappeared, I'd thought he went home to the Subterranean Realms.

"What's Father's message, and why does he think we need a bodyguard?" If I kept the conversation on neutral footing, maybe I'd be safe.

Trillian straightened his shoulders. "Business first, then. As it should be in these . . . uncertain times."

Menolly chose this moment to break in. "So tell us already, *Svartan*."

He gave her a long, speculative look. "Menolly, you're looking almost alive. Met any eligible bats lately?"

She hissed at him, and he grinned.

Delilah broke in. "Stop it, both of you! We don't have time for this, and I don't need to change right now. First Chase, and now you, Trillian. Menolly, why do you hate everybody who's interested in Camille?"

Trillian gave me a sidelong glance but said nothing.

Menolly sighed. "You don't like this black heart either, so don't play all self-righteous with me," she said.

Delilah started to shimmer, but I caught her wrist. "Don't you dare! We need you to hold tight, hon." I glanced at Menolly, who relented.

"Kitten, calm down," she said. "I'm not mad at you, okay?"

With a huff, Delilah flounced to the sofa. Menolly sat beside her, stroking her hand. I motioned to Trillian.

"You might as well sit down too," I said, keeping out of his reach. "Why don't you first explain why our father asked you to play messenger boy. I know exactly what he thinks of you."

Trillian slid into one of the overstuffed armchairs and stretched out his long legs, crossing them at the ankles as he leaned back. "The answer's simple enough. Your father thought my arrival would go unannounced. I don't arouse suspicion, because I can't possibly be a member of the OIA." He grew serious and leaned forward. "Listen, girls, there's trouble in Y'Elestrial. Serious trouble. Your father wants you to know that the OIA may not be able to offer much support in the near future, even though they won't tell you so. He heard Johnson's report, as well as the official response."

"Then Father believes us," I said, relieved. With our father on our side, we stood a better chance of coping with whatever might be headed our way. "We have more. We've confirmed that Shadow Wing has taken over the Subterranean Realms and is planning an attack on both Earth and Otherworld."

Trillian's face clouded over. "I know. I just returned from the Sub Realms, and I've seen the chaos going on there. How do you know all of this?"

I silently walked over to the table where I'd dropped the finger bones and picked them up. "I visited Grandmother Coyote tonight."

Trillian shuddered. "Hell's bells, Camille. The Hags of Fate? You know they're nothing to mess around with. Those visits come with a price."

"I'm aware of that," I said, feeling the smooth ivory roll under my fingers. "And I owe her . . . well . . . what I owe her isn't going to be all that easy to repay, but it was worth it. She provided me with invaluable information that apparently OIA doesn't know—or doesn't care—about." I avoided his eyes. "Have you ever heard of the spirit seals, Trillian?"

He frowned, then nodded. "Vaguely, when I was a child I heard whispered tales about a wondrous treasure that could force the three realms to reunite—either in peace or in war. Why?" he asked, leaning forward. "Did you find one of them?"

"No, but Shadow Wing is searching for them. He means to use them as a key. He can open the portals with them and let his army pass into Earth. To make things worse, he knows where the first one is. And now, so do we. It's up to us to find and retrieve the seal before he does." I filled him in on what I'd learned. Like all Svartans, Trillian was good at hiding his emotions, but I could tell that he was both surprised and concerned.

I picked up the book Grandmother Coyote had given me and headed into the dining room. The others followed me, and we gathered around the table as I flipped open the pages. The text was in an ancient script, but I could read it haltingly, enough to decipher the basics of what it was saying.

In the fourth age of our world, there arose a great leader in the Subterranean Realms named Tagatty. A demon over-lord, he united the lower realms and led a great army into Earth to battle the North men with snow and with fire. The war raged, threatening to spread throughout the lands, until the gods went to the Elemental Lords and begged for help.

*The Elemental Lords agreed to assist, although the
Hags of Fate declined, stating they would only watch as
the situation unfolded. Together, the gods and Elementals
forged a great spirit seal which separated the three Realms
and created the portals—limited nexus points through
which travelers could pass from one world to another.*

Delilah frowned. "So, what happened to the seal? How
did it get lost?"

"How else?" Trillian asked. "Clumsiness. You've got to
admit, when you're facing eternity, you're bound to lose
track of things along the way, and the Elementals and gods
tend to be scatterbrained. Too much power isn't always a
good thing. Look at Earth's history to prove it—Hitler,
Stalin, Good old Vlad."

"Vlad doesn't count; he was a vampire posing as a mortal. But you're right," I said, continuing to read.

*The spirit seal was broken into nine pieces and given to the
Elemental Lords. Guardianship over most of the portals
was given to the Guard Des'Estar, off of which branched
the Otherworld Intelligence Agency thousands of years
later.*

*As eons passed, the Elemental Lords grew careless. The
great wars were forgotten, and the nine seals were lost,
only to be found by mortals who unwittingly became their
hosts. Anyone finding one of the spirit seals can unlock
and use its secrets. If all of the seals are found and once
again joined, the portals will shatter, and the three realms
will again become intimately bound. And there will be no
stopping any wishing to cross between the worlds.*

I pushed the book away. "Before the Great Divide, Otherworld, Earth, and the Subterranean Realms intermingled
freely."

Menolly traced a pattern on the table with her finger.
"Then the Elemental Lords created the seals as a way of
protecting OW and Earth during the great war, and they

left the portals as the only real means to cross between worlds—other than natural nexus points. If Shadow Wing gets hold of the seals, he can tear them apart and allow his armies to ravage the land."

We stared at one another as the ramifications set in. The potential for devastation was tremendous. Unless we could stop him, Shadow Wing could decimate Earth and march on Otherworld. Earth's militaries were no match for a horde of Demonkin, and while OW had an army, it had been a long time since they'd heard any sort of call to battle. It would take time to muster forces.

I cleared my throat. "There are nine parts of the seal. As far as we know, he doesn't have any of them yet. Thanks to Grandmother Coyote, we know the name of the man who possesses the first one, and we know where to find him. Trillian, you have to go back to Father and let him know what's going on. Maybe he can convince the OIA that this is serious. Meanwhile, we'll search for Lane and sneak him to Otherworld before Bad Ass Luke discovers what's going on."

"If Grandmother Coyote told you what's happening, do you think she might tell the demons that you came to her if they asked?" Delilah asked.

When Menolly and Trillian looked at me, waiting, I realized that I'd become the leader of our little group. I shrugged.

"I have no idea. You never can tell what the Hags of Fate will do—she might tell them to balance out the situation, or she might not. Hell, she might even bite off one of Bad Ass Luke's fingers. That's what I owe her—the finger bone of a demon for her collection."

Trillian coughed. "Nice. Simple, but effective."

"Yes, but if I don't pay her, then my own finger is forfeit, so I think I'll do my best to give her what she wants." I grinned at him, and he broke into laughter, his voice echoing through my body. "I thought you'd see the joke in that," I said, waving away Delilah's pale look of surprise.

"What about the other seals?" Menolly asked. "Shouldn't we be finding out where they are?"

I pushed myself out of my chair and peeked through the heavy velvet drapes that closed off the dining room from the outside world. Rain cascaded on the roof in sheets, but a glimmer in the east told me that morning was near.

"We'll deal with them one at a time. That's all we can do. That, and keep hope. Menolly, you'd better get to sleep. Dawn's on the way, and you don't want to be up at sunrise, even if we never do see the sun in this godforsaken place."

"I can feel it," she said. "My body slows. Good night, then, and wake me when it's safe." She raised her hand to her lips and blew us a kiss. I asked Trillian to wait in the living room, and after he was out of view, Menolly glided silently to the bookshelf that stood against the wall. She swung it open and—within seconds—had vanished to the basement, the secret door shutting softly behind her.

The phone rang as I called Trillian back into the dining room. Delilah answered it. "No, I'm sorry, she's out for the day . . . Yes, I'll tell her. What was your name again?" She scratched a message on the notepad by the telephone, then said, "Got it. Buh-bye!"

"Who was that?" I asked.

"Some guy named Wade. Said he wants to ask Menolly out on a date."

"Go figure," I said, grinning as I told her who he was. "I think maybe Menolly will end up joining Vamps Anonymous after all."

Delilah yawned, her eyes weary. "Good for her . . . but honestly, I've got to get to bed. It's been too long since my last nap. Good night," she said, heading up the stairs.

I could feel the same sluggishness coursing through my body. We'd been up all night, and my encounter with Grandmother Coyote had left me drained. I turned to Trillian. "I suppose this is good-bye for now. Father will be waiting."

"Yes, I should go," he whispered, his breath hot in my ear as he slipped around behind me, encircling my waist with his arm. "But first, tell me why you left me, Camille. You aren't prejudiced against my kind like the rest of your family. Did I hurt you?"

I bit down on my lip, hard, and shook my head. "No, but you would have. Eventually. Svartans always hurt those they love. I didn't want to be around when you grew tired of me. I didn't want to be cast aside like yesterday's lunch."

"So you left first, before I could leave you." His lips gently pressed against my neck, nuzzling gently.

I shivered. "Don't do this, Trillian. If we start up, I don't know if I can walk away again. I fell in love with you, and you know what that means."

"Then why leave?" he whispered. "Why walk away when you love me? When you knew I still wanted you? I can feel your body call to me. You want me, inside you, hot and hard. Let me in. I promise, you won't regret it."

Memories of our relationship flared, both the good and the painful. Svartans didn't bind their hearts to one person. To any person, actually. And while I wasn't asking—or looking—for an exclusive relationship, I was addicted to Trillian's power. To be cast away from him was a terrifying thought. I could handle him having other lovers, but I couldn't bear the thought that he might turn his back on me. His race was so intense that one night spent in the arms of a Svartan was all it took to crave another, and yet another. I could barely imagine anyone else touching me. Did I dare let him back in my life now?

I broke away, staring at the door. I wanted to tell him to go. I wanted to order him out and end it right there. Of course, he could command me to undress, to lay myself down, open my legs to him, and I'd have to obey. I was still under thrall, and he knew it. Part of me wished he would—it wouldn't be my fault then.

Trillian scowled. "I won't force you," he said. "I have no desire to force any woman. But Camille, think about it. Remember what it was like?"

Closing my eyes, I wavered. Would it be worth the worry and fear again? I opened my eyes and held out my hand. "Shut up and come upstairs, and fuck me until we shake the stars out of the sky."

* * *

Upstairs, Trillian stayed my hand as I reached for my gown. "Let me look at you first, as you are. It's been so long." His eyes burned with cold fire, and I knew there was no turning back.

He slowly walked around me, reaching out so that his fingers were almost touching me but not quite. I shuddered. Just being near him set me off, and I felt myself flush. My glamour shifted, and I knew my eyes were shining—the silver of the moon reflecting through them as he set my Faerie blood alight.

When Sidhe met Svartan, the magical energy whirled into a vortex that my mother's human blood couldn't stave off. The familiar sweep caught me up as the collision of our opposite natures locked and began their dance.

"Take off your robe," he said, and there was no question that I would not obey. I let the bathrobe drop to the floor.

"Now the gown," he said, his gaze still locked on me.

As I slid the straps over my shoulders and let my night-gown follow the robe, my breasts began to ache. I held my breath as Trillian leaned over and placed a kiss on my neck, so faint I could barely feel his lips.

"What do you want?" he asked.

My voice shook as I answered. "Touch me. Run your tongue and lips over my body. I want to see you naked again, to feel you under my hands."

As he slipped out of the trousers and the shirt that could have come from any menswear shop in the city, my gaze was riveted on his face, his body. His skin was like smooth glass—silken and brilliant and black. He unknotted the braid that held his hair back from his face and it fell in waves around his shoulders, shrouding him in a mirror of the Moon Mother's light. I lowered my gaze and gasped. Though I had seen him naked many times before, I had forgotten just how beautiful he was.

"Don't make me wait. Please . . ." I hated myself for begging, but the pull was too much. It had been so long since I'd had a man—any man—but especially since I'd tasted the wine of my dark lover's passion. Tears welled up as I wondered if he was going to toy with me, to tease me. And then the moonlight broke through the clouds and bathed my room, cloaking me in the Moon Mother's silver lifeblood. Her power strengthened me, and I straightened my shoulders, bringing my gaze to meet Trillian square in the face.

His expression said everything I wanted to hear. "Camille," he said, roughly, reaching for me. I danced back a step and stretched, feeling every muscle in my body crackle with lust and control.

"Do you want me?" I said, holding out my hand to stop him.

Trillian's nostrils flared, and at first I thought he was angry, but then I saw the flicker of delight in his eyes. He enjoyed the game, enjoyed the power play. "I want you. All of you, every inch and niche. Camille, will you have me?"

And then, all play vanished as I opened myself to him, deadly serious, searching for the grail that would carry us out of ourselves and into that realm where our souls could merge. He buried his head in my neck, carrying me to the bed. As I tumbled back, we both knew that our first meeting after so long would not be gentle—the need was too great, the urgency too strong. His eyes flashed as he plunged into my core, driving his cock home again and again as he struggled to find my center. Thick and demanding, he ground his hips against mine, and I felt my thoughts beginning to slide away, leaving an open chasm over which we played out our struggle. And then, we were there—straddling the edge of the cliff, teetering as we fought for control.

With one last thrust, Trillian shuddered. He broke first, his cry echoing to sever the cords that bound me to consciousness. With one sharp gasp, I went tumbling into the abyss.

By the time I opened my eyes, the sunlight was spilling through my curtains, and the smell of bacon and eggs wafted up the stairs. I winced. My neck hurt from being kinked too far to the right, but the ache was nothing in comparison to the sated feel in the pit of my stomach. I luxuriated as I rolled out of bed. I hadn't felt this good in a long, long time.

The other side of my bed was empty. After our tryst, Trillian had returned to OW to talk to my father. So I was back to dancing with the devil. But the smile on my face was too bright for that thought to quench my good mood as I glanced at the clock. Ten A.M. Oh hell, the store!

I slid into a plum chiffon skirt that flirted with the tops of my knees and pulled on a pale gray cashmere sweater. Zipping up my knee-high stiletto suede boots, I hurried downstairs as I fumbled with my hair, managing to corral the tumbling curls into a thick ponytail. Delilah was waiting, bright-eyed, with breakfast on the table.

"I am so hungry." I slid into my chair and snagged a piece of bacon off the platter. "Thanks. I'm running late."

Delilah wrinkled her nose. She was dressed in a pair of flare-legged jeans and a patchwork peasant shirt in shades of blue and ivory. Thick-soled platform ankle boots raised her to soaring heights. "I think you should call Iris today. We have to start looking for Tom Lane."

I'd hoped to find some word waiting from OIA when I woke up, but there were no messages from either Chase or Trillian.

"I guess you're right. We don't have a moment to waste." I picked up the phone and put in a call on the private shop line to Iris.

"Hey, can you run the shop today? We have OIA business."

Iris jotted down notes as I ran through what she needed to know, then promised to call and leave a status report at the end of the day. She spoke perfect English, even though she'd spent most of her life in Finland, where her kin had bound themselves to a family of humans, coexisting peacefully until the family had died out last generation. With no one left to tend, Iris had signed up with the OIA, and they'd left her Earthside, since she knew the world so well.

Delilah and I lingered over breakfast, Delilah writing up a to-do list while I applied my makeup. A sweep of soft brown shadow, an outline of liquid black liner around my eyes, several coats of mascara on my already-lengthy eyelashes. Finally, I rouged my lips with a deep merlot color and blinked.

"That's better," I said, staring in my hand mirror.

"You're chipper this morning," Delilah said. "Now, what do we need to do?" She held her pencil at the ready.

"Well, we need to find out more about Tom Lane, but I'm afraid that may be a common name over here."

"It is," she said. "I already looked him up while waiting for you. There are several Tom Lanes in Seattle and the surrounding areas. And if he truly lives near the mountain, we have to remember that he might not have a phone."

Delilah buttered another piece of toast and bit into it. She had a healthy appetite and worked it off without a problem. "Maybe some of the local Fae have heard of him and know something."

I cautiously licked the taste of bacon off of my fingers, taking care not to muss my lipstick. "You're thinking Tom and the seal might have become an urban legend?"

"Hey, what about Rina? She lives in Seattle, and if I remember right, she was a historian back in OW." Delilah gave a little *purp* of excitement. I could tell she was proud of herself.

"Rina? Who's that?" And then I remembered. A few years back, Rina—a member of the Court and Crown—had slept with the King. That in itself wasn't a crime. The problem was that she'd failed to ask permission from the Queen first, and Lethesanar wasn't known for leniency toward thieves of the royal treasures—be they gemstone or consort. Lethesanar had banished Rina to Earth, forbidding her to return to Otherworld.

"Oh, I'd forgotten about her," I said, wondering what

Rina had been up to since her spectacular—and fiery—departure from the Court. I'd witnessed that blowup, and it taught me a valuable lesson about "borrowing" the property of the royal family. "Do you know where she is?"

Delilah popped open her laptop and began tapping away, her fingers moving with a speed that made me cringe. She'd learned to type the moment she knew we were headed Earthside, but I'd passed on the opportunity.

"Here she is—I've got a file on expatriates living Earthside. Hey, she doesn't live far from the store. She runs an antique shop and lives over it."

"Is she a member of OIA?" I asked.

"Nope," Delilah said, shaking her head. "The Queen would chew a cow if Rina was given any sort of official status. Lethesanar's grudges run deep."

I gathered my purse and keys. "Should we go visit her?"

Delilah closed her laptop and slipped it into her shoulder bag. "Why not? Afterward, we can pop in on Louise Jenkins and talk to her. By the time Menolly wakes up tonight, we should have more information to go on." She followed me to the door, eying me closely. "How are you doing this morning? I notice Trillian wasn't around at breakfast." It was a question, not a statement.

I flashed her a dark look. "Don't start in on me, okay? He stayed for awhile, and yes, we had sex. Then he went back to OW."

"Oh Camille! You really love him, don't you?" she asked, as we clattered down the steps, the downpour soaking us before we could reach my car. I pointed the keychain, pressed a button, and the locks popped. Modern technology wasn't all that far behind magic, I thought. Sometimes, it surpassed it.

As we settled into the car and fastened our seat belts, I shook my head. "I love him, yes, but I don't like him. Not all that much. He's a drug, Delilah. He's passionate and exciting and . . ." I stopped, uncertain of how to explain it.

"And he takes you places nobody else can," she finished for me quietly.

I glanced at her. "Yeah, he does. He did last night. I don't know if I want to give that up."

As I pulled out onto the road and headed toward the center of the Belles-Faire district, Delilah seemed to be searching for words. After a moment, she said, "Maybe it's not so bad to be dependent on somebody else. He made you happy, Camille. I remember when you were together. I don't like him, but if you love him, then I'll support you. You know that."

Raindrops splashed against the windshield, and I flipped the wipers to high speed. The road leading from our house to the middle of the Belles-Faire district led through one suburb after another. Older houses hid behind spacious cedar-lined drives, stately but with that weatherworn look that spoke of genteel poverty, old money running short, families with five or six children who were trying to save a few bucks by getting out of Seattle proper.

"Trillian is Svartan. After a while, he'll leave, and then you'll have to pick up the pieces. It's not in his nature to stick around." I kept my eyes on the road. Wildlife abounded here. It wasn't uncommon to see a dog—or even a coyote—race across the street.

Delilah frowned. "It's not in our nature to remain monogamous either. We are half-Fae, you know."

"I didn't say monogamous," I countered. "What I can't handle is the thought that he might leave me after I've given my heart to him. Remember—we're also half-human."

"But you're more like Father than Mother."

I grinned at her, turning left onto Aurora Boulevard, which would take us into Seattle. "Unfortunately, I seem to have inherited more than Father's looks. I'll walk through fire for a man who can shake my world. I love sex, and the sex with Trillian is better than any drug I've ever had."

"Like you've tried many drugs. You always did sneak out of that part of your training when you were a kid,"

Delilah said. She frowned, her mouth twisting in a particularly endearing way. "You know, to be honest, I don't think I'm really interested in men. Women either. I'm not sure what I'd do with a guy if I had him. Although I am curious. I'd like to have sex at least once . . . to see what the big deal is about."

Startled, I gave her a quick glance. I'd assumed Delilah had her affairs but was just reticent, and I'd never pried. "You mean you're still a virgin?"

She blushed. "Well, in my human form I am."

Wondering at the logistics of her implication, I blinked. Even though I hadn't been with a man since Trillian, I had found plenty of ways to take care of myself. It wasn't enough. Granted, it took the edge off, but in my book, there was nothing that could replace a good, hard man.

"Don't you ever get horny?"

Delilah grinned. "I didn't say that I was frigid, but the whole sex-with-somebody-else scene just seems like so much bother." She stole a sideways glance at me. "So tell me, what's it like with Trillian? What does he do that drives you so crazy?"

This was the first time anybody had ever asked me—without judgment—what drew me to Trillian. Wondering what she'd think, I threw reticence out the window and began to tell her about my Svartan lover.

CHAPTER 6

Our first stop was Rina's store. The Bella Gata Boutique was in what at first appearance seemed to be a run-down part of the city, but the surrounding shops, though drab on the outside, actually housed rather pricey goods. On one side of the Bella Gata stood a restaurant—a dark staircase leading down into a steakhouse, and to the other side, a leather furniture store.

I peeked in the window and saw a lovely hand-worked ottoman in rich burgundy, but when I caught sight of the price tag, I pushed any thought of buying it out of mind. We still had some in savings, but a seven-hundred-dollar footstool was beyond our wish list. And our salary from the OIA didn't translate over Earthside. We'd have to stick to Ikea for awhile, though I preferred Thomasville.

Bella Gata was open for business. A couple of early shoppers browsed the shelves of chintz and china, but for the most part, the shop looked empty. Delilah hung back, allowing me to approach the counter as a woman peeked around the corner. For a moment I thought she might be human, but then I sensed the glamour she was using to cloak herself. Probably trying to avoid the geeks and freaks that liked to glom on to us, but I couldn't help thinking that business at her shop would triple if she let people know what she was. And a good head for business didn't mean you were the bogeyman. In fact, I'd met the bogeyman, and Bill Gates he wasn't.

I leaned on the counter. "We're looking for Rina," I said, keeping my gaze leveled. She flinched, and I knew I'd found her.

"What do you want?" she asked, glancing nervously around.

"Information. We're with the OIA."

At that, she dropped her pretense and her true beauty shimmered forth. As her hair grew blonder, and her eyes darker and more luminous, I began to realize why the Queen had banished her. Rina was one of the most beautiful women I'd ever seen, and I could see how she might pose a threat to the royal ego.

"Did Lethesanar send you?" Her shoulders were defiant, and I sensed that she was poised for a fight.

I snorted. "Do you really think the Queen would have anything to do with us? We're half-human, if you didn't notice. Chill out, we're not here to cause trouble. We just remembered that you were a lore keeper back in OW and wanted to ask if you know anything about a certain legend. My name's Camille D'Artigo," I added, nodding deeply. "And this is my sister Delilah."

Rina blinked. "Now that you mention it, you aren't full-blood, are you? I remember now—you and your sisters were much the topic of conversation back in the Court. There were several there who were bent on dispatching you to the goblin lands. Looks like they did the next best thing." Her voice held a tinge of the old hostility we'd encountered growing up. So Rina didn't like half-breeds.

I narrowed my eyes and leaned across the counter. "Listen, *friend*. Our heritage isn't germane to the discussion. We work for the OIA, and that should be enough for you. Expatriate or not, you owe allegiance to the Court and

Crown. Now, we've run across some potentially dangerous news for both Earth and Otherworld. Are you going to help us voluntarily, or do I have to call HQ?" I was bluffing, but she didn't have to know that.

She paused, and I could tell she was considering all angles. Frankly, she had no reason to love the Queen nor to help out OIA, but if I gave her a little shove, she might just open up.

"What do you want to know?" she finally said.

"We need to know what you've heard about a man named Tom Lane who holds one of the spirit seals. We know he's alive, we know he's near Mount Rainier, and we have to find him."

Rina glanced over at a small handful of customers who were browsing the shelves. "Go wait in my office. I'll be there in a few moments," she said, pointing us to a door down a short hallway behind the counter.

Delilah and I strolled down the hall and into the room. It was sparsely furnished, with an ornate love seat against one wall, a bookshelf next to it, and a big walnut desk and leather chair filling the rest of the cubicle. I curled up on the love seat and glanced at Delilah. The beginnings of a headache were creeping around at the back of my mind, but I had a vague sense that it was connected to something other than lack of sleep. There was something out of whack.

"Do you sense anything strange?" I asked.

"Strange as in how?"

"Oh, energy . . . smell . . . something's wrong, and I'm not sure what."

Delilah paused, sniffing the air. She closed her eyes for a moment and then cocked her head. Her shoulders stiffened, and she rushed to the door, jiggling the knob. "We're locked in," she whispered. "What's going on?"

"I don't know, but I don't like it."

I reached out, trying to figure out what was going down. Inhaling deeply, I let the breath settle into my lungs, but the sound of breaking glass startled me. A muffled scream rang back from the front of the store.

"That's Rina!" I jumped up and looked around wildly for something to open the door with. "We've got to get out of here!"

Delilah motioned for me to stand back. She stared at the door for a moment, contemplating the trajectory, then took aim and let fly with her foot. The heel of her platform boot caught the knob at just the right angle, busting it loose from the wood as the doorframe splintered. She'd learned from the best back in OW, training for a number of years under a martial arts master. Delilah was the equivalent of a black belt kung fu practitioner.

We rushed down the hall into the main room of the store. Rina was sprawled over the counter, all too dead. Blood spatters led from the counter to the middle of the room, and stopped. I sniffed. The metallic smell of blood filled the air. That, and ozone. Somebody had dropped a butt load of magic here in the past few minutes. I glanced down at my feet where a single brown and yellow feather lay. As I bent down to pick it up, Delilah hissed and backed up.

"Demon. That's from a demon," she said. "I can feel it from here."

"It's that freakin' harpy." I turned the feather over in my hand. It felt greasy and dirty and all kinds of nasty. "When we find this bitch, we're going to spit her and roast her over Shadow Wing's fire pit."

"Do you think she was after the same information we were?"

"I don't know, but I'm calling Chase. We have to report this, and I think we should ask him to bring in a Corpse Talker." With a sigh, I pulled out my phone and punched seven on speed dial.

While we waited for Chase, I took a closer look at Rina's body. A few minutes ago, she'd been a gorgeous woman capable of turning a King's head. Now, there wasn't much left that you could even remotely call beautiful. Blood covered the floor from multiple lacerations covering her body

and face. I averted my eyes from her midsection, which
had been eviscerated, leaving nothing to the imagination.
Blood and guts I was used to, but that didn't mean I had to
like it.

Delilah joined me, trying not to look at Rina. We knew
better than to cover the body. There would be evidence to
take, and if we were going to employ a Corpse Talker, then
we needed to leave as few energy imprints as possible.

"You think Bad Ass Luke was with her?" she said.

I shook my head. "I don't smell him here, but I smell
bird."

To be precise, Bad Ass Luke's real name was twenty-eight
letters long and almost unpronounceable. Father had told us
what it really was, but Lucianopoloneelisunekonekari was
just too much of a mouthful, so he'd shortened it to Luke.
Bad Ass had simply been tagged on due to a well-deserved
reputation.

"No, this was the harpy's work." I fingered the feather.
"The coloring's right, and Rina's shredded flesh . . . talons
for sure."

Delilah grimaced. "Dirty, filthy creatures. How the hell
did they sneak through the portal in the first place? Jocko
keeps a good guard on duty."

"The answer to that would be right in line with Chase's
suspicion of an inside job," I said as the shop door opened.
Speak of the devil, Chase peeked inside. I waved him over,
and he cautiously approached Rina's body, a pained look
on his face. Sometimes I forgot FBHs had weaker stom-
achs than we did.

"Jesus, what happened?" he pulled out his notebook,
shaking his head. "She looks like she's been through a
body-count movie."

"Harpy, but we'll need a necromancer to be certain. A
Corpse Talker, to be exact." I handed him the feather. "This
came from her attacker, I believe."

He gingerly took the feather and glanced up at me.
"Where were you during this time?"

I grimaced. "Delilah and I were locked in a back room.

We were waiting for Rina to come talk to us when somebody locked us in."

"You let yourselves get locked in a room? What kind of
agents *are* you?" He stifled a snort.

"Back off, dude. Why do you think we were sent to this
backwater place? Anyway, show some respect. The woman's
dead, and she didn't go gently." I sighed, scratching one of
my ears. My earrings were silver, and I had the feeling they
were only plated. "We were going to ask her some questions, but that's all moot, now. Harpies come from the Subterranean Realms, Chase. They're Demonkin." I stepped
away to give him better access.

"Shit," he said under his breath. "Then you were right.
A demon actually broke through. This isn't that Shadow
Wing fellow you were talking about, is it?"

I shook my head. "No. Shadow Wing makes a harpy look
like a child's toy. Right now, we know that three demons are
running amok Earthside. They're scouts. We think that
you're right, that somebody on the inside helped sneak them
through the portals. Somebody who knows how to open the
gates to the netherworld. Possibly a demon in disguise, or
maybe just one of the Fae, acting in accordance with them.
Either case spells bad news."

"Speaking of news," he said, pulling out his cell phone,
"I received word from HQ today. Menolly is to take over the
bar. It will officially be transferred to her name. She's the
new owner of the Wayfarer as far as Earth is concerned."

"Well, that's different." I frowned. "Not necessarily
good, but different. This could make her a prime target. You
say this was headquarters' idea?"

"That was the directive on my desk when I got to work
this morning. Oh, and there's something else you might
want to know about. Somebody leaked word to the media
that Jocko was murdered. There's going to be a protest
marching through town by the Guardian Watchdogs."

"Are they marching by the Indigo Crescent?" I asked.

He nodded. "That, and every other shop they know to be
run by the Fae. Doesn't matter if you're half-blood or not,

they consider you a threat. The police will try to corral them, but free speech and all that crap."

I frowned. Sometimes, muzzles were an attractive alternative to corral some of the more vocal backlash groups. The Watchdogs thought we were tempting people into the arms of the devil. They'd be singing another tune when Shadow Wing's troops came sweeping through, annihilating everything in their path. Then the Watchdogs would be crawling to us on their bellies, begging for our help.

Chase stood, dialing a number on his cell. "You say we need a Corpse Talker?" he mouthed to me.

I nodded. "Make sure that she's a necromancer too, or we could be dealing with somebody who isn't qualified. And we need her down here before anybody touches the body."

Within minutes he'd summoned both a Corpse Talker and the unit specially designed to clean up after OIA matters such as this. The Court and Crown had specific restrictions on how the bodies of those from Otherworld were to be handled. There were rites that could only be performed if the body had been treated in a certain manner, and while Rina was persona non grata back home, now that she was dead, the exile would be lifted, and she would be returned to spend eternity in the arms of her ancestors.

Let's hear it for hypocrisy, I thought with a shake of my head.

While we waited, Delilah and I filled Chase in on Rina's background and how she came to be living in Seattle.

"I thought that monogamy was unusual among your people," Chase said.

I snorted. "Monogamy has nothing to do with it. She disrespected the Queen—a sovereign offense. If she'd asked for permission to sleep with the King, Lethesanar would have probably given her blessing. Rina basically stole from the Crown."

Chase looked more confused than ever. "But the King agreed. Isn't he also the Crown?" I almost wanted to pat him on the head.

"Yeah, it's confusing. Look at it this way: the King belongs to the Queen. Yes, he's one of our sovereigns, but he doesn't take a piss without Lethesanar's permission."

Chase coughed. "Your society isn't exactly male-oriented, huh?"

"Not so much. The throne passes from mother to daughter. The Queen picks her consort from her cousins—there must always be a blood link—and any children born from a tryst that doesn't involve the King are automatically out of contention for the crown."

"Huh. What if the Queen doesn't have a daughter?"

"Then her sister or her sister's daughter will ascend to the throne. All women in the royal family who stand even within an arm's reach of the throne are required to bear children. At least two, but preferably three if one of the two happens to be a boy. The King has his power, but the Queen is sovereign. Since she chooses whom she will marry, he's subject to her and considered an extension of her. By screwing the King without the Queen's permission, Rina—in essence—raped the Queen."

As I finished explaining, the door swung open, and the OIA medical team burst through, followed by their Earthside OIA counterparts. A short figure in a long, dark shroud led the group, gliding across the floor as if floating. An indigo glow emanated from the chiffon veils that covered both body and face hidden within the multitude of layers.

I took a step back. Corpse Talkers made me nervous, not because they spoke with the dead, but because they were dark, misshapen Faerie who came up to the surface from deep under the ground. Banned from the city of Y'Elestrial except upon summons, their race had no name that we knew of, and no one ever saw their faces. The males remained hidden in the depths of their underground city, and only their women could become Corpse Talkers. Most lived by a set of bound rules and regulations, but a few had gone rogue and were considered wild and dangerous.

The Corpse Talker knelt by Rina's side. "Has anyone

touched her since her death?" Her voice was hollow, almost cavernous from within the folds of the hooded cloak.

Taking a deep breath, I knelt near her, taking care to not even so much as brush my aura against hers. There were stories of very nasty explosions that had happened when the energy of a witch and a Corpse Talker collided, and I had no intention of finding out if they were old wives' tales or true.

"I tested her pulse to see if she was still alive. Otherwise, I don't think anybody but the killer touched her." I held up the feather. "I found this on the ground next to her and picked it up before I thought about it."

The darksome hood turned toward me, and I thought I caught sight of a pair of steel eyes staring out at me, luminous and cold. "Harpy," was all she said, but that was enough to verify what we'd been thinking.

Over the years, I'd seen Corpse Talkers at work, and their dedication and icy passion for their work unnerved me, but I was inexorably fascinated by them. Delilah, on the other hand, watched from beside Chase. She looked nervous; he was totally freaked. Luckily for us, he was enough of a professional to know when to keep his mouth shut.

The shrouded figure bent over Rina's body and slowly pressed her face to Rina's bloody face. Lips to lips, the Corpse Talker kissed Rina deeply, sucking the remnants of the fallen soul out of the body into her own. I knew the drill.

> *Lips to lips, mouth to mouth,*
> *Comes the speaker of the shrouds.*
> *Suck in the spirit, speak the words,*
> *Let secrets of the dead be heard.*

The rhyme echoed in my head; a ditty sung by children hoping to keep the bogeys at bay. But bogeys were child's play compared to these creatures—whatever they were—and bogeys didn't demand flesh as payment for their services. Rina's remains would lie with her ancestors, except for her heart.

We waited in silence, the air growing thick as the Corpse Talker hovered over the body. I glanced up at Chase. He looked faint, and Delilah—who had apparently noticed his expression—silently reached for his hand. Startled, he gave her a quick look and accepted, her touch giving him the strength to straighten his shoulders, though I still heard him gulp down what was likely his breakfast. The scent of his fear mingled with the scent of blood, and I was grateful Menolly wasn't here; she was still so young at the vamp business, and young vamps grew ravenous at the smell of a pricked finger.

After a moment, the Corpse Talker stood, silent as before. I stepped forward. Time to find out if we'd hit the target.

"Rina, can you hear me?"

In a voice that was Rina's and yet not Rina's, the Corpse Talker breathed a soft, "Yes."

We only had a few minutes before the residue from Rina's soul departed, just enough for a couple of quick questions, and then we were out of luck. In some cases, Corpse Talkers weren't able to grab hold of the soul's cord for even that long.

"Who killed you?"

A pause, then again the whisper. "Harpy."

"Do you know why?" I watched the shrouded figure as she swayed, struggling to keep hold of Rina's soul.

"No."

Nice. Short, but sweet. The dead weren't always talkative, which was understandable. We had to make every question count. I thought hard. We had one, perhaps two more chances. What else could I ask that might be of value? And then, I knew. More questions about Rina's death would be a waste of time, but maybe, just maybe I could gain some insight on what we'd come to learn.

"How can I find Tom Lane?"

The Corpse Talker shuddered, as if not expecting the question, but she managed to regain control. After a moment, she said, "He's mad as a hatter, mad as a hare. Go to the woodland, but be you aware. Look for the ancients who shelter from storm, but first you must pass through the lair of the wyrm."

And then Rina's body jerked.

"Oh shit!" Chase blurted out. "What the fuck?"

Delilah dug into his arm as the Corpse Talker jumped back, leaning heavily against one of the OIA members.

I wandered over to Chase and Delilah. "Calm down. That just means the connection was severed. Rina's soul's passed through the veil."

Chase stared at the limp body, and I thought I saw something sparkle in the corner of his eye.

"You okay?" I asked.

He took a deep breath and nodded. "Yeah. I just . . . I'm so used to dealing with murder victims that sometimes I forget that they were people. Hearing her voice come out of that . . . thing . . . seeing the body jump. I've never thought much about the afterlife."

I could see that he was confused, probably even a little scared. I gave him a rough smile. "Don't take it too hard. We believe that the soul just moves on after death. Rina's alive, only not in this body. She's joined her ancestors."

The OIA team was busy making notes as they cleaned up. Chase looked over at the Corpse Talker and shuddered. "How do we pay her?" he asked.

Oh, this was going to be good. "You've never dealt with one of them, have you?"

He shook his head. "No, and I don't want to ever again, though I have the feeling I may be blowing smoke with that wish."

I leaned against one of the display tables and stared at my boots. They were looking a little scuffed, and it occurred to me that I should buy a new pair. Chase cleared his throat, and I blinked, bringing my attention back to matters at hand. How the hell was I supposed to answer without making him toss his cookies? Figuring that sometimes blunt was best, I shrugged.

"She'll take Rina's heart. The medics will give it to her. Corpse Talkers take into themselves a part of everyone for whom they speak. Think of it as a form of communion."

"Oh Jesus, I had to ask, didn't I?"

At his grimace, I jerked him around so that she couldn't see his face. "Don't do that," I said, hissing. "Her job is sacred, and she's as revered as she is avoided. Corpse Talkers speak only to one another unless they have business to transact. We aren't even sure what race they are or what gives them their powers. It's an inborn ability with their women, and so far, no other Sidhe has shown an aptitude for it. Don't make a fool of yourself by turning up your nose. She's one of the keepers of the dead, to be honored. Not despised."

He blinked. "Don't bite my head off. At least your sister understands why I'm so . . ."

"Scared?"

"Try again. I don't scare." Chase gave me a snotty look, but there was a glint in his eye that told me his mind was both on the case yet off in some sleazy corner, squeezing my boobs.

"The hell you don't, Johnson. And look at my face when I'm talking, will you?" Grumbling, I crossed my arms and stared out the window. Delilah was talking to the medics, watching as they prepared Rina for transport back to OW.

Chase cleared his throat and leaned down to whisper in my ear. "But you're so *purtee*, how can I resist? Come on, Camille, admit it. You want me as bad as I want you."

I turned and with an innocent, oh-so-sweet smile, reached out so quickly that he didn't have time to react. I had learned from the best and grabbed his balls, giving them a nasty but not debilitating tweak. He let out a squeak, and I let go. "Keep it up, and you'll be humping my knee, you perv."

As he glanced around frantically for a chair, I grinned

and sauntered over to watch the last of the preparations on Rina's body. By the time I returned, he was glaring but didn't look in pain.

"So," I said in a casual tone. "You ready to trace that harpy? She means trouble for human and Sidhe alike."

I had a feeling he was fuming, but he surprised me. "Camille, I have to give it to you, you've got more guts than anybody I know. Nobody I know would have the courage to do that to me, and I guess I deserved it." He sighed. "I guess I should apologize . . ."

"I guess you should," I said, but smiled. "You okay?"

"Yeah, I'm fine. Say, you need to teach me how you do that. I can see teaching it to my officers."

Raising my eyebrows, I gave a little shrug. "If you want to learn how to grab balls, sure thing, but let's get back to business here." I led him into the back, where I started looking through Rina's desk for any clue to why the harpy might have murdered her. Chase glanced at the items I pulled out of the drawer.

"What exactly is a harpy? Are they like the same thing as harpies from Greek mythology?" He pulled out a stack of small paper bags. "I suppose we should dust these for fingerprints," he said.

"Uh, Chase, harpies don't have fingerprints. Not like humans or Faerie."

"Do they even have fingers?"

"Yeah, and if I can get hold of one, I'm giving it to Grandmother Coyote." I stopped him before he could even say a word. "Don't even ask. I'll explain that one later. Anyway, as far as harpies—they're demons. You might use 'mean' or 'nasty' to describe a killer or a thug, but that doesn't even begin to describe what these creatures are capable of."

I picked up a notebook. Addresses. Might come in handy. I flipped through it, looking for any names that might be familiar, then handed it to him, and he slipped the book into a paper bag.

"Is there a chance they'll work with humans?"

"Oh, there's a chance, but humans who have dealings with Demonkin usually don't last long enough to matter. They trust in fairy stories too much. They believe they'll get what they want if they promise their soul to the devil, but they don't realize that those rules only exist within their own framework of reference. Demonkin use others to their advantage, and when they're done, they simply discard the remains."

I paused, thinking that we had to fill Chase in on Shadow Wing and what he was after. "Chase, we know what the demons are after and why."

He jerked around. "What?"

"Let's go get coffee, and I'll tell you what we learned last night." I wasn't, however, going to tell Chase that I'd slept with Trillian. There were some secrets better left untold.

CHAPTER 7

Delilah and I decided that while I filled Chase in, she'd go check out Louise. As she headed over to the shop to borrow Iris's car, Chase and I agreed to rendezvous at Starbucks. The one thought I dreaded about going back to Otherworld was having to order my coffee from across the portals—we didn't have the plants over there. Yet. And then a lightbulb went on in my head. Maybe I could start a Starbucks franchise in Y'Elestrial, offer mocha frappuccinos and caramel lattes to all the Faerie. With our growing season there, coffee plants would flourish. The potential was mind-boggling.

I stared at the menu board and decided on a quad shot venti caramel mocha with extra whipped cream, while Chase ordered black coffee. As we slid onto the chairs by the corner table, he gave me a sheepish look.

"Listen, thanks for keeping me from making an ass of myself today. I almost fainted when that thing started . . . kissing . . . the body." He fiddled with a packet of sugar before ripping it open and adding it to his coffee.

"That *thing* is a Faerie who is highly respected in Otherworld," I said after a moment. "You were so transparent that even Delilah noticed. Why else do you think she held your hand?" I pulled a long sip on my mocha and shivered as the warm chocolate raced down my throat.

Sighing, I looked at Chase. "Listen, dude. You still think of Otherworld with rose-colored glasses. All elves and unicorns and Faerie princesses. Well, yes, we do have elves and unicorns, and kings and queens, but we also have vampires and shape-shifters and creatures that feast on the flesh of those whom they kill. We run in shades of gray, Chase, most of us who were born there. Stop expecting us to fit your definition of what you think 'Faerie' should be, and you'll rest a lot easier at night."

"Or maybe not," he mumbled. "Seriously, you're half-human, but you don't think like a human, do you? I thought when we first met that I'd be able to understand you better than some of the OIA operatives, but now I'm wondering if the mixture of human and Faerie blood doesn't make you stranger than if you were full-blood Sidhe."

I leaned back, staring out the window at the ever-present drizzle that sprinkled against the city streets. "Why? Because I won't sleep with you?"

Waving aside my comment, he said, "You think everything leads back to that, don't you? I guess I've given you that impression, so I'm sorry. Yes, I want to fuck; you're hot, and I'm not immune to that Faerie charm you have going for you. At least I'm honest about it. But that's not why I said what I did."

He shifted in his seat and squinted. "Here's an example. You didn't even flinch when the Corpse Talker did her thing. To you, this all seems *normal*. I'm beginning to think that maybe I'm in over my head." Pausing for a moment, he added, "I've been thinking about resigning. I don't know how much more I can take. The shocks never stop coming."

Unable to believe what I was about to say, I leaned across the table. "We can't afford to lose you, Chase. *You* created the Faerie-Human Crime Scene Investigations team. You're the underpinning of OIA-Earthside. We need you, especially now. Do you really want your boss taking over and ruining everything you created?"

That was all it took. I knew it would work. Devins was a total ass, and while Chase kept his complaints to a minimum, I'd met the man and wanted to backhand him across the room.

"Thanks," he said gruffly. "Don't worry, I'll stick around. So what have you found out?"

I told him about Shadow Wing and the spirit seals. When I finished, he leaned back in his seat and wiped his hand across his eyes. He looked like he'd aged ten years in the past five minutes.

"So, OIA withheld information from us?"

I shook my head. "Probably not. They aren't that smart. The OIA is slow—bureaucracy to the core, and the Guard Des'Estar not far behind. Over the years, the Court and Crown have left the military to their own devices. The royals have grown lazy and self-important, and our military leaders, even more so."

"Most of the agents I've met seem qualified for their posts," Chase said.

I shook my head. "Listen, Chase, there's a difference between being an operative and being a *warrior*. Most of the agents I know take their job seriously, but they—we—aren't soldiers. And we've been hampered by HQ. My father is with the Guard. He sees the apathy going on. He was very proud of us for following him into service, but even he admits, Otherworld isn't ready to take on Shadow Wing's armies. Neither is Earth, and you'd better trust me on that. The demons could eat your tanks and guns and not even burp. There are hordes of them, Chase. *Hordes*."

Chase eyed me silently, sipping his drink. After a moment, he said, "What can we do? If everything you say is true, then both our worlds are in danger."

I frowned, thinking about what Trillian had said. "It gets worse. If what our sources tell us is true, OIA may not be helping us out much in a while. Something's going on back home, and I'd like to know what." My stomach rumbled.

Breakfast felt a million miles away. "I'll be back in a second."

I grabbed my purse and poked around the cold case, trying to figure out what I wanted to eat. A tuna sandwich and a peppermint fudge bar looked good to go. As I paid for my food, two women in their mid-fifties were staring at me, their jaws agape in surprise. I flashed them an absent smile and headed back to our table. As I took my seat, Chase was shaking his head. "What? You don't like tuna or something?"

"You and Delilah eat like you're starving. Don't they feed you in OW?" He winked, and I realized he was teasing me.

"Our metabolisms are higher than yours, and we need more food," I said, stuffing my face with a bite of the sandwich. I rolled my eyes happily—tuna was as good as naori fish back in OW, though the mercury content worried me a little. But our healers could clear the metal out of us, so I wasn't too worried.

"A lot of women here would love to trade places with you," he said.

"If they'd move around a little more and quit obsessing, they'd be fine. Why you FBHs think everybody should look the same is beyond me. Faeries come in all shapes and sizes and colors, and for us, beauty is more than visual. I can't believe how unhappy most of your females are. It's sad." I took another bite of sandwich and then a swig of mocha to wash it down.

Chase shrugged. "We've got a lot of problems, that's for sure, but I doubt if they're limited to Earthside. Anyway, back to the subject at hand, tell me more about the demons. How do they fit in with Otherworld, and what are they like?"

I blinked. I hadn't expected to be teaching a course in Demonology 101, but it made sense. Chase was on our side, and he deserved to know what he was up against. Though when he found out just what he was facing, he might decide to run for the hills. Clearing my throat, I began.

"Okay, first, there are three categories of demons, and within those three categories, there are numerous varieties. First, you have the Greater Demonkin, like Shadow Wing. They are the biggest of the bad, and killing one is beyond any of our hopes, not without a lot of backup from wizards and sorceresses. Second, we have the Lesser Demonkin. This includes our buddies we're chasing now: creatures like the harpy and Bad Ass Luke. They all inhabit the Subterranean Realms, and that's where they're born. The third category are the minor demons; some aren't even that demonic. We're talking imps and vampires and the like. They may—or may not—live in the Sub Realms."

"Then your sister's considered a demon because she's a vampire?" Chase asked, glancing nervously over his shoulder.

I laughed. "Don't worry, she can't hear you, and I won't tell her you asked. But yes, technically Menolly *is* classified as a demon now. But you know—as I said before, definitions can be tricky. Not all of the minor demons are evil. Some are merely mischievous, and not all of the Faeries and humans are good." The last thing I needed was to make Chase even more afraid of my sister.

He surprised me though. "Well, Menolly scares the shit out of me, but I don't consider her evil."

I smiled at him, grateful. "Thanks. She's nothing to worry about, not in comparison to the Greater and Lesser Demons. But the truth is, most Demonkin tend to be far stronger than humans and have a great deal of destructive magic at their disposal. They're a lot more dangerous than you can imagine. Think fireballs and lightning strikes and poison gas from out of their mouths."

"I see your point," Chase said, reaching over to pick at the half sandwich I'd left on my plate. "You going to eat that?"

With a snort, I pushed the saucer over to his side of the table. "Be my guest."

He laughed. "Oh, man, life was so much simpler before you people decided to put in an appearance. I'm getting another cup of coffee. Want anything else?" he asked, pulling out his wallet.

"Yeah," I said. "Get me another mocha. Triple caramel. Iced this time. And a croissant."

"You sure? That much caffeine's going to send you into overdrive."

"Save the commentary and get me my drink." I waved him away, and he shrugged and headed up to the counter. As he left, the two women who had been staring at me crossed over to our table.

"We don't mean to interrupt," the taller one said, her blue eyes gleaming. Excitement rolled off her like a wave of perfume. "My friend Linda and I were wondering, are you from Otherworld?" She held up a camera and pointed to a button on her shirt. The disk had a dark navy background with the letters FWC emblazoned in silver on it, and little sparkles of color encircling the logo.

Oh great, more Faerie Watchers, though they looked like they were from out of town. I hadn't seen them with Erin Mathews's group before. I gazed at the women. They looked so hopeful that I couldn't disappoint them.

"Yes, I'm from Otherworld. I own the Indigo Crescent here in town."

"I told you, Elizabeth! I knew it—her eyes, you can see the stars in her eyes." Linda, the shorter woman, beamed.

"I thought they might be colored contacts," Elizabeth said, more to Linda than to me. "She doesn't have the same look that the one we met in San Francisco had. But then, I suppose they don't all look alike."

A little tired of being talked over as if I wasn't there, I spoke up. "There are many variations of race and species who live in Otherworld, ladies. We don't come from a cookie cutter mold."

Linda's cheeks flushed crimson. "I'm so sorry, we didn't mean any disrespect. We're from a small town in Iowa, and we're up here to visit a friend. We heard there were quite a few Faeries living in Seattle and were so excited to think we might actually meet a real live one. Where we come from, there aren't many foreigners. A few blacks, but no aliens, so we don't really know your customs."

She babbled on for a few minutes before I stopped her with a raised hand. The taller one—Elizabeth—looked put out, but said nothing. Apparently she'd read the warnings that the Sidhe were unpredictable, because she bit her tongue and bit it good.

"Welcome to Seattle, then. Would you like a picture?" I asked, pointing to their cameras as I eased into a smile. Catch more flies with honey . . . although I'd never quite understood the value of the expression. Mother had used it all the time while we were growing up and even as a child, I'd questioned why anybody would want to catch flies unless you were a goblin and used them for croutons.

Linda and Elizabeth nodded, their smiles returning. Just then, Chase reappeared. He glanced at their buttons and cameras and gave me a sympathetic look. He'd seen the Faerie Watchers in action before.

"Chase, would you mind taking a picture of me and these *lovely* women?"

I had to hand it to him. He caught my sarcasm but merely nodded and accepted the camera. I stood between Elizabeth and Linda, and Chase snapped several shots and then handed it back to them.

"Ladies," he said, flashing his badge. "I'm afraid that Ms. D'Artigo and I have official business to discuss. If you'll excuse us . . . ?"

They reluctantly backed away, shooting thank-yous and nice-to-meet-yous at me all the while. As they exited the coffee shop, I felt an actual surge of gratitude toward Chase.

"Sometimes you're all right," I said, and he flashed me a brilliant grin. His teeth gleamed in the gloom of the afternoon.

"It must be hell," he said, nodding at the retreating women. "You get that everywhere you go, don't you?"

"Not so much as some of the others. After all, I am half-human. But yeah, the Sidhe seem to be the flavor of the year, and I imagine we'll continue to be for some time."

I leaned closer, making sure my voice didn't carry. "Anyway, back to the topic at hand. Our plan is this: we get proof that OIA can't overlook. Proof about the demons and Shadow Wing. We find this Tom Lane guy and take him back to Otherworld. Once they know the extent of what's happening, they'll *have* to act."

As I pulled apart the layers of my croissant, I couldn't help but wonder if we stood a chance in hell of pulling this off. *Hell* being the operative word.

Our next step was to find the harpy, but first Chase had to stop by the station. I decided to run back to the shop.

"Meet me there," I said. "Meanwhile, I'm going to think of a plan to find the harpy." I spoke with more confidence than I felt, but somebody had to take initiative, and it wasn't likely Chase would know how to chase down a giant bird-woman that was running around the city. Of course, it would also be hard for the harpy to hide. How many giant bird-women could there be in Seattle? Somebody was bound to catch sight of her and report her to either the police or Animal Control.

I had to park three blocks away from the Indigo Crescent, but that was okay with me. Between my car and the shop stood The Scarlet Harlot, Erin Mathews's lingerie shop. I'd been meaning to drop in to look at her new stock, and considering Chase had told me he'd be around in about an hour, I had time for a quick look-see.

Erin was behind the counter, looking much more professional than she had at the Faerie Watchers Club meeting. Her eyes lit up when she saw me come through the door, and she gave a bright wave. I'd allowed her to put my picture on the wall along with a caption that read, "Camille D'Artigo—owner of the Indigo Crescent—shops here," and that alone brought in more clientele. Yeah, Faeries were good for business, all right.

She scrambled out from behind the counter. "Camille! So good to see you. How's business?"

I couldn't very well tell her I was on a demon hunt, so I just nodded and murmured as I poked through the racks. "Just thought I'd drop in and take a look at what you might have in the plum or magenta line. Satin or silk would be good." Those were Trillian's favorite colors, but that wasn't why I asked for them. No, not me. I'd halfway decided that I wasn't going to sleep with Trillian again. It had been a mistake, a wonderful, passionate mistake, but a mistake nonetheless. Then again, Delilah was being supportive. Damn, I thought. Why couldn't I just let go of him once and for all?

Erin smiled. "I've got a couple of outfits that might have been made for you. Wait here." While she slipped through the curtains into the back, I flipped through the hangers, looking at the yards of lace and satin and silk and soft cotton. In some ways, I missed Otherworld, with the one-of-a-kind garments sewn by hand. Nobody ever had exactly the same outfit as anybody else . . . but the materials here and the choices were wonderful. You couldn't get PVC in OW, that was for certain.

"Looking for something to drape that gorgeous figure in?"

Startled, I slowly turned to find myself staring at a towering man who was wearing a bouffant blond wig—or at least I thought it was a wig—and who was dressed to the hilt in a skintight, thigh-high sequined orange dress. His skin was so tan that he almost looked brown, and his pink lipstick and green eye shadow were caked on with a spatula. He was in dire need of a *What Not to Wear* overhaul.

"My name's Cleo Blanco," he said. "And you are?" He held out one hand. I saw that his nails were longer—and far more manicured—than my own.

Well, this was an interesting turn of events. In Otherworld, we didn't have drag queens. We had every flavor of the sexual smorgasbord from vanilla to kinked-out peppermint, but very few Faeries dressed like the opposite gender. Of course, our clothes were a little more adventuresome than those Earthside, so maybe we just didn't notice the overlaps.

I took the proffered hand and shook it. "Camille D'Artigo. I own the Indigo Crescent." Curious as to what he wanted, I tilted my head and gazed up at the lanky man. "What can I do for you?"

He laughed, a rich and easy trill that rolled off his tongue like honey. "It's what I can do for you. Honey, I know men who would pay you a thousand a night for your favors. You've got a valuable commodity in that Faerie pussy of yours."

If I were an FBH, I would have been turning bright red. As it was, I just returned his free-and-easy smile with one of my own and wrinkled my nose. "Thanks for the offer, but I think I'll take a pass. My pussy's on exclusive loan right now, and isn't one-size-fits-all." Not technically true, but close enough. I'd had my share of giants and dwarves BT—before Trillian—but Cleo here didn't need to know that.

With a snort, he patted me on the shoulder. His touch was friendly but not invasive, so I let it pass. "Honey, you're all right. I hope you didn't take offense, but I know several girls like you who are living high on the proverbial bacon thanks to their blood. I never like to see opportunity go to waste."

Faerie hookers Earthside? Well, it was bound to happen, I thought. Given the innate charm that we held over FBHs, eventually somebody was going to capitalize on it. While the idea of whoring myself held no interest for me, it didn't offend me either. In our world, sex was open and easy to come by, hence little need for hookers or brothels. At least among the Sidhe. Although it was sometimes used as a weapon, and many a power struggle had been played out in the bedroom, as well as high dramas and duels.

I snorted. "No, I'm not offended. So, Cleo, you work the streets, too?"

Cleo whistled and stared at the ceiling. "No, girl, I do not work the streets. I'm an entertainer—a female impersonator. I work over at Glacier Springs—a nightclub on East Pine, near the Seattle Community College. On Tuesday and

Wednesday nights, I'm Bette Davis, *dahling*, and the rest of the week, I'm Marilyn Monroe." The latter, he said in a breathless and wispy voice. "I take Sundays off to go visit my little girl and her mama."

Just then, Erin came bustling back to the front of the store, several garments in hand. She took one look at Cleo and frowned. "You bothering my customers again, Cleo?" she said, but her tone told me she wasn't serious. He gave her an easy laugh in return.

"He's not being a bother," I said as I took the hangers from her and held up the lingerie. "You didn't lie. These are lovely. May I take them into the back and try them on?"

"Of course." Erin settled herself at the counter again.

Cleo leaned across it, showing off a sizable ruby ring. "Look what Jason gave me. It's real, too. I had it appraised." As I waved at him and headed toward the dressing room, he called out, "You said you work at the Indigo Crescent?"

"I own it. Stop in for a visit sometime," I called back and disappeared into the fitting booth.

The first outfit—a teddy—was too tight to close over my breasts, but the second—a magenta bustier with em-broidered black roses—fit perfectly. It had lace trim and was dressy enough for an evening out if I topped it with a bolero jacket. I set it aside and stared at the other piece that Erin had given me. A swirling gown the color of peacock feathers, the silk was almost see-through but not quite, and it sparkled from the gold beading that went into the eye of the feathers. I slid it over my head, gasping as I looked in the mirror. It bathed me in a wash of jewel tones and shim-mered with every step that I took, the bodice form-fitting, with hidden support that lifted my boobs gently. I had to have it, no matter what the cost.

I reluctantly got dressed, then carried the bustier and gown to the counter. "Okay, you win. I have to have these. I want a dress like that nightgown, Erin, if you can find one that's not see-through." Glancing around, I saw that Cleo had disappeared. "Your friend's gone? He seems nice."

"Cleo's one of the best," she said. "He's confused right

now—not sure just what he is—but he's good-hearted, and every spare cent he gets goes to his kid and her mother. As he told me one day, his daughter and ex-wife didn't know he was gay—or bi—or whatever he is, and he's not about to make them pay the cost for it. So he goes to school in the day and works at the club at night and on Saturdays." She rang up my purchases and wrapped my lingerie in tissue paper, sliding it into a pink bag with red handles. "That will be $257.34."

As I wrote out a check, I asked, "What's he studying?"

"Computer programming. He wants to get on at Microsoft eventually." She handed me the bag. "If you ever need a good techie, he's the one to go to."

I nodded, making a note to remember her advice. You never knew when you'd need a good hacker, and even if we managed to defeat Bad Ass Luke and his cronies, I had the nasty feeling we were settling in for a long fight. I blew Erin a kiss and hit the sidewalk, running the rest of the way to the shop as a flurry of rain sprinkled around me.

Iris looked extremely glad to see me. "You've got a problem," she said when I popped through the door.

"You think? I'm stuck Earthside with three demons running amok through the city. Of course I've got problems!" I shook the water out of my hair and set my shopping bag behind the counter. At Iris's unimpressed look and the tapping of her fingers on the counter, I sighed. "Okay, so what's gone wrong now? We have termites? The roof leaking? Somebody stealing books again?"

"No termites, no leaks, and no thieves. What is wrong is that the Guardian Watchdogs are going to be picketing the shop next week." She held up a flier. "I found this slapped on the door this morning."

I took the paper and glanced at it. In garish tones of blue and white with black lettering, it was a "cease and desist" flier, ordering us to pack up and return to Otherworld or we'd "face the consequences." Which meant that they'd stand around outside the shop with their signs, chanting insults at the top of their lungs, driving customers inside instead of away.

"They're good for business," I said. "Let them come. If they get nasty, I'll call Chase, and he'll haul their asses away."

Iris grinned. "You want me to set a few trip spells out there for them?"

"Now, now," I said, meeting her gleam for gleam, "that wouldn't be very nice. Tell you what, if they get obnoxious enough, you can have a go at them before I pick up the phone. Nothing harmful, mind you, not unless they try to hurt us, but I'll look the other way if you just happen to drop a *clothing optional* spell or something of the sort."

With a giggle, she shook her long hair, which fell to her feet and was caught up in a couple of thick ponytails. "You're bad. That's why I like working here," she said. "How's the investigation going? By the looks of that shopping bag, you weren't out chasing demons." She lowered her voice and pointed to one of the shelves, where Henry Jeffries was standing, peering through the various titles. I had a feeling Henry had a little crush on Iris, but he'd never be the first to say it aloud.

"Chase is supposed to meet me here. He had to meet with his boss first. And once again, I mention his name and there he is," I added as he darted through the door, shaking off his umbrella. He didn't look too happy. I sniffed. Spicy beef tacos, all right, along with a good dose of irritation. "Hey, what gives? Your thundercloud is showing."

He grunted. "Save it. I just got a tongue-lashing from Devins. Apparently, the Guardian Watchdogs are at it again, and Devins wants to know why I haven't figured out some way to shut them up. I told him that I'm not PR, but he seems to have the belief that since the Watchdogs formed because of the appearance of you Faeries, issues with them fall under my jurisdiction."

"Ugh. Sounds absolutely delightful. Maybe this will

make you feel better. I've got an idea on how to track down the harpy." I held up the feather.

"I have a feeling I'm going to regret this," he said. "But it couldn't be worse than facing down that prick of a boss again. Let's take a trip into hell."

With a warning shake of the head, I said, "Don't even joke about that, Chase. Now, do you want to hear my plan or not?"

He shook his head. "Sure, why not make this a complete freak show of a day?" As I glowered, he started to laugh. "Lead on, my dear Camille. I've never tried fried harpy before."

CHAPTER 8

᠆᠆᠆◆᠆᠆᠆

"So what's the big plan?" Chase asked.

"I'm going to cast a spell of Finding on this feather. It might work."

"Oh really." Chase raised one eyebrow. "Should I wear a bulletproof vest and whatever else I can think of to protect myself?" His voice clearly indicated he had his doubts.

"Funny man. My magic works part of the time." I pointed to the door. "Come on. I need to get up on the roof of a tall building where I have a good view of the city."

"Part of the time isn't a good track record," he said. "And does it have to be the roof?"

"Nope, but someplace I can lean outside." I slung my purse over my shoulder and gave Iris a quick hug. "I'll see you later. Don't let anybody paw through my shopping bag."

Chase shook his head. "There's no doubt that I'm going to regret this," he said, holding the door open for me. "If you need a good view of the city from above, I know just the place. But please, for God's sake, don't knock us over the edge."

* * *

Half an hour later we were standing in front of the Space Needle. I hadn't had a chance to visit the Seattle landmark yet. The skyscrapers in the city scared me, though Delilah loved them. In Otherworld, there were castles that were taller than this stark steel structure, but they seemed more fortified, and I had no problem standing on their ramparts.

I gave Chase a long look. "Can you get any more public?"

He grinned. "You said high place, good view. The Space Needle has an observation deck that will give us access to almost the entire city. What more do you want? You don't need to light any fires or burn anything do you? I don't think they'd like it if you did."

"No, I don't need to *burn* anything," I said, exasperated. "How much to get in?"

"I'll get it," he said, shaking his head. He bought us two passes, and we filed through the doors. Luckily, since it was a weekday in October, the lines were short. As we waited for one of the glass elevators to arrive, I suggested taking the stairs.

Chase gave me an *Are you crazy* look. "The observation deck is over five hundred feet up. You think I'm a masochist? You're nuts. My legs are in good enough shape without subjecting them to a brutal workout like that."

I grumbled, allowing him to herd me into the glass-enclosed lift, though I stood well away from the edge. It kept slipping my mind that FBHs didn't have as much endurance as the Sidhe did. Even with half-human blood, I could outwalk just about any person on the planet and go without sleep for several days before dropping from exhaustion. The elevator lurched into action, and I closed my eyes. Forty-one seconds, and we'd ascended over five hundred feet to the observation deck. Slightly dizzy, I stepped out of the elevator.

At least this level didn't rotate three hundred and sixty degrees, like the restaurant did. Grateful for small favors,

I followed Chase through the doors, onto the actual walkway that encircled the Space Needle.

The crowd was light. Everyone seemed to be avoiding the rain-slick catwalk in favor of the windows indoors. Definitely not tourist season, that was for sure. As I clung to the railing and gingerly peeked over the side, the thought crossed my mind that maybe this wasn't such a good idea after all. Five hundred feet was a long ways up. Which, in essence, meant a long ways to fall.

"There don't seem to be any people on the south side," Chase said, pointing.

"That's because there's no protection from the rain over there." But I needed privacy, so we were going to have to settle for drenched. Deciding to get it over with, I led the way, cautiously testing the safety grid that prevented jumpers from throwing themselves over the edge. Content that it was strong enough, I relaxed a little. If somebody was really determined, they could climb over, but they'd have to do some serious maneuvering.

We found a spot that was free from prying eyes. I pulled out the feather and glanced up at the sky. No stars, no moon, just a lot of gray clouds and rain, but at least we were outside where the wind currents would strengthen my magic. Hoping to avoid a misfire, I inhaled deeply, then slowly summoned the magic, feeling it race through my veins as the fire leapt within me. The spark of creation ignited, and I channeled the energy into the feather.

> *Creature of the night, demon harpy.*
> *Where are you? Show me the way,*
> *Feather to flesh, an arrow points*
> *Lady of the Moon, reveal my prey.*

As my voice drifted off, Chase looked around nervously. "Nothing happened," he said.

"No, *really*? Your confidence in my talents astounds me."

"You don't have to be sarcastic." But his expression told

me that he knew he was getting under my skin and enjoying it.

I snapped at him, "Listen, first you worry that something might happen, now you're upset that nothing did. Make up your mind."

He stifled a laugh. "Camille, you're perfect. You're just perfect, misfired magic or—" He stopped abruptly, staring at the feather in my hand. "What's happening?"

The feather was growing in my hand, and the aura emanating from it had taken on an altogether different quality. I cautiously set it down on the walkway, guarding it so the wind didn't blow it away.

"What's going on?" Chase sounded a little choked up, and when I glanced up at him, I saw the definite beginnings of fear in his eyes.

"I don't know," I said. "I guess we'll have to wait and find out."

This wasn't the way the spell was supposed to work. What should have happened was that the feather should have turned into an arrow, pointing in the direction in which the harpy was hiding. Of course, with my spells a lot of things didn't go as planned. As Menolly would say, "Deal with it."

The feather began to stretch and morph, and I backed up, pushing Chase behind me. Magic was my forte, screwups or not. Nervous, I wanted to just forget about it and make tracks, but there were people on the deck, even if it was just a handful. I couldn't leave them to contend with whatever I'd managed to conjure up.

"Oh shit!" Chase's cry broke through my thoughts, and I blinked as a fully formed harpy stepped out of the cloud of sparkles and mist, carrying a wriggling sack. Standing well over six feet high on two taloned feet, the demon had a lower torso that vaguely looked like an ostrich—feathered brown and yellow—and the upper body of a woman. Wings sprouted from her back, her breasts were firm and high, but her face was that of a wrinkled hag. Her eyes glittered as she gave us the once-over.

"Man, you are one ugly sucker," Chase said, whistling through his teeth.

Nervous, unable to stifle it, I broke into a sharp laugh. "Shut up, will you! She's dangerous."

A couple of girls who were near enough to see what was happening screamed and raced off in the other direction.

"Damned spell worked all right, but instead of leading us to the harpy, it brought the harpy to us," I muttered.

"Whatever the case, she doesn't look happy. Oh shit— look out!"

Chase's shout roused me from my shock. A good thing, since the harpy chose that moment to take a swipe at me. I ducked as her claws ripped past. Her fingernails were the length of small paring knives—and just as sharp. I didn't relish being on the receiving end of one of her love pats. Rina was not-so-living proof to what this demon could do.

I sucked in a deep breath and called out to the Moon Mother. I might not be able to see her, but I knew she was there, above the layer of clouds and daylight, and I could feel her energy resonate in response to my touch. "Lady, don't fail me now," I whispered as I brought up my hands to catch the ball of glowing moonlight that was forming in front of me.

"Attack and subdue!" I shouted, commanding the energy to attack.

The glowing orb stretched out like a luminous blade and slashed at the harpy. She shrieked and took a step back, her gaze fastened on me. Just then, Chase leaned around my right side, and an explosion rang out, startling the hell out of me as he aimed and fired his gun.

"Damn it, you'll ruin my control of the energy—" I said, but it was too late. The ball of moonlight had taken on a mind of its own and it apparently decided that it wanted whatever was in the bag the harpy was holding. It lashed at her, and she dropped the sack on the walkway. Chase's bullet had done no damage whatsoever to the demon.

I pushed him out of the way, trying to regain control of the moonlight but to no avail. I'd lost it, and it would go on doing whatever it wanted to do. And what it wanted to do was to curl around the sack and shield it. The harpy hissed, then apparently decided she'd lost that battle. She turned back to me.

"We need her alive, Chase." I sidestepped the glowing circlet of moonlight, focusing on the harpy, as I once again called out to the Moon Mother. Light raced down my arms into my hands, and I brought them up, pointing at her.

"Attack and subdue!" A beam of quicksilver poured from my hands, taking aim at the harpy, and this time it met her full-force. She soared into the air and hovered over the edge of the guardrails as the ray streamed toward her. I only meant to contain her, but apparently I'd put a little too much *oomph* behind it, because the light enveloped her, draining the flight from her wings. With a long, echoing shriek, she fell out of the sky and barreled to the ground below.

"Oh hell and bother!" I raced to the safety rail and peered over the side, Chase right behind me. The harpy had landed full-force on the sidewalk and was now one big red splat. The sound of scurrying feet told us that security guards weren't far behind. I turned to Chase. "What should we do? We can't let them find out about the demons."

"I'll talk to them. I'll tell them it was a Faerie who committed suicide," he said. "I'll get the OIA team out here. Go on!"

I grabbed the sack that the harpy had been holding and did the only thing I could think of. Hoping that my magic would work without a glitch this time, I gathered the light in the air around me and cloaked myself. Thank the gods, more than my clothes vanished from sight. Stepping between shadows as silently as I could, I crept toward the stairs, leaving Chase to clean up the mess.

As soon as I slinked back to my car, I leaned against the seat and closed my eyes, waiting for the spell to wear off. With my luck, it would take all day, and I'd be stuck until somebody came to pick me up. Cars didn't drive down the street by themselves, and I didn't want to draw any attention, considering the fact that at least two more demons were prowling the city. We might have taken care of the harpy, but Bad Ass Luke and the Psycho Babbler were still on the loose.

I'd never had to tangle with an actual demon before, and the encounter had left me unnerved. Not something I cared to repeat, but somehow I didn't think my wishes counted for much.

However, today luck was with me. My hands began to fade back into sight, and as I stared at my fingers, I had one of those aha moments and groaned. I had to remember to call Chase—if he could get the medical examiner to chop off one of the harpy's talons, I might be able to use that as my payment to Grandmother Coyote.

I thought about returning to the shop but shifted gears when the bundle that I'd snatched away from the harpy started to wriggle in my lap. What the hell? Cautiously, I untied the knot on the cloth and opened it. What had the moonlight been protecting from the demon?

A baby gargoyle stared up at me, her eyes glowing a brilliant topaz. A tortoiseshell, she was covered with a soft, downy fur, and on her face was the sweetest look that I'd ever seen.

"Well, hello," I said, gently lifting her up. Her wings were still far too small to carry her; she wouldn't be flying anywhere soon. In fact, she looked too young to be away from her mother. As I gazed at the cub, I had one of those flashes that told me more than I wanted to know.

Gargoyles and unicorns tended to be among the favorite foods of some demons, and rumors had been circulating for years that they kept them like livestock in the Subterranean Realms. If so, the cub had probably been intended as the harpy's midafternoon snack. Cringing, I gathered the gargoyle to my chest and held her tight. She let loose with a loud burp and then a faint cry as she clawed at my breasts.

"You're hungry. I'm afraid I don't make milk, little one," I said, holding her up. "But I bet we can find you something at home." She clutched at my hair as I disentangled her and set her back in the scrap of cloth that the harpy had carried her in. I finally figured out how to fix the seat belt so it held her tight, and then as the last bit of my toes flickered into sight, I pulled out of the parking garage and headed for home.

"What are you going to name her?" Chase asked. He'd arrived at the house as soon as he finished wrapping up things with the harpy, and now sat at the table, playing with the gargoyle cub, trying not to look astonished. I could see the laughter—and shock—in his eyes.

"Maggie," I said. "She just looks like a Maggie to me."

"I thought gargoyles were just statues carved out of stone," he said, tickling her tummy as I carried a bowl over to the table and placed it near her. She took a hesitant step, then her tongue flickered out and she leaned over the bowl, clutching the edges with her tiny hands. As she lapped up the liquid, Chase asked, "What are you feeding her?"

I settled into the chair next to him and leaned forward, staring at the creature who was now slurping up her lunch. "A mixture of cream, sugar, cinnamon, and sage. I have to get her started on the sage right now."

"Why?"

"Because gargoyles need it to further their development. This cub will never see her mother again, so I'm going to have to do what I can to make sure she develops as normally as possible. There's something odd about her, though . . ."

"You mean besides the fact that she looks like a bewinged, misshapen cat?" Chase snickered, but I noticed his gaze was firmly latched to Maggie, and I realized that he was enchanted by her. So Chase liked animals, be they Earthside or from Otherworld. The thought made me like him a little bit better.

"Gargoyles only look and feel like stone when they're bound to a quest. By nature, they're watchers—observers. The creatures are intelligent to a degree and have a limited vocabulary, but they don't think like we do. They're also incredibly long-lived, even more so than the Sidhe. Some of the gargoyles you see on the walls of Notre Dame and other cathedrals are in stasis, watching and keeping track of what goes on Earthside. They've been there so long among the statues that they may never be able to change back. I don't know their whole history, but I should start reading up on it now that Maggie's here."

Chase ran his fingers lightly over her back. "She's soft. Are you going to keep her or send her back to Otherworld?"

I shrugged. If I sent her home, there was no guarantee she'd be looked after. The Court and Crown didn't care much about Cryptos, except for unicorns and pegasi. Some time in the far distant past, gargoyles had been pressed into service and stripped of their rights in Y'Elestrial. They were often used like animals—intelligent ones—but animals nonetheless.

"Maggie's a Crypto, creatures most humans think of as imaginary but that have a vivid history of legend and lore Earthside. Most of the time, they're solitary and keep to themselves. I think I'll keep her. At least I know she'll be safe that way." I absently stroked her fur. "Tell me what happened with the harpy. And you didn't happen to think of cutting off one of her fingers, did you? I could really use it."

The look on his face was priceless. "Oh yeah, demon finger. No, sorry, the thought didn't occur to me. Tell me, just what the hell do you need a demon's finger for anyway?"

"As payment for information. If I don't come up with one, I've got to forfeit one of my own fingers. I forgot to ask you for it earlier, I was in such a hurry to get down out of that damned Needle. I don't ever want to go up there again, by the way," I said, shivering. "I'm afraid of heights, if you haven't figured that out by now. So tell me what you found out."

He stared at me like I was nuts. "You owe somebody a demon's finger as payment for information? What kind of freak show games do you play, Camille? Oh never mind," he quickly added. "I don't want to know. Here's the rundown: the cops backed off when they saw my badge. I contacted the OIA team, so there wasn't much of a problem."

"Well, the agency will damned right know there are demons on the prowl now," I said. "This should convince them we have a real threat. Did they find out anything special about the harpy that we should know about?"

Chase glanced toward the kitchen. "You got anything to drink? I brought their report with me. I put a rush on the autopsy. They didn't bring in a . . . what did you call it? Corpse Talker . . . that's it, though."

"They wouldn't. Corpse Talkers have no power over Demonkin."

"Ah, I didn't realize that," he said. "They did bring a wizard with them, though. He was there to . . . let me see." He consulted the file. "Oh yeah, he was there to examine the demon's *magical signature*. Make sense to you?"

"That would be standard practice," I said, leaving the table long enough to poke around in the refrigerator. "Lemonade okay? Or would you prefer something harder? Wine? Absinthe—the nectar of the Green Faerie?"

Chase blinked. "Absinthe is illegal."

"Not in Otherworld, and technically, any house of an OIA agent is considered OW territory for as long as we're here. Like an embassy. I can have absinthe on the premises, but I can't take it off our land." One of the few comforts from home, absinthe had originally come Earthside via the Faerie Queen hundreds of years ago. It had been a gift from the Sidhe to mortals.

"Maybe later," Chase said. "I could go for a glass of wine, though. I prefer red, if you have it."

I pulled out a bottle of wine that had been a gift in the last care package our father sent us. It was made from the finest grapes in Otherworld, as rich and as red as blood, and as smooth as brandy. Pouring two glasses, I handed one to Chase and cradled the other in my hand.

He sipped, and his eyes grew round. "I've never tasted anything quite like this," he said, his voice suddenly deepening.

"You're drinking Faerie wine. Now, about the harpy?" I glanced at Maggie, who had finished her meal and curled in a ball on a throw pillow that I'd placed on the table.

"She was a demon, all right, and Jacinth said—do you recognize that name? She's the attendant who worked on the harpy; she also examined Jocko."

I nodded. Jacinth and I knew each other from childhood. She was one of the good ones—she'd never taunted us because of our mixed blood, and I both respected and liked her.

"Jacinth said that it looks like the harpy has only been Earthside a few days, which would coincide with the sighting of the demons coming out of the Wayfarer." He flipped through the report. "It says here that she had a collar on that marks her as being part of something called a Degath Squad."

Oh hell. "The Degath Squads' prime tasks are to scout ahead for information. That clinches it. Grandmother Coyote is right—Shadow Wing did send scouts in, and they are looking for the spirit seals."

Chase gazed at me, his eyes shrouded and dark. "So what's our next step?"

"Find Tom Lane. Get the seal before they do. Somehow, kill the demons before they get to anybody else. I just hope we manage to find them before they find us."

"You and me both. How long till Delilah comes home?"

"I'll find out," I said, pulling my cell phone out of my purse. I punched in Delilah's number, and she answered on the third ring. "You need to come home," I said. "We found the harpy and killed her."

She sounded relieved. "Thank gods you did, because the harpy got hold of Louise Jenkins before I could get there. I'm on the way home. I'll be there in ten minutes."

"Oh hell, Louise is dead?" I glanced over at Chase, who jerked his head up. He pushed a pad of paper in front of me, and I scribbled Louise's name on it.

"Yeah. Chase might want to send a crew out there. I don't think anybody's missed her because there were no signs of the cops or anything. I used gloves, made sure not to touch a thing with bare hands."

"Chase is already here, so I'll tell him. What's her apartment number again?" I jotted down the information. "Okay, thanks. Say, would you stop and grab a couple of pizzas for dinner? Sausage, ham, pineapple, whatever else you can think of that's good." As I flipped the phone closed, I noticed that little Maggie was breathing deeply, sound asleep.

Chase was on the phone as soon as I gave him all the information, and once again, the OIA team was activated. He told them to call him as soon as they knew what was going on.

As we waited for Delilah, I fixed up a little box for the gargoyle, and Maggie snuggled happily in her bed. Chase and I sat in the living room, watching the news on TV. There was a short segment on the "strange Faerie" who fell over the side of the Space Needle. At least reporters weren't onto the fact that the harpy had been a demon, although they made a few ill-advised chicken jokes. Louise Jenkins wasn't mentioned; the team must still be investigating.

By the time my sister slipped through the door, I was starving. I took the pizza boxes from Delilah and set them on the coffee table. "Hey, go in the kitchen and take a look at what I found. If she's awake, bring her back with you."

Delilah headed into the dining room while I opened one box and sniffed at the thick sausage and mushroom pizza, long strings of extra cheese glistening on the top. "You have the best-tasting food, Chase. I could get used to living Earthside, if only for that reason."

He snorted as Delilah returned, Maggie snuggled in her arms. "She's adorable. Where did you find her?" She settled into the rocker, chucking the chin of the wide-awake and bewildered gargoyle.

We filled her in on our encounter with the demon. "My spell backfired, but at least we were able to make use of the results," I said. "She was part of a Degath Squad. You know what that means."

Delilah's smile faded. "Hell Scouts."

"Yeah, and even though she's dead, that leaves us the two most dangerous ones to contend with. We have to solidify our plans to find Lane. I don't think we have much time. So tell us about Louise."

Delilah rolled her eyes. "Talk about bad news all the way around. I'd like to wait until Menolly's awake, though." She glanced at Chase, who gave her a frustrated nod.

I reached for Maggie and wandered over to the window. Dusk was starting to fall. "I'm hungry," I said. "Chase, you hold Maggie while Delilah and I set the table."

He started to protest, but I plunked the gargoyle in his arms, handed him the remote, picked up the pizzas, and motioned for Delilah to follow me into the kitchen. As I arranged the plates and napkins on the table, Delilah poured more wine for Chase and me, and milk for herself.

"I'm so hungry," Delilah said, licking her lips. She set the parmesan shaker on the table. "Chase seems awfully nice tonight. He didn't act like I was a freak at all."

I glanced at her, grinning. "Maybe seeing the harpy made him realize how normal you really are."

Delilah laughed as she tucked a bowl of broccoli in the microwave and punched it on for three minutes.

"You know, as homesick as I am," I said, "I have to admit how much easier technology makes things. I'll miss electricity when we go back."

"We had servants there," Delilah countered. "But thank heavens for Mother. At least we understood the language and culture before we came here."

Mother had brought us up bilingual, and had taught us about Earthside customs from the time we could walk.

"True. I suppose we were the logical choices for this assignment. Maybe headquarters wasn't punishing us after all. Most of the agents assigned Earthside go through long periods of transition, but we already knew a lot about life here before we ever joined the OIA."

"It's a comforting thought." Delilah peeked down the hall into the living room. "Chase and Maggie are asleep. She's such a cutie. Can we really keep her?" The wistful tone to her voice made me smile. Delilah always brought home stray animals when she was young, and Mother had asked Father to build a shed out in back of our home specifically for Delilah's menagerie.

"Yes, we can keep her. Her mother's probably churning out babies for some demon's sweet tooth, and HQ isn't going to want her. I don't know how Menolly will feel about it, but she'll come around."

"Everything's ready. Let's eat." With that, she went to wake Chase. While he washed his hands, I showed her how to mix up the cream for Maggie, and we fed her, then put her to bed before settling in at the table for our own meal.

"Are gargoyles intelligent?" Chase asked, taking his third piece of pizza.

"Some are," I said cautiously, in case Maggie could understand the rudiments of language. "They can be brilliant, or they can have the brainpower of the average cat. A lot depends on the nutrition their mother gets during pregnancy, the clan their bloodline hearkens from, and whether they were handled roughly at birth. Considering the harpy had her, I'm not at all sure Maggie will grow up to be much more than a pet. She may never be able to go into stasis."

If she couldn't, then she wouldn't be of any use to the OIA. Which, considering the way gargoyles were forced to live when they went Earthside, was probably the best thing that could happen to her. Some gargoyles, especially those with lower intelligence, didn't possess the ability to freeze-frame.

Chase blinked when a loud snore cut through the air from Maggie's box. "She sounds a little like a cat, a little like a pig."

"They snuffle when they're happy." I glanced at the clock. "Time to wake Menolly. We have plans to make."

"Just so long as we find Tom Lane before Bad Ass Luke does," Delilah said.

"And just so long as we find him before Bad Ass Luke finds *us*," I said. Neither she nor Chase had much of an answer to that.

CHAPTER 9

Menolly stretched, shaking her braids to a loud clatter. "So what's on the agenda tonight?" She shimmied into skintight jeans and a cami top, giving me a toothy grin. Her fangs glistened in the dim light, and once again, I found myself a little queasy. She looked at me. "What happened with Trillian? Is he back in your life?"

I leaned back on her bed. "Yeah, I'm weak. So sue me."

"Couldn't you just find one of our cousins to hook up with? Or even a vampire? I know several lesser vamps that aren't too objectionable." Her eyes twinkled, and I knew she was teasing me.

"Yeah, I need an undead lover just about as bad as I need another hole in my . . . head. Speaking of vamps, you got a call from Wade. I think somebody's smitten," I said, teasing her.

"You're kidding. He called here?" She did her best to look pissed, but I could tell she was interested. An excited light flickered in her eyes, and she was trying to hide a smile.

"I see that grin, so don't try to bluff me, because you can't. You gave him your number, so you were obviously interested. Now, come on, there's a lot to fill you in on. Chase and I took out the harpy today, but not before she killed both Louise Jenkins and an exiled Faerie."

Menolly followed me upstairs, glancing at Chase as she took a seat opposite him. I introduced her to Maggie, and she seemed surprisingly delighted, holding the little gargoyle in her arms with a tender smile flickering at the corners of her lips. While she snuggled Maggie, Chase and I launched into what had happened with Rina and the harpy.

"We enlisted a Corpse Talker, and I asked Rina how to find Tom."

"What did she tell you?" Menolly asked.

"A riddle. 'He's mad as a hatter, mad as a hare. Go to the woodland, but be you aware. Look for the ancients who shelter from storm, but first you must pass through the lair of the wyrm.' If you can figure out what it means, be my guest."

"Wyrm?" Delilah frowned. "Dragon?"

"No dragons around the Pacific Northwest as far as I know," I said. "Of course, OIA also told us that the demons would never break through onto Earth."

Menolly snorted. "The OIA has been sloppy on a number of things lately. I agree with Delilah. Best guess is that a dragon of some sort's hanging out there. Possibly he's protecting this Tom?"

I groaned. A dragon was so not what we needed. Generally selfish and greedy, they made wonderful mercenaries and were nearly impossible to kill. If Tom had hired one to protect him—or somebody hired the wyrm for him—then we were going to have a fight on our hands. And considering the state of our little ragtag band, I knew that none of us had what it took to take on a dragon.

"Okay, so let's call that roadblock number one," I said. "I wonder if Bad Ass Luke and the Psycho Babbler know about this. The question is, how do we find Tom? He's supposed to be living near Mount Rainier, either on the edge of the national park's borders, or hiding within."

"It's too late to drive out there tonight, and the roads are going to be difficult—parts of the park are already closed for the winter. Tomorrow we'll make the trip," Chase said. "Delilah, can you help me do some sleuthing on him before then? We can go through everything at my office. Then tomorrow, we'll meet here before heading out. I'll drive. Say we get started around eight tomorrow morning?"

"Sounds good," Delilah said. "Now, do you want to hear everything that happened at Louise Jenkins's apartment? As I said, the harpy was a step ahead of us there, too. Actually several steps. Louise was a mess. She'd been dead long enough for rigor mortis to set in, so the harpy may have gotten to her before she stopped at Rina's. I searched the apartment but found nothing. I took a long look at Louise, or at what remained of her, that is." She winced and shook her head. "Bloody, terribly bloody. Anyway, I noticed there was a ring on her finger. Gold and diamond."

"Wedding finger?" I asked.

"You got it. I wonder if Jocko married her and conveniently forgot to tell the OIA. They would have kicked him out for that."

"Or maybe they were engaged," Menolly said slowly. "I remember several times he mentioned that he was getting used to life Earthside, and how it wasn't so bad. He was respected because of his size here. Back in OW, he was ridiculed for being so short."

I turned to Delilah. "Did you notice anything else? Pictures? Anything to give us a clue of what kind of a connection Louise and Jocko had?"

Delilah squinted, thinking. After a moment, she said, "Her apartment was trashed, so I couldn't make out much about what she was like. No pictures that I could see, but I didn't want to disturb the scene any more than necessary."

Menolly snapped her fingers. "Wait a second. Jocko had a diary. I saw him writing in a journal a few weeks ago. It was small, with a drawing of . . . it looked like an antique map on the cover. Did you find anything like that in his room when you searched it after he was murdered?" She turned to Chase, who looked surprised.

"No. Not at all. In fact, it barely looked like he lived there. I was surprised that giants could be so clean. Could the diary be at the bar? An undercover OIA team member searched his office, but I don't remember anything like that in the evidence they brought back. By the way, has Camille told you about your promotion?"

Blinking, Menolly shook her head. "Promotion? What are you talking about?" Then understanding flooded her face, and her pale skin glowed even brighter. "Oh crap and hell. They've put me in charge of the bar, haven't they?"

"You got it," Chase said. "So I guess you have to go back to work tonight. While you're there, take a look around and find out if the diary is hidden behind the bar. Take Camille with you, and both of you be careful—if there's an inside man, we haven't found him yet. And if he knows you're an agent, you could be in a lot of danger."

"Chase is right," I broke in. "Only Jocko knew that we're sisters, so I can just be a local bookstore owner, out for a drink. Then, tomorrow, we'll drive out to Mount Rainier. Okay, Chase and Delilah, get busy with your research. Two heads are better than one. Just ask any dubba-troll."

Delilah glanced at Maggie. "What about her?"

"She should be okay until I get home. She's sound asleep."

"Okay. Get your butt in gear, Chase."

Chase broke into a smile. "My pleasure. Just don't go shifting on me when I'm not prepared for it."

I waved my hand. "Get out of here, both of you. If there's trouble, call me on my cell phone."

Once they left, I hurried upstairs and slipped on a tight, thigh-high black leather skirt, then laced up my new magenta and black bustier, jiggling so my boobs were ready to bust out. I slid my feet into a pair of round-toed pumps with four-inch stiletto heels and twirled in front of the mirror. Woo-hoo, good enough to eat!

We needed all the information we could get. If there was an inside person at the bar, they wouldn't talk to Menolly, but they might talk to me. Especially if I turned on the charm.

I wrapped a velvet stole around my shoulders and cautiously descended the stairs, careful to avoid catching my heels on the numerous cracks that split the wood.

Menolly glanced up at me as I entered the kitchen. Her jaw dropped, and she coughed. "Damn good thing Trillian isn't here to see you. I'd never get you out of the bedroom."

"You may have that trouble soon enough. I just can't get him out of my system. So, you ready?"

"Whenever you are." She held up the keys to her truck.

"I'll take my car. If we're seen entering together, whoever's working on the inside might get suspicious." I made sure I had everything and nodded toward the door. "After you." And we headed out into the stormy night.

The Wayfarer was rocking as usual. It had real Otherworld feel—the lights were fashioned to look like kerosene lamps, and the décor appeared rustic on the surface but was polished when you looked closely. Long benches and tables served the crowds, as well as booths for private parties. In addition to the standard beer and wine, the bartender kept a few goodies such as Cryptozoid Ale and Brownie Beer behind the bar, all pricey and in high demand.

A staircase ran along the back wall, leading up to two floors of rooms that were always full. The portal itself was secreted in the basement, and an OIA agent was on guard night and day to process the passports of those entering from OW. It was where we'd first made our appearance Earthside.

Menolly was in full swing at the bar. The lights were dim, and she was working like crazy. The crowd of subculture FBHs who thronged to the bar loved the fact that she was a vampire, though they kept a respectful distance, except for the few who were hung up on the mystique of vamp lore.

While acceptance of the undead was still sorely lacking, things were slowly changing, although their reputation hadn't been helped by all the horror movies and vamps who loved to play up the whole ooo-spooky image. Dracula, for instance, had been a resident of OW, and during his deportation to the Subterranean Realms, he managed to escape and to flee Earthside before the guards could stop him. He'd single-handedly destroyed potential relations between vamps and humans for hundreds of years.

I wandered up to the counter and pushed through the crowd. Women dressed so skimpy they made me look like a nun clustered in groups at the tables, alert for any sign of Sidhe men who might wander through. They weren't Faerie Watchers though. No, the Faerie Watchers Club preferred to focus on the magic and sparkles and unicorns. These women were looking for a party and maybe a little more. They called themselves Faerie Maids and a few—usually the most interesting—had enough success that they'd become addicted to sex with the Sidhe. Gods only knew what they'd do if they ever slept with a Svartan.

The women weren't the only ones looking for a little action. Several men wandered through the bar, but most of them knew they didn't have a chance in hell. Menolly told me they picked up the women who were left sitting alone at the end of the night. It was sad, really, but overall, very few of the Sidhe paid any attention to the open invitations.

I slid onto a stool, glancing around. Here and there, I spotted another Faerie or two. Even a few Weres were hanging around the outskirts of the room—you could tell them from the gleam in their eyes. They met my gaze, and some nodded, a few gave me a half wave, acknowledging our common roots.

Where should I start? A tingle in the back of my neck alerted me, and I turned around. In the corner booth, I spotted a young man. He looked Japanese, but a glamour around him caught my attention.

"A glass of white wine," I murmured to Menolly when she finally made her way over to me. "And who's that? Over there in the booth?"

She glanced at the man as she set the Riesling down in front of me. In a whisper, she said, "I've never seen him in here before tonight. I *can* tell you, he didn't come over from OW. He smells like a demon, but I'd bet my fangs that he's not from the Subterranean Realms."

I sipped my wine and slowly pushed myself off the stool, strolling over to the booth. As I approached, the man looked up, and I saw that he wasn't quite as young as I thought. His face was smooth and unlined, but his eyes were far older than twenty-something. I leaned against the wall separating his booth from the next one.

"Won't you sit down, beautiful lady?" he asked.

I accepted his invitation, sliding into the opposite seat. As I cradled my wineglass in my hands, it dawned on me that this was no chance meeting. He'd been waiting for me, though I didn't know how or why. After a moment's silence the air around him rippled. Magic, all right.

"Grandmother Coyote said you might be able to use my help," he said abruptly. As he blinked, his chocolate eyes turned a startling shade of topaz.

Bingo. I knew I sensed something familiar about him. His scent was thick with musk, but beneath the masculine odor, I could detect the subtle smell of Grandmother Coyote's energy mingling in his aura—as if she'd leaned against his shoulder or patted him on the back.

I took a sip of my wine and contemplated this odd turn of events. "Perhaps." Toying with my drink, I gazed at him, trying to figure out just who he was. Menolly was right. He wasn't from the Sub Realms. That much I could tell, so he couldn't be the Psycho Babbler, as charming as he might seem.

That left the question as to whether he was in league with Bad Ass Luke. Whoever he was, he was handsome, with shoulder-length hair the color of charcoal, smooth and shining and gathered back in a ponytail. He had no facial hair save for a small goatee and a pencil-thin mustache, and while his build was slight, he looked wiry under the green cable-knit sweater. Hmm . . . he really was cute. What might he be wearing below that sweater? I couldn't very well ask him to stand up so I could see his pants.

Shaking myself out of my reverie, I said, "So, who are you?"

The corner of his lips crooked into a cunning smile. My pulse revved, and I shifted in my seat, wondering if he could read me.

He gave a little laugh. "Morio. I just arrived in town."

Morio? That was a Japanese name.

"Not from Otherworld, you didn't," I said before I could stop myself. "You aren't one of the Sidhe. What are you?" Whoops . . . very rude. In Otherworld it was considered the height of bad manners to ask what someone was upon first greeting. I backtracked. "Excuse me . . . bad manners. My name's Camille. So Grandmother Coyote pointed you my way? How did you know I'd be here tonight?"

"I followed you from your house." He brushed away a shoulder-length strand of hair that had come loose from his ponytail.

Shit, then he also knew that Menolly and I were connected. I prayed that he was really on our side. "You've been watching me? I don't appreciate that."

Morio shrugged. "You wouldn't have noticed me if I hadn't told you, so don't worry about it. I arrived from Japan yesterday." He glanced around the tavern. "I haven't been here in a while. The giant's gone." With a quick gesture at Menolly, he leaned forward. "I won't tell your secret. Or hers."

I sucked in a deep breath. Direct questioning wasn't going to work on him. "What do you want with me?"

He traced an intricate pattern on the table. I tensed—the weave looked like spell work, but I couldn't feel any magic emanating from it, so I tried to relax. "It's not what I want with you," he said. "It's what I can do for you."

"And *what* can you do for me?" I leaned forward, realizing that I was asking more than one question.

"I can help you find that which you seek," he said. "I know the forest. I know how to track, to sniff out and seek."

He lifted his head, locking me in with his gaze. His slow smile ran through my veins like fine wine, disorienting me as the energy of the woodland closed in around us. Dark and deep, old and wild, it wove itself like a cloak around his shoulders. "Whatever you want beyond that, I'm sure I can provide."

As I caught my breath, I realized he was an Earthside spirit and that he belonged to this world. "Did Grandmother Coyote call you in on our behalf?"

Another smile, another yank into a swirling kaleidoscope of leaves and twigs and roots plunging deep into the earth. "Not exactly, but she showed me those who threaten this world. *My world.* I'm at your disposal. Put me to work."

He lifted his glass to salute me, and I returned the compliment, wondering what to do next. My question was answered when Menolly caught my attention. She hadn't lifted a finger, but we were sisters, and I could feel when she called me. I glanced over at the bar to where she stood, a small book in her hand. A traveler's notebook, an elastic band held the pages closed. Jocko's diary.

"You'd better go talk to her. I'll wait for you," Morio said.

As I slowly stood, keeping my eye on my new companion, it occurred to me that Morio had affected me in a way no man had since before I'd met Trillian. Whether that boded for good or ill remained to be seen.

Menolly gave me a quizzical look as I approached the bar. I asked for another white wine, then leaned over the counter. "We need to talk."

"I can't get off duty right now, and after work I want to look around and see if I can figure out who was helping Bad Ass Luke from here. But take the journal with you. By the way, who's the hot-to-trot? Please don't tell me he's on Shadow Wing's side."

I raised one eyebrow and glanced back at Morio, who lifted his glass in my direction. "I'm not sure yet, but he's an emissary from Grandmother Coyote, and if he's a demon, he's an earthbound one. I'm certain he's not in league with our big bad boys from the netherworlds. I'd smell them on him."

"Really?" Menolly topped off my glass and pushed it across the counter, along with the diary. "I've been watching you two. You've got something going on there. Be interesting to find out just what he is . . . maybe a wizard?"

I shook my head. "Don't think so, but can't tell yet. Okay, I'm leaving, and I'll probably take him with me."

"Planning on doing some undercover work?" she asked, snickering.

I started to make a smart-assed retort, but who was I kidding? "I wouldn't mind finding out what's under that smooth exterior, I'll tell you that. His name's Morio, by the way. If anything happens to me, go to Grandmother Coyote and ask her what's going down." Sliding the diary into my purse, I drained the glass, then strode back over to the booth, where I nodded to Morio. "You coming?"

Without a word, he stood, slid his shoulder bag, and followed.

The rain whipped so hard that I cringed; my legs felt like they were under attack by a swarm of bees. Morio didn't seem to notice, but he did know where I'd parked and led me directly to my car. As I unlocked the doors, I wondered if I was crazy getting behind the wheel with this strange creature by my side. Inhaling deeply to calm myself, I fastened my seat belt and waited while he did the same.

"We're going back to your house?" he asked.

I glanced at him quickly. "Why?"

"That seems most logical. You need to sleep before tomorrow. We are going looking for Tom Lane, aren't we?"

I sighed. "Listen, I don't know what you are, or how you know so much, but bad manners or not—I want some straight answers. You say Grandmother Coyote told you about me, you say you watched our house, and you knew which car was mine. What's going on?"

He grinned then, a full-fledged, delightful grin that made me want to lean over and kiss him. "Camille, your temper's showing."

Charmer or not, I was at the point of ordering him out of the car when I caught a glimpse of something darting toward us from the alley. I gasped as a large black silhouette leapt toward the front of the car and smashed a rock into the windshield. The glass shook but didn't shatter, although a crack slowly streaked from one side to the other. Dazed, I stared dumbly at the creature who loomed in my headlights. That is, until I realized that it was coming around to my side.

"Fucking hell!" I screamed, suddenly noticing that Morio had hold of my wrist and was yanking me over the gearshift onto his seat. He'd already thrown his door wide and was outside like a light, dragging me with him.

"Run," he said, pushing me toward the lighted intersection. "Run!"

I had only taken a few steps before my heel caught on a hole in the sidewalk and I went sliding, face-first, along the concrete. Wincing as wet gravel lodged itself into my palms and chin, I forced myself to roll to my feet, kicking off my shoes as I did so. I whirled around, but all I could see was a blur.

Then, in the midst of the downpour, I caught sight of Morio. Our attacker was nowhere to be seen. Morio glanced around, then turned my way. I saw that he was holding something, trying to get it into the shoulder bag. I managed to catch a glimpse of an ivory rounded object with glowing red eyes. A skull? I couldn't be certain, but it looked like it.

He closed the bag, then leaned his head back, as if sniffing the air. After a moment, he strode over to me and held out his hand. Still wary, I took it, and he scooped me into his arms with no more effort than I'd have scooping up Maggie. It would seem that Morio was a lot stronger than he looked.

"What the hell was that thing?" I asked, not bothering to ask why he was carrying me. I figured he had his reasons, and I had no objections to being in his arms. In fact, it felt pretty damned good.

"A skinwalker. Earthbound, but probably in league with darker forces. I warded it off, but it won't stay away long. Come, we have to get out of here before it returns with re-inforcements." He carried me back to the driver's side of the car. As soon as he was in, I peered around the cracks in the windshield, pulled into traffic, and shot off.

Along the way, Morio remained silent, enjoining me to wait until we were safe to ask any more questions. I had to warn Menolly, though, so pulled out my cell phone and punched number three on the speed dial.

Two rings later, Menolly answered.

"Listen, we've got trouble."

"Morio?" As usual, she was blunt and to the point.

"No. We're on the way home right now. We were attacked by something called a skinwalker after we left the bar. It was only a few blocks from the Wayfarer, so you need to be care-ful. Get someone you trust to walk you to your car when your shift is over. If you have to, call Chase, but I don't know if bullets would work on that thing. Call me before you leave and again when you're safely on the road."

I could hear the hesitation in her voice. "Are you sure you're safe with Morio?"

With a laugh, I shook my head, even though she couldn't see me. "I'm not sure we're safe anywhere," I said. "Talk to you later."

The rest of the ride was uneventful. As I pulled into our driveway, I tuned in to the wards I'd set up around the property. They glowed at the corners of the land, a soft white, holding fast. Nothing happened to Morio as we passed through them, so he couldn't be *too* bad.

I parked and turned off the ignition. Thank the gods we'd made it home safe. But if Morio had found our house, had anybody else? I thought about Maggie, in there alone, and bounded up the porch stairs, barefoot. I fumbled with the key, finally managing to unlock the door, and hurried into the darkened hallway.

Morio was right behind me. "I'll help you check the house," he said, as easily as if he lived here.

"Okay, you can help, but no going through things that are none of your business. Got it? No funny stuff."

He shrugged. "Funny is good, it keeps a soul healthy. Lead on, lady."

We searched the house from top to bottom, although I conveniently ignored the basement. The entrance, hidden behind the bookcase door, stayed safely off-limits. Menolly's lair was sacrosanct.

As we returned to the living room, satisfied that nobody was lurking in the hall closet or under the beds, Morio set his bag down on the love seat and quickly assumed the lotus position next to it. *Mighty flexible,* I thought, wondering in what other ways he might be flexible. My body was jumping on the bandwagon my mind had already commissioned and set into motion.

I offered him a drink, and he accepted a beer. As I handed it to him, he stared at me, appraising me from head to toe, and the appraisal looked good. I licked my lips. While I was used to men staring at me—if only for the size of my breasts—this was different. This could lead to something, and coming so soon on the trail of Trillian's visit, I wasn't sure whether that was a good idea or not.

I settled down in the recliner. "All manners aside, tell me who you are."

He cracked a smile. "I can see you won't be satisfied with a simple explanation."

"Not on your life. Spill it, as the locals say."

He shrugged. "You know my name—Morio—and I told you the truth. Grandmother Coyote sent me to help you. I'm one of the yokai-kitsune."

"Kit what?" For all I knew, it could be a family clan name, a tribe, or some secret fraternal order.

"Yokai-kitsune. Fox demon would be a close translation."

Demon? Oh shit! I jumped up and looked around wildly for the nearest weapon. The silver short swords my father had given to each of us were safely ensconced in a cabinet in the parlor. Since the closest thing I could reach was a sofa cushion, I held out my hands to gather the moon's energy, hoping that she wouldn't fail me now.

He cocked one eyebrow. "You're going to attack me? Oh, that's nice."

Hesitating, I stared at him, waiting. "Then you really aren't from the Subterranean Realms? Why would Grandmother Coyote send you here?"

Morio snorted. "No, I'm not from down under, and she sent me because you obviously can't handle this situation on your own. If I'd been from the netherworlds, you'd be toast by now, and I'd be feasting on your bones." He patted the seat beside him. "Now, sit down and quit being a drama queen!"

Of all the arrogant, smarmy—I paused when I looked into his upturned face. He was patiently waiting for me to do as told. I wanted to stomp off into the kitchen; however, this situation was going from bad to worse, and we needed all the help we could get. I sat down, sighing.

He smiled, satisfied. "Good. You know how to listen. As I said, I'm a yokai-kitsune. I come from Japan, though I've been to the U.S. several times before. I owe Grandmother Coyote a big favor, and she's calling it in, so here I am. She wants me to help you find the spirit seals. After hearing about what's going on, I am more than happy to be of service. Nobody's going to invade my world and get away with it."

I examined his face. Now that I had a chance to look closer, I could see that his ears were slightly pointed and that his teeth seemed a little sharp for a human. But he wasn't Faerie—not in the sense that my father was.

"You say you're a demon?" I asked.

"In a manner of speaking. Demon, nature spirit, what have you. The terms aren't important. What matters is that I'm not human, even though I take the form for the most part."

"A Were?"

Again, a shake of the head. "No. Demon."

I could see I wasn't going to get much else out of him, so changed the subject. "I thought Grandmother Coyote wouldn't interfere."

"She won't, but she *can* ask others to step in. Shadow Wing is upsetting the balance, and the Hags of Fate don't like it when the scales are off-kilter." He opened his bag and pulled out the object he'd been holding earlier. As I'd suspected, it was a skull. "This is my familiar. I have to have this in order to change into a human. If I lose it, the next time I change into a fox, I can't change back until it's returned to me. It was given to me at birth. I'm telling you this so you don't get any bright ideas about swiping it for one of your spells."

I blushed. "I'd never think of it," I said, though it occurred to me that I still owed Grandmother Coyote the finger bone of a demon, and here was one, sitting in my living room. But I was a good hostess. I wasn't going to conk this guy over the head and make off with his skull, let alone cut off his finger, especially after she'd asked him to help us fight Shadow Wing. Besides, I was more interested in other body parts.

"So, what did she tell you?"

"Everything I need to know. You're looking for the spirit seals that have been lost. If you don't find them before Shadow Wing does, we're in big trouble. What I don't understand is why the OIA won't step in with a mass attack and take care of this problem."

"Because they can't." The voice from the front door startled us both, and I leapt up, catching my breath. Trillian. Again. And he didn't look happy to see Morio sitting there.

CHAPTER 10

～⊷⊶～

"Will you stop that? Next time ring the bell!" I glared at him as he wandered in and slid into a chair, his eyes never leaving me after a single glance in Morio's direction.

"Why should I?" he asked. "You know you'll let me in, so why bother with outdated niceties?"

"And *that* is one of the reasons we're no longer together," I said, exasperated.

"We were together last night, and you had no complaints, I noticed." He turned to Morio. "Let me introduce myself. I'm Trillian. Camille's lover."

"Stop right there! I may have slipped and slept with you again, but I'm *not* your lover. Not anymore." I sighed. "You're boorish and arrogant. And terribly rude."

"And your point is . . . ?" he asked, eyeing me with a speculative look. Irritated, I turned away as he continued. "The OIA can't intervene directly because the Queen has her head so far up her ass that she can't see what's going on. And the generals are sitting tight and cozy in their fancy homes with their stashes of opium and their feasts and orgies. Even if they figure out what the hell's happening, the troops aren't equipped to do battle. I hate to tell you this, but that ragtag army couldn't fight their way out of a box. The only hope is subterfuge, because by the time the royals figure out something's wrong, Shadow Wing will have discovered the spirit seals *and it will all be too late."*

He leaned back, his gaze flickering around the room.

"Did Father tell you all that?" If that's what my father was saying, we were in real trouble.

"Your father isn't alone in his assessment. There's trouble on the wind for the Queen. Old enemies just don't fade away, even after a thousand years. She needs to remember those she's crossed in the past." After a moment, Trillian looked over at Morio. "So the old hag sent you? A wolf cub to do a man's work? Well, I suppose you're better than nothing."

"Yokai-kitsune, thank you." Morio bristled, and his pupils narrowed. "I know what you are. I've seen your kind in the northern mountains before. Don't push me, Svartan."

Great, a testosterone match. Just what we needed. "Chill out, both of you. Morio, I welcome your help, and my sisters will too. Trillian, back off."

Trillian arched his eyebrows and gave me a slow, sensuous grin. "Do you welcome my help, too? You did last night."

His eyes were gleaming. Uh-oh. I caught my breath, forcing myself to shake my head. The next moment, Trillian had slid in beside me, his fingers running up my arm.

"Stop it!"

"Your feelings are transparent—" he started to say, but before he could get the rest of his words out, Morio's hand latched on to my other wrist, dragging me out of Trillian's grasp.

"Leave her alone. It's obvious the lady doesn't want your attention." Morio pushed me behind him as he glared at Trillian.

"Cub, you've just overstepped your boundaries. You'd better keep your nose out of situations that don't concern you." Trillian was standing, hands on hips, at the ready.

I knew that he carried a long knife in his boot, and I had the feeling he'd upgraded to more modern weaponry since coming Earthside. The last thing I needed was for him to take a potshot at Morio with some purloined handgun.

"Enough!" Thoroughly irritated, I squeezed between them and glared at them until they both backed away. "Take it down a notch, boys. I mean it."

When they were sitting again, albeit grumpy and eyeing each other like hostile dogs, I headed toward the kitchen. "I need to check on Maggie. If either of you starts up again, I'm going to come in here and blast you both. And you know you can't count on the side effects of my spells—you could end up a couple of puffballs, for all I care!"

Trillian's gaze burned into me, and he gave me a sly smile, then returned to staring down Morio. I paused to make sure they were really in truce mode, then slipped into the kitchen.

Maggie was snuggled in her box, curled up asleep on an old blanket. My irritation evaporated as I looked down at the beautiful swirls of orange and black and white downy fur covering her little body. Gargoyles were small when born, and they aged so slowly that it would be years before she grew to adulthood. I knelt beside the box and gently stroked her fur. She snuffled in her sleep.

While I'd wanted a cat—a black one who stayed a cat and didn't turn into a person—felines didn't like being around Menolly. And Delilah would have been jealous and territorial. So Maggie was a perfect compromise. She wouldn't be afraid of vampires unless she'd already been treated badly by one, and she wouldn't threaten Delilah's seniority. The last thing we needed was a litter box dispute. Maggie turned, blinked once, then closed her eyes and fell back asleep.

I made sure there was water in her bowl and then chopped up a few ounces of steak and added some bread and milk. As I set the saucer down next to the box, Maggie's eyes opened, and she peeked over the edge. She let out a little *mooph*, then yawned as I lifted her over the edge. She lapped up the water and the food.

When she'd finished, I rubbed her belly, then carried her outside and set her on the ground. She dribbled a few pellets and a puddle on the grass near the steps, and I picked her up again and carried her back inside. It would be a long time before her wings were big enough or strong enough to carry her weight, and I didn't want her crawling around by herself outside.

After I put her back in the box, I poured myself a glass of wine and returned to the living room, hoping that Trillian and Morio had been able to restrain themselves. Apparently, my absence had been too taxing. They'd started talking to fill the silence.

"The Queen will never understand how much danger there really is," Trillian was saying. "She's too caught up in her opium dreams to pay attention. The General Commander is trying to whip things into shape, but he's getting a fight every step of the way. The last meeting of the ruling council was a farce. Men are leaving the Guard in droves because of poor management and lack of organization. And the OIA is divided in its loyalties."

"What's this?" I asked. "How in the world did you find that out?"

"I don't just talk to your father," he said, snorting. "I have my spies. One of the Council members is a good friend of mine. I'm serious, Camille. Don't expect help from the Crown and Court—they've become so corrupt over the years that there isn't a person there who has the authority to change matters. Not yet."

I jerked my head up to stare at him. *Not yet?* Trillian never said anything without reason, but until I knew what was going on, I decided to keep my mouth shut. I still didn't know Morio well enough to trust that he might not repeat what he heard. And if word got back to the Queen that her competence was being questioned, we were all so much dead meat—or would wish we were. Lethesanar was an expert at persuading her prisoners that they'd be better off dead. A number of them took that route—using whatever method they could find to kill themselves before her next round of amusements.

"So you're saying OIA is on its own?"

Trillian inclined his head. "I'm saying OIA will do what it can to help you, but that may not be for much longer. Don't put your trust in them, and for the sake of the gods, don't count on the Court and Crown to back you up."

Slumping in my chair, I let out a long sigh. My family had never been close enough to the Court to be privy to its inner workings. Mother's presence had been enough to keep my father out of the loop. And as lower-echelon operatives, my sisters and I weren't privy to the relationship between the Court and Crown and the OIA.

I suddenly wished my father was here. He knew something, or he wouldn't have sent Trillian. But I also knew that he would take his own time about telling us what was going down. Father was loyal to his beloved Guard. Whatever was happening *must* be bad, for him to admit to Trillian that there was need for secrecy.

"What's next?" Morio said as the door opened and Delilah rushed in. She slammed it behind her, then turned to stare at all of us.

"I see we have company," she said, dropping her backpack on a chair.

I stared at her. Something was different, but I couldn't figure out what. Her cheeks were flushed, but since the temperature was dropping, I could chalk that up to being cold. There was something else, though. She was walking differently, and she sounded breathless.

All of a sudden I knew. Chase and Delilah had slept together! Chase, who for months had been spooked by the idea of the werecat, and who had been chasing after my skirts, had fucked my sister. I took her by the elbow.

"Come with me; I want to talk to you."

Trillian groaned. "You're going to leave me alone with wolf boy again?"

"Fox, you imbecile—I'm a yokai-kitsune, not some lycanthrope!" Morio growled and held out his hands. As I watched, his nails lengthened into long claws, and his eyes sparkled.

"Down, boys." I stepped in between them again. "Do I need to hire a babysitter to keep the two of you civil?"

Morio gazed at me for a moment, an insolent look on his face, then he retracted his claws. "No problem, Camille."

Not to be outdone, Trillian jumped on the bandwagon. "We'll be good. Go gossip all you want."

Delilah stared at them both, clearly confused, as I steered her into the kitchen, where we sat down next to Maggie. Delilah petted her for a moment, then sucked in a deep breath. She met my eyes.

"You know, don't you? You can tell?" She ducked her head.

"Of course I can tell. I can smell him on you." And indeed, Chase's cologne lingered on her skin. I braced her by the shoulders. "The only thing that matters to me is that you're happy and safe. He didn't hurt you, did he?"

Her eyes went wide. "Hurt me? No, in fact I accidentally scratched him." She sobered, and I had a sudden flash.

"Oh no, you didn't?" I saw where this was leading and wasn't sure I wanted to go there.

Delilah looked scandalized. "No! At least not during . . . but afterward, I guess the tension got to me. We were cuddling when I shifted. I scared Chase so bad that he fell out of bed," she said, giggling.

I stifled a laugh. Old Chase got more than he bargained for. Humans always underestimated the power sex held for the Faerie, even a half-breed. More lives in Otherworld had been lost to primal lust than in all the wars combined.

"Are you upset?" Delilah rummaged through the cupboards for a bag of chips and opened them with her teeth. "I know he's been after you for a long time. I wasn't sure . . ."

"You know perfectly well I'm not interested in Chase," I said, grabbing the bag from her and filching a handful.

"I know you are . . . were . . . a virgin. Are you okay?" She didn't have to worry about pregnancy or disease—we'd been to the Medicine Mother before we left Otherworld and had our fertility temporarily stopped and been magically enchanted against illness. But her emotional state could be at risk.

She nodded. "Yes, I'm fine. I'll keep watch, though. This was my first time and, even though it was with an FBH, I know the risks." About one in ten thousand Sidhe went stark raving mad from their first sexual encounter, usually ending up wandering the world as a crazed seer.

"Chase is really quite a sweetie," she added. "And I just wanted to find out what it was like."

"So, what do you think? Was he any good?" I pulled a carton of milk out of the fridge and poured her a glass.

"I don't have much to compare him to," she said, taking the milk. "It was fun—nothing earthshaking, so I'm not sure what all the brouhaha is about. I have more fun chasing mice, to tell you the truth, but I didn't want to trounce Chase's ego, so I told him he was great."

I gazed at her, wondering just how bad in bed Chase must be. The Fae usually responded to most sexual encounters in a way that left porn stars looking like Pollyanna. Or maybe it was that Chase was human and Delilah was . . . well . . . only half-human. Whatever the case, I hoped that she wouldn't regret her actions.

"As long as you're okay. We have some serious problems going down." I filled her in on what had happened at the bar, and about the skinwalker. "So Morio's here to help us, thanks to Grandmother Coyote, but it sounds like we can't count on either OIA or the Court and Crown. Whatever's happening there, it doesn't sound good."

Delilah was about to say something when a fracas sounded from the front door. She raced down the hall, and I followed, close on her heels.

"You idiot, don't kill him! Jesus, he got away—can't you do anything right? I'll go get him!" Morio's voice rang.

Delilah and I collided at the entryway. The front door

was wide open, and Trillian was standing on the porch, holding a jacket, a confused look on his face. Morio was racing down the driveway faster than I'd seen any human or Faerie run, but I couldn't see who or what he was following. Had the skinwalker found us? But the creature hadn't been wearing clothes, that was for sure. I quietly took the jacket from Trillian's hand and, with a glance at Morio, who had apparently given up the chase and was headed back to the house, motioned for Delilah to follow me.

Once back in the living room, we checked out the coat, finding two things: a knife and a small notebook. As I pressed a hidden switch, a nasty seven-inch blade sprang forth, barely missing my fingers.

"That's no pocket knife," I said, gazing at the switch-blade as I closed my eyes, examining the energy of the knife. No dangerous aura, although it didn't feel all that clear, either. No sign of demon-light or Faerie-fire.

"Whoever he was, I think he was human," I said. "The knife isn't enhanced. No magic running through it."

Delilah flipped through the notebook. "There's a name written in the front. Georgio Profeta. No phone number or address, though." She gasped, and I peeked over her shoulder. There, in neat and tidy printing on the page, was an exact copy of what we'd read about the spirit seals. And taped below the writing was a photograph that showed a very large, very snaky, brilliantly white dragon hovering next to one very tired-looking lumberjack. The name next to the photograph read Tom Lane.

I stared at Delilah. "What the hell is going on?" Taking the notebook from her, I skimmed through the rest of the contents, but beyond a few incomprehensible poems, there was little more than the info about the spirit seals and the picture. I held the photo up to the light. The dragon appeared to be a blend of Eastern and Western heritage, a white, snaky beast with majestic wings and long whiskers and horns. The lumberjack was a tall mountain of a man with a wild look in his eye, unkempt beard, and long, flowing hair.

"He looks three sheets off the mainsail," Delilah said. "There's something about his eyes."

I squinted. She was right. An otherworldly glow filled his eyes. And then I caught a glimpse of a chain hanging around his neck. "Want to make a bet this really *is* Tom Lane? If he's been wearing one of the spirit seals for a long time, it's probably had an effect on his mind."

Just then, Morio and Trillian came trooping back through the door. I motioned them into the living room. "What happened?"

"Your guess is as good as mine," Trillian said. "I heard somebody outside on the porch, and when we got there, that little weasel was sneaking around. But wolf-boy here lost him."

Morio shot him a withering look. "*Fox*, Svartan. *Fox*. And yes, I lost him. I've never known a human to run that fast, nor have I ever lost a scent so quickly. It's like he vanished into thin air. But he wouldn't have if *you* hadn't let him get away." He turned to me. "This idiot had hold of the man's coat, but he didn't have hold of the man. The guy slid right out of the jacket and was off the porch like a jackrabbit."

"How was I to know he'd be so slippery?" Trillian jabbed his finger at Morio's chest. "You weren't much help either—"

"And again, chill out!" My voice echoed through the room. Trillian and Morio backed away, darting accusatory stares at one another. When they'd gone to their corners, I continued. "Nothing tripped my wards, so I'm thinking he's not really a threat. We'll figure out who he is tomorrow. We can ask Chase to run a check on him before he comes over. Meanwhile, Trillian, you and Morio take turns watching the house—make sure nobody gets in. Delilah, before you head to bed, give Menolly a call to make sure she's okay. That skinwalker is still out there. I've got to get some sleep so I can recharge. The fight with the harpy wiped me out, and I can barely keep my eyes open."

The weight of the day suddenly came crashing down on

me. I sorely needed to lie down in a quiet, dark room. Heading for the stairs, I was grateful for the sturdy railing, grateful that Delilah had the third story of the house and not me, grateful that there was somebody to keep watch so I didn't have to.

In my room, I stripped off my clothes and climbed under the covers, after making sure the door to the balcony was firmly locked and that nobody was out there hiding. Within moments, my eyes had closed, and I drifted off to sleep.

I don't know how long it was before I sensed a presence in the room. Still dazed, I fought through the layers of consciousness while images of the skinwalker and Rina and Bad Ass Luke raced through my mind as I struggled to wake up. And then, as my eyes fluttered open and I started to sit up, the bed creaked as someone crawled in behind me.

Frantic, I pushed myself to a sitting position, but hands reached out to pull me down and roll me over onto my back. And then I knew who it was. Trillian leaned over me, one hand holding me fast by my waist as the other stroked my hair.

"Oh good gods, can't you wait? I was asleep," I said weakly.

Trillian just shook his head. "Shush . . . you know we're meant to be together. Let me in." His voice was like smooth velvet.

"Trillian, you're incorrigible. Let me go back to sleep." I pushed against him, but my body rebelled against my mind, and he seemed to sense my ambivalence as he sought my lips, fastening his mouth to mine.

He loomed above me, and I melted into the kiss, which went on and on, his tongue darting like quicksilver to touch my own, his icy eyes glowing against the jet black of his skin. He had unbound his silver hair from the braid, and now it cascaded around me, tickling me with its soft strands.

I thought of all the reasons why this wasn't a good idea, why it had been a mistake the night before and was still a mistake, but none of that seemed to matter. When he touched me it was with a silken fire, and our auras flowed together. I gasped as his mouth slid along my breasts and shoved aside all the reasons why I shouldn't be doing this. What we had between us was too good to deny, and I wanted him, wanted his heart, wanted his body, his cock inside me.

Reaching down, I clasped hold of him. He was rigid and firm, ready at the helm, but then he pushed my arms over my head, holding me down by my wrists as he covered me with kisses, lingering at my breasts, then sliding his lips along my belly. I moaned, and the sparks we created lit up the room. As I spread my legs, he nuzzled me, lingering over the neatly trimmed hair, then pressed my thighs open and plunged his tongue into the nexus of my body, sweeping me into a vortex of pleasure.

"For the sake of the gods, don't stop," I said, my hands gripping the long strands of his hair as his head bobbed up and down between my legs. The fire between us built, lightning and ice, and I cried out once, then twice, as I neared the peak. He raised his head to stare at me with a triumphant gleam in his eyes, and then quickly plunged himself deep within my core. At first thrust, I let out a choked scream, and then I was moving, riding him as he rode me, and all the gods in the heavens couldn't have torn me away.

I could feel him nearing the edge even as I teetered on the cliff, and then we let go, falling. Trillian let out a muffled shout, his head buried between my breasts, as I let down my last guard and gave in to *le petit mort*.

As the shock waves rolled away, I fell back on the pillows, savoring the ripples racing through my body. Trillian murmured something I couldn't hear, then curled up next to me, his arms wrapping around me like a comfortable and well-worn cloak.

"I've missed you so much," he said. "It hasn't been the same without you. No other woman can do to me what you can, and believe me, I've tried to fill your place."

I stared at him. Trillian was admitting to having feelings for me? I knew he enjoyed me in bed, but to hear him say he missed me was like hearing Donald Trump say he was giving up his empire to join a commune.

"Did you really miss me?" Sleepy and sated, I snuggled deeper under the covers. Damn, it felt good to lie next to somebody.

He nodded, slowly at first. The flicker of a scowl passed over his face. "Nobody's ever left me before, though I've left plenty of women behind. But Camille, there's something about you. I couldn't stop thinking about you while we were together, and I couldn't stop thinking about you after you left. You're like the honeysuckle wine the dryads make—one sip and you never forget."

"I thought that was the peril of loving a Svartan," I said, pushing myself up to a sitting position. I slipped a couple of pillows behind my back to cushion myself. "Trillian, do you know why I left?"

"You told me once, but I didn't pay any attention," he said and for a moment, the Trillian I knew so well shone through. Unless it pertained to his comfort, he never listened to anybody else. At the core, he was selfish, as to some degree were all Faerie.

"I left you because I knew you'd leave me. Svartans are notorious for casting away their partners. In fact, most of your people are so hedonistic you make the Sidhe look like saints. I was trying to protect my heart, Trillian. I am Sidhe; I don't have a problem playing with a crowd. But I'm also human, and when I fall, I fall hard. I couldn't face rejection."

Thirsty, I slipped out of bed and padded into the bathroom, where I poured myself a glass of water. Technology and its wonders. *Gotta love it,* I thought.

Trillian rose, and once again, I found myself mesmerized by him. His muscles rippled under the moonlight shining through the window, and he stretched, luxuriating like a cat. He gave me a sly smile.

"Camille, oh my Camille . . . I told you before that I wouldn't cast you away like the others. Why won't you trust me?" As he took a step forward, there was a knock on the door, and it opened. Morio peeked around the corner.

Trillian whirled around, an angry look on his face. Before he could yell at Morio, I stepped between them, unfazed. I was seldom embarrassed by nudity, unless the voyeur showed discomfort. Morio perked up. In fact, he looked downright pleased when he caught sight of me.

"What's up?" I asked.

"Your sister Menolly's on the phone. She wants to talk to you. And the gargoyle is whimpering. I think she's hungry." He glanced at Trillian, and his expression changed to one of boredom. "You're due to relieve my watch in ten minutes," he added, then closed the door behind him.

Trillian gazed at the bed, then looked at me. "You want to fuck him, don't you? I could sense the spark between you downstairs."

I sighed. "What can I say? He's the first man since you that I've found attractive."

He cleared his throat. "Play with the fox if you want. Just don't let him get in the way of us." I heard a warning note in his voice.

I held up my hand before he could go on. "Get dressed. You need to let him get some sleep. I don't want the two of you fighting."

Sliding into my new nightgown—which Trillian liked as much as I thought he was going to—I slid into a pair of fuzzy slippers, then headed downstairs to find out what Menolly wanted.

CHAPTER 11

The minute I picked up the phone and said hello, Menolly snorted.

"I know what you've been doing, but the question is, with who?" Ever since she'd become a vampire, Menolly had the uncanny ability to ferret out sex, whether it be by smell, sound, or maybe just a buzzing in her head. "Never mind. I'll get the juicy details later. I just called to let you know that I'm headed to my car now. You wanted me to let you know when I left the bar."

I glanced at the clock. Two A.M. Right on schedule. "Okay, but call me when you get in your car and are on the road. Where did you park, by the way? That *thing*—that skinwalker—is still out there. Also, somebody was prowling around the house tonight. Trillian and Morio couldn't catch him, but we have his jacket and one very interesting notebook."

"Hmmm . . ." I could almost hear the wheels turn in her head. "I'm parked in Ayers Garage, the one on the corner of Broadway." She hung up, and I slowly replaced the receiver in the cradle. The Capitol Hill district was home to the tattooed freaks and gothic geeks who were about as on the fringe as you could get and still be considered human. They were a lot of fun to hang out with, but the area also housed the junkies and lowlifes.

I glanced up at Morio, who was leaning against the wall, staring at me. "What? What is it?" I asked, uncomfortably aware of his scrutiny.

He raised one eyebrow, shrugged, and said, "I don't know what you see in him, but you obviously have some connection. If you ever want to talk, just tap on my shoulder."

I had a feeling the word *talk* was fraught with meaning for the fox demon, but he turned away as Trillian lightly ran down the steps, fully dressed, with his smug smile back in place.

"All right, go on, get some sleep," Trillian said.

Morio glanced around, then looked at me. I pointed to our rarely used parlor. "You can stretch out in there. The sofa's comfortable, and you won't be bothered unless Mr. Profeta decides to make a return visit."

He nodded and withdrew as I stared at the phone, willing it to ring. *Come on, Menolly,* I thought. *Be careful.* Even vampires could be taken down by some of the creatures we were facing. Trillian seemed to sense my worry, because he slid an arm around my waist and just held me against him, for once not pushing. I rested my head against his shoulder, trying to breathe. Maybe things were different. Maybe he'd changed. But that would be like a leopard changing its spots, wouldn't it?

Before I could quiet the argument taking place in my head, the phone rang. I snatched it up. "Menolly? Is that you?"

She laughed. "No, it's Santa Claus. Yes, it's me. I'm safe in the car and on the way home. I'll be there in half an hour. You should get some sleep, unless you have other plans, that is. Who's there, by the way? Just Morio?" Aha, she was fishing to find out if I'd slept with the fox demon.

"No," I said slowly. "Delilah's asleep . . . Morio's

resting . . . and Trillian's here." I let out a long sigh, and she caught it.

"Oh good gods, you slept with the Svartan again!" Exasperation filled her voice, along with a touch of irritability. "Well, tell him that I said if he hurts you, I'll drain him dry of blood and hang him out for the vultures."

I swallowed the lump in my throat. "I don't think that's a good idea—"

"Do it!" When Menolly wanted something, she usually got it. While I was the oldest, when she was feeling her oats, we all ate oatmeal.

"Okay, but if he gets mad, it's your fault." I leaned back to look at Trillian. "Menolly says that if you hurt me, she'll drain you dry and leave you out for the vultures."

A brief flare of anger flashed across his face, then disappeared as he began to laugh. "Give me the phone," he said.

I handed him the receiver.

"My dear, lovely, *deadly* Menolly, I'll have you know that I plan to treat your sister as honorably as I'd treat any lady of the high Court." Trillian paused as she said something, then laughed again—his voice rich and deep and racing through me from breast to toe. "I'll count on it."

Gods above, I thought as I took the phone back and hung up. I really was in trouble if they were joking together.

Trillian kept watch, occasionally stepping outside to see if he could pick up any unwelcome scents or sounds, while I padded into the kitchen to check on Maggie. She was curled in her box but awake. She reached for me, and I lifted her to my breast, then settled in the rocking chair to doze for a few minutes.

The sound of Menolly's car pulling into the driveway startled me awake. Smoothing my robe, I set Maggie back in her box and put on the teakettle. I'd grown fond of orange spice tea since coming Earthside, and kept seven different brands of it in the cupboard. I dropped four teabags into the teapot and poured the steaming water over them, closing my eyes as the fragrance drifted up to envelop my senses. While the tea steeped, I mixed up a batch of formula for Maggie, setting the bowl inside the box so she could reach it. She would eat two semisolid meals and drink three bowls of formula a day until more teeth came in.

I'd barely settled at the table with my mug of tea when Menolly entered the kitchen, Trillian right behind her. Her eyes slid over me, then back to him, and she shook her head.

"I still think you're nuts," she said. "Trillian, no offense, but you're bad news all the way around. Don't take it personally."

He snorted. "Of course not, my dear. I'll take it for what it's worth—coming from a *vampire*."

"Enough, both of you." I lifted my cup. "We're facing a long day tomorrow, and I need some more sleep, but first I wanted to fill you in on what we're planning, since you won't be able to come with us, Menolly."

She slid into the chair opposite me and reached for my hand. Her own was cool and bloodless, but she was my sister, and that was enough.

As I gazed into her eyes, I thought about all the late-night talks we'd had when we were young, sometimes giggling and giddy, other times somber and in tears, trying to sort out the taunts thrown our way because of our human heritage. Now she faced far worse. Vampires weren't respected anywhere except in the Subterranean Realms. In Otherworld, lesser vamps were merely tolerated. And Earthside, they were mostly feared.

I squeezed her hand. Vampire or not, I loved her and considered myself lucky to still have her around. The Elwing Clan could have let her die. Perhaps that would have been for the best, but we'd never know. She was here now, and that was all that mattered.

Trillian watched us in silence. After a moment, he leaned forward. "Shall we fill her in?"

I took a deep breath and told her everything that had

happened, showing her the blade and the notebook. "We have a skinwalker after us—although I suppose that could be coincidence. And we have somebody prowling around our house who knows about the spirit seals. I don't like the idea of leaving you home while we're looking for Tom Lane."

"Well, I can't very well go with you," she said.

Trillian cleared his throat. "I'll stay and watch over the house and your gargoyle. You've got this Chase person going, and wolf-boy is champing at the bit to help—"

"You'd better quit calling him that," I said, glancing toward the hall. "One of these times Morio's going to take a swipe at you, and even though he looks wiry, my guess is that he's pretty damned strong."

"I'm sure you'll find out soon enough," Trillian said with a grin. "Be that as it may, I'll stay here while you and Delilah go with the others."

I let out a long sigh. Trillian was good to his word, if nothing else. His ethics might come into question, and any move he made had to have ulterior motives, but he wouldn't let us down.

"That would make me feel better," I said. "I'll show you how to mix up Maggie's cream, and what to feed her, and you can keep an eye on things."

"Then it's settled." He leaned forward, sniffing at my tea. "I don't see how you can drink that stuff."

"Wait a minute," Menolly broke in. "You mean you're asking this Svartan to babysit me? I don't think so."

"It's either that or we leave Chase here."

She let out a loud sigh but backed off. I debated on whether to give her the scoop about Chase and Delilah but decided to leave it up to our golden-haired sister. Menolly would pick up on it soon enough on her own.

"Okay, I guess that's it." I drained the last of my tea. The knots in my shoulders were beginning to work their way out, and I was ready for more sleep. "Off to bed. Thank the gods the full moon isn't for another couple of days, or we'd be facing one hell of a mess tomorrow. Night, Menolly."

She nodded. "What about Maggie? Will she be safe down here?"

"Trillian's keeping watch the rest of the night. She'll be fine."

As I stretched, Menolly leaned over and cooed a few words in Maggie's ear. Maggie reached out with her long pink tongue and licked Menolly's face, and my sister laughed, without the grating cynicism I'd grown accustomed to since the Elwing Blood Clan changed her. Maybe, just maybe, Maggie and Menolly could help each other cope with the fates that had played into their lives. I headed up to my room.

I'd barely fallen asleep again when an earsplitting screech broke through my dreams, and I shot out of bed. The noise echoed up the stairs. I glanced at the clock. Five A.M. Dawn had broken, though the sun wouldn't be up for an hour or so. I was still in my gorgeous nightgown, so didn't bother to stop for a robe; instead, I just went racing down the steps. I almost collided with Delilah as she turned the bend from the third floor, dressed in her Hello Kitty pajamas.

"What's going on?" she said, scampering down the stairs ahead of me.

"I don't know—" I grasped the railing as something clanged my inner alarm with a piercing shriek. As I doubled over and clung to the newel post, Delilah grabbed my arm to keep me from tumbling down the stairs.

"What happened?" she asked.

I shook my head, clearing away the fog. Warning bells were ringing so loud that I thought I'd go deaf. "Something's broken through the wards and is in the house. I hope to hell it's not Bad Ass Luke!"

Another earsplitting shriek broke the silence as we hit the bottom step and raced down the hall. We entered the living room just in time to see Morio go flying through the air to land against the opposite wall. A large, hairy creature turned his attention away from the yokai-kitsune to hunker down over Trillian, who lay on the floor, still as death.

"The skinwalker," I gasped.

"Die, you bastard!" Morio shouted as he picked himself up. His hair was loose and rippled around his shoulders. His ears had grown longer and tufted, and his nails were gleaming, long, razorlike claws. Eyes shimmering with a golden light, he leapt forward again and sliced through the air, catching the skinwalker across the back, ripping into the flesh. Dark blood oozed from the wound, matting into the wiry hair that covered the creature.

I tore my attention away from Trillian and stretched out my hands. Chance of backfire or not, I had to do something. The clouds outside the window roiled with energy, so I called on the lightning instead of the moonlight. A flash echoed through the room as it answered, and fire raced down my arms, into my hands. I couldn't aim and shoot; I might hit Morio. Instead, I'd have to actually touch the creature.

Delilah raced back into the room, carrying a huge cleaver from the kitchen. She raised the blade and brought it down just as the skinwalker backhanded her, knocking her over the sofa. I heard a loud thud and an "Oh fuck!"

As she pulled herself up using the back of the couch, I took a chance and leapt forward, hands out. The lightning branched from my palms as I made contact against the creature's side, and forks of the white-hot energy shot through him, the smell of singed hair choking the air.

The skinwalker howled and turned on me, catching hold of my wrist with one hairy paw, the other wrapping around my neck.

"*Kitsune-bi!*" Morio shouted, and an orb of light came racing my way. It missed me and hit the skinwalker's eyes. He shrieked and let go, struggling to cover his face as the brilliant fox lantern blinded him.

As the skinwalker stumbled, I slapped my hands against him, and the lightning that coiled in my body again jumped from my fingers to his skin. Full-force, a bolt of pure power knocked him off his feet, and the creature fell backward onto the floor, where Delilah thrust her cleaver deep into his chest.

I slumped back, breathing hard. "Is he dead?"

Morio scrambled over to check. "Yeah, he's dead. Very much."

"What's going on?" Menolly drifted into the room, looking haggard. "I was almost asleep when I heard a ruckus—well, I see we have a visitor."

I crawled over to Trillian's side. The skinwalker had left a bruise around my neck that I could feel growing darker, and I was pretty sure that both Morio and Delilah were covered with bruises too. As Menolly tended to Delilah, Morio knelt next to me.

"Is he—?" Morio's eyes asked the question his lips would not.

I leaned over my dark beloved, listening for breath. There—faint, but definite. "He's breathing, but he's badly injured. He needs help, now. Delilah! Call Chase, tell him to send an OIA medical team over here, *stat*. It's an emergency." Forcing myself to remain calm, I took Trillian's hand in mine and held tight. "What did the skinwalker do to him?"

Morio shook his head grimly. "I think he hit him with those claws. Skinwalkers are filled with venom. If they bite or scratch someone, there's a good chance they'll poison them." He searched Trillian's other arm. "Here it is—a long gash. Not much blood, but see how it oozes?"

The wound was shallow but covered with a thin layer of bubbling pus. My stomach lurched as I watched it fester up and trickle across Trillian's beautiful skin.

"Will he die?" I whispered. "Svartans have a natural immunity to so many things. The skinwalker's venom must be terribly potent."

"It is. Think komodo dragon on two legs. Trillian has a chance if help reaches him in time. He can't stay here, though. He'll need care that isn't available Earthside."

Frowning, I nodded. I didn't like the thought, but if he

was to survive, he was going to need stronger magic than they could work here.

"You're right, of course. He has to return to Other-world." And then a faint odor caught my attention. I turned back to the skinwalker and leaned close, still nervous, even though I knew it was dead. "Demon scent. This thing isn't a demon itself, but it's crossed paths with one. I didn't get close enough downtown to smell it, but . . . Menolly, can you identify the type?"

Menolly knelt by the creature and sniffed, a disgusted look on her face. "Demon, yes. A lesser one. My guess is that Bad Ass Luke had a hand in this. He's probably paying the dregs around Belles-Faire to keep an eye on us. And to come after us. Which means he knows we're OIA."

I glanced outside. Dawn was breaking in the east, and I could see the glimmer of sunlight on the horizon. Though clouds were coming in, we wouldn't see rain for a few hours. "First light! Menolly, you have to get downstairs. Go, and make sure you barricade the doorway."

She stroked my face. "I wish I could help you today, but I can't. Be careful, all of you. I'll see you tonight."

As she disappeared into the kitchen, Delilah sat next to me as I clutched Trillian's hand. I might be making a huge mistake by getting involved with him again, but damned if I'd give him up to his ancestors without a fight.

"I called Iris," she said. "She'll watch the house and Maggie while we're gone today. The shop can stay closed for once."

I nodded, unable to speak. Morio slid down on my other side and wrapped his arm around my shoulders. Wearily, I leaned my head against his chest. As we sat there, watching Trillian's breath grow frail, the sound of sirens echoed in the distance. Help was on the way, but would they be too late to save him?

Chase came rushing in, an OIA emergency team behind him in a scene that was beginning to look all too familiar.

I forced myself to move so they could examine Trillian. One of the medics, a youngish elf whom I recognized as being Sharah, a niece in the elfin high court, patted me on the arm. If she felt any distaste over treating a Svartan, she kept it well hidden.

Morio and I told them what happened. One of the medics looked over the skinwalker, while the others concentrated on Trillian. I stood back, watching with a muted sense of horror as they stripped off his robes and jabbed his arm with a syringe full of a shimmering blue liquid. The elixir would keep his heart going while his body fought against the neurotoxin.

As I glanced over at Chase, I saw that his arm was around Delilah's waist. Neither one noticed me looking at them, and I suddenly felt very much alone. If only Menolly could have stayed up longer. Just then, Morio edged in next to me, and I reached for his hand as we watched the frantic scurry to save Trillian's life.

Finally, one of the techs sat back and wiped his forehead with a cloth. "He's stable enough to transport, but we have to get him back to OW immediately. If we don't, his condition will deteriorate, and he'll die. He received a lethal dose of the skinwalker's poison. If he wasn't so strong, he'd already be dead." The medic glanced at the rest of us. "Did anybody else get cut? Even a minor scratch?"

Morio shook his head. "I got bruised up, but no cuts. Not that I know of. Camille? Delilah? You were both attacked. Are you all right?"

Dazed, I glanced down at my body. My neck was tender, but I had no idea whether I'd received any gashes from the skinwalker.

"I don't know," I said.

"Come on." Delilah broke away from Chase and held out her hand. "Let's go in the other room and we can check each other for cuts."

I gave one more look at Trillian, whose eyes were closed in deep slumber, before letting her lead me away.

In the bathroom we stripped and looked each other over

carefully. A few scratches on my shoulder, but those were from Delilah in kitten form and were almost healed. No new gashes, cuts, or anything that looked like an abrasion. I slid back into my nightgown, which was now shredded, and slumped on the edge of the tub as Delilah pulled on her pajamas.

She sat down next to me and took my hand. "They'll save him. He'll be okay once he gets back to Otherworld."

"If they treat him right when he gets there. Svartans aren't looked on highly, you know." I stared at the floor bleakly.

"The healers don't all answer to Court and Crown," she argued. "He'll be okay, Camille. He's tough. And he's in love with you. Why else would he come back? Svartans never go back to their lovers, but he came back to you."

I shook my head. "No, I'm not going to convince myself of something that might not be true. Especially when his life hangs in the balance. I can't let myself believe that he loves me. If he lives, then we'll figure this out." But in the silence of my heart, I begged the gods to let him live. Even if I never saw him again, I didn't want him to die.

Delilah pulled me to my feet. "Come on. We'd better get back out there so you can . . . so you can say good-bye to him before they take him away."

As we headed back into the living room, I wondered if it would be the last time I'd ever see Trillian alive.

Once the medics had attended to our bruises they took Trillian and the skinwalker with them. Sirens screaming, they headed for the Wayfarer. They'd have to take him through the most accessible portal, and while Grandmother Coyote could lead them to her portal in the woods, the trip through the undergrowth might be enough to kill Trillian before they got there.

When the medics had gone, Delilah and I went upstairs to change. We left Chase and Morio to clean up. As I brushed my hair, I glanced over at Delilah, who had swapped her PJs for jeans and a sweatshirt. I dressed in a cotton gauze walking skirt, a cami top, and then a gossamer-weave jacket over everything. As I buckled my ankle boots, I looked up to find Delilah smiling gently.

"What is it?" I asked. Her smile had startled me, reminding me so much of Mother's. And right now I wanted nothing more than to run home, to leave Earth and the demons behind, and cuddle in the bosom of my family. But Mother was dead, and we were duty bound to protect both this world and our own.

"I was just thinking how pretty you are. You know, you remind me of Aunt Rythwar."

Aunt Rythwar was one of the Court and Crown beauties. She was more securely placed than Father, having married up in caste, but she was also unpredictable, and I'd heard that she'd killed more than one lover who displeased her. No proof, however, meant no charges. And even if they'd had proof, she might have been excused if the Queen thought she was justified. Her current husband was well-behaved and never raised his voice in complaint.

"I haven't seen her in ages. Thank you, by the way. I consider that a compliment. So tell me, how do you think you'll handle Chase now?"

Delilah shook her head. "What's to handle? We had sex. We may have sex again. We may not. I don't think it gets much simpler than that."

I shook my head. Bone-weary to the core, I dreaded the rest of the day. "Don't be so certain. One thing I've learned the past few days is *never to say never*. Especially when it comes to friends and lovers."

Grabbing my purse, I headed for the stairs. Delilah followed, backpack in hand. When we reached the living room, the mess had been cleaned up and the furniture was back in place. I smelled something good coming from the kitchen, and we peeked around the corner. Chase was frying up scrambled eggs and bacon, while Morio was feeding Maggie. Touched by the gentle way in which he patted her as she lapped up her cream, I knelt beside him and gave him a quick kiss, which he returned without hesitation.

"For everything, thank you." I said. "Without you we would have died."

Morio held my gaze. I couldn't read what was behind those ancient eyes, but he winked at me. "My pleasure to be of service. Anything you need me to do . . . *anything* . . . just ask."

Chase held out his arm to Delilah, but she just wrinkled her nose and blew him a kiss. "Food, man. Give us food. That smells wonderful, and I'm starved."

Looking mildly confused, he turned back to the range. "Not a problem. I figured we might as well get an early start, especially after what just happened."

Delilah and I set the table.

After we ate, Chase pushed back his plate. "I received notification from the OIA headquarters today. They've officially acknowledged that three demons broke through the portals. They do not, however, acknowledge that Shadow Wing sent them."

I slammed my fork down. "Fools. They'd better get off their asses and smell the brimstone. So what do they recommend we do about this situation?"

"They want you three to track down the other demons and terminate them. However, they specifically told me that they have no official resources to offer you at this point. And that's *all* they said."

Chase offered me another slice of toast. I shook my head, and he handed it to Morio.

"Did they say anything about Tom Lane and the spirit seals?" I asked. "Do you know if they heard anything about what the Corpse Talker said?"

"They didn't mention it, so I'm betting the answer is no."

"So . . . our assignment calls for us to wipe out the demons that aren't supposed to get through the portals in the first place?" My bet was that until we had the spirit seal in hand and rubbed their noses in it, HQ would chalk the whole thing up as a fluke. But Father had dealt with Bad

Ass Luke before. And Father already suspected something was drastically wrong.

Chase shrugged. "Sounds like it. They made it abundantly clear that going through the official channels won't do us any good."

"Right," I said, staring at my plate.

Delilah carried our plates to the counter. "So, did you find out anything more about Tom Lane and where he lives? We were at a dry well when I left last night." She flushed, a smile creeping to her lips.

Chase ran his gaze over her in the way he had been running it over me, but with less "letch" and more "like." "Yeah, actually I did. I slept for a couple hours, then woke up early and hunted through some old databases. There's a Tom Lane that lives just outside the national park. His house is located a half mile from Goat Creek, although from what I can ascertain, it's more of a shack than a house. He doesn't seem to have a regular job, but he's not on any of the welfare rolls or food stamp programs. That's about all I know."

"At least it gives us something to go on," I said.

Chase pointed at the calendar. "We're deep into October, and by now, a good share of Rainier's roads are closed. We'd play hell trying to get through the park, so I'm hoping we find Lane where we need him to be."

A knock at the door told us Iris had arrived. She radiated concern and compassion, and just being in her presence made me feel better. Through those brilliant blue eyes, she'd seen a lifetime of misery, war, and famine, yet she still maintained her love of humans, for all their foibles.

Chase had arrived in a big old SUV so that we could travel together. While he and Delilah loaded it with supplies and—I assumed—discussed their tryst together, Morio and I showed Iris how to feed Maggie and keep an eye on the house. Despite her stature, Iris was more than capable of bringing down an assailant, and since she was of Faerie blood, she was adept in defense magic at a startling level of skill. As we finished up, I took one last look around the house, hoping that it would still be in one piece when we returned—and Menolly still as alive as she'd ever be.

Jocko's diary was still on the table. With all the excitement over the skinwalker, I'd forgotten all about it. I jammed it in my tote bag before heading out the door. We clambered into the SUV. Chase and Morio sat up front and Delilah and I behind them, as we set out on our quest to find Tom Lane.

CHAPTER 12

~◆~

Along the way, we told Chase about our mysterious visitor and the notebook we'd found in his jacket pocket. He pulled to the side of the road when I flipped the notebook open to the picture and handed it up to the front seat.

"Shit, is that a dragon?" He looked ready to jump out of the car and, in the infamous words of the Monty Python clan, *"Run away!"*

"Chase, your powers of observation astound me." I shook my head. "Of course it's a dragon. What did you think it might be? A gecko?"

Chase flashed me a scathing look. "I've changed my mind. I like your sister better than you. She's not so abrasive."

"She slept with you," I said, snorting. "Of course you like her better."

"Hey, I have ears, you two!" Delilah said, blushing. I realized that her nonchalance over Chase might just be a put-on. She had that smitten look in her eye, and so I flashed her a smile to let her know I'd been kidding.

"The dude beside the dragon's a big muthah," Chase said. "Faerie?"

I shrugged. "Hard to tell. Doesn't look like it, but that doesn't mean I'm right. Or, he could be just human."

"Okay then," he said, handing the picture back to me and starting up the car again. "Say, what happens if we come face-to-face with the big lizard? How do you subdue one, anyway?"

I groaned. None of us were ready to take on something of that size. "You don't, unless you happen to be a powerful wizard or witch. And I'm not nearly strong enough, even *if* my powers weren't subject to short-circuiting. If a dragon attacks, your only hope is to either beg for mercy, outrun it, hide until it gets bored—which may be weeks—or kill it."

Morio cleared his throat. "Killing a dragon is bad luck. Its kin will know who did it, and they will hunt you down for the rest of their lives. The only way to stay in one piece after you've slain a dragon is to vanish. Change your name, go undercover, and hope that you're lucky."

I leaned forward, peering around the headrest to look at him. "That's true, especially with Eastern dragons. They're a different breed than Western ones. Some of them aren't as bad-tempered, but they're all arrogant." Turning to Chase, I added, "Remember this: do not tromp on a dragon's ego. Bite your tongue, let them insult you, whatever they want. Just don't challenge them, because that's the quickest way to become a crispy critter."

He glanced at me in the mirror, then at Morio, who nodded. "Point taken. I won't forget it. Tell me, do you think the dragon's mixed up with the demons?"

"No," I said, settling back in my seat. "I doubt it. Dragons eat lesser and minor demons for lunch. If we could cajole one onto our side, we'd have no problem until we ran up against Shadow Wing, but I'm afraid we don't have much to offer. Dragons are mercenary creatures. You have to make it worth their while to help you."

Chase shifted gears as we exited off I-405, onto SR 167. "We're headed toward the Nisqually entrance to the park. Goat Creek is somewhere before there, and we'll be looking for a graveled path leading into a tangle of bushes."

"Road have a name?" Morio asked.

"Nope. Maybe a mailbox, though Mr. Lane may get his mail at the nearest post office. I did find out that there are two giant holly trees on either side of the road. That shouldn't be too hard to spot."

I fished through my tote bag for Jocko's diary and opened it up. Delilah leaned over to get a better view, and we began thumbing through the pages. Most giants spoke in a guttural dialect of Faerie, and their writing was a phonetic version of their speech. Jocko was no exception. While translating took a little time, we could read the entries if we transposed some of the verbs and nouns. When we were able to decipher his handwriting, that is.

The first few months of entries were pretty standard fare for someone who was worlds away from his home. Jocko had been lonely, he'd missed the mountain air even though he didn't miss being picked on for his size. He missed his mother but was glad to be out of his father's reach. Apparently Jocko, Sr., had a tendency to violence. Jocko was loyal to the OIA, but even he seemed to notice the lack of support foreign-based operatives got.

And then, about midway through the diary, we came to the first mention of Louise.

She came in again today and I asked her for her name. Louise. What a strange name, but beautiful. She's so nice, and she told me that she likes hanging around with Faeries. I said, "I'm just a giant, and not a very good one at that," but then she said I was cute. She's going to take me to a movie this week. I've never been to one. I've heard of them, but was too nervous to go by myself. Everything still seems so strange.

Delilah gave me a broad smile. "He had a crush on her."

"And it sounds like she might have returned the feeling." I glanced out the window. I was uncomfortable prying into Jocko's personal affairs. Even though he was dead, it went against my nature to snoop into thoughts that he had expected to remain private. But we had to know what went on and why Louise had been killed.

"We're almost at Puyallup," Chase said.

"This is where that big fair is, right?" In September, Chase had invited me to go to the Puyallup Fair with him, but I had declined. Now, as the highway raced beneath the wheels, I could see that the city had that just-passing-by feel to it. Automobile dealerships lined the highway, and the requisite convenience stores, gas stations, taverns, casinos—all the road stops that would beckon a weary traveler driving long stretches in the night.

"Right. And over there's Rainier," he said, nodding to the southeast. "We're about an hour or so away from the entrance to the park."

After staring at the glacier-covered mountain for a few minutes, I went back to Jocko's diary, skimming pages again until about a week before his death. There, I found an interesting entry.

Louise loved the ring and as soon as I can put away enough money, I'm going to sneak her through the portal. She spends just about every evening with me. I know my family won't accept her, so we'll strike out on our own when we get home. OIA will be pissed, but I don't care. They don't do nothing for me anyways.

Last night, Louise caught Wisteria in the basement. I warned Wisteria to quit going down there. She's not authorized to be around the portal. Neither is Louise, but I know she won't touch nothing. Wisteria said that she just wanted to check on some inventory she thought was down there so I guess it's okay.

I don't know what HQ was thinking sending her to me—she's not much help, and she's a bitch. Won't work nights when Menolly's around, says she hates vamps. I tried to tell her that Menolly isn't like the other vampires, she's good people, but Wisteria won't listen.

"So Jocko was planning on sneaking back through the portal with Louise, and they were going to vanish after that. And who the hell is Wisteria? Did you ever hear Menolly mention her?" I frowned as I thought back, trying to recall if I'd ever heard the name before.

Delilah squinted. "Not that I can remember, but then I never paid much attention to the goings-on at the Wayfarer. Do you think she's our leak?"

"Maybe. We have to look into it when we get home, that's for certain." I glanced at Jocko's last entry. He'd been planning on taking Louise out for takeout the night he died, and then going bowling. It was so routine, so daily-grind life, that my stomach knotted. Jocko hadn't a clue that his life was about to end. He hadn't realized that his presence put Louise in danger. If he would have known that he and Louise were about to die, they would have crossed through the portal and disappeared. Of that much, I was certain. So Jocko was clueless, and now he was dead.

When I looked up again, we were pulling to a stop at a convenience store in a small town named Elbe, whose main claim to fame was the Mount Rainier Scenic Railroad Excursion, a one-and-a-half-hour, fourteen-mile round-trip train ride through the lower-lying foothills surrounding the mountain. It actually sounded fun, and I made a note to come back later, once things had calmed down, and take the ride. I could do with a bit more wild energy than was provided by the woodlands surrounding our home.

"Anybody need to use the restroom? Get a bite to eat?" Chase opened the door and went to fill the gas tank. Delilah and I hopped out and wandered around.

Set near Alder Lake, the little town managed to keep afloat, thanks to the numerous tourists on their way through to see Mount Rainier. The Ashland Market, the store at which we'd stopped, overlooked the lake, and I meandered over to the edge, staring at the wide expanse of water. The clouds were thick, threatening to break open with a deluge at any moment, and the wind whipped the waves on the surface of the lake into a nice froth.

Delilah joined me, though she hung back a few feet from the bank. Like the majority of catkin, she had a natural reluctance to go near the water, and though she bathed without a problem—thank the gods—she had only learned to swim through the insistence of the OIA. Since she received her certification, she hadn't set foot in a body of water bigger than a hot tub.

She tightened her jacket, stuffing her hands under her arms. "Damn, it's cold. I don't like it here. It's too wild, too old."

I stared at her. "Too old? We come from Otherworld, and you think this place is too old?"

With a shrug, she said, "Maybe not that . . . I guess . . . it's just that this area feels wild in a way Otherworld doesn't. The magic in Otherworld's forests makes the trees sparkle and brings them to life. Here, the trees don't talk to people. They grow in their own dark realms, and I can't hear what they're thinking."

What she said was true. In Otherworld the land was so linked to the inhabitants that it felt like a community. Even in the dark woods, there existed a sense of comprehension and understanding. Earthside, a great chasm divided the forest from the people, underscoring the sense of distrust that I felt from the majority of humans that I met. They didn't trust the wild, they feared the primal, and went out of their way to tame everything within reach. It was as if the wild places were at war with humanity. If only a compromise could be reached.

We watched as a hawk flew low over the lake, hunting. "Sometimes," I said, "I wonder what it would be like if Otherworld and Earth were freely linked once again, like they were in the past, with no rules or regulations about who came and went. How would that change things?"

"It would be death to both worlds." Morio had crept up behind us, so silent that neither one of us had heard him. Startled, I jumped, but he put his hand on my shoulder. "Sorry, didn't mean to scare you." He glanced at Delilah, then back at me. "With the progression Earth has taken, it would be a huge mistake to open free movement between the worlds at this point. Maybe sometime in the future, when both sides are ready for the culture shock."

"Ready?" Chase called to us from beside the SUV, looking vaguely disconcerted. We hustled back to the car. He was holding a bag full of snacks, but a disturbed look told me that he had more on his mind than potato chips.

"What's wrong?" I glanced around, wondering what had happened in the past fifteen minutes.

"I was chatting up the clerk. There have been some pretty strange goings-on around here lately. Abandoned buildings burned to the ground, a few cows and sheep missing, and some blood splattered in the area. Strange UFO sightings being reported. What's that sound like to you?"

"Dragon on the loose, that's what." I glanced at Morio and Delilah. "I have the nasty feeling we're going to meet old smoky."

The prospect of battling a dragon made me queasy. And for that matter, what the hell was it doing around here? And how was it connected to Tom Lane? The photograph in Georgio Profeta's notebook seemed to indicate they were linked. And what was so special about Lane, anyway, that he possessed one of the spirit seals?

As we climbed back into the SUV, the clouds darkened, and the storm finally broke, sending sheets of rain to pound the pavement, the fat droplets bouncing as they hit the road. Chase navigated carefully. The highway was far narrower than the freeway as it curved through the rural area.

"Once more, tell me exactly what I should do if we run into the dragon," Chase said, glancing in the rearview mirror.

"If you see it first, cautiously and quietly back away. Hide if possible. If it sees you, it may immediately attack—in which case you're toast. Or, it may try to talk to you. If it speaks, listen, and don't argue. Don't let your pride get in the way, don't threaten, and don't give it your real name. That's asking for trouble. Apologize for entering its territory, ask politely if you may leave. Whatever you do, don't

draw your gun or that's all she wrote, folks." I picked
through the snacks and found a Milky Way bar.

Chase coughed. "Sounds lovely. I take it that for humans, it's a lose-lose situation all the way around?

"Actually," Morio said, clearing his throat, "I've met
one dragon that was quite friendly."

I stared at him. "You've faced a dragon before?"

"A couple, but don't get your hopes up. I lucked out
with the friendly one. He was looking for dinner, and I happened to know where a farmer with a herd of cows lived.
The other time wasn't quite so bloodless." He grimaced. "I
was traveling with a young priest who decided he was more
powerful than the dragon. He wasn't."

"Oh Jesus, that's just what I needed to hear," Chase
said, slowing as we came to a turnoff to the left. A graveled
road led us through a tangle of undergrowth. Huckleberry
and bracken, brambles and juniper encroached on the road,
and giant Douglas firs rose out of the thicket, along with
wild crab apple, vine maple, and red cedar. Here and there,
patches of fireweed long gone to seed dappled the area. As
we bumped along, the wild energy that Delilah had mentioned spread like mist rolling along the ground.

When we rounded a bend, to the left up ahead we saw
an old house. The road ended in a circular driveway, where
a couple of old trucks sat, rusted out from the looks of
things. Further back, three outbuildings looked ready to
tumble. I scanned the area, looking for any sign of the lumberjack. Chase was craning his neck, probably looking for
the dragon.

The SUV coasted to a stop, and we piled out. Chase
lightly tripped up the steps to the house, skirting a broken
patch that threatened to cave in under him. He knocked on
the door, but nobody answered.

I slipped around the side, veering toward the tenuous
outbuildings, looking for any sign of life. As I approached
the smallest one covered with moss, Chase screamed as an
explosion rocked the area. Hell and high water!

Racing back to the house, I saw that Chase had been

thrown clear of the porch by some sort of blast, and the sparkles that indicated magic at play were flying everywhere. He was lying on the ground with Delilah kneeling beside him. Morio was cautiously approaching what had been the door. I dashed up the stairs, taking them two at a time, skidding to a halt beside the yokai-kitsune. He held his fingers to his lips.

"There's someone inside," he whispered.

Inhaling deeply, I mustered up as much energy as I could. Even though it was raining, lightning felt a long way off, but the Moon Mother—invisible as she was behind the cloud cover and daylight—ran strong and clear. I summoned her power, and it raced through my body, into my hands.

"Okay." I nodded at Morio. "I'm ready. Let's go see what we're up against."

As we rounded the archway, we found ourselves face-to-face with one of the Fae. She had pale mint-colored skin, and her eyes were the same color as mine, lilac and lavender. Tiny shoots, tendrils of some plant, emerged from various parts of her body, peeking from beneath a dress so sheer that she looked more naked than if she'd been nude.

Magnetic and lovely, she gave us a long look and then motioned to Morio, who took a step toward her. I grabbed his arm.

"No! I smell demon," I said. And then I knew who we were facing. It was Wisteria, from Jocko's journal. And as far as I was concerned, that meant Bad Ass Luke couldn't be far behind.

Wisteria shifted her attention to Morio. She held out a finger and again crooked it. I glanced at his glazed eyes and jabbed him in the arm.

"Snap out of it; she's using a glamour on you!"

Morio shook his head and blinked. Wisteria gave me a dirty look and pulled her lips back, showing sharp little teeth. Oh yeah, she wasn't on our side; that much was obvious.

Just then, Delilah and Chase pushed through the door.

Seeing the four of us standing there, Wisteria seemed to think the better of a fight and turned to run.

I was on her like snow on a mountain, sending a bolt of energy zinging in her direction. I hit her square in the small of the back, shoving her a good ten feet forward, but then to my horror, the bolt continued to ricochet off the walls. Before I could stop it, the energy slammed into Chase, knocking him off his feet.

"Crap! Chase, are you okay?" As I knelt beside him, Morio and Delilah converged on Wisteria. I heard a scuffle and glanced their way. They had managed to catch her. Morio was holding her down, while Delilah attempted to muzzle her mouth with the sleeve of her coat.

Chase blinked a couple of times, then slowly sat up. Thank the gods, he hadn't received the full blast, or he could have died. He glanced down at his shirt, which was scorched, and winced.

"Anything broken? Do you need a doctor?" I helped him to his feet.

He dusted off his jeans, then gingerly prodded his stomach, where the material had turned soil brown. "Thanks a lot. I loved this shirt. Damn, that stings. You pack a wallop, girl."

"You didn't get the full effect. Be grateful for small favors," I said grimly. In the best of all possible worlds, the bolt shouldn't have ricocheted like that, but considering the haywire effect of my magic, there was always a chance for something to go awry. Actually, in the best of all possible worlds, Menolly would still be alive, my magic would work perfectly, my sisters and I would be at the top of the OIA food chain, and we wouldn't be stuck running after a Degath Squad of demons who'd decided the time was ripe to take over Earth.

After making sure that Chase would survive, I turned my attention to Wisteria. Delilah and Morio had managed to restrain her near a big oaken table that was covered with a faded linen cloth. A place mat and napkin sat neatly in front of a chair. I shook out the napkin and advanced on our prisoner.

Delilah pulled her hand away as I slid the cloth in place over Wisteria's mouth. "She's strong," Delilah warned. Just then, the Faerie twisted savagely, attempting to free herself. My sister slammed Wisteria against the floor as Morio strengthened his grip.

I knelt down, trying to get a handle on just what race Wisteria hearkened from. She was obviously connected with the woodland. The vines and leaves weren't adornments on her dress; they were part of her flesh, part of her very essence. I stroked her hair, smoothing the long, wheat strands away from her eyes. The faint outlines of a brand appeared in the center of her forehead—a trefoil leaf.

"An offshoot of the dryads, I think." I struggled to remember my schooling.

"A maenad?" Morio asked. "She's volatile enough."

I shook my head. "I don't smell any meat, and maenads eat meat. She's never touched a hamburger in her life, I'd stake my reputation on it. No, I think Wisteria here is a dryad who's gotten into a snit over something and fallen in with the wrong crowd. Problem is, now she's linked to two murders."

Chase joined us and stared down at the Faerie. "She's got plants growing out of her."

"Genius, aren't you?"

"Hey, give me a break. After all, you almost killed me."

I glanced at him quickly but saw that he was teasing. Then, snapping my fingers, I said, "I know what she is! She's one of the floraeds, a rare branch of the dryad family. They really hate humans." I frowned. What to do with her? Floraeds were fairly powerful when they were near enough foliage, and we were smack in the middle of woodland central.

Morio seemed to grasp the situation. "We can't let her go. She's dangerous to both us and the mission."

"Do you think she'll understand what's at stake if we talk to her?" Delilah asked.

"Doubt it, but I suppose it's worth a try," I said. Wisteria struggled, and I gave her a cold smile. "Hold your horses, sister. Just chill out and listen to us."

I patted her down, looking for any weapons. Floraeds didn't usually carry them, but it couldn't hurt to check. When I withdrew a long, narrow tube and several wicked-looking darts from the folds of her gown, I was glad I'd taken the time to frisk her. Better safe than sorry. I sniffed the tips of the darts.

"Poison, and a deadly one at that. We're lucky we caught her before she shot one of us, or it would be all over." I motioned to Chase. "Tear that tablecloth into strips, please. We need something to tie her hands with, because if they're free, she can cast spells. We have to question her."

"Will my handcuffs work?" Chase asked, holding them out. I glanced at them. Cold steel. They wouldn't be comfortable, but they wouldn't burn her like iron. Even my sisters and I got a nasty rash from the metal, and we were only half-breed.

"They should work, but we need to bind her hands behind her back." I took the cuffs from Chase and glanced around the room, assessing our options.

Freestanding floor-to-ceiling beams were spaced evenly through the living room. I had them hold Wisteria so that her back was flat to one of the posts, then pulled her arms around back of the beam and handcuffed her. She struggled, her skin smooth as silk under my fingers. I gauged the size of her hands, reassuring myself that she wouldn't be able to slide out of the cuffs. Her fingers were slender, but not that slender.

"Okay," I said, standing back. "We're about as safe as we're going to be around her. Remove the gag, but watch her feet."

Morio lowered the gag. Wisteria coughed several times, then yanked her head up, fixing her glare on me.

"Bitch," she said, eyes narrowing. "You don't belong here—this isn't your home."

"My mother was human. Earth is my home as much as Otherworld." I leaned in, examining her trefoil, which had started to glow. "Again, just chill. We know you're in league with the demons, and we know you were involved with Jocko's death. Probably Louise's death, too."

She flinched. A true flinch. While most of the Fae could lie without blinking, surprise lit up her expression, and I realized that she had no idea Jocko had been murdered.

"What do you mean?" she said. "Jocko and Louise are dead? Who killed them?"

"Your pals. The deviants *you* snuck through the portal. You told them about Louise, didn't you? That she saw you near the portal? I bet that's why she was murdered. To shut her up."

The look on Wisteria's face told me everything I needed to know.

"Wonderful," I said. "So you not only turned traitor and, by your actions, inadvertently helped murder a fellow OIA agent, but you also were instrumental in the death of a human. What happened after you let them through? Did Bad Ass Luke and his cronies tell you to go home and forget you ever saw them? Did they promise you nobody else would get hurt? Maybe feed you some line about restoring earth to her former glory? Is that what happened?"

She didn't answer, but I could tell I'd struck a nerve. I was so angry that I wanted to dispatch her right there, but I restrained myself.

"Is it true?" she asked, looking at Morio. "You're earthbound. You wouldn't lie to me, would you?"

Morio's gaze flickered my way, and I kept my mouth shut. Fox demons were excellent at illusion and camouflage. Deception went hand in hand with their nature, though I hadn't picked up on any lies from him yet. Some of the fox demons used their powers for harm; Morio had chosen a higher path.

He crossed his arms and stared at Wisteria for a moment before speaking. "I swear on Inari's heartbeat that I'm not lying. Jocko is dead, and the demons killed him." He held up one hand in a sign that I didn't recognize. "By the breath of the Rice Maiden, it's true."

Wisteria stared at her feet. "I didn't know they were going to hurt him. He was nice enough to me . . ." I wondered if she regretted her actions enough to cooperate with us, but then she lifted her head, her eyes cold as glacier water.

"The giant's death is regrettable, but as the humans would say, consider it collateral damage. As for Louise, what do I care? She's human, and that's all that matters. The days of raping the earth are soon to be over. We're taking it back, and this time, we won't let go so easily."

Chase sputtered, but I held up my hand for him to be quiet.

"Wisteria, when the demons get through with the land, there won't be anything for you to protect. You know what they're like," I said. "Most of them hate growing things. They despise life and abundance and have as little regard for the birds of the air and the beasts of the forest as they do human and Faerie alike."

I narrowed my eyes. "You might say they have the same regard for the natural world that you did for Louise. Shadow Wing and his crew won't rest until the land is razed. Life under the demons will be worse than life under any human you could ever despair to know."

"Bullshit!" She struggled against the cuffs. "They gave me their word—"

"Are you too stupid to live?" Morio slammed his fist against the beam next to her. "Do you really believe they're telling you the truth? Grandmother Coyote was right—the balance is totally out of whack, and nut jobs like you aren't doing anything to help. Sure, humans have wrecked the land, but what they've done won't even begin to compare to what Shadow Wing has in mind. Who are you working with? Who contacted you about helping Bad Ass Luke?"

Wisteria spat at him, hitting him square in the face. As he turned away, fists clenched, I stepped in again. "If you don't believe him, there's not much we can do, but you're abandoning both our worlds to hell by refusing to tell us what you know." When she stubbornly shook her head, I turned back to the others.

"She's not going to budge. Floraeds are stubborn as ticks, and she's got it in that pea brain of hers that the demons are going to sashay up to the nature spirits and turn the keys to Earth back over to them once all the humans are dead or subjugated. If our efforts fail, I only hope I get to see her face when she understands what's really going down. Because, with the gods as my witness, I swear I'll tear her apart with my bare hands that day."

Furious at the veg-head, I delegated Delilah and Morio to search the house for anything that might tell us where Tom Lane was. Meanwhile, I stepped outside to see if I could conjure up a spell that might help rather than bite us in the butt.

The wind had picked up; it had passed chilly and was downright cold. Blowing in from the southwest, a downpour threatened to swamp us before nightfall. I sucked in a deep breath, inhaling the scent of mossy trees and Douglas fir and molding fungi that padded the ground and made walking slippery.

The maples and oaks and other deciduous trees were almost bare now, their leaves whipped off by the frenzied gusts that swept through the area. Otherworld had its storms, some of them violent and awe-inspiring, but I had never experienced the continual drenching that the Pacific Northwest received for a good nine months out of the year. I longed for the sun, but according to Chase, that wouldn't be happening in any measurable amount, anytime soon.

As I stood in the soggy afternoon, shivering despite the thick weave of my jacket, I began to sense the presence of magic. Old magic, deep from the forest, deep from the ground. It wasn't the magic of wizards or witches. No, this was the magic from beneath the soil, growing out of the very element from which it was born. Earth magic—dark and loamy, filled with secrets buried under the years of leaves and branches that had decayed back into the planet herself.

There was something ponderous about the energy, something so heavy that it muffled my hearing and sucked me under. Dark as in deep nights in the thick of the woods, dark as in the wild hunt that raced across the sky. Dark as in ancient secrets that worked neither for good nor evil, but were simply a force unto themselves. A sparkle of green flared around me, and I understood that I'd contacted a minor earth elemental.

I knelt, steering clear of a puddle forming in one of the wheel ruts in the drive, and placed my hand on the slick earth. *Listen,* I told myself. *Just listen. No casting spells, no calling down the moonbeams or starlight. Just tune in and respectfully ask where we might find the man called Tom Lane.*

And then, I saw him—clear as a vision. Lumberjack, yes, but not a logger at heart. He was tall and strong, and beneath the grizzled beard, he bore a nobility born in another time and place. His eyes were lit with the sparkle of madness culled from living too long and seeing too much. I gasped as he reached out to me with an outstretched hand and begged for help.

Who *was* he? And why did he have the spirit seal?

As I watched, the dark maw of a cave opened up, and I understood that he was hiding inside it. I fine-tuned my internal radar and was pleased when I received a strong signal leading into the woods toward the side of a foothill. Tom Lane wasn't far, but it would take some navigation to get there, and the rain wasn't going to make it a whole lot of fun.

As I shook myself free of the lingering tendrils of energy, a hoarse shout from the house startled me, and I turned to race back inside.

CHAPTER 13

Wisteria was laughing. I glanced around to find Chase, doubled over on the floor. Delilah and Morio knelt beside him.

"What the hell happened?"

"We should have gagged her again," Delilah said. "Apparently, Wisteria can charm with her words. Chase got too close, and she managed to kick him in the balls. Hard."

Morio was trying to help him sit up, but it was obvious the kick had been perfectly aimed. Chase was so pale I wondered if he was going to be okay. His face was one big knot of pain.

I glanced over at Wisteria, who had a triumphant look in her eyes. Furious, I slammed her head against the beam, holding her by the throat.

"Try anything more, and you die. That's just the way it is. I'll let our sister come have some fun with you. You know Menolly? And you know that she's a vampire? Wouldn't you be a tasty treat for her?"

I could tell I'd made an impression. Wisteria swallowed—I felt her throat move—and I stepped away slowly, keeping an eye on her feet. "Delilah, tear up that tablecloth and tie her feet to the beam." I repositioned the gag on Wisteria's mouth. By the time we were done, she'd be trussed tight as a turkey.

As Delilah jumped to obey, Morio motioned me to Chase's side. "I think he'll be okay, but he's not going to be hiking around the woods today, that much I can tell you. What should we do?"

I sighed. "Leave him here to watch Wisteria. Secure him with some sort of cover. Morio, aren't your kind good at illusionary magic?"

He nodded. "*Mekuramashi*. The illusion-maker. I can fix it so Chase appears to be a pile of clothes. That way he can sit on the sofa and rest while we're out hunting."

"Good. Get him up there, then. I know where to look for Tom Lane, but I think he's in trouble and needs our help. We have to get to him as fast as possible." I helped Morio gather Chase up and gently transfer him to the sofa. Chase was trying to hold on to his dignity. He glanced up at me, and I gave him a tentative smile.

"Just sit here and rest. Everything will be okay. I've gagged Wisteria again. Apparently, floraeds are a lot like the sirens. Not a good thing when you're a human." I fixed a pillow behind his head as Delilah joined me, taking Chase's hands in hers. I discreetly withdrew, leaving them to speak in private.

I joined Morio, who was sitting at the table. "I guess we're about ready," I said. "What do you need for this spell of yours?"

He shook his head and said in a low voice, "I just need my skull familiar, but I don't want her seeing it. What she doesn't know, she can't use against me. Can you blindfold her?"

"Not a problem." I sighed. "She's far more dangerous than I suspected. I had no idea floraeds wielded this much power."

"She's definitely not your typical wood sprite," he said. "There's more to this one than meets the eye. I tell you, Camille, we'd be better off if we killed her. This is a war, and she's on the side of the enemy. I think she can cause a lot worse havoc than this, and I don't want to see it play out."

I bit my lip. He was right. I knew he was and yet . . . she wasn't a demon or a rogue vampire or a harpy. She was one of the Faerie. Evil, yes, but it was hard for me to raise my hand against my own kind.

But then again—was she really one of my own? She hated me for my human side, that much was obvious, but even had I been full-blood Sidhe, she'd find a reason to stand against me. Perhaps it was that I didn't know just how much more violence I could stomach. After seeing the skinwalker attack Trillian, I was running on empty.

"I know you're right and yet . . . I don't know if I can do it."

"I can," he said, and I knew it was an offer.

I bit my lip, wavering. But I was a member of the OIA and my father's daughter. If we decided to kill the floraed, it would be my responsibility to carry out the deed. I shook my head. "Let me think for a bit. We still may be able to learn more about the demons' plans from her. If we wrap her in iron cuffs and gag her, then she won't be able to do anything."

"If *you* try to wrap her in iron, you'll only be hurting yourself." He was frustrated, that much was obvious, but then he shrugged. "Okay. We'll figure out what to do with her when we come back from looking for this Lane dude. Deal?"

"Deal," I said, relieved that I'd bought a little more time to make up my mind. I blindfolded Wisteria. Morio focused on Chase, creating an illusion that the detective was a pile of clean clothes. Even with my Sight, I couldn't tell just what lay under the illusion.

"You're good," I said, glancing at Morio.

He cocked his head to the side, contemplating the illusion. "Not bad if I say so myself." And then a sly smile stole across his face. "I'm good in other ways, too, if you're ever inclined to find out. Very good. You know, Svartans don't hold the trophy when it comes to passion."

Before I could say a word, he motioned to Delilah and headed for the door. Wondering if he'd meant what I heard, and wondering if I had the guts to find out, I followed.

We set off in the direction that I'd been shown. Delilah glanced back at the house, a worried look on her face.

"Do you think Chase will be okay?" Raindrops streaked her face, and she'd pulled up the hood on her jacket. Not only did she avoid lakes, ponds, and oceans, but she wasn't all that fond of rain, either.

"I hope so," I muttered, gliding through the copse. "If he leaves Wisteria alone, and if nobody shows up at the house, he should be fine. Morio's illusion was pretty damned good."

The undergrowth was so thick that even with our advantages, it took us time to wade our way through. I wasn't too thrilled about leading the way, but since I was the one who knew where we were going, it didn't exactly take a genius to figure out that I was the best choice.

"Morio, you've lived Earthside all of your life. How have you managed to keep your nature hidden from humans?" I asked, pushing between a huckleberry bush and a large fern. Water splashed in my eyes as a frond smacked me in the face, but with the pouring rain I barely noticed.

"I was born in a small village—there are still villages in Japan—and lived there most of my life. My grandfather taught me at home, and I recently got my degree from an online accredited university."

"Are you out, now that the Sidhe have shown up from Otherworld?" In a way, our appearance had made things easier for the earthbound Fae and other Cryptos. It allowed them to come forward. It was exotic to be different now, and humans all over the world were suddenly in search of mysterious ancestors who might have originally come from Otherworld. Of course, the vampires and undead hadn't found the same acceptance yet, but that was understandable.

He shrugged. "To some, but I don't announce it to the world."

"Are you sorry we showed up?" I asked.

Close behind me, he answered, "That's a double-edged question. No, I'm not, because it was time we let humans in on our existence. And yes, I am, because it's turned all that is magical and mystical into a consumer circus."

I snorted. "Like it wasn't before? People have been longing for magic since the beginning of time. I think there's a universal memory that remembers the days when Otherworld was just a step away and before Avalon traveled into the mists. Lord of the Rings, Harry Potter . . . all of these books I've been reading tell me that my mother's people need us. They need to rediscover their sense of wonder about the world and to develop their own innate powers that all mortals possess. And perhaps *we* need humans to remind *us* of what it means to be frail, to be vulnerable."

"I think we can learn a lot from FBHs. Compassion is more of a human trait than one belonging to the Sidhe. Surely you would acknowledge that," Delilah broke in.

I thought about what she said. Our mother had been fiery and quick-tempered, but she had a heart of gold. Our father was unusual among the Court and Crown in that he shared the latter quality. "You may be right, little sister."

Just then, we broke through the thicket into an open meadow. Surrounded on all sides by a ring of cedar trees, it bore the markings of magic. A clearing, and one specifically dedicated to some deity or being, at that. I felt like I was trespassing as we entered the ring of trees. Toadstools formed an inner circle, and a mound of grass rose slightly in the center.

"A barrow?" Delilah asked, frowning. "I didn't think the barrows were used much anymore, and I had no idea they were found on this continent."

"As far as I've read, most of them were abandoned during the Great Divide. But this—this one has the energy of a portal. Not an OW portal, though. Where are we? And what is this place?" I slowly advanced on the slope of grass, looking for any sign of an entrance. "I can almost hear argentine pipes."

And listening, I realized that I actually did hear music. There—whispering on the wind—a trilling melody so wrapped in magic that each note quavered in the air, alive and vibrant, bidding me to dance. My feet urged me to shed shoes and jacket and go skipping across the lea. I sucked in a deep breath and threw back my head, laughing, suddenly lighthearted and fancy-free.

As I turned, Delilah leapt in the air and shifted into her golden tabby form. She began racing around the meadow, chasing after raindrops and imaginary mice. I vaguely felt that I should stop her for some reason, but the music was so compelling that I turned back to the barrow. If only I could find the entrance, I could find out just who was playing those pipes.

"Camille—Camille! Can you hear me?" Morio was at my side, a feral look on his face. I gave him the once-over. He was looking pretty good, that was for sure, and I became aware of a tingling that was focused somewhere below my belly button. In fact, my entire body was buzzing, and I realized that the only thing that would stop the itch was . . . I licked my lips and held out my hand.

"I need you. Right now, right here." I reached for him, my breath quickening as my pulse began to beat a staccato of desire that reverberated through my breasts, my stomach, my thighs. His dark hair and haunting eyes drew me in, and I wanted to throw him to the ground and climb aboard.

Morio let out a low growl, and he took a step toward me. "Be careful what you ask for," he said in a husky voice. "Because I'll give it to you. I don't play games. You want me, you've got me, but there's no stopping once we begin."

I could smell his musky scent. He was primed and ready; I didn't have to see him naked to know that. The thought of him bearing down on me made me shiver with anticipation. My mind sputtered, asking me what the hell I was doing, but my body egged me on. I decided my brain could use a breather and shoved any last reservations aside. Not that there were many to begin with.

"I don't want gentle. Take me here. Now. Forwards, backwards, any way you want," I whispered. Ready to explode, I shivered as his eyes glinted with a primal hunger.

"Let's see how far you're willing to go," he said, and he was on me, grabbing my wrist as he fastened his mouth on mine. I fell into his kiss, melting in the raging fire that roared to life between us. He braced my shoulders, encircled my waist to pull me tight against him.

I struggled with my dress, but Morio slapped my hand away and pushed me to the ground, shoving my skirt up as he yanked down his zipper. He tore open my shirt and sought my breasts, covering me with love bites that only fueled my need. As his dark eyes slanted dangerously, I felt myself being swept under by the wave of passion rolling through the meadow.

And then Morio was ready, and I opened myself to him, sinking into the rich loam of the earth as he drove deep within me, thrusting with long, powerful strokes. I yielded to him, to the music, to my own need. All the pretense and reserve of the fox demon disappeared then, and his eyes gleamed as he threw back his head and let out a *yip* of victory.

The music grew louder, and Morio smiled then, his teeth sharp and needlelike as his fingernails extended into claws. He nipped at my shoulder, and a glimmer of fear raced through me as it filtered through my sex-addled brain as to just how alien he was. Fae? In a sense, but earthbound and connected to the primal energy that permeated the world.

Suddenly frantic and wondering what had gotten into me, I began to struggle, but the more I squirmed, the harder he got. As I fought to free myself, a backlash of energy hit me, and I surrendered, soaring higher than Trillian had ever taken me. I hovered, unable to breathe, wondering just who and what I was, and the scent of rain-drenched roses washed over me as I slowly sank back into my body, touching down with a sense of power that I hadn't felt in a long time. Immediately, I wanted more. Morio must have felt the increased desire, too, because he panted raggedly in my ear.

"Stop," he said, his voice cracking. "We have to stop *now*—this is a glamour, and it's a dangerous one." He forced himself to roll away, struggling to keep his hands off me. "Get away from the mound, get out of the ring of toadstools."

Startled by his angry bark, I scrambled to my feet.

He leapt up, eyes blazing. "I said run—-now!"

And I ran. I raced toward the ring of cedars. The moment my feet passed the edge of the toadstool circle I felt as though I'd ripped myself out of some hedonistic womb. Stumbling to a halt, I dropped to my knees, my head pounding like somebody had taken a sledgehammer to it. My body had taken a pounding, too, but of quite another kind. As the world swirled around me, I sucked in several ragged, deep breaths, and reality slowly fell back into place.

"What the hell?" I mumbled.

From where I was, I could see Morio chasing Delilah. He suddenly vanished, and a mouse appeared where he'd been standing. Delilah flicked her tail and began stalking the rodent, paws slowly inching forward, whiskers twitching. As she pounced, the illusion broke, and Morio appeared, grabbing her by the scruff of the neck. He jogged back to my side.

The moment he crossed the toadstool ring, Delilah began to shimmer, and he set her on the ground a few feet away, toward the cedar grove. As she shifted back, the surprise on her face made me want to laugh. Almost. Whoever had put up this barrier had done a damned good job of it.

"Okay, what just happened?" Still flushed, I accepted Morio's hand, and he pulled me to my feet. As his fingers met mine, we sparked, and I realized that we had managed to tangle ourselves together all too tightly. We'd play havoc trying to unknot this web, that much was certain. Especially since we'd been attracted to each other to begin with.

Morio held my gaze for a moment, then glanced back at the mound. "Sidhe magic, but different from yours. How many Sidhe stayed Earthside when Otherworld broke away and went into the mists?"

I shook my head. "It was so long ago, no one knows. There are a lot of nature spirits here, and a lot of Cryptos were left behind—or chose to stay. We're related, but it's been a long time since the initial divide. Do you think this is where Wisteria makes her home?"

He shook his head. "Since she works at the Wayfarer and is aligned with the OIA, chances are she probably has a tree somewhere near Seattle. No, this magic is too powerful for her. The music makes me think of Pan, but it's rumored that Old Shag has been staying close to home in Greece."

I took a step closer, and we locked eyes. Morio held out his arms, and I stepped into his embrace. He kissed me, long and slow, tender without the fury that had spurred us on earlier.

"We're going to have to discuss this later," I said. Thoughts of Trillian filled my mind, but even as I worried over his life, my body had a will of its own and I'd responded so strongly to the fox demon that it made me afraid. And I liked Morio. Trillian thrilled me to the core. I loved him and I hated him. But I really didn't like him. Whatever came out of this mix was going to be interesting, that was for sure.

"I know." Morio let out a long sigh. "But right now we need to focus on matters at hand and avoid being caught up by that whimsy spell again."

"Excuse me," Delilah piped up. "But what the hell are you two doing?"

I broke away from Morio and jerked my head toward the mound. "While you decided to take a kitten break, we ended up in a lip-lock that would hit a triple-X rating. Didn't you notice the nice layer of mud I decided to add to my outfit?" Unfortunately, *that* wasn't a joke. Thanks to Mr. Fox's wild ride, the back of my jacket and skirt were soaked with dew and mud and soggy leaves.

"I was wondering but was too polite to ask," Delilah said with a cough. "Uh-oh. I can't wait to see the fallout on this one," she said, a snarky grin creeping across her face. "Well, I'm just glad you guys caught me before I took off into the woods and got myself lost."

"Thanks, wild child. Back to the matter at hand. If this isn't Wisteria's doing, then whose? It's Sidhe magic, but linked to Earth, not to OW."

Morio knelt to examine the toadstools. "Camille's right. This is very powerful magic and dangerous to leave unattended."

With a frown, Delilah stared at the barrow. "Then the question is, how do we break the illusion? I want to know what's under there."

I studied the mound. "I can probably break through, but there's a very real chance that when my magic comes into contact with the barriers, I might cause some sort of an implosion. I'm not sure it's worth the risk. Maybe we can just go around it?"

Morio cocked his head to one side. "I can try to banish the force field, but I don't know if I'm strong enough. This isn't just illusion. What about if we try it together? Maybe I can deflect any misfire from your magic, Camille."

"Brave, aren't you?" I rubbed my backside. I'd really taken a pounding. Morio was stronger than I'd given him credit for. It was going to take a lot of stretching to work out the knots in my inner thighs. "You sure you want to chance it? If something goes wrong, I can't guarantee your safety."

He noticed my discomfort. "Need a little massage there to straighten out the kinks?" he said, winking. As I sputtered, he added, "Don't sweat it. I think I can protect myself from anything you can manage to botch up."

"Gee, thanks, I love you, too." I frowned. My back felt like it was being pricked by a hot needle. "What the hell? Delilah, do I have anything under my shirt?" I lifted the cami so she could take a look. Morio stared with an unabashed leer. I stuck my tongue out at him while Delilah checked my back.

"Yeah, you managed to get a blackberry bramble under there." With a quick jerk, she yanked, and I let out a yelp as the thorn dislodged itself from my skin. "So much for sex in the woods," I muttered. Except for the wild places of Otherworld, brambles stayed in nice, tidy patches at home.

"Okay, let's get back to business. Chase is going to be wondering where the hell we are if we don't hurry up." I studied the barrow. "I'll focus on disrupting the barrier, you focus on sweeping aside any illusions that might be linked to it. You stand over there, a good arm's length away."

We took up position, with Delilah guarding the rear. As I raised my arms and summoned the Moon Mother's power, the energy of the lea shimmered. The rain stopped as a cold wind blew up, shaking the trees. I focused my concentration on boring a hole through the force field, turning myself into a magical power drill. Morio worked alongside me, dispersing the illusions that bound the area, breaking their hold on the land.

As the barrier began to weaken and we drove a wedge in it, a low rumble began to vibrate through the air, and the earth shook, waves rippling beneath our feet. I swayed, trying to keep my footing, but the quake magnified and sent both Morio and me sprawling. The force field cracked, shattering into a thousand invisible shards and then the lea was silent once more.

"Talk about shake, rattle, and roll," I said as I staggered to my feet.

"What the hell? Are we in the middle of a war zone?" Delilah asked.

The lovely grassland was now a blackened mound in the center of a ring of sickly trees that murmured dark thoughts and desires. The ground had been scorched, and tree trunks charred into carbon lay scattered around the area.

"Holy crap. Look at this place." Delilah sucked in a deep breath, her eyes wide.

"That about says it all." I looked around for Morio, who was rubbing his shoulder from where the quake had tossed him. "What happened here?"

"Look," he said, pointing to a darkened hole against the mound. It led deep within the earth. "Is that a cave?"

As I squinted through the rain—which was once again pounding the area—I saw that he was right. It was a cave. *The cave.* And I knew that somewhere within, Tom Lane was hiding.

"That's where we want to go. This is it, folks. Let's move." But as I moved forward, the rustle of wings caught my attention. Before we could take another step, a shadow rose up from behind the mound. There, snaky and huge and milky white, hovered a dragon. And he looked hungry.

CHAPTER 14

"Dragon!" Delilah fell back, a terrified look on her face.

"Stop shouting. I see it." What the hell were we going to do now? The pastoral woodland setting had suddenly become a field full of land mines, and any residual urge to dance had turned into an even stronger urge to turn tail and run. But that wouldn't help matters. Dragons were big. Dragons were strong. Dragons were fast. And most of all—dragons made lunch out of witches like me.

The wyrm was a blend of Asian and Western heritage. His body was long and snakelike, and his wings were large but ornamental; he didn't need them to fly. What looked like horns but were really antennae graced the beast's forehead. The reptilian grace hovered above us, milky and pearlescent, shimmering between pale pink and ivory.

As I stared into his icy gray eyes that were ringed with black and held twin diamonds in the center of each pupil, I couldn't help but wonder at how beautiful he was. It had been many years since I'd seen a dragon, and never this close. Part of me just wanted to stand in awe, but I shook myself out of my trance. Dragons were notorious for being able to hypnotize their prey—it made for an easier time of preparing crispy critters for lunch.

Actually, maybe I was doing him a disservice. After all, not all dragons breathed fire, but by the looks of the surrounding countryside I wouldn't put it past him. The meadow had been razed, and the perfect circle of debris convinced me that a forest fire hadn't been responsible for the damage.

I carefully stepped back, one foot at a time, my gaze fastened on the face of the dragon as I prepared to run or freeze-frame, whichever my gut told me would save my life.

The dragon let out a low rumble that sounded suspiciously like a laugh. An ominous laugh. Dragon jokes were usually at the expense of the listener, and little good could come out of a dragon's mirth, except for his own amusement.

I glanced briefly at Morio. He, too, was playing statue. Delilah was nowhere to be seen, and I hoped she'd had the chance to duck behind a tree. Out of sight, out of mind, out of stomach.

"So, should I eat you here or save you for later?" His voice was lower than any bass I'd ever heard. "You've had your last feast—each other—so now it's my turn."

I struggled to remember everything I knew about the beasts. What had I told Chase? Don't try to outshine a dragon, don't puff up in his face. Dragons were so arrogant that they'd make quick work of anybody who challenged their superiority. Yada yada yada. On the other hand, some seemed to value courage. Cowards weren't known for their luck in walking away from a dragon-fest, at least not with all their parts still intact. I cleared my throat.

"We apologize. We had no idea we were intruding in your territory. Please, if you let us go, we'll leave and never return." Compromise—that might just be the ticket. *We made a mistake, we screwed up, take mercy on us, and let us go about our business. Grovel, grovel, beg, beg.*

The dragon snorted, and puffs of steam flared out from

his nostrils. "You expect me to believe that, little witch? You're one of those pesky Sidhe, aren't you?" His luminous eyes whirled, and once again, I found myself staring into them, but as his mind touched my own, I jerked away.

He laughed again. "Not *full-blooded* Sidhe after all. Half-breed. Human and Faerie . . . delicious combination. Dessert, that's what you are. But tell me, Witchling, what are you doing here? You're not earthbound, unlike your companion." The winding neck swerved in Morio's direction.

I let my breath out. I'd been holding it so tightly I felt like I'd just busted out of a corset. Morio casually slid his hands in his pockets and gave the dragon a nod. He was going for the buddy-buddy routine. I silently wished him luck.

"Greetings, Ancient One. We're truly sorry for the interruption. We were searching for someone and were led astray." Morio's voice was smooth and silken. He couldn't be trying to use his illusion to deceive the wyrm, could he? Dragons were immune to most charm. I forced myself to keep my mouth shut. Morio knew what he was doing. At least I hoped so.

The dragon hiccupped, and another cloud of smoke emerged, smelling decidedly like roast meat. Definitely, I did *not* want to meet his last meal on a face-to-face basis. I just prayed that Tom Lane wasn't down there in his belly, along with the spirit seal. Gutting a deer was hard enough; gutting a dragon was a full-blown expedition into monster surgery, and first we'd have to kill him.

After another moment's pause, the dragon said, "Foxman, you'd better cease your attempts to enchant me, or I'll start with your head and pick my teeth with your bones. Now, tell me the truth, why are you in my territory?"

Morio glanced at me, a question on his face. We had all of about three minutes before old Smoky here was going to start blasting. If the dragon was in league with the demons, we were dead. If the dragon was out for himself—a distinct possibility—then who knew? What I did know was that dragons were terribly clever at sniffing out liars.

I finally shrugged and said, "We're looking for a man named Tom Lane. We need to talk to him."

Smoky's eyes lit up. "You want to talk to that meddlesome idiot?"

Uh-oh. By the tone of his voice, it was obvious he wasn't Tom's friend, but I didn't sense a demonic aura around the dragon. Maybe he and Tom just had issues. But why hadn't Smoky already resolved them with a puff of fire? I couldn't be sure, and I didn't think it was diplomatic to ask.

"We need to find him," I said. Then a stroke of genius hit me. "If you tell us where he is, we'll take him away, and he'll never bother you again."

The dragon shifted, hunkering down on the mound. His neck bobbed like a king cobra in a snake charmer's basket before stretching out to zero in on my face. Those glittering, glacial eyes were about ten feet away, the dragon's head huge in comparison to me. He was scrutinizing me. I did my best to appear wide-eyed and innocent.

"Witchling, what's your name?"

Another no-no. Never give a dragon your real name. Not a good idea. I shook my head. "I'm not that stupid. You know I'm not going to give you my name, so don't even bother."

A deep rumble filled the air as he huffed and then laughed. "I like you. Funny and brave, a rare combination. Your quarry ran into the cave early in the day. I chased him as far as I could, but he got away. If you take him with you, I'll let you live and walk in my forest. If you fail, then I'll eat you for breakfast."

I sighed. I was starting to feel like the universal stooge on the end of the bad-deal train. *Bring me a demon's finger bone, or I'll take one of yours. Terminate the demons, or they'll destroy the world. Get Tom Lane out of my sight, or I'll eat you for breakfast.*

"I guess that's our only choice. It's a deal." What more could I say? "But you have to let us into the cave so we can go find him. And no scaring him off while we're trying to catch him. And no funny business."

Morio suppressed a snort, and I knew what he was thinking. We'd really dug ourselves in with this one. I still couldn't sense where Delilah was.

The dragon gave his best imitation of a shrug. "My word of honor, on my smokestacks and whiskers, little witch."

Word of honor indeed. Dragons were good at twisting words, and I didn't trust Smoky's jovial nature. But it was the best we were going to get, barring the protection of a wizard or a witch far stronger than I.

He dipped his head and pointed toward the cave in the mound. "I chased him in there. Just get busy and find him. I'm feeling irritable today."

As Morio and I cautiously approached the cave, I forced myself to stare straight ahead. I wanted to look for Delilah, but the dragon would suspect something. We were at the mouth of the dark tunnel when I glanced back.

"So tell me something. Why didn't you catch Tom yourself? Why haven't you eaten him yet?"

Smoky's eyes sparkled, scintillating and brilliant. "I didn't fancy a bout of indigestion," was all he said.

As we passed by him, I could feel his hot breath warming the air. Actually, compared to the rain it was pleasant, and part of me wanted to stand there for a moment to dry off from the downpour, but then I thought the better of it. After all, a dragon giving you a pet name like *Witchling* only spelled trouble. The smell of charcoal and meat was so thick around him, though, that I shuddered and hurried past.

Morio followed close behind, his hand on my shoulder. As we came to the entrance of the cave, I forced myself to walk sedately. No use in exciting the dragon into a mistake that we'd regret. Once inside, however, I slumped against the wall, shivering.

"That was one encounter I never expected to have. Nor do I fancy a repeat. Okay, where the hell is Tom? Let's find him and get out of here." I shook my head and looked around.

The walls of the cave glistened. Phosphorescence, perhaps? Faerie fire? I closed my eyes and reached out, searching for any sign of life. There—a flicker, just a mind's touch, down the tunnel and to the right.

"Someone's in here, that's for certain," I said, not exactly keen on the idea of tramping through the dark. I didn't like caves. I preferred the open sky or at least a house where I knew I wouldn't be falling down any mine shafts or tripping over rocks or getting squashed by rockslides.

Morio glanced at me. "You're claustrophobic, aren't you?"

Shrugging, I stared at the floor. "Kind of. And I've got vertigo, and I'm squeamish when it comes to babies' diapers. I'm just a mess, aren't I?" I let out a sigh and reluctantly leaned against the wall of the cavern. "Actually, I'm not claustrophobic in the truest sense of the word, but my magic comes from the moon and stars. I don't like being trapped under the earth. "I never went to visit the dwarven city back in Otherworld because most of it's buried in the mountain. My father took Delilah and Menolly, but I couldn't face it."

"Did your mother go?" Morio asked.

"No, she didn't want to go either, so I stayed with her, and we went on a weeklong shopping spree in Aladril, the city of Seers by the ocean." We'd come away with some pretty good deals, too, although Father had choked when he saw the bills come in. But he paid them without a word. He never denied Mother anything she might want.

"I'd like to visit Otherworld someday," Morio said, looking around the cave. "Here, help me find a stick or twig, and I can illuminate it."

"With fox fire?" I squinted, looking around. There, a branch that must have been about a foot long. I handed it to him, and within seconds he had enchanted it so that we could almost see the entire chamber. The sparkling ball of light on the end of the bough was brighter than candlelight but didn't shed quite as much light as a kerosene lantern.

"Fox fire is a common term for it, though not totally accurate," Morio said. "In Japan, we call it *kitsune-bi*. Here, let me lead the way."

He brushed past me, and the scent of his sweat set me off again. I fought the desire to reach out and touch him. Great, what would I do when Trillian returned? *If Trillian returned*, I thought somberly. If he even lived. That thought snapped my mind out of the sheets like a bucket of ice water.

"You'd like Otherworld, I think." I swung in behind him and cautiously picked my way along the corridor. The cave was damp and chilly. The moisture in the air had condensed along the walls, and I could see patches of slime mold clinging to the rock in some places, along with bloated white fungi and a lot of creepy crawlies.

The bugs didn't bother me—I was used to them from childhood—but the mold made me nervous. Back home in Otherworld, it took on a life of its own with a rudimentary consciousness and could be dangerous to the unwary traveler. Even though it was different here, I couldn't help but shrink away from the walls when we passed by.

"What's it like?" Morio asked.

"Otherworld? It's open and vast. The Court and Crown holds sway over Y'Elestrial, the home city of the Sidhe, but there are so many other cities and lands. The cities are lovely, for the most part, but the villages are another matter. Most are dirt poor, and the people live hand to mouth."

"Is there one governing council for Otherworld?"

I shook my head. "No. Each city-state is self-contained. However, the inhabitants of Y'Elestrial are the ones who have the most interaction with humans, and we're the ones who control the portals. Otherworld also has a vast network of wild woods and dark lands that house odd species of Fae. They seldom have much to do with the Sidhe. Or anybody else for that matter."

Once again I wished I was home, not trekking through an Earthside cavern in search of a mysterious man running from demons. A change in career seemed like just the ticket at this point, but I knew I wouldn't do it. My father wasn't a quitter, and he'd raised his daughters with the same sense of loyalty.

Morio said nothing, and I wondered if he could read my thoughts.

"There, ahead about ten yards, a T in the passage. Do we go left or right?" He motioned toward the end of the corridor.

"Stop for a moment, and I'll find out." Hesitantly, I leaned against the wall, taking care to avoid a patch of white fungi. I closed my eyes and reached out, trying to touch the spark I'd felt earlier. There, behind the cavern wall? No, it was only a scurrying, a couple of rats looking for lunch. To the right I sensed the movement of some specter—a ghost or spirit that was passing through. Probably the remains of one of Smoky's lunches, I thought.

As I cast around, I began to sense a slow, steady pulsing of magic. Heavy magic, to the left. Ancient magic, so strong that it almost floored me. Earth magic, deep and resonant, emanating from the very core of the world. And yet a top note played over it, sparkling with stars and the movement of the wind through the trees. And connected to this force in a way I didn't understand beat the heart of a man. He, too, felt old—far older than me. *Tom Lane.* It had to be him.

"This way," I said, mesmerized. As we hurried down the passage, I told Morio what I'd felt.

"If it's Tom you're sensing, then I'll bet the other energy belongs to the spirit seal. Didn't the history say that the seals were given to the Elemental Lords? That each Elemental Lord received one, and they all lost them over the eons? Deep earth energy could indicate this was the seal given to Robyn, the Prince of Oaks."

Of course! Robyn, who ruled the forests of Earth, who walked between worlds, dancing in the woodlands. "That makes a lot sense."

The Prince of Oaks spent more time with humans over the years than almost any other Elemental. He loved mortals, he cared for them, and the destruction of the jungles and forests wounded his heart. I'd met him once, long ago, when he came to pay homage to the Court and Crown.

Morio's foxfire led him around the bend, but he held up a hand as I followed. "Wait for a moment. I sense an illusion nearby. Let me feel this out."

I hung back as he tentatively moved forward, one slow step at a time, testing the ground before him before putting his weight down. Suddenly, he teetered and almost lost balance. I jumped forward and grabbed him by the elbow, holding him steady.

"What happened?" I couldn't see anything that might have thrown him off balance.

"There's a pit just ahead of us in the center of the passageway. It's been covered over with an illusion so we can't see it, but it's there, and probably deep enough to break our necks. Give me a moment, and I'll do what I can to dispel the mirage." He handed me the light and mumbled a low chant that seemed to go on and on. After a moment, the ground began to shimmer, and I could see the vague outline of an abyss. Then the illusion broke, and the pit was there, easily visible.

"Hell, that looks nasty," I whispered.

Morio took the branch back and cautiously held it toward the mouth of the hole. He peeked over the edge. "It is nasty. Watch your step."

I edged over to him, wary. As I inched forward enough to see over the edge, a long, dark shaft opened up into a pit that was a good hundred feet deep, if not more. From the bottom, the sound of rushing water burbled up. An underground stream of some sort. The fall would be deadly.

"Oh joy. So this is a sure sign that we aren't welcome, but I can't sense Tom down there. I don't think he fell in." The pit took up a good two-thirds of the corridor; it would be slippery footing to skirt it. The very thought of tiptoeing around the edge gave me the heebie-jeebies.

Morio examined the edges of the chasm. "I wonder if he's the one who created it. Could he know the demons are after him and be trying to hide from them? The dragon didn't seem all that concerned about him, and there's no way the wyrm can fit in this hallway. But a demon . . ."

"A demon could. But Tom is human. How could he create an illusion like this? Most of the humans who work with magic only have rudimentary skills. There are a few adepts, but very few." I stared at the pit, trying to figure out what was going on. "Could the illusion be a permanent fixture? Maybe Tom already knew about it?"

Morio shook his head. "Illusions wear off. The pit is probably an ancient sinkhole, but the illusion couldn't have been here longer than a few hours. Come on, let's get a move on. If Tom thinks demons are close, then they probably are, and the last thing we need is an underground duel to the death."

"I don't like those words," I muttered.

"What words?"

"*To the death.* There's such a ring of finality about them, and I don't have Delilah or Menolly here. Speaking of, I wonder how Delilah's doing. I just hope she managed to avoid Smoky out there."

"She probably went back to the house to check on Chase once she saw what was happening. She's a smart girl. Don't write her off as too naïve."

I shrugged. "Smart, yes. Wise? Not so much. Okay, so how do we get me around the pit?"

Morio laughed, then lightly tripped around the edges, showing no sign of unsteadiness. Once he reached the other side, he set the light on the ground and braced his back against the wall, his left hand outstretched toward me.

"Face the wall and take my hand. Then inch across. I'm strong, I'll be able to hold you if you fall."

"Right, just like I can fit in a size two dress." But with no other choice, I pressed my face against the stone wall and began a shuffling side step along the lip of the pit. Morio grasped my fingers, giving me enough sense of balance that I was able to scoot the rest of the way across without incident. I was *not* looking forward to the return trip.

When we were on solid ground again, Morio picked up the light, and we slowly progressed along the corridor. Morio tested each step before putting his weight down. Where there was one trap, there might be more.

We'd traveled another thirty yards when the passage branched again, this time with our path leading straight ahead, and a fork to the right. The fork would take us deeper into the mountain. Again, I reached out. This time, the energy was stronger and to the right.

"Take the fork," I told Morio.

We had barely turned onto the branch in the road when Morio stopped. "Look—straight ahead. See the light? That's no illusion." Sure enough, a faint glimmer of light filtered through a crack in the solid rock. We hurried along to the end of the passage, which stopped short. A dead end. End of the line.

"There has to be a hidden door," he said, running his hands over the crack. "But I don't sense an illusion. At least not any I'm familiar with."

I stood back, thinking. If there wasn't a door on the *end* of the passage, had we missed one coming down the hall? I began to hunt around, listening closely. At first, all I could hear was a gentle susurration as the air currents shifted, but then I began to hear breathing—slow and rhythmic.

I spread my hands against the rock, and sure enough, a thin stream of air flowed over my hand. The rough granite was cool against my skin as I squinted, trying to see the edges of the door. Sure enough, there it was—faint but still visible in the dim light. The door was roughly six feet tall by three feet wide. The question was, how to open it?

I motioned to Morio. As I traced the outline, he held up the foxfire light, and we inspected the rock for any sense of indentation or latch.

Near the ground, we found a handhold. I swallowed hard and reached into the dark opening. My fingers met a cold lever and—damn! I snatched them out and held them up to the light. Faint red blisters were beginning to form along the pads of my fingertips. Iron welts. The metal burn hurt like a son of a bitch, but I managed to keep my mouth shut. Morio gestured for me to stand back.

He reached down. I heard a faint click, and the door began to swing out, the stone block swiveling on its hinges.

We jumped out of the way, and the minute it was open, we squeezed through to the other side.

I gasped. The chamber into which we had stumbled was huge. Stalagmites and stalactites formed a forest of columns throughout the cavern, but most of the chamber was open and glistening. Limestone waterfalls cascaded in frozen brilliance down the walls, and a rim stone pool sat off to one side, pearls of calcite creating a glistening stone bubble bath around the edges of the mineral tub. A faint illumination emanated from the walls.

"We aren't in Kansas anymore, Toto," I muttered, glancing back at the door. Sure enough, a sparkling barrier confirmed that we'd entered a different realm. This part of the cave wouldn't be found on any map or surveyor's guide. We'd crossed through a natural portal into . . . where? Could we be in Otherworld? Or was this someplace entirely different?

"Where are we?" I whispered. Even the low flutter of my voice echoed throughout the chamber. I stepped closer to Morio, who was gazing at the alabaster beauty of the walls.

His arm curved protectively around my shoulders, and I felt his lips press gently against the top of my head. "I'm not sure, Camille. I've never felt this type of energy before, and it makes me nervous. Are you sure that Tom is here?"

I nodded. "I sense him. But how did he find this place? This portal isn't listed with the OIA, that much I can tell you." Snuggling closer, I shivered. The damp air was gone, but the tingle of magic rippled up and down my arms. Whatever had created this place—or whoever—was powerful indeed.

And then, before Morio could answer, a noise caught our attention. I stepped away, readying myself for an attack. But it wasn't a demon we were facing. A voluptuous woman over six feet tall and awe-striking stepped from behind one of the limestone pillars in the center of the room. Her dress flowed like cobwebs draping down from her shoulders, and she stood regal and serene.

"Who are you?" The words tumbled out of my mouth before I could stop them. "And where is Tom Lane?"

She blinked once, then a smile broke across her face. "You mean my pet? My poor precious boy?"

I glanced at Morio, who shook his head, as obviously confused as I was. "I don't understand. Your pet? Who are you?"

As she smiled, I saw the flecks of silver in her eyes. Was she one of the Sidhe? But then my memory sparked to life, and I knew who she was. The legends were true. So she'd refused to cross over when Otherworld severed connections with Earth.

"You're Titania, aren't you?"

As she gently inclined her head, my stomach flipped. The Faerie Queen emeritus, Titania was dangerous and unpredictable. She was far less human than the Sidhe of my own world, even though she'd remained Earthside.

Titania's gaze never left my face. "And now would you tell me," she said, "what you want with my poor, besieged, gone mad as a March hare, Tam Lin?"

CHAPTER 15

Tam Lin? Tom Lane? It all made sense now. But Tam Lin had been returned to the mortal world eons ago. Tom couldn't be Tam Lin, who lore said had lived out the rest of his life with his wife and children. Or could he?

"How is that possible? Tam Lin's been dead for hundreds of years." I slowly skirted to the left, not trusting Titania to play fair. Rumor had it she'd gone over the edge and had lost all sense of reason.

"Has he now?" Titania spoke to me, but her eyes were on Morio, and I sensed a danger in the making.

Morio must have sensed the same thing because he seemed to grow taller, more imposing. "Let us speak to Tom."

She ducked her head and smiled. Glamour, I thought. She was becoming more seductive by the moment, her face softening, the glow in her eyes growing brighter. Her breasts seemed to swell just enough to make it look as though she'd taken a long breath and held it. "Our Witchling won't tell me her name, but I know who she is. Camille, am I right?"

I blinked. So much for secrecy. "How did you find out?"

Ignoring me, Titania homed in on Morio. "You, however, I don't know. Perhaps you'll be gracious enough to give me your name?"

I glanced at him. Titania sounded three sheets to the wind. Maybe she was drunk, or the magic in the room had clouded her sight. Or maybe the years spent alone cut off from Otherworld had been too much for her to bear. Or perhaps, just perhaps, Titania had tripped off the deep end and gone mad. Whatever the case, I didn't feel safe around her.

Morio seemed to be thinking the same thing I was, because he warily held his ground. "It's a trick. He's probably *not* Tam Lin."

Titania took his bait. "Are you calling me a liar, mortal?"

"Prove you're not." The gauntlet, thrown down. Morio was a handsome man, and Titania liked handsome young men.

After a moment's hesitation, she narrowed her eyes. "You know there's no way I can prove such a thing, nor do I need to. I'm the Queen of Faerie here, and don't you forget it. When the Elemental Lords divided the realms, I chose to remain with this world and with my roots."

"Tell us about Tom," I said softly. "Please?"

She sighed, then like a drowning woman clutching at a lifesaver, slumped down on one of the limestone benches and began to talk. I had the feeling she had few friends or companions left in whom she could confide.

"I knew after a few years of brats and a nagging wife who grew older day by day, Tam Lin would return to me. And I was right. One day, he was outside the barrow, waiting for me. I took him back and kept him here for hundreds of years, feeding him my Faerie bread and letting him sip from the nectar of life. Over the years, Tam Lin lost his mortality. He now belongs to me, wholly and fully and forever." But there was a catch in her voice.

"Something went wrong, didn't it?" I asked. "What happened?"

She flashed me a cunning look, but then her eyes softened.

"Girl, half-human or not, you have the sight and no small amount of power. Consider this. You were born to your life between worlds, you know how to cope with the passing of years and the growing weight of your thoughts. Tam Lin was born mortal. *He* couldn't adjust as time went on."

I nodded, understanding. My father had offered Mother the option of drinking the nectar of life to extend her life far beyond her allotted years, but she'd been smart enough to recognize the pitfalls. She'd refused, and when she was thrown from the horse, death claimed her.

"What happened to him?" Morio's voice was gentle. He, too, understood the implications of what Titania had done.

A single tear trickled down her cheek, gleaming like a diamond, faceted with a hundred perfect prisms. "He lost his mind. He ran in the woods for months at a time with the animals. One day the Prince of Oaks found him and brought him back to my barrow. He chastised me—me! Titania, Queen of Faerie. He scolded me like a wayward child." Her voice rose, and her cheeks flushed. She paused a moment, then continued.

"He made me promise to try to help Tam adapt, and he gave him a pendant to protect him. So Tam Lin became Tom Lane, and for a time each century, he resides in the world. I use my contacts to get him the accoutrements he needs for human society. It's harder now that humans require such extensive identification. Then, we find him a simple job that keeps him occupied. Near the end of each cycle, when he begins to tire or when someone gets suspicious, my darling comes home with me, and I wipe his memory of that life. After a time spent in my chambers sleeping, he wakes to yet a new life."

Speechless, I stared at her. How selfish could you get? First, she'd bound Tom to her when she snatched him out of his world and kept him captive. Then after he escaped and returned home, she encouraged him to come back to her. Instead of wiping his memory and sending him back to his family, she'd given him a life span his mind couldn't cope with.

"By all the gods, why don't you just let him sleep? Put him in stasis until the end of time? He'd probably be happier." She could blast me if she wanted, but what she'd done went against every code I'd been raised with. Unfortunately, a lot of my full-blood kin would have a good laugh at the situation.

Titania shot off the bench. A nimbus of anger flared around her, and I automatically shielded myself.

"You're so righteous, so virtuous, are you? I can smell the Svartan on you. Don't play coy. You're playing the devil's mistress, so what gives you the right to judge me, you *half-breed*? I am Titania, Queen of Faerie. Tremble before me!" Her eyes flared with magic, but there was no oomph behind the fireworks, and I realized that all Titania had left were illusions and memories. A faded beauty queen, clinging to old photos.

"I'm not compromising anyone else with my actions," I said, striding forward. "I didn't deceive anyone." I pushed her back down on the bench and leaned over her. "Listen to me, and listen good. You chose to give up your crown and remain earthbound. Well, I've got news. The Queen of Elves adapted. And there's a new Queen of Sidhe and she'd eat you alive."

Titania's glamour wavered in the wake of my words. Yep, I knew how to pitch a fit, all right. "You're alone, Titania. Your time is past and you'd better walk into the shadows gracefully before I report your actions, in OW. Now, let us talk to Tom. By the powers of the Y'Elestrial, the OIA, and the Guard Des'Estar, *I will take him with me.*"

Morio stepped up to my side. The Queen emeritus hung her head as I pulled out my badge. Leather-worked, it was enchanted so that if it were out of my reach for more than a day, the emblem would self-destruct. That I held it in my hands was enough to prove authenticity.

Titania wrung her hands, and I almost felt sorry for her. For a good share of history she'd been the most beautiful creature on earth, commanding thousands of the Fae. Now she was forgotten. A dinosaur.

"What if we take her—" Morio started, but I stopped him, knowing what he was going to say. I pulled him off to one side and kept my voice low.

"She'd never fit into Otherworld. She'd lose it for good, just like Tam Lin lost it. Titania has too much pride to admit that she's outlived her time. Some of the Sidhe drag on millennia, but most choose to exit mortal life far earlier, when they grow tired or bored."

"I'll call Tom," Titania said, looking up. I had a feeling she'd heard us. "You may do as you like with him. We've played this game for a thousand years. I suppose it's time to call it a draw."

She rose and glided to the far wall of the cave, peering down a tunnel. I could hear her whisper faintly on the wind, calling for Tom to join us. Returning to us, she gazed into my eyes, and all artifice was gone.

"I suppose I should thank you, Witchling. You've reminded me of what I was. I will not fade into a walking shadow, nor will I subject myself to the rule of a jaded Queen who deserted the world to which she was born. Take Tam Lin and leave. The dragon will let you pass if you present him with this." She held out a sigil, cast in silver that had been forged under the moon. I could feel the power coursing within the talisman, and glanced up at her.

"You don't have to do this," I said, and she understood I wasn't talking about Tom.

"Oh, but I do," she countered. "The world has grown too small, and with Otherworld rejoining the human race, there's no place for me. I couldn't walk in the cities if I wanted to, and the wild places of the Earth are few and far between."

I turned the talisman over in my hand. Dragon rune. So Smoky had formed an alliance with Titania. Without the talisman, Titania would have no leverage to protect herself. Slipping it in my pocket, I noticed that Tom was standing in the archway to the cavern. Grizzled and worn, he was a true lumberjack, a man who had once been a knight. But his eyes were empty, and I realized that he'd long ago left the world. Where Tom's soul roamed, I wasn't sure, but he was walking wounded, half a man, his spirit existing only in the fragments of selves that the Faerie Queen had provided for him.

A pendant hung around his neck, an emerald cabochon caught in a gold and silver weave. The gem flickered, swirling into a new pattern every time I looked at it. The first spirit seal.

"My Tom, listen to me," Titania said, her voice gentle.

Morio and I exchanged looks. Regardless of her reckless choices, Titania cared for Tom. She had loved him once. Now, fractured into a hundred lifetimes, I had the feeling he'd become her pet, a beloved old lapdog whom one took care of until the end.

"You are to go with these people. They will treat you well."

He looked confused. "Where will I sleep? Who will feed me?"

Morio stepped up and gently tapped him on the shoulder. "We'll make sure you have all the comfort you need, Tom. Will you come with us?"

Tom hesitated. Then, with a prompting from Titania, he nodded. "All right, I'll go."

I drew Morio to one side. "We could just take the pendant. That's what we're after. Now that I've seen him, it seems wrong to separate them."

Morio shook his head. "I think the seal is connected to him. If we separate the two before consulting a wizard, we could drive him utterly mad. We have to take him with us."

"This just keeps getting worse and worse. What was the Prince of Oaks thinking?" I could only see chaos and destruction coming from the mess we were in. "A lot of innocent people are going to be hurt before this is over."

I glanced back at Tom and Titania. She had brushed aside a lock of hair that fell across his forehead, and he caught her hand, bringing it to his lips.

"I wish we didn't have to do this," I said. "I was wrong to speak so harshly to her. But I guess there's no going back."

"Tom will forget," Morio said, lifting my chin so that I was staring into his eyes. "He always does, you know, each time she wipes his memory. Perhaps your healers will be able to free him from the wine of life, or they may be able to send him to his final slumber."

Rip Van Winkle, only sleeping for a thousand years instead of twenty. Or, they might just kill him—swiftly and without pain. The Court and Crown seldom concerned itself with humans, and this would be another blot on our history when the truth came out.

"All right, let's take him and get back home. I'll go as escort when we ship him through the portal. I just wish Trillian were here," I said, rubbing my head. What I wouldn't give for some ibuprofen. "I'd feel a lot safer with him around." Trillian had no compunctions about defending himself and those he was sworn to protect, even if it meant fighting dirty. And now, we didn't even know if he was going to live.

Morio seemed to understand what I was thinking. "As much as I resent his presence, I wish only the best for him. We'll find out how he's doing. I promise you that. And if necessary, I'll go with you to Otherworld to deliver Tom to the OIA."

We turned back to Titania, who reached up on tiptoes to kiss Tom gently on the lips. "Farewell, my brave knight. We've had a long run of it, but the play is over, the curtain falls, and it's time for the actors to go home." She cocked her head, looking me in the eye. "Take care of him, please. Don't let anything happen to him."

I nodded, my mood plummeting even farther into the black. "I'll do my best to keep him safe. Titania, know that you're helping to save two worlds by letting us take him. He carries a vital secret, even if he doesn't know it. I'll let you know what happens to him."

She shook her head. "No, it's better that he just be cut out of my life. Go now, please just go, and leave me to my silence."

Morio took Tom gently by the arm and, with me leading

the way, we headed out of the cavern, leaving the ancient Queen behind. I hadn't thought her capable of love, and perhaps I was right, but apparently she had more feelings than I gave her credit for.

The trek back seemed quicker than finding our way into the barrow. The pits that guarded the passageway were still an obstacle, but together Morio and I helped Tom make it past without incident. I wanted to touch the spirit seal, to feel the power that resided within, but was smart enough to keep my fingers out of the cookie jar.

Tom seemed rather chipper for leaving his ladylove. At first, he acted like he'd been drugged, but the farther away from Titania we got, the more alert he became. As we approached the entrance to the cave, he stopped, staring at the opening.

"I don't want to go out there," he said, his gaze locked on the entrance.

"Why? What's wrong?"

"They'll be coming to get me," he said.

I glanced at Morio. Just what did we have here? "Who's coming to get you, Tom? Is somebody after you?"

He hesitated, then—like a child deciding to put his trust in an authority figure—shrugged. "I don't know who they are, but early this morning, somebody was sneaking around outside the house, and I got scared. So I ran through the woods and hid with Titania."

I stared at Tom for a moment. He wasn't as out of it as I'd thought. Maybe being near Titania acted like a drug in his bloodstream. "Did you see what they looked like? Do you know how many were out there?"

Tom scrunched his lower lip, thinking. After a moment he said, "I think there were three of them. Two men and a woman."

Two men and a woman. I looked over at Morio. "Has to be Bad Ass Luke, the Psycho Babbler, and Wisteria. Once the harpy died, they must have recruited Wisteria for more than helping them slip through the portal. I'll bet they threatened to kill her if she didn't do what they wanted."

Morio concurred. "You're probably right." He turned to Tom. "They were outside your house?"

"Yep," Tom said, shaking his head. "I was out in the woods fishing for breakfast. The trout run real good in a stream that I found. When I was coming back with my catch, I heard something in the driveway. I snuck up along the trail first to see who it was. I don't like strangers. I saw three people near my place. It was still too dark to get a good look at them, and I didn't stick around 'cause they felt nasty," he said, almost apologetically.

I sighed. Obviously, the demons had come looking for him. We were lucky that Tom had been foraging for his breakfast. Otherwise, they'd have the spirit seal and be on their way back to the Subterranean Realms. But where were they now? They'd left Wisteria in the house, but what about Bad Ass Luke and the Psycho Babbler? Would we be able to smuggle Tom back to the city before they tried to snatch him from us? I bit my lip, trying to decide what to do next.

Morio peeked out of the cave. "Smoky's still out there," he said.

I glanced at the dragon. "I wonder . . . Titania gave us an emblem to pass as friends. I wonder if that might be enough to convince him to guard us while we hustle Tom back to the car?"

"Can't hurt to try. Or rather, we don't have a choice, so we might as well ask him." Morio turned to Tom. "Are you afraid of that dragon out there?"

Tom shook his head. "Nope. He's a good sort, for a dragon. I always come out here and have a chat with him when I'm lonely. He threatens to eat me a lot, but since I belong to Titania, he won't do it."

"Well, we can't just stay here all day," I said. "You two wait while I go have a talk with Mr. Fire-breath." I stepped out of the cave and whistled to Smoky. "Hey you, dragon!"

He swiveled his head to stare down at me. "Where's the pest?"

"Inside the cave." I held up the emblem. "Titania said to show you this."

That had an effect. Smoky blinked and reared back. "She gave you her pass? Well then, little Witchling, you must be special indeed. Go on your way, and I won't make you my dinner."

All the talk about dinners and desserts was beginning to annoy me. "Listen, *Smoky*—"

"What did you call me?" He leaned in, and I found myself staring into a giant eyeball that looked like a wall of ice. "Little witch, don't be too forward."

"I don't know your name, so I have to call you something other than 'hey you' or 'dragon,' don't I? So I'm calling you Smoky as long as you refuse to give us your name." I sighed. This was getting us nowhere, or worse—could be netting us an invitation to dinner.

But he laughed. "Too bad you can't stay awhile and play."

"Listen, we could really use your help," I said. "You could do wonders for us if you'd be willing to give us a hand."

"So now you need my help, do you?" He blinked; the gust from his eyelids actually ruffled my hair. "What do you want?"

I cleared my throat. "We have Tom, and we're taking him with us. We need an escort to his house. There are demons prowling the woods, Smoky, and they're bent on capturing Tom. They're not exactly planning a picnic for him, either. If they take him away from us, the whole world's going to suffer."

Sure, dragons could be downright mean, and they often snatched up passersby for a snack, but they weren't evil in the way that demons were evil. And lucky for us, they usually didn't like Demonkin. I'd studied my dragon lore in school.

Smoky frowned—not an easy task for a dragon—and after a pause that seemed to last forever, said, "Demons, is it? They're bloody well unwelcome in *my* woodland. Come on, I'll guard you on the way back to the house."

I whistled for Morio and Tom as the dragon drew back. A brilliant flash of light blinded me, and when it dissipated and

I could see again, a tall man in a long white cloak was standing next to me. He had flowing silver hair that reached his ankles, and his skin might have been made of alabaster. But his eyes were those same twin glacial pools that had stared me down. I'd heard that dragons could take human form—at least the older ones—but had never known whether it was true or not. I guess this answered my question.

Morio's eyes went wide as he looked up at the lean giant. "You are—"

The man gave us a thin smile. "Smoky, apparently. Come then, let's get you back to Tom's house before I get bored."

We traipsed through the woodland with Smoky in the lead. I hung back a little, studying the creature-turned-human. He was handsome, though stern, but there was far more to his aura than to his looks. That ancient dragon energy imbued him with a regal stance. While he might eat me up in dragon form, he would never be rude or crude as a human. He might take what or who he desired without a second thought, but he would do so with courtesy.

"You find me perplexing?" he said without turning around.

I blushed. Somehow he'd sensed my fascination. "Just . . . different," I said, stumbling over my words. All my charm, poise, and experience seemed to have just flown the coop. Out with the bathwater, just like the baby.

Morio stared at him openly. "So tell me, if a human were to stumble on you in the woods, and you knew they were coming, what would they find?"

Smoky chuckled. "Why me, of course. As I am now. They'd find me a pleasantly eccentric hiker, out for a jaunt. Of course, I'd be wearing jeans and a leather jacket. Unless, of course, I was hungry and they were alone and there was no chance of me being caught." He let out a laugh that reminded me I was talking to a dragon, not a man.

"Do you eat a lot of people?" I asked, not sure if I wanted to know.

"The question is, how many do you consider *a lot*?"

I glanced at him, and he flashed me a smooth grin. Oh yeah, dragons were charming, all right.

"I find my food as I need it," he said.

I could tell I wasn't going to get a straight answer out of him on that question. Or probably many others. Dragons loved to speak in riddles.

As we came up on the edge of the path leading to Tom's house, I began to get nervous. What would we find? Would the demons be there? Were Delilah and Chase okay? Smoky went first, his long white robe swishing around his legs as he strode out in the open.

"Well, he's not afraid," Morio said in a low voice.

"He doesn't need to be afraid," Tom answered.

I laughed. "You're absolutely right, Tom. Say, listen to me for a minute," I said, sobering. "You have to stay with us. Unless we tell you that somebody's safe, don't go off with anybody else, and don't let yourself trail behind. You need to be with us at all times."

"Okay, but I wish I knew what you guys wanted me for. I'm nothing special." He frowned, looking vaguely disconcerted.

I tried to think of a reasonable explanation that would hold him off until we got back to Otherworld. I didn't want Tom knowing anything about the pendant hanging around his neck for now. He might get some half-cocked idea to play hero and try to use whatever other powers the pendant might have. I could sense that there were strengths hidden in that stone that hadn't been mentioned in the book that Grandmother Coyote gave to me.

Smoky whistled, and we slipped out of the undergrowth. As we entered the clearing, the door to the house opened, and Delilah came out, followed by Chase, who had apparently recovered enough to walk. They looked from Smoky to Tom, and started down the stairs.

"Everything's okay—" I started to say when I was startled by a noise from behind an ancient cedar growing near the house. In unison, we turned to look as a man stumbled out from behind the tree.

He was wild-eyed, with hair sticking out from his head, a real Albert Einstein type, and he wore a crazy getup that looked a lot like chain mail. On closer look, I had the sneaking suspicion it was made of tinfoil.

"Oh boy," I muttered under my breath. "Just what we need—another Froot Loop."

"Froot Loop is right," Smoky said, turning a bland eye to our visitor, who was busy trying to extricate what looked like a long knife out of a sheath attached to his leg. "I see my buddy's back."

"Your buddy?" Morio asked, inserting himself in front of Tom. "You know this guy?"

"He's not one of the demons," I said.

Smoky snorted. "Demon? Hardly. No, I have a run-in with this little fellow every few months. He must have at least twenty tries under his belt."

"Twenty tries?" I said, feeling a little lost. "Tries to what?"

"To kill me," Smoky said, striding forward. "Witchling, meet Saint George. Good old George has been trying to kill a dragon for the past fifteen years, and apparently I am still his target of choice."

CHAPTER 16

~~~~~

Saint George? I stared at him, confused for a moment, then snapped my fingers. "Georgio Profeta—that's his name, isn't it?"

At that moment, Delilah came running down from the steps. Georgio—or Saint George, whatever his name might be—didn't notice her until she'd leapt on his back, knocking him to the ground. Chase followed more sedately. He still looked a little green around the gills, and I had a feeling he'd have his jewels on ice before the day was out. Delilah wouldn't be getting any tonight, that was for sure.

Smoky sauntered up to the would-be hero. He knelt down, giving Delilah a quick look before turning his attention to the man sprawled out beneath her. "George, George, George. What am I going to do with you? I told you to give it up. You're never going to kill me, so just go home, forget this happened, and next time go hunt windmills." He sounded almost fond of the man.

Delilah jumped up as I skidded to a halt next to them. "Who are these people?" she asked.

I blinked. "Well, I think that we've seen Mr. Profeta

before—or at least his jacket. And this," I indicated Smoky, who had crossed his arms and was observing the whole scene with a look of mild amusement. "Meet Smoky the dragon."

"I thought Smoky was a bear," she said, snickering.

"No, no, no. D-r-a-g-o-n, *dragon*. Meaning no names, got it?"

She clapped her hand to her mouth. "Oh . . . oh! Yeah, got it."

Dragons were cunning, and as much as I was beginning to like Smoky, it wouldn't do us any good if he had our names.

"You're a harsh-hearted woman, my little Witchling," he said, leaning down to plant a faint kiss on my forehead. I almost swooned under the swirl of energy as his lips met my skin but managed to backtrack from *that* thought quick enough to keep it from getting me in trouble. The edges of a grin played around his lips as he motioned to Delilah, who was staring at us with an incredulous look on her face. "You—girl—help him up. He can't hurt me, and he won't hurt you."

Delilah looked at me. I nodded. She reached down and grabbed Georgio by the elbow, helping him up. As he tried to smooth his wannabe chain mail, she helped him shake out the armor. Chase had reached us by then, and as he reached for his gun, I shook my head.

"Not a good idea," I said, giving a little jerk of my head in Smoky's direction.

Smoky took a long look at Chase and flashed him a wide, beguiling smile. "How do you do. You must be—?" He let his voice drift. It was a charming voice, an inviting one, one that made you want to spill your guts to the person speaking.

Chase started to open his mouth, but I grabbed his arm and yanked him off to the side, reaping an "Ouch" for my troubles.

"I'm sorry, I know you must still be hurting, but trust me, you do not want to give that man your name. And whatever you do, don't address any of us by name in front of him. Remember the dragon we were talking about? Welcome to his world."

"Dragon?" Chase's look changed from confused to *Oh God, not again.*

"Yes, I said *dragon*. And a powerful one at that. Smoky may look all man, but trust me, under that gorgeous hunk of man flesh is a pure, fire-breathing dragon. And if he learns your name, he can use it to control you."

Chase glanced at Smoky, then back at me. "Gorgeous, huh? He doesn't look like a dragon, although I'll admit he has an arrogant enough stance to him."

"Yeah, well, an hour ago he was big enough to squash your house."

"You mean dragons can change shape into humans?" He groaned. "Oh great, so I may have talked to a dragon say . . . oh . . . twenty years ago and never known it?"

"That about sums it up," I said. "Though most of them don't make a point of meandering through the city streets chatting up humans. They tend to . . . well . . . to eat them instead. Or enslave them."

Once again he flashed me a dry smirk that held just enough fear behind it to tell me that Chase believed me. "Say," he said, so casually that I knew he was putting up a front. "You don't think Delilah thinks he's cute?"

I repressed a snicker. "Chase, dude . . . get real. Do you drool after supermodels? Heidi Klum? Tyra Banks?"

For once he blushed and stared at the ground. "Uh . . . uh . . ."

"Yeah, that's what I thought. So just deal with the fact that Smoky's a supermodel to the Faerie world. Gorgeous, sexy, and as alpha-male as you can get. He makes Trillian look like a Boy Scout, and trust me, that's hard to do." Once again, the thought of my Svartan lover hanging between life and death choked me up, but I managed to push the thought to the side. Grief later. Take care of business now.

Chase grimaced. "Okay, okay. So, who's the dude on the ground?"

"Georgio Profeta, our mysterious visitor who had the

picture of Tom Lane in his notebook. By the way, we've found out something about Tom. He's actually Tam Lin of legend. He was ensnared by the Faerie Queen's spell centuries ago and has been living a series of well-planned lives since then, though he doesn't remember who he was originally or how old he is."

"Oh, this is just getting better and better," Chase said, groaning. "So he's like some sort of *Highlander* character?"

I frowned, then understood the reference. A movie that Chase had recommended some time back. Delilah and I'd watched it but had been relatively unimpressed except by what a great voice Christopher Lambert had.

"Well, not exactly. Tom's not going to end up ruling the world, and he's not immortal, though he's probably one of the oldest humans on record, thanks to some well-timed nectar of life."

"Nectar of life?" Chase's eyebrows did a little dance. "We really have to have a long talk at some point. Okay, so what do we do? Have the demons been out here? And what do we do with veggie-girl, who's still tied up inside?"

I frowned. By all rights, we should return her to Otherworld for questioning. "We'll take her with us, which means making sure she's bound and gagged all the way. This is turning into a real joyride, isn't it? I'm going to go question Georgio and find out just what he was doing outside our house. Why don't you take Delilah and Morio inside and truss up Wisteria for traveling?"

Chase glanced at Smoky. "Will you be safe with that thing?"

I grinned. "Yeah, I think he likes me. Whether or not that's a good thing, I'm not entirely sure. Go on, we want to get out of here before Bad Ass Luke et al. return. I'd sure like to have Smoky on my side when they do."

Chase motioned to Delilah and Morio, and they took the steps two at a time. Tom sat down, digging at the ground with the heel of one boot. Smoky gave me a veiled look that I could barely decipher, though what little I could made me nervous.

Dragons sometimes took human form to lure in mates—they were all as lecherous as they were powerful. While no children were born of the unions, it could be a bizarre and frightening match. Not that I'd ever experienced it, mind you—though looking at the tall, lean, absolutely beautiful form Smoky had taken, I understood the temptation.

I shook my head to clear my thoughts. Apparently my paralyzed libido had been thawed full force, thanks to Trillian and Morio, but it looked like I was leaning toward dangerous—albeit fun—territory. I edged over to Georgio, who was slumped on the ground staring up at Smoky. Kneeling beside him, I tapped him on the shoulder. He looked like a little boy who'd managed to get aboard the carousel but who'd lost the brass ring.

He looked up at me, his expression both sweet and bewildered. "Yes?"

"Your name is Georgio, isn't it? Georgio Profeta."

He blinked, as if thinking about the question, then nodded.

Not very talkative. I tried again. "What were you doing outside my house? We have your notebook and jacket."

After another moment, he said in a whisper, "I was in the bar when you were talking to that Japanese man about how you were looking for Tom Lane. I thought you were coming out here to kill the dragon, and I couldn't let you do that. It's *my* destiny, so I followed you home to find out who you were."

So he thought we were out to vanquish Smoky? "Georgio, we didn't even know about the dragon until we found your notebook. How long have you known about him?"

"A long time," he said, his eyes downcast.

I glanced up at Smoky, who was listening with interest. "Just how many people know about you?"

He winked, one lip curling into a smile. "Too many. I've been around here a long time. But most people don't ever find a trace of me. I'm good with illusion, as you and your boyfriend know."

"He's just a friend," I said.

"If he's just a friend, then I'd love to see how you treat a lover," Smoky said with a snort. A faint wash of smoke wafted out from his nose, and I blinked, wondering just where the line stopped between dragon and man. In a persuasive voice, he added, "You don't have a boyfriend, Witchling?"

"Wipe that smirk off your face," I said. It just occurred to me that Smoky had probably had a perfect view of Morio and me having sex. If so, he must have gotten an eyeful. "I do have a boyfriend, and he's a Svartan, so play nice, because he won't if he thinks somebody's bothering me."

Smoky's eyes flashed. "Don't threaten me, girl. Don't you ever, ever forget who you're talking to when you talk to me."

I cringed. Not good, nope, not good. No matter how smarmy they got, a dragon was a dragon, whether in human form or not. "I'm sorry," I said in a little voice. "Don't toast me."

He let out a loud grunt. "Faeries . . . you're all a bunch of pests." After a pause, he said. "So, you have a Svartan boyfriend, and you're cavorting with a fox demon? That's a new one."

I held my tongue. Sometimes silence really was the better part of valor.

He continued. "Anyway, I've been mistaken for a flying saucer more than once, which just goes to show you how people see what they want to see. Humans are a fanciful bunch."

Turning back to Georgio, I said, "My friend, we aren't out to kill Smoky here. We were looking for Tom, that's all. But listen. You can't go around slaying dragons. It's dangerous, and you'll end up getting eaten."

Georgio's lower lip trembled. "But I'm Saint George. It's my destiny to slay dragons."

As I stared into his eyes, I realized that Georgio truly believed what he was saying. Unlike Tom's prestigious past, however, Georgio wasn't the actual saint he purported to be, and if he tried to slay the dragon, he'd be dead before he could lift his sword. He needed to be home safe, watched so he couldn't hurt himself. I reached out and fingered his chain mail. As I'd suspected, it was a replica, spray-painted plastic—uncomfortable and of utterly no protection.

I stood up and walked over to Smoky, my nose quivering as I drew near. The smell of smoke and musk filled the air, and I straightened my shoulders.

"Tell me more about him," I said, nodding at Georgio, who was playing with the rings of his armor.

Smoky frowned, a look of distaste crossing his face. "He thinks he's a dragon slayer. When he first started coming around I was wary, but for some reason the man fascinated me, and I let him live. After the second time, I went into the city in disguise to do a little digging. Turns out Georgio has a few bolts loose in his head, but he's not dangerous. He lives with his grandmother and works in a market, sweeping floors and doing other simple tasks."

Any other dragon would have already snarfed down the poor man without a second thought. Before I realized what I was doing, I reached out and rested my fingers on Smoky's arm.

"You feel sorry for him, don't you? That's why you don't kill him."

Smoky gazed at my hand for a long minute, then gently shrugged me off. "I feel pity for no man." But the look on his face told me I was right. "Besides, he'd be too tough and stringy."

"You didn't kill Tom either, though you had the chance," I said. "Face it—you have a soft spot for humans. When's the last time you ate one?"

Smoky grabbed me around the waist and yanked me close to him. My feet dangled off the ground. His breath thick, he pressed his forehead against mine, staring into my eyes.

"Witchling, once again I warn you: don't press your luck."

I struggled, but he held fast. Feeling like an idiot, I stammered out a contrite apology. "I'm sorry, really. Please, let me go."

Smoky squeezed me tighter. "I could carry you off," he murmured, sniffing my hair. "No one would dare try to stop me. After all, you owe me for my protection."

"Smoky," I said, trying to keep my voice even. "Please let me go. So much depends on getting Tom Lane away from here before the demons return." I wasn't about to tell him that Tom's pendant carried a hefty power behind it— that would ensure that Smoky became the new guardian of the seal.

His eyes shifted, a dizzying array of colors swirling in the icy depths of the glacier. I felt myself being sucked in as I lost interest in freeing myself. He buried his nose in my hair and slowly, deliberately, licked my ear. I closed my eyes, but then he let go, setting me down gently.

Shaking, I said, "Thank you for letting me go. Again, I'm sorry."

The dragon gazed at me with eyes that were aloof and cool. "Go," he said. "Don't worry about young George here; I'll see that he goes home without being scratched. But, little witch, I'll see you soon. I guarantee it."

I hastily backed away. "Come on, Tom, we have to hurry," I said. As we headed toward the house, I glanced over my shoulder. Smoky stood at the edge of the wood, and I could feel him watching every step I took. When he saw me looking, he briefly raised one hand, then vanished into the forest with Georgio following him like a puppy dog.

We hurried up the stairs just in time to see Delilah and Chase guiding Morio down the stairs. He'd thrown Wisteria over his shoulder. She was trussed up tight as a turkey, and her mouth was firmly gagged.

"Let's get moving," I said, a sense of urgency pushing me on. "Events are moving. I can feel them on the wind."

We piled in the car. Delilah volunteered to drive, since Chase was still coping with his bruises. Wisteria had come very close to ensuring he never fathered a child. As we swung out of the drive, back onto the graveled road, I thanked my lucky stars that we'd managed to get Tom away from Titania. All in all, things had gone more smoothly than I expected, but we weren't home free by any means.

The mood on the drive home was heavy. For one thing, we had a gagged and bound floraed with us who was intent on helping the demons wipe out the human race. For another, Bad Ass Luke knew we had Tom. A whisper on the breeze going past told me he'd found out and was cursing our names. The more I thought about it, the more worried I became. Frustrated, I looked out the window.

"Can't this car move any faster?"

Chase shook his head from the passenger seat next to Delilah. "Not a good idea, Camille. We don't want the State Patrol stopping us. I have my badge, but even so, with Wisteria tied up in the back, it wouldn't look good."

He had a point. I glanced back at Morio, who sat next to the bound and gagged floraed in the back of the SUV. He kept his gaze trained on her, alert for the slightest hint that she might be up to something. The OIA would need to know that there was a spy in their midst. And Wisteria could potentially shed a lot of light on what Shadow Wing's plans were.

"Should I drive straight to the Wayfarer?" Delilah asked.

I mulled it over. That would be the most expedient route, but chances were, at least one of the two remaining demons would be there waiting for us. I shook my head. "No. Menolly said there are a couple of secret entrances to the bar, but to find them we'll need her. I think we should hole up at home until she wakes, and then she can lead us in a roundabout way."

"We may have killed the skinwalker, but I'm pretty sure the demons have other allies besides plant-girl here," Morio interjected. "So we'd better be on alert for more than just Bad Ass Luke and the Psycho Babbler."

"Good point," I said. "Head home, Delilah, but take the

side roads and enter via the driveway in the back. We don't want to announce our arrival."

The first edges of dusk were creeping across the sky when we pulled into the rough driveway that led through the acreage to our back door. As I slowly scanned the area, a tingle raced from the back of my neck down through my arms. Demonic aura, that much I could tell.

"Somebody's here," I muttered. "I hope to hell everybody's okay."

Delilah eased her foot off the gas pedal, and we coasted to a stop next to a huge oak tree whose limbs and boughs spread up and over the top of our house. She let the engine idle as she glanced back at me.

"What now? Do we just get out and go in?"

I considered our options. "I think I'd better go in. Chase, you come with me. Delilah and Morio stay here to keep a watch on Wisteria and Tom. If anything happens to us, get out of here fast. Head for the Wayfarer."

Chase and I stepped out onto the muddy ground. He was still looking pained but seemed to be okay overall. When he reached inside his jacket and pulled out his gun, I sidled up to him.

"Bullets won't do you any good against a demon unless you've got blessed water on them."

He blinked. "Holy water?"

I shook my head. "Blessed—holy water may work, but blessed water is enchanted by wizards who specifically know how to handle demons."

Chase cleared his throat. "I don't suppose you have any on hand?"

"No," I said. "And I don't happen to have a wizard of that caliber on hand, either. I wish we did; this would be so much easier. But OIA has grown so lazy over the years that we aren't prepared for things like this. However . . ." I paused, thinking about the Wayfarer. "Maybe there's a bottle or two down at the bar. I doubt it, but maybe we'll luck out."

"Should we head there now?" He hesitated, staring at the back porch. I realized that Chase was afraid. Belonging to OIA had been a fun game, one that felt powerful and important, but now that we were actually facing an enemy, his job had lost some of its appeal.

I took the lead and headed up the stairs. "We don't have that luxury. We'd put them on guard for sure. Come on, Chase. Just keep your wits about you. Maybe I'm smelling the aura of some lesser creature that wandered through our grounds. An imp or something."

I cautiously edged the screen door open. We kept a lot of our outdoor wear on the back porch, as well as a freezer and other odds and ends—the same as any human family would do. Though I had to admit, most families didn't have hundred-pound bags of rock salt sitting around, nor a litter box for one of their sisters. Chase followed, his gaze never leaving my back. I sensed that he was taking his cues from me and hoped I wouldn't let either of us down.

The door to the kitchen was locked. I silently inserted the key, trying to peer through the crack where the curtains didn't quite fall together. From what I could see, the way looked clear, but that didn't prove anything, and I knew that some demons could blend into their environments.

Before I pushed the door open, I took a deep breath and summoned the power of the Moon Mother. The charge built in my hands, and when I felt armed and ready, I gently pushed the door open with my shoulder and slipped into the kitchen, taking in the entire room in one glance.

The kitchen was empty, but something felt off. As I looked around, trying to place the out-of-synch energy, I realized Maggie's box was gone. And no sign of Iris, who normally would have her head stuck in the refrigerator. House sprites liked to eat. *Hell, what had happened to them?*

Chase crowded up behind me.

"Step back a couple feet, I've got energy hanging on my hands that could blast you in two—you don't want to accidentally get in the way," I said, keeping my voice low.

He complied, his gun cautiously pointed to the ceiling as he looked around nervously. "What next?"

"I want to know where Maggie and Iris are," I said, narrowing my eyes. "I expected to find them both in the kitchen, but they aren't. There may be a logical explanation, but I don't like the energy that's floating around."

When I tuned in, it was as if static had overtaken the airwaves. I couldn't sense Maggie anywhere, nor Iris or Menolly. I stared down the hall toward the living room. The demonic aura was coming from there and was growing in intensity. Whoever we were facing had more power than I wanted to meet at the end of a wand.

I debated summoning Delilah and Morio, but that would leave Tom unattended. We didn't dare bring him in until we'd made sure the house was secure. The nasty thought that the demons had split up occurred to me—it would be just like them. In which case, defeating one would be easier than two, but it also meant we would have to be on guard for that much longer.

Step by step I made my way down the hall, praying that the demons hadn't found Iris and Maggie. I hadn't thought about them being in danger this morning—our house was warded. But something had gotten through. My stomach fluttered as I thought about the possibilities, and I breathed a silent prayer that my imagination was working overtime. I'd been stupid to leave them unprotected.

Chase followed me. I could smell both his fear and his anticipation, and I knew there was a part of him enjoying this. *The hunt, the chase.* I understood that side all too well. The Moon Mother and all who followed her—be they moon witch or Were or member of the Hunt—could be a bloodthirsty crew. She was no gentle goddess watching over children and whispering Faerie stories, but a cold and stark mistress who demanded her due.

We approached the end of the hallway leading into the living room, and I sensed movement nearby. I inhaled deeply, readying myself.

As I swung around the corner into the living room, I saw

a tall man standing in the middle of the room. A shocking gold spiky haircut topped his head, and his eyes were brilliant crimson, with no pupils to be seen. He was wearing a silk shirt and brown trousers, but they phased in and out along with his body, and I realized that I was looking at an illusion. If Morio had been with me, he would have been able to dispel it so we could see the creature's true form, but Chase pulled up short, fully taken in by the sight.

"He's beautiful—" Chase started to say.

"No," I cut him off. "It's an illusion. He's a Psycho Babbler, and he can charm you, so be cautious."

The golden man laughed, but it wasn't friendly. Definitely not Santa Claus, I thought. I'd met Santa, and he was truly a saint in rough clothing. This man . . . not man— demon—this demon was wrapped up in a pretty package, but he was evil incarnate, and if I didn't keep my focus, he'd take advantage of any slip or opening. And we'd be on a one-way ride to hell.

"Don't look him in the face," I said to Chase, keeping my gaze on the Psycho Babbler's hands. I suddenly realized that I had no idea what powers this creature had besides his ability to charm humans and half-humans. For all I knew, he was as dangerous as Smoky. What I wouldn't give to have that dragon standing beside me right now.

"Give me the man, and I'll let you live," the demon said.

"What man? This man?" I nodded at Chase, playing dumb. I wanted to ask about Iris and Maggie, but on the off chance that they'd managed to hide, I didn't want to alert the creature to their presence.

The Babbler looked at Chase and snorted. For just a moment, his illusion wavered, and I saw his true form. He was dark and thick, with reptilian hide, and looked like a bipedal gecko with fangs curving out of his mouth like warthog tusks. His fingers were tipped with razor-sharp claws. One swipe could gut me.

"Hell. Chase, get out of here and go get Morio and Delilah. Take their place and lock the car doors." I blocked the way, inserting myself between the two men. When

Chase hesitated, I said, "Now! Do as I say, or you're going to die. Trust me."

Chase turned and ran as I focused on the glowing balls of moonlight that were balanced on my fingertips. Enough talk.

"Burn!" I yelled, thrusting my palms toward the Psycho Babbler. The force shot out from my hands, striking him full in the chest. He staggered back as a swirl of smoke rose from his skin, and the illusion he'd been projecting vanished. I darted back around the doorway, hiding behind the arch that led into the living room as I summoned more power. As I drew the moonlight into my hands, I ran through my repertoire of spells, but none were as direct as the energy blasts. They were the least likely to backfire, too.

I listened, trying to pinpoint the heavy breathing of the demon, but the air was silent. That was strange. I *should* be able to hear him, especially with the wards I'd set up in the house. I knew better than to just peek around the corner, but I had to find out where he'd gone. If he was just on the other side of the doorway, all it would take was one swipe from around the corner. However, he might have climbed through the window out onto the porch.

Steeling my courage, I cautiously inched around the corner, peering into the empty room. The windows were closed, yet there was no sign of him. Where the hell had he gone? It shouldn't be too hard to follow his signature, but doing so would leave me vulnerable, because I couldn't keep my spell at the ready and locate him at the same time.

I reluctantly shifted focus and began looking for the auric signature of the creature. There! He'd moved toward the center of the room, the sparkles of purple and crimson were as clear as footprints in wet sand, but then they abruptly vanished. Damn it. He'd teleported or muted his trail in some other manner. He could be anywhere.

Frustrated, I dropped my guard. My first mistake. My second mistake almost killed me. I was so immersed in wondering where the Psycho Babbler had gone that I didn't notice a rustling behind me. The next thing I knew, thick hands wrapped themselves around my waist as the demon caught me up.

"Give me the man, and I won't tear you to shreds," he said, his voice raspy. But even as he spoke, I heard another sound from behind us. The Psycho Babbler let out a short scream as I fell to the floor. Catching myself, I whirled around in time to see him towering over Iris, who had stabbed him in the back with a pair of pruning shears. He took a step toward her as she backed away, a terrified look in her eyes.

CHAPTER 17

"Iris, run! Go get help!"

Before he could hit her, I dropped to the floor, rolling my full weight against the back of his legs. The Psycho Babbler wavered, then began to fall forward, cursing in the Hellanic tongue—not to be confused with Hellenic. As he thundered to the floor, I crouched, squatting as I called down the lightning. No time for a slow, steady build, I willed the crackling forks to shoot from the heavens.

The demon flicked his tongue as he staggered to his feet. His skin was like armor, scaled and leathery and a coppery shade of rust, and as he opened his mouth, I could see gleaming droplets clinging to his tusks and teeth. Great, the dude had envenomed saliva, a common trait with minor demons.

"Ugly bugger, aren't you?" I felt the niggling kiss of the lightning and opened wide to the power. As the full fury slammed through my body, I struggled to keep conscious. If I passed out, the energy would turn on me and crisp me alive.

I staggered to my feet. The Psycho Babbler did the

same, and we squared off, like Jukon fighters from the island nations of Otherworld, awaiting the signal to begin. And, like Jukon fighters, we were in this to the death. *Unlike* the ocean warriors, I wasn't ready to die at a moment's notice.

"Give it up, girl. You know you can't win against me," the demon said, his voice thick and whistling around his big, sloppy tongue.

I ignored the taunt, narrowing my concentration as the charge built in my body. I felt myself growing tall and terrifying as forks began to flicker off my body. Inhaling, I whispered a prayer to the Moon Mother, and she answered. Strong, she was, and her quicksilver blood flowed through my body, blood to blood, breath to breath, flesh to flesh. With one last breath, I raised my hands. Demon he may be, but I was half-Faerie and a witch, and even if my powers did short-circuit on occasion, I still summoned the moon and lightning to do my bidding.

He paused, his eyes narrowing. "Witch—"

"You've got that right," I said. "And you forgot Etiquette Lesson 101. Never, *ever* make a witch angry." And then I loosed the lightning. Twin forks shot out of my hands, catching him square in the chest. He grunted, stumbling as the smell of burning flesh hit my nostrils. I immediately began readying for another attack.

He lurched forward, swiping at me with one of his great paws, and I nimbly dodged the attack. The demon took another swing, this time missing me by mere inches. I hastily jumped aside, trying not to lose my balance. If I didn't get somebody in here fast, I was going to end up on the bad end of the shish kebab.

I strained my ears, listening for the sound of approaching help. Nada. And then I heard something—a faint clicking from the kitchen. I shot a quick glance out the window and saw that dusk had fallen early, thanks to the heavy cloud cover.

"Yo! Demon! Come kiss my ass," a familiar voice sliced through the room. As the Psycho Babbler turned, I caught a glimpse of Menolly, her eyes glowing crimson, fangs fully extended. As she vaulted toward him, I hit him with another blast, aiming for his legs. His hide was so tough that the energy charred his skin but did little other damage.

Thunder rumbled through the room as the lightning raced through his body. Menolly grunted—the lightning wouldn't hurt her, but she didn't like it. The demon apparently liked it even less. He swung around, and his claws barely missed me, but he managed to fall on me, knocking me to the ground. I screamed as his toothy grin came within inches of my face, but then he rose in the air as if a marionette on a string, and I saw that Menolly, my slight, petite sister, had hold of him with one hand.

I made tracks, backpedaling out of the way. As I watched, Menolly reared back, mouth open. Her fangs glistened like deadly needles. Enthralled by the bloodlust, she tossed the demon to the ground and fell on him, biting deep into his neck. The Psycho Babbler struggled, but she held him down, and I could hear the sucking noise as she gorged herself on his blood.

Queasy, I stared at her in morbid fascination. I'd never seen Menolly feed before—at least not like this. I'd seen her take blood from strangers, but she always left them alive and relatively unharmed when I was with her. This time, her intent wasn't to feed but to kill. I knew vampires were strong, but I hadn't realized she was this strong. And even though it was a him-or-us situation, the sight of her thrall bothered me, but I pushed aside my distaste. There was no room for mercy here, nor compassion. The Psycho Babbler would have killed all of us if he had the chance.

Besides, I was having my own problems. I began to shake as cramps raced through my body. Calling down the lightning had its drawbacks, especially when I summoned so much in such a short amount of time. As I leaned against the doorframe, Morio raced in. He took in the situation and crossed to my side.

"Are you okay?" he asked.

I nodded, cringing as the demon gurgled and collapsed.

Menolly leaned over him in a preternatural stance, bent almost double, on her tiptoes. Blood trickled down her chin . . . dark blood, almost black, but blood nonetheless. A wild look filled her eyes, and she held out her hand, warning us to keep away.

"Don't come near me yet," she said, her voice hoarse. "I'll be back in a moment." She eased out of the room, retreating to the kitchen.

"Is she all right?" Morio whispered.

"She's still in the grips of her bloodlust," I said, wincing as a spasm hit my back. "Cripes, this hurts. Anyway, Menolly will be back when she's regained control. Meanwhile, we might as well have a look at the Psycho Babbler." I stretched, arching my back as I tried to work out the kinks.

"Ready?" Morio asked.

I nodded, and with Morio guarding my back, slowly approached the prone figure, kicking it gently to see if any life remained.

"I think he's dead." Morio knelt beside the creature. He gingerly flipped the Babbler's head to the side. Two fang marks still dribbled a few drops of black blood, but it looked like Menolly had finished him off by breaking his neck. And since he hadn't drunk any of her blood, he wouldn't be coming back. Two down. Bad Ass Luke to go.

"Well, that takes care of one of our remaining problems," I said, dropping onto the bench in the foyer. "Let's get Tom in here and plan how to smuggle him down to the Wayfarer. Luke's still out there, and he's far worse than either the harpy or the Psycho Babbler. My father was almost killed by him, and Luke got away from the entire division unscathed."

A noise startled me, and I jumped, but it was only Menolly, peeking around the corner. "He's dead?" she asked, her voice somber.

"Yes, he is. Are you okay?" She looked even more pale than usual, and I wondered just what drinking demon blood might do to a vampire.

With a shrug, she said, "I suppose. Nasty-tasting creature. I'm rather queasy, actually. I think I'll go get rid of this crap." And with that, she headed back to the basement. I wanted to go after her, but she needed to be alone. Nobody wanted to be seen when they were tossing their cookies, vampire or not.

"Morio, go bring everybody inside. I'll look for Maggie and Iris."

"Iris is safe. She ran out to the car when you told her to get out of the way." He kicked the demon again, just to be sure. The Psycho Babbler didn't move. "Back in a few," he said, heading for the door.

Hoping that nobody would show up to gather the body—meaning Bad Ass Luke—I cautiously approached the kitchen. The secret compartment leading to the basement was open, and I slowly descended the steps. When I entered Menolly's bedroom, I heard retching sounds from the blood room. Great, I thought as my stomach churned. Now I was a bad doughnut away from losing it myself. Even thinking about the taste of demon blood made me queasy, and for some strange reason, I was glad that it disagreed with her. Not that I wanted her to be sick, but . . .

"Mooph, mooph . . ."

The sound came from the other side of Menolly's bed, near the wall. I hurried over. There, snug in her box and wide awake, Maggie was playing with a Rubik's Cube. She hadn't solved it, but she was having fun sucking on the corner. She reached for me, and I bundled her into my arms.

"Hey, sweet thing. Did Iris bring you down here?"

"I thought we'd be safe here, when the demon came in." Iris was standing on the bottom stair. She was the only one outside the three of us who knew the secret entrance to Menolly's room, and she was sworn to silence.

"Good thinking," I said. "I'm so grateful neither of you was hurt. What happened?" Before she could speak, I held up one hand. "Wait, you can tell all of us together. Let's go. Menolly will be along in a few minutes."

Making sure the entrance to Menolly's lair was closed, we returned to the living room. Delilah and Chase were sitting on the sofa, Wisteria still bound and gagged on the floor between them. Morio was keeping watch out the windows. Tom sat in the rocking chair, looking confused and a little tired.

As I nestled on the floor in front of Delilah with Maggie in my arms, I gingerly stretched my neck. If I'd been an FBH, I'd probably be sporting at least one broken bone, if not a broken neck. As it was, I was going to need a good masseuse as soon as possible. I leaned back against Delilah's legs, and she began to rub my shoulders. Maggie *moophed* again and snuggled deeper into my arms. Nobody said anything at first, then everybody started talking at once.

"Whoa—hold on there, people. One at a time, please. I have the beginnings of a headache, and I hurt like hell from where the Psycho Babbler body-slammed me." I handed Maggie to Delilah as I eased my way to my feet.

Menolly entered the room at that moment, catching my gaze with her own. We didn't speak, but an unspoken understanding passed between us. When things calmed down, we'd have a long talk about the Psycho Babbler's death. Until then, I motioned for her to sit down.

Menolly glanced at Wisteria. "What's she doing here? And why is she tied up?"

I shook my head. "Wait a bit," I said. We needed to discuss what we'd learned, but it occurred to me that doing so in front of Wisteria would be a stupid—and potentially deadly—mistake. We had to store her somewhere while we talked, but I didn't want to leave her where Bad Ass Luke or any of his other cronies might find her.

"We have to do something with Wisteria," I said, pointing at the floraed. Her eyes glowered, and I had the feeling that she'd take the first opportunity that came her way to wipe every one of us out of existence.

"I still say we should just kill her," Morio said impassively. "She's a danger to both our mission and to us. We can't chance her getting free."

While I knew he was right, it was hard for me to face yet

more death and destruction. I glanced at Menolly, who stared at the floraed with a puzzled look on her face.

Delilah frowned. She gave him a firm shake of the head. "We can't do that, as logical as it sounds. The best thing to do is turn her over to OIA and let them deal with her. They might be able to dredge up some useful information that will lead them to more spies."

"Spy? That's what this is about?" Menolly asked. She turned on Wisteria. "You've been a spy this whole time you've been at the bar? Jocko trusted you! If you had anything to do with his death—" Her fangs came out as she hissed. "I warn you, even if you don't have warm blood running through your veins, I can as easily kill you as I can kill a fly."

"Hold on!" My headache was full-blown now, and all I wanted to do was crawl under the covers. "Menolly, she had a hand in Jocko's death, yes, but I don't think she knew the demons were planning it. She's more useful to us alive than she is dead. But we need to find a place to stash her while we talk."

"That's easy enough," my delicate, porcelain sister said, and promptly backhanded the floraed with a blow strong enough to knock her out. "There. Problem solved. Dump her in the parlor for a few minutes while we talk if you're still worried about her presence."

Delilah raised one eyebrow, handing Maggie to Chase, but she said nothing as she and Morio carried the limp figure of the floraed into the other room. I followed, wishing we had somebody to stand guard, but since we didn't, I closed the curtains and left the door cracked.

As we headed back to the living room, Delilah pulled me aside. "Menolly's sure high-strung today. What happened?"

"She killed the Psycho Babbler when he was attacking me. Maybe drinking demon blood agitates the temper?"

As we settled down in the living room, I thought about it. What would drinking the blood of a demon do to a vampire, other than give her an upset stomach? Menolly fed on the miscreants of society. Did their blood affect her in negative ways? It was something I'd never before considered, and I made a note to ask later when we were done with this whole fiasco.

Morio and I ran through what had happened at Tom's cabin, introducing him gently to Menolly. She gave him a quiet nod, as Iris scurried over to his side.

"Would you like some tea?" she asked him, ever the nurturer.

He gave her a faint smile and nodded. "Thank you. I'd like that."

"Iris, first tell us what happened, then you can make tea for all of us if you would." I winked at her, and she flashed me a broad smile of her own. It was nice to have someone around who liked to mother her friends. It had been so many years since our own mother had died. As young as she might look, Iris was far older than we were.

She took a deep breath and let it out slowly, folding her hands together in her lap as if she were about to begin a recitation. "I was feeding the last of Maggie's breakfast to her when I heard a noise in the living room. I peeked in and saw the demon, and before he could smell me, I grabbed Maggie and her box and—" Pausing, she glanced at Chase and Morio. "And hid out where you found me. I heard you fighting with him and came out to help."

The Talon-haltija had very good hearing; they could pinpoint a mouse at a hundred yards. I wasn't surprised that she'd heard me, even through a secret passage. Grateful she hadn't given away Menolly's hiding place, I cleared my throat.

"As far as we know, the Psycho Babbler was alone," I said. "Which may mean that Bad Ass Luke is probably hiding down at the Wayfarer. I wonder if he's got any way of knowing that his buddy just bit the dust."

"You think they might be telepathically linked?" Chase asked.

I shrugged. "I have no idea. Nobody from OIA has dealt with demons for a long time except our father and

the rest of his regiment, and he was the only survivor. Demonkin have a variety of powers, and they delight in using
them to the detriment of everybody else. I just wish we'd
paid more attention to Father's story about his fight with
Luke. Maybe there was something in there that would
help us now."

I glanced at my sisters. "Can you remember anything
that might come in handy?" With luck, they'd paid more
attention than I had.

Menolly squinted, leaning back in her chair. "Just that
he almost lost his life." She sucked on her lip. "Hey, do you
remember that he said that the demon had a sword that
could slice with a blade of fire?"

Blade of fire? What? And then I remembered. Father
had said something about Bad Ass Luke and his fiery
sword.

"You're right. Father said that Bad Ass Luke cut down
ten guards with a single stroke—all ancient Sidhe who had
outlived battles that had felled countless of their kin. And
Luke had managed to kill them all with his sword. A brilliant blade of fire attached to a carved bone hilt."

"Crap." Delilah's shoulders drooped. "I'd forgotten all
about that. The only thing I remember is that Father said
every time he went to make a move, it seemed like Luke
was one step ahead of him." She looked up at me. "That
doesn't sound good, does it?"

"Not really," I muttered. A blade of fire? The ability to
predict the moves of your enemies? Each by itself was
daunting, but together, the two abilities scared me out of
my wits. I coughed, trying to find something hopeful to say
about the situation, but all I could muster was, "Maybe we
should rethink this? Maybe Shadow Wing is just looking
for a vacation spot for his crew?"

"I wish," Morio said. "Any chance you can get through
to OIA from here? Tell them about the Psycho Babbler?"

Chase looked at me. "You have a Whispering Mirror,
don't you?"

I gestured toward the stairs. "In my study. Come on.

Let's get this over with. Somebody better stay downstairs and watch Wisteria and Tom, though." I glanced at our guest, who had fallen asleep in the rocking chair. His head rested against the back of the chair as he gently snored.

Morio raised his hand. "Iris and I will stay here and keep watch. Go now. We shouldn't linger around here for much longer." He took up guard at the window, and Iris retreated to the kitchen to make sure the back door was locked and warded. Talon-haltija were creatures of many talents, and Iris was at the top of her class. For a house sprite, she packed one hell of a magical punch.

I led the way with Delilah, Chase, and Menolly following. Chase looked around, a curious light in his eye. I had to give him kudos. Since he'd discovered the delights of Delilah, he hadn't tried to flirt with me. He had more class than I would have given him credit for a few days ago.

My study was where I worked on my magic, made my potions, and spent a good deal of time curled up in the overstuffed armchair, reading. My Whispering Mirror was in the corner of the room, covered by a black cloth. I pulled back the velvet. The size of a vanity mirror, the frame had been worked from silver delved from the Nebelvuori Mountains—the lands of the dwarves.

The silver had been wrought into an interweaving knot work pattern, with delicate roses and leaves ornamenting the frame. It was stronger than it looked, thanks to the Wizards Guild, and it would last until either the charms were broken or until the winds of time wore away the world. The glass inside was tempered, though it could be shattered by a blow from a magical creature.

The mirror was voice-activated and specifically tuned to the frequencies of our voices—the only three who could use it were my sisters and me. Chase had a similar mirror in his home. The OIA decided it was safer there than in a public office and had charged him with keeping it secret from all but OIA members. I knew he kept it inside a locked closet and that he'd installed a highly sensitive security monitoring system.

I slid onto the chair and said, "Camille."

The mirror began to mist over. We waited, Delilah, Menolly, and Chase crowding in behind me. After a few moments, a voice from the other side of the glass said, "How may I direct your call?"

"Earthside Division reporting in." As I said, humans had nothing on the Sidhe when it came to bureaucracy. The mists began to lift, and my reflection disappeared, replaced by an image I'd been longing to see for months.

"Father!" I almost jumped out of the chair, but that wouldn't be protocol. I forced myself to sit still. After all, he was a senior officer, and we owed him respect. Besides, he'd write me up if I didn't follow procedure, and the last thing I needed were any more demerits in my file.

Delilah, however, couldn't restrain herself. She jumped up and down and waved behind me. Menolly leaned in over my shoulder, her face eagerly soaking in the sights of Otherworld. Homesickness oozed off of her like honey, and in that moment, I realized that she, more than any of us, had lost the most by accepting this assignment.

"Camille!" Father broke out in a smile, his eyes crinkling around the edges as he leaned forward. He was a handsome man, looking young by human standards but he was far older than any human walking the planet. Except for Tom Lane. Of medium height, he was trim and fit, muscled in a lanky way, and he wore his hair in a long, raven-blue braid. My own hair was this color, and my violet eyes matched his. I was surprised that he hadn't started dating again. Our mother had been gone a long time, but he only mingled with other women at parties and social functions.

"I'm so glad to see you girls," he said. "I volunteered for communications duty today because I've got a cough, but I never dreamed I'd get a chance to talk to you." His gaze flickered over Delilah, Menolly, and Chase. "My girls, how are you doing?"

I let out a long sigh. "Have you seen Trillian? Is he alive? Did he tell you what's happening here?" *Please, please, please,* I thought, *please tell me that Trillian's still alive.*

Father nodded. "Yes. He was seriously injured, but he lives. The doctors managed to counter the poison." He glanced over his shoulder, then leaned toward the mirror, lowering his voice. "I'm making certain he returns to you by way of the Grandmother Coyote's portal tomorrow. You'll have to look out for him while he heals, and that's going to take at least a month."

Breathing easier, I relaxed. "Thank the gods, but why are they discharging him from the infirmary so quickly?"

"The gods had nothing to do with it," Father said, shaking his head. "You can thank the medics who went to great lengths—over their personal distaste—to keep him alive. We're in trouble here, Camille, and I don't think he'll be safe here for much longer. In a few days . . . it won't be safe for him or any of his kind."

I narrowed my eyes. "What's going on? Headquarters doesn't seem to care about the potential disaster we're facing here. Otherworld—Earth—both worlds are in danger. The demons are sneaking into Earth and looking for the spirit seals so they can rip open the portals. Shadow Wing's on the move, and he means to invade Earth and then Otherworld. And we're facing a showdown with Bad Ass Luke."

Father gave us a brief nod. "I know. Trillian told me. What's happened since the fight with the skinwalker? Hurry and don't leave anything out."

I filled him in on what had happened since then.

"And you have Tom with you?"

"Yes," I said. "He's downstairs. Morio's guarding him—a yokai-kitsune who's working with us, compliments of Grandmother Coyote. Thank the gods she got involved, because Morio saved our butt more than once. But Bad Ass Luke is out there, and we know he's going to interfere before we manage to send Tom through the portal at the Wayfarer."

Father frowned, thinking. I glanced back at Delilah, who was raptly staring at the mirror. Menolly, too, for all of her suppressed anger over the way Father reacted to her when she'd been turned into a vampire. We all needed reassurance, and Father's face was the most comfort we'd had in several days.

As I glanced at Chase, who was hanging toward the back, I realized that I hadn't introduced him yet. "I'm sorry, I forgot my manners," I said. "Father, this is Chase Johnson. Chase is the director of OIA affairs, Earthside. Chase, this is our father, Sephreh ob Tanu. He's a member of the Guard and reports to the ruling council as an auxiliary delegate."

Father gave Chase a brief nod. "Our surname system would be confusing for you to understand. You may call me Captain Sephreh."

Chase cleared his throat and straightened his shoulders. "Nice to meet you, sir. I just wish it wasn't under these circumstances." He fidgeted, running his hand through his hair, and I repressed a laugh. Meeting the parents was always awkward.

"What do you think we should do?" I asked. "Can you give us any clue that might help defeat Bad Ass Luke? If he's worse than the Psycho Babbler, then we're in big trouble."

Still looking uncomfortable, Father shifted in his chair. He finally leaned close to the mirror, his voice a whisper. "I've been debating whether to tell you, but I suppose I have to. The Court and Crown are in an uproar, and the OIA has been left to its own devices."

"What's going on?" I asked, a cold chill running down my back. "Are you safe?"

He nodded. "Don't worry about me. I'm fine at the moment, but something's happened that will affect every branch of government, including the military. Shadow Wing has picked the perfect time to make his attempt."

I wet my lips, afraid to ask but knowing I had no choice. "What is it?"

"The Court is in chaos. Queen Lethesanar's sister has come forward and claimed the crown for herself. Tanaquar's accusing the Queen of being so drugged that she can no longer rule. And Tanaquar has a vast array of support, including anybody who's ever been harmed or punished by

Lethesanar. We're on the brink of civil war, and until things are sorted out, I doubt if anybody beyond the oldest of the Guard will pay any attention to talk about demons and invasion."

I stared at him, openmouthed. "Civil war? But . . . the Queen *is* the Court."

"Who's backing Tanaquar besides the Queen's victims?" Delilah asked.

Glancing up at her, I said, "That's a good question. Who?"

Father let out a low sigh. "That's why I'm sending Trillian back to you as soon as he's able to stand. The entire city of Svartalfheim is relocating to Otherworld from the Subterranean Realms to get away from Shadow Wing. They've been talking to Tanaquar about what's going down under, and she's promised to do something about the demons if they help her win the Crown. They've forged an alliance. Trillian informed me a few days ago. He wanted to give me the chance to get away."

Unable to process everything he was saying, I sucked in a deep breath. "Did you tell the Court about this?" My father was the most loyal of the Guard. If he'd kept the information silent, then I knew all hell was about to break loose.

He shook his head. "Camille . . . girls . . . I am loyal to the Court and Crown, but Lethesanar has brought dishonor to the city. She's sullied Y'Elestrial's name with her disregard for its citizens. Since you left, things have gotten far worse. Anyone disagreeing with the Queen faces torture. The Court's opium parties bankrupt the city. This is not the Crown to whom I pledged an oath of fealty."

My father was an ethical man. He would remain loyal to Court and Crown, but not necessarily to she who wore the crown.

"Yesterday, Tanaquar went public with her accusations, and it was then that the emissaries from Svartalfheim arrived. The Queen's livid, and she's banned all Svartans from the city, but she can't stop them from coming to Otherworld. They've already contacted the dwarves about this and have formed an alliance. And you know how much the

Elves hate their darker brothers, but the Elfin Queen must believe the stories about Shadow Wing, because she's forged a truce with the King of Svartalfheim."

I stared at the mirror, unable to comprehend just what I was hearing. Such an alliance was unheard of in history. "Holy crap. Father, we have to get Tom back to OW— neither he nor the spirit seal are safe here."

He shook his head. "I can tell you what I know about Bad Ass Luke's weaknesses, but you must not bring the spirit seal to Y'Elestrial. The Queen would attempt to use it against her sister, as futile as that might be."

I stared at the mirror, a wave of helplessness pouring over me. "Then what do we do? Where can we hide it?"

He stared at me, his face a blank slate. "Take it through Grandmother Coyote's portal. On this end, it's guarded by Great Mother Bear and is out of the OIA's jurisdiction. From there, take the seal to Asteria, the Elfin Queen. She has the least to gain with it in her possession, and I think you can trust her. Tell no one in OIA what you know. Kill Luke, and report it as an isolated incident."

I knew it hurt him to go behind the OIA's back. I also knew that our father wouldn't order us to do something like this unless our lives depended on it.

Nodding, I sat back. "As you say, Father. Now tell us about Luke. Does he have any weaknesses?"

My father closed his eyes, and he looked tired and worn-out. "I'll tell you again what happened when I fought him, but I fear that eliminating this demon will be the hardest thing you've ever done," he said.

CHAPTER 18

By the time we signed off, we were all as weary as Father had looked. Chase was obviously shaken. He was a by-the-book cop until he'd joined the OIA, and now he was being told that his beloved new agency was corrupt and that civil war threatened to interfere with everything that he'd helped build Earthside during the past few years.

While Delilah and Chase made sandwiches for us, I filled Morio and Iris in on what was going down. We hauled Wisteria into the living room, where it was easier to keep an eye on her and yet she still wouldn't be within earshot.

Tom was another matter. He hadn't spoken much, merely humming to himself under his breath. But when he saw Maggie, his face lit up, and he asked if he could hold her. I watched as they snuggled together in the rocking chair that sat near the kitchen range. He played with her little hands, smiling as she wrapped tiny claws around one of his fingers. I wiped my eyes, feeling weary and sad. The evil we were facing threatened to overrun the Toms and Maggies of the world. It would chew them up and spit them out bleeding and raw without a second thought. And that was why we would stay and fight.

"We're going to need the cooperation of Grandmother Coyote. We need her portal to get Tom over to Otherworld." I drummed my fingers on the table, trying to think out the logistics. "Then we track down Luke and dispatch him as quickly as possible."

Morio shook his head, a worried light glimmering in his eye. "I have the feeling that Luke will be coming to us before we ever reach Grandmother Coyote's woods. For one thing, his buddy should probably have checked in with him by now, but instead he's lying dead in your living room. For another, you know that by now Luke has to have figured out that we have Tom."

"Can you sneak through to convince Grandmother Coyote to help us—to let us use her portal?" I stared at him, and images of our hot-to-trot liaison out on the mound flickered through my head. Once Trillian was back, I was going to be walking a tightrope between the two men because I really didn't want to give up either of them.

He glanced over to the counter where Delilah was putting the finishing touches on our lunch. "As soon as I eat. Meanwhile, I suggest that you cast a tracking spell to locate Luke. I'll bet you anything he's on his way here. The last thing you want is to be caught unprepared."

"Oh, that's *just* what we need," I said. "And if it works as well as the one I cast on the harpy, then all our troubles will be over because good ol' Luke will appear right in our living room."

Chase snorted, and Delilah laughed outright. But Morio was right, I thought. We just couldn't sit around and wait for Luke to come to us. I accepted the turkey sandwich Delilah handed me and morosely bit into it.

"Yeah, yeah, I'm good for a laugh," I said. "But Morio does have a point. I'll give it a try, but we all need to be prepared, because if my spell backfires and he shows up in the living room, we need to take him down then and there. This is to the death, people."

Chase slid into the chair next to mine. "Camille, how long has this civil war thing been brewing in Y'Elestrial?"

I shrugged. "Who knows? Probably hundreds of years. Lethesanar is an opium addict; we knew that growing up."

"We should untie Wisteria," Delilah said. She had hopped onto the counter, and her long legs dangled over the edge.

"Huh? Why the hell would we do that? That bitch is dangerous." I stared at her, wondering where she'd left her brain.

"She's been tied up for several hours now. She has to be getting cramps."

Ever the compassionate heart, my sister. I sighed. Even though she meant well, it was too dangerous. "Delilah, hon, think for a moment. Wisteria tried to kill us. She's in league with the demons. She *hates* us. And you want us to untie her? Remember what she did to Chase."

"I'm with Camille on this one, Delilah." Chase didn't look happy about agreeing with me, either. "We can't chance it. With everything that's going down, we run a big risk if we let her loose—even for a few minutes."

Delilah glanced over at Menolly, who only had to shake her head to voice her opinion. "I understand that, but it just seems cruel, keeping her tied up without a break. Can we at least ask her if she wants some water?"

I pressed my lips together, not wanting to play the bad cop. Chase glanced at me, and I saw that he wasn't willing to, either.

Menolly swatted at a gnat. "She's no princess, Kitten. She's a bloodthirsty wood sprite who's lost her marbles," she said. "She'd as soon rip off your head as look at you."

Delilah stared at her with that wide-eyed ingénue look she had. Finally, Menolly shrugged. "Whatever, but don't blame me when something goes bad. Come on, I'll help you. We'll offer her some water, and if she moves a muscle, I'll break her neck."

"I'm not sure if I feel better or not," Delilah muttered as they rose and headed into the parlor.

Iris was at the sink, standing on a stool to wash dishes. I

started to tell her not to bother, then stopped. House sprites reveled in helping those they cared for. It was part of their nature, just as being a lug had been part of Jocko's, or being sarcastic was part of Trillian's.

She turned around and, wiping her hands on a dishcloth, asked, "What should I do while you're fighting this demon?"

"Hide with Maggie and Tom. You'll have to protect both of them. We'll secure you safely, though." I played with the last of my sandwich, thinking about our predicament. If our father could have crossed over to help, I would have felt so much safer, but that wasn't going to happen.

Wondering if Trillian's part in matters—whatever that might be—had been discovered by the Queen, I tried to figure out how we might go home after Tom was secured within the Elfin city's walls. If we returned to Y'Elestrial, the OIA would require us to fight against Tanaquar. And frankly, when I admitted my true feelings to myself, I was hoping Tanaquar would win.

The Queen's younger sister was brilliant and strong, and while she, too, had her cruel side—as did most of the Sidhe—she possessed a sense of justice that made me trust in her judgment far more than that of the opium-dazed Lethesanar. But we weren't home right now, not yet. We had to focus on the impending battle.

I shook myself out of my reverie and stood up. "Chase, you and Morio leave the kitchen, please. I'm going to hide Iris, Tom, and Maggie. Then I'll cast a location spell to find Bad Ass Luke."

"I've got to head out to talk to Grandmother Coyote anyway," Morio said, giving me a quick kiss. "Stay safe till I get back." He dashed out the door. As I watched through the kitchen window, he was there one second, and the next a sleek red fox was darting into the woods.

Chase left the room, and I gently walked over to Tom. "Take Maggie, would you?" I whispered to Iris. She obliged as Tom looked up at me from the rocking chair with the sweetest smile I'd seen in a long time.

"You've sure been nice to me, miss. Can I do anything

to help you?" That endeared him to me even more. I was beginning to see why Titania had kept him around.

"Trust me, Tom, you're helping us even if you don't know it. Now I want you to lean back and close your eyes. It's time for a nap." I ran through the spell, hoping to hell I'd get it right. When he complied, I placed one hand on his forehead, and the other on his shoulder. "Hear but forget. Follow but sleep, Mother Moon."

The words drifted on the air for a moment, then settled down over him like a shroud, embracing his body. No mix-ups this time. Within seconds, Tom was breathing softly. I leaned down to whisper in his ear.

"Come with me, and watch your step, Tom."

He stood. I took his hand and led him over to the secret entrance, which Iris had opened. She held Maggie firmly in one arm, waiting for me to lead Tom down the steps, then fell in behind me. We reached Menolly's sitting room, and I helped Tom sit down in the upholstered recliner. Iris covered him with an afghan.

"He'll sleep for several hours," I said. "Whatever you do, don't bring him upstairs until we return. If something goes wrong and you suspect danger, take his necklace and Maggie and hide yourself as best as possible. If we don't return, go to Grandmother Coyote, and take the necklace through the portal to the Elfin Queen." I gave her and the now-snoring gargoyle cub a hug, then returned to the kitchen, shutting the bookcase door behind me.

Before I could reach the living room, Menolly came charging into the kitchen, cursing a blue streak. She was pissed, that much was obvious. Her eyes were glowing red, and her fangs were out.

"Uh-oh, what happened?"

"Wisteria decided to try and play vampire," Menolly said, glaring over her shoulder.

Delilah entered the kitchen more slowly. One hand was on her neck, and I saw a trickle of blood streaming between her fingers.

"What in the seven stars happened to you?" I rushed over and yanked her hand away from the wound. Menolly was right. Wisteria had obviously planted her lips on my sister's neck, but it wasn't exactly a love bite. Blood seeped from the wound, and a strange green pus was already oozing out of the jagged edges.

"Cabbage-breath wanted a drink of water, all right. Then she attacked Delilah, who was holding the cup." Menolly huffed herself into a chair, crossing her legs with a graceful kick.

"Is she still alive?" Having seen my sister in action, I wasn't holding out much hope, but Menolly surprised me.

"Yes, I left our precious hostage alive. She's not getting free without help, though," she said, a wicked grin playing on her face. "I know how to bind knots, and believe me, she'll feel every muscle in her body for days."

Delilah gave in to my fussing and let me wash and dress the wound. It looked nasty, but I sprinkled an all-inclusive antibacterial powder on it that we'd been given by the healers back in Otherworld and covered it with gauze.

"I could say I told you so," I muttered. "When will you learn to listen to me?"

"Eh, shut up," Delilah said, a smile playing on the corners of her lips. "Don't worry, I'm over feeling sorry for her," she added. "I can't believe she tried to tear a chunk out of my neck."

"You sound surprised."

"I just thought . . . I never thought . . ." Delilah's gaze flashed down at me, and I knew what was bothering her.

"Honey, you may play fair, but Wisteria's our enemy. Never forget that," I said, carefully taping the edges of the gauze. "These demons are out for blood. They're out to take over this world, and our world, and they aren't going to make nice-nice and leave women and children alive. We can't allow them to succeed."

Her lips quivered. My softhearted sister, who always wanted to believe the best, to focus on the positive, to eliminate the negative by pretending it wasn't there, was beginning to understand the seamy underside of war. A harsh lesson, but one she needed to learn.

"I guess you're right," she said. "But I just can't imagine how one of our own would go in league with them. Doesn't Wisteria understand that the demons will kill her? I tried to tell her that, and she laughed in my face."

"Before she bit you in the neck?" I put away the gauze and antibiotic powder and washed my hands. "Listen to me. People—humans and Faerie and Sidhe included—hear what they want to hear and believe what they want to believe. It's the nature of life. Now, we need to stash Wisteria somewhere before I cast the location spell to pinpoint Luke's whereabouts. Any ideas would be muchly appreciated."

"I don't think we should put her outside. If Luke shows up, he'll set her free, and then we'll be dealing with two whack-jobs." Menolly glanced around, frowning. "What about the broom closet? You could lock her in there with one of your magic locks."

"Uh-huh. Like that's ever worked for me." My mentor's attempts to teach me how to cast magic locks had been one big waste of time for us both. To date, I'd managed to get it right exactly three times out of a hundred serious tries. "I can give it a shot, but I don't guarantee results."

"That's comforting. Oh hell, there's a chance, and it won't take much time to find out if you can make it work." She stood up. "I'll volunteer to carry the monster in here if you'll give it a shot."

I shook my head. "Menolly, you either have a lot of confidence in me, or you think you're strong enough to withstand anything I can throw at you. Okay, go get her, and I'll try. I promise you nothing, however."

As she carried the bound-and-gagged Wisteria into the kitchen, Delilah scowled but happily opened the closet door. Menolly tossed Wisteria inside, none too gently. She was about to slam the closet shut when a knock on the kitchen door stopped her.

Chase and Delilah drew their guns. Menolly paused, waiting, as I edged my way to the porch and peered through the curtains. It was Morio. I cautiously opened the door, and he hustled inside, stopping with a puzzled look when he saw the open closet, the pissed-off floraed, and Delilah's bandaged neck.

"What happened?"

"Wisteria decided to try her hand at sucking blood. We're locking her in the closet, and you're just in time to join us. After that, I'll cast the location spell to find Bad Ass Luke." I shut the door and locked it tightly. "Did you talk to Grandmother Coyote? What did she say?"

"I'm fast in my fox form," Morio said. "And yes, I found her. She's willing to let us use the portal. I assume one of you knows the mechanics of transfer?"

Menolly raised her hand. "I do. I learned at the Wayfarer. Speaking of which, I can probably kiss my job goodbye when the OIA finds out I didn't show up tonight."

"I doubt it, considering . . ." I stopped, noticing that Wisteria had perked up. "Shush. Our spy is listening."

With that, Menolly slammed the closet door and stood back. "Fire at will."

"Thank you, Madame Vamp." I couldn't believe I was going to try this again. I'd all but given up on ever mastering it. "As I said, I usually get this wrong, so I suggest all of you take cover to avoid getting hit by a backlash if this thing blows up in my face."

When everyone had retreated to the living room, I focused on summoning the magic that froze situations, that locked doors and barred gates and sealed secrets. It flowed through me clear at first, running thick in my veins. My father was a master of this spell—it was an innate ability with him, and I'd inherited the power, but with a pathetic twist.

I tried to bring my attention away from the possibility of failure, to concentrate on success, but once again, there was a familiar jog, as if the energy reached a certain point and then stalled out. The next thing I knew, the force that came rushing from my hands enveloped the closet door and the hinges exploded, a shard of shrapnel catching me in the arm.

"Damn it to high hell!" My arm burned like a mother-sucker. I clasped the forearm, where a two-inch shard of metal had lodged itself in my flesh. The door, freed from hinges or any other locking mechanism, teetered and fell toward me, and I barely managed to jump out of the way before it landed on the floor with a resounding thud. And *that* took care of any hopes of magically entrapping Wisteria in the closet.

The others rushed in. When he saw the blood, Morio grabbed my arm and inspected it. He motioned for me to sit at the table, and Delilah promptly fetched the same supplies I'd just finished using on her.

"You just couldn't stand the fact that I'm wearing such a haute couture bandage, could you?" she teased.

I snorted. "Oh yes, it's all the rage at Court and Crown this year. I heard the Queen will be sporting one just like it when Tanaquar gets done with her." I sighed, depressed. "My magic's been working pretty good the past couple of days. I'm getting good at blasting people, but I guess it couldn't last forever."

Menolly yanked Wisteria out of the closet. The floraed had a triumphant gleam in her eye, and I wanted to smack her a good one but refrained.

"I'll take our visitor here into the storage room," Menolly said. "There aren't any windows, and we'll just lock the door with a key and hope for the best." She trudged away, carrying the woman over her shoulder like she might carry a baseball bat.

"Good idea," I muttered. "I just hope my sudden flop doesn't presage the same failure in locating Mr. Bad Ass."

Morio held up a wicked looking pair of tweezers. "Inhale, then exhale sharply while I pull this thing out of your arm."

I obeyed, screeching as he ripped the barb of metal out of my flesh. "You could have been a little more gentle," I said, but he shook his head.

"It would have hurt more that way. This is going to sting

when I clean it, but we have to make sure there aren't any metal shavings in there."

As he poured water over the wound, I gritted my teeth, promising myself I wouldn't scream. When he dried it and sprinkled on the antibiotic powder, I decided to forget my dignity.

"Great Mother, are you trying to torture me?"

"Breathe, breathe," he said, stroking the palm of my hand with one finger. As his flesh met mine, I began to lose track of the pain, and when he ran his fingers up my wrist, I had totally lost track of it, instead following the silken movements of his skin grazing my own.

"That's right, just follow my voice, breathe out the pain, feel only pleasure." His gaze met mine, and I wanted to jump him then and there. It was only with difficulty that I pulled my attention away.

"Feel better?" he asked, a smile playing on the corners of his lips, and the warm glow of his body receded back out of my aura.

I looked around the room. Delilah and Chase were watching me, and I wondered if they knew just how close I'd come to having an orgasm right there in the kitchen. Morio had been using his powers of *mekuramashi* on me.

"You should bottle that and sell it," I said hoarsely. "I'd buy a whole case."

"Only too happy to help. I'll help more, later." His voice was low enough so that only I could hear.

I swallowed hard, thinking that when we were done with Luke, there was only one sure way to relieve the tension we were under. "When we have the time," I said, and he leaned over and placed a light kiss on my lips.

Just then, Menolly returned. "Wisteria's locked up and the key is safe with me." She held it up for us to see, then slid it into her pocket. "Now, what about Luke?"

What about Luke, indeed?

"I guess there's no putting it off." I motioned to the living room, and we gathered around the fireplace. "If this works like it did with the harpy, then we're in trouble."

Delilah pulled out her long knife. Guns wouldn't work on Luke, unless we happened to have an AK-47, and that wasn't even in Chase's arsenal. Menolly extended her nails. Morio closed his eyes, and I could feel the energy rise around him as he summoned his magic. And Chase pulled a weapon out of his jacket, one I'd never seen him wield. A steel pair of nunchakus. I gave him a questioning look.

He smiled. "I do have a background in defense *other* than just pulling a trigger, Camille. Trust me, I know how to use these. You said bullets won't be effective against a demon of Luke's caliber, and somehow, I don't think bitch-slapping him will do any good, will it?"

I laughed. "Chase, you're all right. Okay, we're ready. I just wish Trillian was here with us—we could use his talents. Let's see," I said, looking around. "I need my scrying bowl, along with a bottle of clear spring water."

"I'll get it," Delilah said, taking the stairs two at a time.

"Anything I can do?" Chase asked, looking around the room. "Need any furniture moved or anything?"

"Thanks. I'd normally light candles, but Luke is a creature of fire, and if he shows up in the living room, I don't want any flames going. He could use them in his attack and burn down the house just that much easier." I frowned, looking around as I tried to assess what we might need. "I know. You can get the fire extinguisher from the kitchen. We could probably blind him with it. At least temporarily." The truth was, I had no idea what effect the foam would have on a demon, but it couldn't hurt to try.

Chase trotted into the kitchen and brought back the extinguisher. As he set it down next to me, I caught his hand in mine.

"Chase, I hope you and Delilah enjoy what you've found together—for however long it lasts," I said, keeping my voice low. For all I knew, Menolly and Morio were both listening in. All of us had better hearing than an FBH, but Chase didn't have to know that.

"I've been pretty snide to you over the months," I continued. "But Delilah likes you, and you seem to have lost your fear of being around her."

His eyes glimmered. "I know I've been a pain in your side since we met. You're just so . . . I don't know. Vital? Alive? But the other night when Delilah and I were working together alone, something just happened. I've never looked at her before like that, but without you around, I could see her for who she is."

I wanted to tell him he had no idea who she really was, that he'd barely scratched the surface. And I'd be right. But I also knew that was for him to discover, and for Delilah to reveal.

"Just remember, she's half-Sidhe. And the Sidhe may look human, but we're not." His expression told me I was about to overstep my bounds, so I cleared my throat and changed the subject.

"Okay, I'll want the coffee table in front of the armchair and—here comes Delilah with the bowl."

Delilah bounded into the room, my scrying bowl in one hand and in the other, a bottle of water that came from the Tygerian River back in Otherworld.

The Tygerian Well was a holy spring that bubbled up from a place high in the mountains. It flowed so quickly and so fast that it had become a river. The water and well were continually blessed by a group of priests who lived far up the slopes of Mount Tygera in an ancient monastery. The Order of the Crystal Dagger was one of the oldest spiritual brotherhoods in Otherworld, and the monks were as reclusive as they were deadly. However, they had no objection to people using the blessed water, as long as no one harmed or defiled the river, the monastery, or the mountain.

I poured the water into the bowl and set it on the table, waiting a moment for the ripples to settle. A few sparkles of light played on the surface. I motioned for everyone to be seated. "When I start, please be quiet. If Luke comes rampaging through some gateway from hell, then you'll be the first to attack because it will take me a moment to break out of trance. Are you ready?"

Everybody nodded.

Taking a deep breath, I closed my eyes. Since I didn't have anything that had belonged to Luke, I'd have to use a variation of the location spell. I lowered myself into the whirl of energy, and liquid silver raced through my veins as I formed a question in my mind.

"Where is the demon Lucianopoloneelisunekonekari? Where is he, right now?" I opened my eyes and looked into the water. After a moment, a mist began to form above the surface, spiraling like a DNA helix. Miniature tornadoes swept across the bowl as the mist bubbled, growing to form an oval frame above the table. Within the frame, a dizzying parade of Faerie fire danced.

I slowly stood, my body quivering. While I'd cast this spell a few times before, I'd never seen this sort of response and wasn't sure what to expect. Should I yell for everybody to run for the hills, or would I finally be able to say I'd performed a magnificent feat of magic and make my mentor proud?

Five seconds passed, then ten, then half a minute. Still the mist coiled, mirroring the oval of lights. Just as I was about to write it off to a pretty show and nothing more, the Faerie fire began to coalesce. A scene formed, remarkably like a television screen, but we weren't watching Leno or Letterman.

A house rose in the near distance, and I immediately recognized it as our own house, looming large under the full moon. Thick clouds built, threatening to cover the sky. A copse of cedar and fir and birch ringed the backyard, and a bird feeder hung on one of the larger firs that buttressed the dirt path that led from the fence surrounding the house down to the tree line.

I snapped my fingers. "Bingo, we're seeing the house from within the woods. Out back." Even as I spoke, a surge of anger raced through me and then passed on—it had to be Luke. He was out there, somewhere.

"I know what's going on! Rather than showing us where he is, the spell is showing us what *he's* seeing." Excited, I dropped my focus, and the mist immediately dissipated. "He's out back in the woods."

"He's hiding in the cedar grove," Delilah added. "And I know exactly where he's at. You know the path that leads down to Birchwater Pond? That's the trail. I recognize that bird feeder." A guilty look flashed over her face, and I had the feeling she'd been prowling around that woods in cat form. She caught my expression and grinned. Yep, the cat ate the canary all right.

"We're going out to meet him," I said. "I don't want him getting close enough to destroy our home."

"Forget the house. I don't want him destroying *us*," Menolly muttered. She flexed her back, arching lightly. "All right, shall we take the rumble to him?"

Resigned to our impending doom, I nodded. "Let's get moving."

We were about to head out when the doorbell rang. I cautiously peeked through the peephole. Surely Bad Ass Luke wouldn't come ringing the bell like some Avon lady? Startled, I yanked open the door.

"What the—?"

Smoky broke out in a wide and toothy grin. "I thought you could use a little help," he said. "I had a feeling something was going down, so I'm offering my services."

Speechless, I stared at the dragon. Man. Dragon-man? His gaze never left my own as I ushered him through the door and into the living room.

CHAPTER 19

"What the hell are you doing here?" I finally found my voice.

"Ah, Camille," he said. "Lovely to see you, too."

I flinched. He knew my name? Not a good sign, not a good sign at all. "How did you—"

"Find out your name? It wasn't difficult. Titania and I had a little talk. She can be very verbose when she's lonely and drunk. She misses her Tom, so she was nipping at the nectar. She doesn't have the capability to hold her liquor the way she used to," he added. I couldn't tell whether he was laughing or not behind those glacial eyes.

Somehow Titania had known my name and so, of course, Smoky did, too. In fact, he probably knew all our names by now, but I was betting that he wouldn't abuse that knowledge. At least, not until Luke was well and truly out of the way. After that, we'd have to be cautious.

"You're going to help us kill Luke?"

"I suppose, though I've heard rumors that the demon who walks your woods out there is a bundle of laughs." Smoky snorted at my sharp glance. "Don't think I'm clueless as to what's going on. I won't be able to shift into my natural form inside the forest, only in a clearing. But I've got other tricks up my sleeve that you'll find useful."

After introducing him to Menolly, we headed out the back door. The moon was riding high in the sky, she was a sliver away from being full, and I could feel her pull on me. Delilah could, too; her form shivered and trembled as if she could barely keep herself together. She'd be okay tonight, but tomorrow would be another story. We had to finish this before morning.

The woodland that buttressed against our backyard was a good twenty-acre patch with a path leading down to Birchwater Pond. Overgrown, the thicket was mostly composed of cedar and fir, of birch and huckleberry and fern. Vine maples looped their way through the copse, and an oak stood sentinel here and there, but for the most part, the tangle was so dense that it was nigh to impossible to travel off the path.

"How far is that bird feeder along the path?" I asked. Luke couldn't be very far in to have been looking at our house. In fact, chances were, he was watching us approach right now. There wasn't much we could do about that, but every second that passed gave him that much more time to gather his strength.

"A few yards," Delilah said. "Not far. I hope he didn't slip around through the undergrowth with the idea that he could sneak in the house while we were out."

I frowned. I hadn't thought of that possibility. "We just have to hope and pray that Bad Ass isn't as smart as you are."

Closing my eyes for a brief moment, I searched the area for any sign of demonic activity. Bingo! Over near the gazebo. He wasn't in the woods anymore, and he *was* headed for the house. Turning direction, I broke into a sprint, yelling at the top of my lungs. No use trying to surprise him, but perhaps we could engage him before he got inside and tore the place to the ground.

The others, taken off guard, followed a beat behind me. I could hear the fall of their shoes on the wet grass as

I neared the gazebo. And then Luke stepped out from behind the ornamental pagoda. I skidded to a halt, and Smoky bumped into me. I felt his hand on my ass but didn't have time to shake him off.

Bad Ass Luke was a misnomer. *Bad Ass Luke* brought to mind a drunken football player, or a hotheaded biker. But Lucianopoloneelisunekonekari was no human thug. Standing a good eight feet high, Luke might be human in shape and form, but all resemblance ended there. No simple demon, either. Hollow eyes reflected the fires of the nether realms, and his arms and legs were vein-shrouded and engorged, muscle-bound beyond any steroid dream. He wore no clothes, and that he was male was rock-hard obvious. It was also apparent that he was strong enough to rip the head off an ox. Poor Jocko hadn't stood a chance, so where did that leave us?

I froze, paralyzed by a vast flow of fear. Smoky broke away, and I wondered if he was going to cut and run, but then I saw that he was trying to gain some distance so he could transform into his dragon self.

Morio pushed his way around me, moving to the side as he stared at the hulk who was slowly striding our way.

"What do we do? Oh, Great Mother, how can we take down that beast? He's *huge*!" Delilah sounded on the verge of panic. She squeaked again when Luke opened his mouth, and a billow of gas emerged.

"Poison!" Morio said. "He can use poison—I can smell it from here. Do your best to get behind him, because you don't want him breathing on you!"

Holy mother of mountains. Just what we needed. Poison gas, and arms strong enough to crush us. I shook myself out of my paralysis and summoned the Moon Mother.

"I need you tonight, Mother Moon. Pour everything you have into me, even if it tears me apart. Lady, send me your power!" I raised my arms to the sky as the clouds that had drifted over the moon parted. Silver beams shot down to touch my fingertips, and a well of energy rushed through my arms, into my heart, staggering me under the wild night.

Chase pulled out his nunchakus, holding one stick while twirling the other on the chain that connected them. He sidestepped to the left.

"If we fan out, he can't kill us all at once," he said, and I could hear the quaver of fear in his voice. But I marveled that an FBH could face such an enemy and not be cowering under the nearest bush.

"You're right—spread out!" There was no room for doubt, no room for fear. We had a job to do and a duty to both Otherworld and Earth.

Menolly strode past me. "Well, *I* can't be affected by his poison," she said without stopping. I started to grab her arm but let go when she gave me a little shake. She stormed toward him.

Luke paused, staring at the petite, pale woman who stood before him, her head lowered.

"Sending me the weakest to begin with?" His voice echoed through the yard, but when Menolly raised her head, he stopped laughing. I couldn't see her face from where I stood, but I knew what she looked like in hunting mode. I'd seen it when she attacked the Psycho Babbler. Glowing eyes. Mouth drawn back to reveal long, glistening fangs. Luke took an unsteady step back, and I could hear the sharp intake of breath as he eyed her uncertainly.

"Vampire?" Looking puzzled, he cocked his head for a fraction of a second. That pause was all Menolly needed. She flew in, launching herself into the air with a speed that was breathtaking. Luke roared and tried to leap to the side, but my sister was faster, and she landed on his chest, clinging to him with her claws. She reared her head back, then plunged her teeth directly into his face.

Good girl, I thought. She was trying to prevent him from breathing his poison so we could get in there. His hands were around her waist, trying to pry her off, but she held fast, fangs lodged within his cheek. She ripped at his eyes with her nails, and he roared again.

I broke into a sprint and circled around to the right. As I readied the lightning in my hands, I saw that Smoky had found a place large enough in which to complete his transformation. A majestic white dragon was now rumbling around in our backyard, crushing the rosebushes.

He took aim at Luke, and a buildup of smoke puffed out of his nostrils, but instead of fire—which would have done no good whatsoever—he let out a low roar and stamped the ground, quaking the yard. Everybody stumbled.

I managed to catch myself, and the moment I was steady enough, I aimed for Luke and let the lightning fly from my hands, striking him in the back. Combined with the earthquake caused by Smoky's tail thwack, the attack forced Luke to let go of Menolly. She dropped to the ground, stumbling away to vomit. Good ol' demon blood, all right.

The moment Menolly was out of the way, Morio let loose with *"Kitsune-bi!"* and a bolt of fox fire flashed in Luke's face. He bellowed, shaking his head as the blinding light lit up the night.

While Luke was rubbing his eyes, Delilah bounded in. I thought she was going to slash at him with her knife, but instead she pulled out a large bottle from her pocket and splashed him with water. Luke's skin sizzled where it hit—she must be using the blessed Tygerian water! He roared again, swinging wildly, and caught her in the side, knocking her a good twenty feet back. Delilah spun in the air, landing in a crouch. Leave it to a cat to land on her feet.

Just then, Luke turned, and I found myself facing him in his full fury. Terrified, for his sight seemed to have cleared and there was nothing to prevent him from breathing his poison in my face or smashing me with one of those humongous fists, I stumbled away, racing for the woods.

As I reached the tree line, I felt the wave of a heat blast behind me and heard the crackle of flames. I didn't have time to glance over my shoulder, but I knew that Luke had let loose his fiery blade. I leapt over a bramble bush, only to find myself ankle deep in a mud hole.

As I freed myself from the muck, the rattle of trees told me the demon was coming my way. I plunged off in another direction, darting around the windfalls and snags until I found myself face-to-face with a log that must have been four feet in diameter. Covered with moss, it was slippery, and as I tried to scramble over it, I could hear Luke's garbled curses as he thrashed through the woods.

What was I going to do? Father had warned us that fire wouldn't work against the demon, nor would charms or guns. Unless we happened to have a tank turret or a hulking big cannon handy, we were plumb out of luck. I finally found a toehold and scrambled over the log, crouching on the forest floor behind the tree trunk. Not the greatest cover, but better than nothing.

Sudden silence. I steadied myself so that I was taking shallow, even breaths that might be soft enough to escape his notice. After a moment, I heard him take one step, then another. He must not have seen me when I slipped behind the tree, and it was blocking him from seeing my body heat. I hunkered lower and ran through my available options.

I could shoot another blast of energy at him, but it wouldn't take him down. What would put out a demon's fire? Water . . . blessed water. But we'd need a swimming pool full of it. What else might affect Luke? I racked my brain and then—then I knew.

The one weakness the demon had.

My father had been the sole survivor of the guards who attacked Luke. The demon had mowed them down with his poison gas, and my father had been lucky enough to be standing out of reach. He'd told us that the only way he'd escaped was when he managed to stab Luke with his sword. The demon was about to swing on him when Father took a blind swing. His sword connected with the demon, plunging the tip into Luke's side.

Luke had dropped him, and Father had managed to get away while the demon was doubled over. Father hadn't been able to figure out why exactly that had happened, because the knife hadn't hit any vital organs or really done much damage at all, but he didn't stay to figure it out. He barely escaped with his life.

When I was a child, I was in charge of polishing Father's

sword for him. I'd carefully spread a mixture of beeswax and oil on the blade and wipe it to a high sheen. It tarnished easily because it was silver. And that's what had done the damage—not Father's actual strike but the silver inherent within the blade.

Luke was as vulnerable to silver as the Sidhe were to iron! I was sure of it. So what we needed were silver weapons. Or silver bullets. One swipe caused pain. Enough blows, and we should be able to kill Luke.

I had to get the information back to the others, but how? Should I try to transform myself or make myself invisible? A movement in front of me caught my attention. A cat, a golden tabby to be exact, crawled into my lap. She had a blue collar on.

I knew that Delilah could understand me in her transformed shape, so I leaned as close to her ear as I could, and as softly as possible, said, "Silver weapons will kill Luke if we hit him enough times." Delilah blinked and licked my face, then slinked off through the trees and vanished into the night.

Another thump told me that Luke was getting antsy. "Come out now, and I'll make it quick," he said.

I decided to forgo his charming invitation. Maybe I could turn into a bug or something—anything—small enough to scuttle off. But what if it didn't work? What if I turned into a giant bull's-eye, or just managed to unleash a huge puff of smoke? I'd be dead.

And then the forest shuddered with the groaning of trees and the snapping of branches. What the hell?

"Grrmph?" Luke sounded like he'd taken a nasty thud on the back.

I straightened my shoulders just as all hell broke loose. The woods lit up like Washington, D.C., on the Fourth of July, and much to my chagrin, a flaming branch landed next to me. Scrambling to my feet, I swung around.

Luke was embroiled in a battle with Smoky, who had managed to wedge himself through the forest, knocking over several trees in the process. Luke had let go with a blast of fire, which did nothing but ash up Smoky's leathery hide, and now Smoky was tearing at Luke with his claws in a scene remarkably reminiscent of Godzilla versus King Kong.

Just then, Morio, Chase, and Delilah came racing onto the scene, carrying the silver swords that we kept in the living room cabinet. They attacked, with Chase and Morio swinging in from behind. Smoky fell back as Delilah went in from the front, her sword in hand.

I scrambled back over the log and summoned the lightning again. As Luke bellowed, they stabbed at him, the sharp, short cuts causing more damage from the silver than from the actual blood lost.

And then I knew what I could do. Instead of firing forks of lightning, I formed them into a giant arrow of shimmering silver light and aimed for his eyes. It flew in true aim, striking dead center on his forehead, where it drove itself deep. Luke screamed and then, teetering, crashed backward to the ground. Delilah launched herself at his heart, her sword driving deep into his body. Luke arched, howled once, and collapsed. It was over.

"Is he really dead?" Delilah asked, prodding him with her sword.

Smoky shimmered and once again stood there in all his buff glory. He leaned over Luke, performing several checks that I had no desire to partake in.

"He's dead." He stood up and wiped his hands on the mossy ground cover.

"I was afraid that we were all going to be dead meat." Delilah dropped onto the nearest log and looked at the sword. "Thank the gods Father made us bring these when we came Earthside."

I stumbled over to them and dropped to my knees next to the dragon. "Father's sword was silver. Remember he told us how he managed to get away from Luke? When I thought about it, the only conclusion I could come to was that it was the metal, because it sure wasn't the blow, not after the attacks this creature took." A sudden thought occurred to me, and I glanced up at Morio. "Sword, please?"

With a knowing look on his face, he handed it to me. I spread out old Bad Ass's hand and brought the sword down across four of his fingers. Chase grimaced, and even Smoky looked askance.

"You never know when you're going to need an extra," I said, pocketing them. "One for Grandmother Coyote, and three for the spell cabinet."

"Oh boy, I wish I hadn't seen that," Chase muttered. Delilah slipped up next to him, and he instinctively curled his arm around her waist.

I grinned. "Wait until you see Delilah go after a mouse. You're going to just love *that*."

"So what do we do with his body—and that of the Psycho Babbler?" Morio asked.

"I'd say take them through the portal with us to the Elfin Queen. If Lethesanar is too busy to pay attention to the OIA's sacred duty in guarding the portals, then we have to convince somebody else in Otherworld that things here are heating up."

"But we killed the demons and found the seal," Chase said.

"One out of nine." A stab of fear shot through me, but I brushed it away. We'd survived this battle; it was time for celebration. "Chase, we aren't done yet. We may have stopped Shadow Wing from getting the first seal, but there are eight more, and each one can give him a terrible advantage against Earth and OW."

"Okay, who's going to drag him back?" Chase nudged Luke with his toe. "I don't think I can even budge him."

"Oh, Great Mother," Menolly said. "Get out of my way." And with a blink of the eye, she hoisted Luke over her shoulder and silently stalked out of the forest toward the house.

Chase gave me a startled look. "She's strong."

"She's a vampire," I said.

"Are all vampires that strong?" he asked, looking slightly green.

I gave him a slow smile. "Chase, my dear, Menolly's still young and weak. She'll grow in strength as the centuries move on. Right now, she's a neophyte. Which is why you don't ever want to cross a vampire unless you've got garlic in your pocket or silver around your neck."

"What about a cross?" he asked.

"A nice old wives' tale, but that's all it is." And with that, I turned to follow her.

We had a portal to cross, and until we were in the courts of the Elfin Queen, I wouldn't feel secure. By the time we reached the house, Menolly had alerted Iris that all was secure, and the Talon-haltija sat in the rocking chair with Maggie on her lap, wide-eyed and ready to hear about the battle.

We gave her the rundown, and I glanced at the clock. Well past the witching hour. "Menolly, if you travel through the portal, you risk coming back here during the daylight. I don't think it's safe for you to go."

"Not a problem. Just take the floraed with you, or I'll make her my appetizer."

"Say, did you ever return Wade's call?" I asked.

"Talk about non sequiturs," she said, but I could see the wheels turning in her head. "I will before I go to bed this morning. He seems a good sort, and I might as well get to know some of the vamps around here."

She leaned against the desk, eyeing the clock. "I have to feed on something a lot more appetizing than that stupid Psycho Babbler. He and his buddy made me sick to my stomach. And I want to drop in at the Wayfarer. Maybe I can salvage the situation there."

"Then you'd better hurry. You only have a few hours till first light. And be careful, there are still a lot of unanswered questions."

She nodded and slipped out the door, as silent as the grave. After she left, I turned to Delilah. "We'll have to figure out some way to transport these demons with us. We can't carry them like Menolly can."

"No, but I can," Smoky spoke up. I gave him a questioning look. "I've never seen Otherworld," he said. "Though of course I know about it. I think I'll come along. I can carry both of the dead demons without a problem, if you can take care of the floraed."

I could see by the look on his face that the matter was settled. "Okay, I guess that takes care of that. Chase, you and Iris stay here until Menolly returns. Morio, I'd like you to come with us to Grandmother Coyote's and then return home to keep watch on the house. Delilah, Smoky, and I will deliver Tom and the seal."

The last thing I felt like was another tromp through the woods, but the longer we kept Tom with us, the more likely someone from the Sub Realms would come gunning for him.

Iris scurried off to fetch him, while Delilah and I went upstairs to make ourselves presentable enough for a Queen's court. As I pulled on a dress of spun silver and a peacock-colored cloak, I reflected that this was going to be a far different trip than I'd hoped.

I'd been looking forward to seeing Father, but with everything in chaos, we'd better avoid Y'Elestrial like the plague. Instead, we'd head directly for Elqaneve, the city of the Elves. It was simply too dangerous to return home now. And if Lethesanar found out what we were doing, we'd end up in her dungeons, a fate worse than death.

Delilah's expression told me she was thinking along the same line. She dressed in her best silken leggings with a glittering gold tunic over the top and slung a turquoise belt around her hips. "I'd better leave my gun at home," she said as she fastened on her silver sword.

"Are you ready?" I asked. She nodded, and we hurried downstairs. Along with Smoky, who carried the dead demons, and Morio, who helped us keep Wisteria in check, we slipped back into the night and into the woods.

CHAPTER 20

Traveling through a portal is a little like falling into a drug-induced sleep for the barest fraction of a second, leaving behind a nasty hangover and the distinct sense that the laws of nature have been violated one too many times.

Grandmother Coyote had gleefully accepted the demon's finger and marked our deal finished. She led us to the tree in which the portal had been secreted. As we hoisted ourselves and the demons into the streaming light that raced up and down the core of the giant oak, I held out a faint hope that perhaps Father had been wrong, that we'd find out from the Elfin Queen that everything was all right in Y'Elestrial.

The trip itself only lasted a flash, but when we stepped out of the portal on the other end—a large cavern set in the middle of the Barrow Mounds outside of Elqaneve—the day had already begun, and sunlight streamed around us. The air was clean and held a magical charge that told me we were once again back in Otherworld. The countryside vibrated with life; here oak and beech, rock and crystal, all had their own sentience.

While they also did Earthside, it was easy to miss with the static from all the people and electricity and sheer noise generated by day-to-day life.

It didn't take long for the guards to find us and escort us through the crowd of onlookers. They swept us through the streets, carrying the demons and Wisteria on a cart drawn by horses. The streets of Elqaneve were paved in cobblestone, and flowers dappled the roadsides. In the evening, shimmering Faerie lights glowed to guide those hard of night sight.

Vendors were thick in the streets, hawking their wares. Apparently we'd hit the city on market day. Mothers led their children to school, while Brownies and house sprites shopped for the day. Elves weren't above owning servants, but they treated them well for the most part.

Everyone turned to watch as we passed. They were polite yet aloof, but beneath the surface I could feel their questions bubbling. Delilah and I were obviously half-Sidhe. Tom was human, but not so much. And Smoky . . . it wouldn't be too difficult for most of the folk to peg him as some sort of magical creature in disguise.

Tom looked around, his eyes sparkling like a kid who had just discovered a secret candy cupboard. It occurred to me that he must have lived in a place like this when Titania first took him into her Barrow City. Even if he couldn't remember, the magic must have sparked some sense of recognition.

When we arrived at the base of the palace, I was struck by how modest the royal court was compared to that of Y'Elestrial. Queen Lethesanar loved pomp and pageantry. The palace here, though, while large and gleaming of alabaster, was also simple in design and surrounded by gardens rather than fancy statues and subcourts. The guards led us into the great hall, where we were searched for weapons, and then escorted us to Queen Asteria's chamber.

The Elfin Queen sat upon her throne of oak and holly, as brilliant as the moon, and as aged as the world. She had been the queen of Elfland even before the Great Divide, and there was no talk of her stepping down over the millennia that had passed. She stood as we entered. Beside me, I felt Tom tremble.

"You bring me no good tidings," she said. "You bring dead demons into my city, and a chained wood sprite who seems to have gone mad?"

I curtsied. "May we talk in private? We have so much to tell you."

She took us into a closed chamber and there, with one of her advisors and three guards present, we told her everything, including what our father had said was happening in Y'Elestrial. By the end of our account, she was leaning back in her chair, drumming her fingers on the table, her face looming somewhere between disgust and distress.

"I was afraid of something like that," she said. "The Subterranean Realms are active, so active that we've been forced to make a truce with our born enemies. I don't like being put in that position, and it's all Shadow Wing's fault. Lethesanar is a fool. She cares more about her own pleasures than she does her people, and she's going to be taken down a peg or two until she relinquishes the throne to her sister. If she refuses . . ."

I cleared my throat, knowing all too well what she'd left unsaid, but I kept my mouth shut. I didn't want to agree, in case this was a trap to see how loyal we were to the Court and Crown. And I didn't want to disagree for the opposite reason. After a moment, the Queen tapped her silver-headed walking stick on the ground. Even Elves and Sidhe and Faeries aged over the eons, and bones eventually wore out and grew brittle.

"Well then, I suppose we'll have to see what we can do," she said. "In the meantime, you should return Earthside. I'll find out more about the seals and assign my own guardians to keep watch on the demons. You'll be our agents, as well as agents of the OIA."

"Double agents?" I asked, aghast. Traitorous. And yet, we had no real choice in the matter.

"Yes, double agents. When he recovers, send this Trillian

to me. He'll be our go-between. He'll accept the job, if he knows what is good for him."

Oh yeah. Trillian was going to love that, I thought. Delilah gave me a nudge and a wink.

The Queen ignored our interplay. "You may go. An emissary will be in contact with you within a few days. This isn't over yet, my girls. Shadow Wing will be sending more scouts, and he won't rest as long as there are seals in the world. No, a skirmish is over and you were victorious, but as for the battle—it's only just begun."

"What will you do with the spirit seal?" I asked.

The Elfin Queen pressed her lips together. "We have a place of refuge in which we will store and guard it. I won't tell you where it is because the less you know about the whereabouts of the seals we find, the safer you—and they—will be. What you do not know, you cannot reveal."

Though she smiled, I sensed a veiled threat back there and realized she was thinking that if we were caught and tortured by Shadow Wing, we wouldn't be able to spill secrets. The thought sobered me, and I stared at the ground for a moment. Shadow Wing was bound to figure out that we'd killed his scouts. We'd be primary targets before long.

"Go now," the Queen said softly. "Don't dwell on what may be. Apply yourself to the task at hand. The Hags of Fate may predict the future, but there is always free will, and that is your saving grace, my dear."

With that, she ushered us out. As we left, I glanced at Tom. "What will become of him?" I asked her.

She gave me a gentle smile. "He'll enjoy his days here, and we'll do what we can to reverse the effects of the nectar of life. He needs to sleep, as do all creatures when it is their time. He's long outlived his legends."

"You won't hurt him, will you?" I asked her, catching her gaze. "He didn't do anything wrong, and he protected the seal for hundreds of years."

She beamed at me then, brilliant and wise, and for a moment, I could see why her people loved her so much. "We won't hurt him. You have my word. Now take your dragon friend—yes, I know what you are, young beast—and return through the portals. There's so much work ahead. But you have an ally in me, as long as Lethesanar is kept ignorant of our agreement."

Delilah and I murmured our assent, and together with Smoky, who had the audacity to blow a kiss at the old Queen, were led back to the portal. I stopped long enough to replenish my stash of Tygerian water, but before long, we were standing back by the entrance to the cave.

I looked back, not wanting to leave. Otherworld was the home of my father, and I wanted to stay. And yet Earth was my mother's home, and together with my sisters, I owed it allegiance as well. And Earth needed us now.

"Are you ready?" I asked Delilah.

She nodded, though I could see the same conflicting emotions playing over her face. We held hands, she and Smoky and I, and stepped through the portal, emerging once again into a rain-filled forest. I shivered and pulled my robes tighter. The Lexus was waiting just off the road up ahead where Morio had left it for us. I winced as the dirty rain splashed on my face.

Yes, Earth was my home as much as Otherworld, and though it was filled with pollution and horrendous weaponry and a sense of hopelessness, it had a magic all its own. If we could keep the demons at bay, if we could bring to life that magic and make it thrive once again, then maybe our mother's world would survive.

"You know, even though I have use of your names, I give you my word that I'll hold them in honor," Smoky whispered to me before climbing in the backseat. "I won't abuse them."

Suddenly feeling lighthearted, I fastened my seat belt.

"Let's go home," I said. "Trillian will be here tonight, and we all need rest. We should contact Father later in the day to find out what's happening in Y'Elestrial. Menolly needs to sort out matters at the Wayfarer . . . Queen Asteria was right. We've got a butt load of work to do."

Delilah snapped her seat belt closed. "I don't think

that's quite what she meant. But you're right, we do have a lot to do. We should also build a little house for Maggie in the parlor to give her some privacy."

"That's not a bad idea," I said, turning on the radio station. "I bet she'd like that. Did you notice how much Menolly took to her?"

"Yeah, I did . . . I think it will be good for both of them," Delilah said, turning up the volume. And as we pulled out onto the road, lilting tones of the Gorillaz's "Demon Days" began to fill the car.

I glanced at Delilah. "Our anthem?" I asked.

She let out a long sigh and leaned her head against the headrest. "Yeah, and, I fear, a prediction of things to come."

As I eased out onto the road, I knew she was right.

And now . . .
a special preview of the next book
in the Otherworld series
by Yasmine Galenorn . . .

CHANGELING

Coming July 2007
from Berkley!

The moon was high overhead, rounded and full like one of those snow globes human children like to play with at Christmastime. I could barely see her up there watching over me as I slipped through the thick grass, padding lightly on the frost-shrouded ground. The night was clear but bitterly cold, and my breath formed little puffs of air as it spiraled out of my mouth.

I was freezing, but it was better than staying inside where Maggie could get hold of me and slobber her kisses all over my fur, or where Iris could trap me inside that stupid cat bag and forcibly clip my claws. Her manicures always left me with stubby nails the next day. And nobody but nobody was going to ruin the French manicure I'd just paid fifty bucks for at the local salon.

As I rounded the gazebo near the path leading to Birchwater Pond, a movement from within the trees alerted me and I paused midstep, listening. The noise repeated itself: a ruffling of leaves, the snapping of brittle twigs on the forest floor. Oh great Bastus . . . please don't let it be Speedo, the neighbor's dog. That little pisser was the most tenacious basset hound I'd ever met. The *only* basset hound I'd ever met, to be honest. He delighted in chasing me whenever I showed up on all fours, baying like a drunken troglodyte. While I could easily outrun the mutt, I didn't trust him. Of course, to be fair, he wasn't a Were, just a regular old dog. Probably a good thing, now that I thought about it, considering that he was shy a few bolts in the bucket, but still . . . I glanced around, looking for the nearest tall tree. It never hurt to be prepared.

When Speedo didn't break through the undergrowth but the noises continued, I reconsidered. Possum, maybe. Or skunk. Skunk would be bad, but *this time* I'd fight my instincts and leave it alone. Skunk me once, shame on the skunk. Skunk me twice, and I'd be the butt of my sisters' jokes for weeks.

As I searched my gut, something told me that my stalker wasn't an animal. At least not your everyday furball running through the woods. I might not be a witch like my sister Camille, but I had my own set of instincts, and they were whispering loud and clear that somebody was out there. I raised my head and sniffed, inhaling deeply. *There*. The faint scent of big cat, but behind that, something stronger. And then I knew what it was that I sensed. *Cat magic*.

Cautiously, I made my way to the gazebo and loped up the stairs. I didn't want to be caught unarmed in the grass. There wasn't much I could do in this state if a demon happened to pop out of the woods to attack me. Turn into a ball of fur and razorblades, maybe, but considering my size, fighting back promised a quick and painful end to my existence. Once I was in the gazebo I'd be able to scramble up on the railing, which would give me a better vantage point from which to observe.

I lowered myself into a pouncing position and wiggled my butt, preparing for the pounce-and-leap, but as I sailed into the air toward the third step, my big old fluffy tail decided to play tease-and-tickle with a patch of spiny cockleburs that were growing near the edge of the gazebo. *Oh shit!* I thought, as I went thudding to the ground, belly first, feet splayed out like some cartoon cat from *Tweety and Sylvester.*

I blinked as my dignity took a direct hit. As I shook my head and pushed myself to all four feet, I found—much to my dismay—that the tufts of my tail fur were knotted up in the prickly plants. I let out a little growl of frustration. Why did I have to have such long fur? Granted, I was the prettiest golden tabby around, but sometimes looks were overrated. I tugged, trying to free myself but no luck. The fur was stuck and not coming loose.

An insect that hadn't bitten the dust during the cold snap buzzed around my head, and I twitched my ears, resisting the urge to bat at it. *Nope, leave it alone*, I thought. *I've got bigger concerns than a flutterbug. Like getting loose from this fucking plant.* When I was in cat form, it was always harder to control my urges. Beetles distracted me, and spiders . . . leaves flying in the wind, a dandelion going to seed . . . oh yeah, I was a sucker for anything that promised to put up a good chase.

I tugged again but a sharp pain at the base of my tail told me that maybe that wasn't the best idea in the world. Now what? I couldn't transform back while the moon was full, not until morning. And with Camille off racing with the Hunt as it streaked through the night woods, and Menolly in town at a Vamps Anonymous meeting, my family sure wasn't going to come to my rescue.

With a little huff, I tried again and almost ripped out a wad of fur. Well, shit. Frustrated, I crouched, trying to avoid getting any more entangled than I already was. The night was just getting better and better. First, I had to miss my late-night fix of trash TV. I couldn't get enough of *Jerry Springer*, *Maury Povich*, and *Blind Date* and watched them every night, making Menolly join me. We did our nails, I ate tons of popcorn, and we gossiped about Camille and her lovers. If I didn't get my boob-tube fix, I was a grumpy girl in the morning.

And then I'd been all set to take out a mouse that was

gnawing at Camille's comfrey plant. I had the rodent down, under my paw, when she began spieling out a sob story about a litter of munchkins at home. Camille always said I was too softhearted, and I guess she was right. I let the mouse go free, albeit with a grumpy "Get out of here before you're toast."

My sisters didn't know that I could talk to animals when I was in my Were-form. The subject had never come up, and for some reason, I found myself reluctant to tell them. This was my own special world, one they couldn't enter. Camille had her connection with the Moon Mother, and Menolly had her bloodlusts . . . although that was a rather recent addition to her life. It wasn't like she'd asked to be turned into a bloodsucker, the Elwing Clan had turned her into a vampire against her will. But, for whatever the reason, I'd kept my ability a secret.

After the mouse ran off, I stopped to groom and damned if I didn't find that I'd picked up a thriving patch of fleas from the rodent. Now I'd need a flea dip or some Advantage, and both clashed with my DKNY Be Delicious perfume and left me with dry skin and a mild rash.

Which brought me to the here and now: host to a flea circus, stuck to a cocklebur plant, with an unknown intruder, who was packing a butt load of cat magic, watching me from the woods. Woo-hoo and oh yeah. Now we were having big fun! It always irked me when people assumed that Weres just spent the nights of the full moon partying hearty and getting down with their bad selves.

Another crackle from the woods caught my attention, and I decided that—whatever I was going to do—I'd better get on with it. I gingerly tested the burs again. Nope, the prickly heads had me but good. It would hurt like a son of a bitch, but I was going to have to just yank myself free. I couldn't take the chance that whoever was out in those woods was friendly. I closed my eyes to steel myself for the rip when a different noise, directly to my left, startled me. I whipped around, nerves jangled.

There, illuminated in the light of the moon, sat the

mouse that I'd released. She rose up on her hindquarters, quivering, her nose and whiskers twitching as she stared at me. I swallowed every instinct in the world that told me to bat her a good one, and tried to exert a pleasant, how-*you*-doin' smile.

"You need help?" she squeaked.

"What do you think? Do I *look* like I need help?" I said.

She gave me a pained look. "I don't have time for this. My children are hungry. Do you need help, or don't you?"

Oh Great Mother, the gods save me now. It was bad enough that I'd been softhearted enough to let her go, but to be forced into accepting a favor from an entrée? "Beggars can't be choosers, I guess," I muttered, ego shot to hell.

A twinkle raced through her eyes, and she tittered and puffed up her chest. "Say it then."

"Say what?"

"Mice rule, cats drool."

I huffed. "What? You expect me to"—she turned tail at my outburst and was sauntering off—"Wait! Come back."

"You going to say it?" she asked over her shoulder.

I squirmed. With no choice, I hung my head and hoped to hell that nobody ever caught wind of this. "Mice rule, cats drool." That was it. Utter humiliation. My night was complete.

She sniffed, satisfied, then slowly examined my tail. A nibble here, a nibble there, and she broke through the twigs attached to the cockleburs that were entangled in my fur. I swished my tail back and forth. The weight of the burs threw me off balance a little, but I was free and that's all that mattered. I grudgingly thanked the mouse as she skittered away.

Another shuffle from the woods, and I made tracks, too. While I had the suspicion there might be a Were hiding in the forest, I also knew that some demons also had the ability to use cat magic, so I wasn't about to count on whatever was stalking me being feline-friendly. Taking a deep breath, I loped across the lawn toward the house.

The back door on the porch was locked, but I'd installed a cat door, and after one or two mishaps, Camille had warded it to match my aura. The alarms would be set off by anybody who crept through it except me. We kept it locked to keep out other four-legged visitors except on the nights of the full moon or when I wanted to go out and check the grounds without being noticed. There was always the chance that a raccoon might be an intruder in disguise.

Once inside the enclosed back porch, I scratched at the kitchen door until Iris opened it. She picked me up and chucked me under the chin. I gave in without a fight. Iris loved cats and she treated me like her personal puss. The Talon-haltija was short and stocky, milkmaid pretty with a smile that would melt a glacier. She'd been bound to a family in Finland until they all died out, and then the house sprite joined the OIA, for which my sisters and I worked. They had assigned her to remain Earthside as our assistant.

At first, she just worked in Camille's store, but after a nasty encounter with the demon Bad Ass Luke, Iris moved in with us. She took care of the house and helped us out when we needed it. It was kind of like having our favorite aunt around.

"You have a rough night?" she asked, examining my fur. "What do we have here? A tail full of stickers? And fleas?" She wrinkled her nose. "What have you been doing, girl? Come on, Delilah, we better get you cleaned up. I'll have to cut these burs out before you shift back, but I think you'll still end up with one seriously sore rear end."

I squirmed, wanting to tell her about the presence I'd felt, but she couldn't understand me. I could hear and understand both the Fae and humans while in Were-form, but hadn't been able to figure out a way to make the communication a two-way street.

As she carried me over to the counter and held up the scissors, I quieted down. As long as she didn't try to clip my claws, she could pamper me all she wanted. When Camille or Menolly returned, they might be able to pick up a bead on whatever it was I'd been sensing, and do something about it before the magical signature faded away.

By the time the moon went to bed, I was curled up by the fire, purring heavily as I drifted in and out of my nap. I'd tried to wait up for Camille and Menolly, but the pull from the flames was too strong. The minute I snuggled up in my cushioned slumber ball Camille had bought for my birthday, I slid right into the arms of Morpheus. Which is why I woke up with one paw still furry, and the other rapidly shifting into a hand.

Nobody ever believed me when I told them it wasn't painful. Oh, it might be if you weren't a Were, but for us, it was as simple as changing clothes. Speaking of clothes, my collar had disappeared and was just as quickly transforming back into my sweatpants and tank top. Iris had been right. My butt hurt.

"Seems my Kitten is back from her journey." Menolly's voice echoed in my ears as I rolled off the slumber ball and thudded to the floor, fully transformed as the last whisker vanished.

I blinked, squinting at the window. First light was about an hour away. "Cutting it thin, aren't you?" I said, my throat a little raw. My stomach rumbled, and I discovered that I was a little queasy, too. What *had* I eaten during the night? Definitely not Miss House Mouse. My mind a little less engaged in feline pursuits, I decided to drop off some Cheese Nips where I knew she and her family lived. Poor little thing. I must have given her a good scare, even if she had taken advantage of my situation.

"You don't look so hot," Menolly said. She was sitting on the sofa with Maggie in her lap. The baby Crypto was slurping away at the contents of the bowl of cream, cinnamon, sugar, and sage that Menolly held.

The pair had become inseparable since Camille had first rescued the calico gargoyle from a demon's lunch box, and now both vamp and gargoyle had happily bonded in one of the strangest friendships I'd ever seen. Not that Maggie was all that bright—it would be years before we knew if she would develop past the stage of a smart cat or a slow dolphin, but that didn't matter to us. She was a rambunctious little sweetheart, and Menolly adored her. We all did.

"Speak for yourself," I grumbled, rubbing my backside. "You didn't get a butt full of thorns last night."

"No, but I didn't get a bellyful of blood, either, and I'm hungry."

I grimaced, but Menolly waved away my protest. "At least I'm always beautiful," she said, looking over my bedraggled state. "Even after a hunt. But you look like something the cat dragged in." She opened her mouth to complete the joke, but I shot her a nasty glare and she stopped. "Your sense of humor vanish overnight?"

"Give me a break," I said. "I'm hungry, I need a shower, and Iris had to cut off a pile of fur when I came home." The morning after a transformation was never a pretty sight for most Weres. I was ready to head upstairs for a shower and then spend the morning in my Hello Kitty pajamas. "I'll bet you aren't all that pretty to your victims," I added, feeling snarky.

Giving me a wicked grin, Menolly said, "Most of my victims are so enthralled, they come on demand. Trust me, they love it." Even though Camille had convinced her to join Vampires Anonymous, Menolly's cutting sarcasm had remained intact. Sister or not, Menolly was one freaky badass chick. Gorgeous, but scary.

"Yeah, they love it till they find out you sucked them dry." I shook my head, reaching for the doughnut box sitting on the coffee table. Chase, who fancied himself my boyfriend because we had sex once a week, had sent them to me. It was sweet, really, and he knew my taste for Twinkies and Ding Dongs, so he'd gotten the gift right.

"So what happened? No pervs out last night?" I winced as I stretched. My muscles needed a good workout. I'd head down to the gym toward evening. They loved me there and had given me a free lifetime membership because men signed up just to watch me work out. Being half-Faerie in a world enchanted with our presence had its perks. All Fae made a strong impact on FBHs. Full-blooded humans either loved us or hated us, but very few were immune to our presence.

"I drank enough to stave off the worst of my thirst, but I'm going to need a real hunt in a few nights." Her emerald eyes flashed against the copper of her Bo Derek braids. As she shook her head, the ivory beads she'd had woven into the braids clattered like the bones of a dancing skeleton. Menolly made no noise, except when she chose to. The beads reminded her that she had once been alive. That she hadn't always been a vampire.

"You mean a full kill," I said. The phone rang, but stopped after one ring. Iris must have picked up.

"You nailed it." Menolly shrugged, but I could hear the craving in her voice. A young vampire, she still needed to drink deep and often.

Looking at her, it was hard to believe Menolly was a vamp, except for that Butoh dancer complexion. Petite, she barely made five three, if that, but she could toss a dead demon over one shoulder and carry him like a child, and she could drain a person of blood without blinking. She was the youngest, but sometimes she seemed as old as the hills to me.

Camille, the oldest, was a buxom and curvy five-foot-seven witch. Long waves of curly black hair cascaded down her back, and her eyes were violet with silver flecks. She was the practical one, although you wouldn't know it by the way she dressed, which was one step shy of a fetish bar.

And me? I was the middle child, though both Camille and Menolly treated me like I was the baby. At least I had them both beat in the height department. I topped six one, and my body was muscled and lean. No couch potato kitty for me, except during my late-night TV binges. My hair would have been called flaxen by a poet, and until recently had fallen almost to my waist. Tired of the constant upkeep, I'd marched into a salon and asked for a layered shag that barely skimmed my shoulders.

The three of us looked about as much like sisters as we did like goblins. Our mother had been human, and our father was one of the Sidhe. We fell at odd points along the spectrum. Unfortunately, our half-breed status upset the status quo with Father's relatives. Worse, it upset our internal balance.

Camille's magic proved chaotic and was as erratic as her choice in men. Menolly could climb a hundred-foot tree, but she fell off a simple perch when spying on a rogue clan of vampires. They, in turn, tortured and turned her into one of them.

As for me . . . my shape-shifting was unpredictable, and I couldn't always control it. And even though I was a Were, no gorgeous lioness appeared when I transformed. Just a golden long-haired tabby, whose tail occasionally got stuck in a briar bush and who ended up with . . . fleas. Damn it. I smelled like Advantage and the beginning of a rash was climbing up my back. It seemed Iris had dosed me a good one. I needed to take a shower before I broke out in hives.

"Where's Camille? I have to talk to her about something I felt out in the woods last night." I glanced around, looking for signs that she might be home. No stilettos, no corsets lying around, no stench of sulfur from misfired magic.

"She said she was stopping off at Trillian's before coming home," Menolly said. Just then Iris appeared in the doorway.

"Camille called a few minutes ago. She's on her way now. I'm going to take off for the shop. She should rest for awhile before coming in," the house sprite said. "Tell her I'll expect her in around one?"

I nodded, watching as Iris bustled off. Camille ostensibly owned the Indigo Crescent, a bookstore in downtown Belles-Faire, a grimy suburb of Seattle. In truth, it was a front for the OIA—the Otherworld Intelligence Agency, for which we worked. They'd sent us Earthside because, bluntly, they thought we were a bunch of bumbling bimbos. Klutzes we might be, but a pack of vacuous T&A? Never. We had brains! We had looks! We had . . . the worst record in the service. However, thanks to the bureaucracy, instead of getting us out of the way, the OIA had put us right on the fast-track to Hell.

A few months ago, we'd had a nasty bit of business with a Degath Squad—a trio of demons on a scouting mission. We'd barely managed to squeak through the assault alive.

When we returned to Otherworld to prove that things weren't so hunky-dory back on Earth, we found our home city in an uproar with a full-fledged civil war going on. We ended up dragging with us two dead demons; one gagged and bound floraed—a rare offshoot of the dryads—who had decided to pull a Darth Vader and betray both humans and Faeries; one dazed thousand-year-old human straight out of legend; and a spirit seal. We left the partridge and pear tree home.

The spirit seals, if all nine were joined together, formed an ancient artifact, and that artifact—or any portion thereof—would give the leader of the Subterranean Realms a significant advantage in his goal to raze both Earth and OW.

Considering our own drug-addled Queen was duking it out with her sister in a civil war, we showed up on the doorstep of the Elfin Queen on the advice of our father. When we dropped the demons and other assorted goodies at her feet, Queen Asteria promptly proclaimed that, like it or not, as of that moment we were double agents and would be acting for her as well as for the OIA.

Oh, and one other thing, a little thing really—just don't tell the OIA about this arrangement. And when a millennia-old magic-wielding queen tells you to do something, you don't argue.

One thing we knew for sure: Where there was one demon, there were bound to be more. Where there was one Degath Squad, other Hell Scouts would follow and, eventually, with an army to back them up. With the Otherworld Intelligence Agency embroiled in civil matters, we were pretty much on our own.

Granted, Camille's boyfriends, Trillian and Morio, had joined forces with us. And somehow we'd warranted the attentions of a gorgeous hunk of dragon flesh we knew only by the name of Smoky. On the Earthside side of things, my boyfriend, Chase Johnson—an FBH, a detective, and a member of the Earthside division of the Otherworld Intelligence Agency—was also on our side. Still . . . not a great lineup against a Soul Eater with hundreds of thousands of demons at his command. With Shadow Wing on the rampage, we were a pale wall of defense.

The door opened and Camille blew through. She was in full getup—flowing plum chiffon skirt, black lace bustier, black PVC boots that laced up her calves, their heels a mile high. Her eyes sparkled with silver. She'd been running magic, all right. Her glamour was so strong that I was amazed she didn't have a pack of men following her home.

Of the three of us, she had the most appeal to the FBHs. Her very scent invited them to come play, and her voluptuous curves left little to the imagination.

Camille had another side, though. She'd taken care of me after our mother died. Menolly was off in her own little world by then, though not yet a vampire, but Camille held it together for our father and for the three of us.

"Something tripped the wards," she said. "I can feel it. Anything happen tonight I should know about?"

I jumped up. "I've been waiting for you to get home." I glanced out the window. First light was only moments away. "I want you to come out back with me. I smelled cat magic last night and I think a Were may have been in the forest, but I'm not sure. I was in cat form, and the full moon can cloud my senses."

She ruffled my hair, a habit that I both loved and hated. "Let's go check it out, sweetie." With a glance at Menolly, she added, "You need to get downstairs. The sky's clear and the sun will be up soon. I'm surprised you aren't already feeling it."

Menolly brushed her eyes. "I am, actually. I'll put Maggie in her box and go to bed." Unlike most vampires, Menolly used an actual bed to rest in, and her lair—very Martha Stewart—was hidden in the basement. We'd turned the door into a secret passageway so she'd be safe from random intruders, and no one else but Iris knew that the bookshelves in the kitchen actually opened up to reveal the staircase leading to Menolly's apartment.

Camille followed me out to the backyard. Everything looked so different from this height, but the minute I saw the cockleburs, I felt my dander rise. I stopped to root them out.

"What are you doing?" Camille asked.

I grunted. "Got them stuck in my tail last night. I'm going to hire a gardener to come in and clear the yard of anything remotely nasty."

"Just don't get rid of my belladonna or wolfsbane," she said, choking back a snort as I led her to the path where I'd sensed the intruder. "So I take it your butt's sore?"

"Worse than diaper rash," I said. "So, are the wards sounding an alarm, or were they just tripped?" They were Camille's spell, and she was the only one who'd be able to sort through the variances of disruption that happened when they'd been detonated.

She closed her eyes. "No demons at play, but that doesn't mean much, considering how Bad Ass Luke conned Wisteria into working with them." Stopping suddenly, she blinked and said, "Did you know that Trillian and Morio are roommates now? They decided to save money and rent a two-bedroom apartment together."

"Good gods, there's gonna be a bloodbath."

Trillian was a Svartan, one of the elves' darker-souled cousins, and he'd been playing Camille for years. They were lovers, though she wasn't sure if she even liked him. But the old saw went *Once you've bedded a Svartan, you'll never go back*. Apparently, it was pretty much on the nose. I wasn't interested in finding out for myself.

Morio, a yokai-kitsune from Japan—a fox demon, but

not the big-bad kind of demon—had hooked up with her when they accidentally tripped a lust spell out near Mount Rainier. It seemed that the results were good enough to go back for seconds, and thirds, and who knew how many servings?

Trillian and Morio kept a cautious truce because of Camille, but they were clear rivals for her affection. The Sidhe weren't monogamous by nature, a good thing or there would have been bloodshed by now, considering the amount of testosterone involved.

"And how do they expect to pull off being roomies? Bet you it lasts less than two weeks," I said, fishing a twenty out of my pocket.

"You're on," Camille said, grinning. "I'll give it a month."

I could tell she didn't think much of the arrangement, either, and I wondered what it meant in terms of sleeping arrangements, but the possibilities were too much to envision on an empty stomach, so I left it alone for now. After a moment, she raised her head.

"Hold on, there's something here. It's faint . . . but definite . . ."

She plunged into the bushes and knelt near the base of a large oak that watched over the wooded acreage that spread out next to our land. As she examined the tree, I scouted around the path, finding a line of footprints. The night had been clear, with no rain to wash them away. They led up to the tree, then away from it again and disappeared in the middle of the tangle of huckleberry, brambles, Oregon grape, and fern.

Just then, a Steller's Jay dive-bombed me from the branches of a fir, scolding at the top of its lungs. Little bugger, I thought as I waved it away. It could smell the cat on me. I wrinkled my nose and let out a little hiss, and it screeched even louder. Another jay joined it on the branch, and both perched there, eyeballing me.

"Don't you dare unless you want to become my breakfast," I muttered.

"Delilah!" Camille's voice brought me out of my spar-

ring match. Her face was a mixture of disbelief and wariness. "I know what was here."

"What? What was it?" I leaned against the oak, waiting. *Not a demon. Please don't let it be a demon,* I thought. I was tired of demons. While I could kick ass with the best, I didn't like conflict. When my sisters got into arguments, the stress turned me into a pussycat.

"You were right, there was another Were here last night," she said, her eyes flashing with silver. "And unless I'm off my game, I think it was a werepuma. A male." She looked up at me. "He's marked the tree."

A werepuma? I stared at the trunk, then at our house, which you could just see from this vantage point. The fact that he'd marked the tree meant he was claiming territory. But why? Was he in league with Shadow Wing and the demons? Or was he a free agent? And if he wasn't aligned with our hellion friends, just what did he want?